Local Honey

Local Honey

Shawn P McCarthy

Dark Spark Press

Book cover design by Miracle Marvel
Printed in the United States of America
First Printing, 2025
ISBN-13: 979-8-9856882-3-8 (Dark Spark Press)

Dark Spark Press
www.DarkSparkPress.com
Publisher.DarkSparkPress@gmail.com

For

Margaux
&
John

Chapter 1

For the Money

The big road rose from the east and stole Jim Yarrow's brother on the coldest day of nineteen fifty-one.

Hissing and clanking, the construction advanced with smoking yellow machines, a swarm of workers, and fresh scars across the landscape. The mid-point of the "American Century" had arrived with a bold confidence and a tangle of new highways. Post-war cities pushed through their old perimeters. Young couples migrated outward, seeking to consume. It seemed like new roads were being built everywhere, including the Town of Riverbend.

Even when the big road was out of view, Sergeant Jim Yarrow still felt its presence. He fielded complaints when heavy trucks cut through residential neighborhoods. Construction noises echoed for miles, and the dust was ever-present.

The highway also arrived with a heavier weight for Yarrow: the loss of his younger brother Will. He worked on the big road, though not for long. It was January when they lost him. By June, the pain had faded some. But not the memories.

As he piloted his cruiser through the small hills and the lush greenness above the Merrimack River, Yarrow tried not to dwell on Will or any other burden. It was sunny, and he just wanted to enjoy the beauty of the day. He hoped to see an elusive wood duck on the water or maybe an eagle roosting in the branches of an eastern white pine.

His police radio had been silent for half an hour, so he listened to the Philco dash radio instead. Art Mooney and His Orchestra sang about looking over a four-leaf clover. The tune caught his attention, and he tapped the steering wheel. Together with the sun, the music slightly lifted his spirits. He tried to remember whether he and his wife Linda once danced to that song. He decided they had. Probably at the Hampton Beach Casino Ballroom, back before they were married. She was still in her sundress, shoulders slightly pink from the bright afternoon.

The recollection made him smile, but his thoughts were interrupted by a voice that squawked from his receiver. He turned down the music and picked up the mic.

"I'm sorry Tina. What was that?"

She repeated the message. "Someone's reported an illegal farm stand operating on the outskirts of town."

"A farm stand? You mean, like, a place selling produce and stuff?" It was a strange complaint, and it caught him by surprise.

"I guess so."

"Why would that bother anyone?"

"Who knows? I guess people have their reasons."

As Yarrow gripped the mic, the ring and middle fingers on his right hand remained straight and stiff. The damage came from a bullet that passed through his palm during the Battle of Anzio. That was the spring of 1944, when he was just 21 years old. The army field hospital gave him a quick rebuild and sent him on his way. The other three digits still worked, and when he came home he was glad to have a hand that looked relatively normal.

"Tina? Do you know who called in the complaint?"

He heard her chuckle. "Yes. It came from our old friend, Mary Jane Danforth."

If the dispatcher could have seen him, his look of disgust would have made her laugh.

"Come on, Tina, can't you just point her to the office of permits? Or maybe zoning?"

"She insisted on a police response. And, you'll like this, the chief was standing behind me when she called. He just rolled his eyes and left the room."

She read the street address then added, "Just stop by, see what's there, then file a quick report. There's nothing else going on anyway."

He sighed. "Yeah. Ten-four."

He knew the location. Dusty gravel lot, half a mile south of Route 110. It was little more than a wide spot near the old Coal Ferry Road.

In his high school days, Yarrow and his friends sometimes parked there and walked down a trail toward the river. Decades of sediment had pushed up against the bank, creating a small sandy beach on a curve of the Merrimack.

The place also held another attraction back then. They'd try to catch a glimpse of the Bivens girls. There seemed to be several of them, living in a shack near the water. One in particular always caught his eye. But that family was gone now, and so was their decrepit home.

As he drove, he tried to remember if they ever brought his brother along on their river visits.

Will.

Yarrow couldn't help but think of him.

Will was the baby of the family. Just nineteen when the big road took him. After that, Yarrow watched as his Ma grew somber and empty. Losing Will made him examine his own life. Prices paid. Paths chosen. Months after the death, Yarrow still felt the heavy weight.

So, Yarrow retreated too. Into family. Then into himself.

Endless patrolling became his escape. He requested reassignment to the rural side of town where he could just cruise the low knolls and shallow valleys near the river. It gave him time to think.

As he drove toward the old Bivens place, he thought about the woman whose complaint prompted this visit.

Mary Jane.

Jesus.

He had a strained history with Mary Jane Danforth. He'd known her since childhood and they were in the same class in high school. Back then, she was the boisterous head of the student body. A few years later, she became the founder and president of the Riverbend Improvement Society. In that role, she produced a steady string of suggestions and complaints, supposedly in the interest of civic improvement.

As he reached his destination, Yarrow downshifted and let the Ford Super Deluxe roll into the parking area. The gravel lot was just as he remembered. At the far end, he saw a card table topped with yellow gingham. Amber jars stood in neat lines and a hand-painted sign leaned against the table. It read *Local Honey*, with a hastily sketched bee.

That was it. No other produce. No other tables or crates or anything. Just honey.

Wow, he thought. *This is what bothers you, Mary Jane?* This little table?

But he knew the farm's history all too well and he had his suspicions about what might be driving the complaint.

As Yarrow exited his cruiser, he spotted the proprietor talking to a customer. Her back was turned. But as he walked closer, he recognized her. That triggered a strange elation, tempered by a sobering trepidation.

It had been ten years, but he knew that hair and the delicate curve of her waist. For a moment, he considered retreating back to his black-and-white. He could ask Tina to send a different officer. But, he steeled himself and called out.

"Well, my goodness, is that Rebecca Bivens?"

She handed a bag to her customer, slid some money into her pocket, then slowly turned in his direction. She wore a white dress with dark blue polka dots. A blue belt was cinched tightly around her waist. The outfit made her look wonderful, but she also looked quite thin—to the point where it startled him. He told himself it was just the light.

A puff of wind blew a lock of hair from beneath her red scarf. Then her eyes brightened, and a smile spread over her lips.

"Jim Yarrow!" she exclaimed. "I don't believe it. It's so good to see you again."

She stepped forward and hugged him. He accepted it awkwardly. The curious elation bubbled up again, and the feeling bewildered him.

"Good to see you … too," he stammered. "Wow. How long has it been, Becky?"

She adjusted her scarf. "Well, my family left town in July of forty-one. Quite hastily, you may remember."

"I do remember." He tried to smile, but that summer and that memory were tough for him. The weight of it tugged at the corners of his mouth.

"Wow. Ten years. So, welcome back, I guess?"

"Thank you."

He walked with her toward the tiny table. "You know, Becky, we never had a chance to talk after everything happened. A lot of us felt bad about it. I was only eighteen then, but I should have—"

Becky held up a finger. "No more mention of it. Okay, Jim? That was a long time ago. I was young too. None of what happened was our fault."

Yarrow nodded. He still felt like he should say something. Maybe pull an apology out of his pocket and deliver it on behalf of the whole town. But he knew he wouldn't find the right words.

Instead, he gestured toward the path that led to the river. "Have you been down there yet? After your family left, someone burned down your old house."

"It was just a shack, Jim. And yes, I know."

Yarrow ran his fingers through his hair. "I never saw the inside. But I do remember it. It was expanded and modified so many times, that house looked like a big drooping peanut."

She laughed, then caught his gaze. She held it. "This isn't my first time back here. I've slipped in and out of town a few times over the years. I needed to revisit it."

Then she reached out and took his hand. "Anyway, I was so sorry to hear about Will. To me, he was always your pesky younger brother. But I did like him."

He was surprised she knew. "Thanks, Becky. That's kind of you."

"What happened?"

He didn't like talking about it. But for her, he would.

"Will found work as a laborer on the highway construction. He was excited to be part of it. But a few weeks into it, he was working at the bottom of a trench on a bitter cold day, trying to square it off with a pick. A big Link-Belt excavator sat next to the trench, swinging back and forth. They assured us that bucket followed the same arc dozens of times. But that one time, a basketball-size rock tumbled out, and it struck Will in the head. Hard hats were not a job site requirement. I don't know if a hat would have saved him anyway."

"Goodness, that's awful."

"Yeah. So, that was that. Less than a month after signing up for the highest-paying job of his life, Will was gone. Never even reached the end of his teens." Yarrow shrugged, then forced a smile.

"I'm so sorry, Jim. And how about your mom?"

"I think she's all right. She had pneumonia last month and she's still coughing. But I think maybe she's improving now."

"Good. I'd say she deserves a break."

Except for her obvious thinness Becky was just as he remembered. She still had the same great confidence. And she still looked so ...

He forced himself to look away. "Where are you staying now?"

"Right here. There's a flat spot a little up the hill from where our shack used to be. I went to an auction in Boston last month and bought an old bakery truck. I removed all the racks and added a bed. Built a small counter too, and a place to sit."

"You're living in a truck? Good Lord Becky, you should—"

She held up her hand.

"Don't worry, Jim. It's actually nice. And that truck is more than I've had for a long time. When I sleep out here, I can hear the owls and crickets. I hear the rain fall on the metal roof. It's quite enchanting."

Jim said no more. He stepped toward the table to examine the jars. "It looks like you're back in the honey business. I have to say, I'm surprised." He glanced over to see her reaction, but she remained inscrutable. "There are people in town who still remember those days with a bit of anger. You know, because of what selling honey actually meant."

"Is that so? I only remember selling jars of sweet amber liquid, right from the hives."

He gave her a quizzical look. "Some have a much different memory."

Becky laughed in that demure way he always found charming. "Well, I hope they do remember. I still offer a quality product. And, if you can't afford to buy a jar, we're always willing to extend credit." She gave him a big smile.

Knowing her family history, Yarrow found that mention of credit unnerving.

He studied the labels on the jars. They looked a bit different than the old version. But the message was the same.

Bivens Farm

Best Honey for Your Money

Becky walked over and stood beside him. "I brought seven hives with me. You can see them in the field over there. Not a huge number, but it's a good start. It shouldn't take me long to expand. Making proper investments is just smart business, don't you think?"

Yarrow looked toward the hives. "Yeah, well about your business. That's what brought me here. Someone filed a complaint about your operation."

She looked surprised. "What's there to complain about? I have every right to sell my products."

Yarrow tried to put on his best public-official voice. "Well, maybe. But you're supposed to have permission from the property owner."

"I have that."

"You do?"

"Yes, Jim. My mother only rented this land. But now, I own it." She spoke with pride. "I signed the papers weeks ago. It took years of saving, but here I am."

Yarrow couldn't hide his surprise. When he thought of the Bivens family he remembered them living hand-to-mouth. Old dresses. Worn trucks. Patched roofs. He suspected there were times when they went to bed hungry. Looking at her now, he still wondered.

"That's great, Becky. Good for you, for managing that."

"I thought it was time to come home."

He nodded. "You're right, of course. Farms are allowed to sell their own produce. But this town can be difficult. They'll make you get a license for your stand. A health inspection too."

She walked to her local honey sign and flipped it around. A business license and a small card from the local health department were taped to the back. "I hope these will do, Jim. I don't have a wall yet where I can hang them."

He lifted his hands in surrender. "Well, look at that. You're way ahead of me."

Becky laughed. "Not always. But today? Maybe I am."

They talked for a few minutes until more people rolled into the lot.

"Looks like I have some customers. But it's great to see you, Jim. I hope you'll stop by again. And if you ever need honey, you know where to find it."

Her comment caught him off guard, and he offered a stammering reply. "Yes, I ... I guess I do." Then he hastily added, "And I'll bring my wife."

By that time, Becky was facing away from him. He couldn't see her reaction. But he knew she heard him. He also knew her return to Riverbend would change everything for the coming summer. Not just for him but for many people.

"One more thing, Becky," he called out. "Be careful with the credit. And please, avoid those creative ledgers like your mom kept."

She was silent.

"And you certainly know what else you need to avoid. So, please? That's where things went off track for your mom. That can't happen again."

She looked back over her shoulder, gave him a slow wink, and walked on.

Chapter 2

Intersection

The Merrimack River begins at the confluence of the Pemigewasset and Winnipesaukee Rivers. It flows southeast from central New Hampshire, then turns abruptly eastward as it enters Massachusetts. The drastic bend is a legacy of ancient glaciers. Miles of rocks and sludge damned the river and forced it toward the coast. Millennia later, the mouth of the Merrimack provided a gateway for European explorers to enter deep into the land, exploring the area that would come to be called New England.

Where the River Ends, Merrimack Imprints, 1946

For three years, a bell hung above the door of Rocco's Grill, where each swing grazed its lip, sounding a chime. It rang as Jim Yarrow entered, causing him to close his eyes and shake his head.

"That damn thing."

Rocco waved hello. "You know I'm leaving it there just to bug you, Jim."

"It's working."

As Yarrow sat at the counter, Rocco placed a steaming cup of coffee in front of him. "Pecan pie today?"

"You really are trying to bug me, aren't you?"

"You're the only customer who never orders the pecan pie, Jim. I keep hoping you'll surprise me."

"Nope. I'm mister steady and predictable."

Yarrow and Rocco had known each other for years, starting with Miss Amesbury's third-grade class. They were solid friends by the seventh grade. Yarrow often ate lunch at the big U-shaped counter. Breakfast and lunch were offered on one side. By mid-afternoon, beer and liquor were available on the other. It was an unusual set-up for a grill, but the building had a shady history. During the Prohibition era sliding doors were added to one side, providing a place where booze could quickly be concealed. When the bottles were covered, both sides retained the look of a regular restaurant.

As he wiped down the counter, Rocco looked toward the partially fogged windows. "Uh oh, Jim. I think you may be in trouble."

"Hum?"

"Mary Jane. She looks pissed and she's headed this way. You can sneak out the back door if you want. Coffee's on me."

Yarrow shook his head. "Let her come. I'll have to face her eventually."

The bell chimed. Heads turned as Mary Jane stormed in. When she saw Yarrow, her face changed. She forced a half-smile.

"Jim! I was hoping to run into you."

"Really?" came his unenthusiastic response. Their relationship was complicated and he kept their interactions to a minimum. But she was a tough person to avoid. As she slid into the stool next to him, Yarrow stared at the Formica counter, focusing on the spinning reflection of an overhead fan.

"I heard you paid a visit to the old Bivens Farm this morning. Is that right?"

"That is correct, MJ. But I'm sure you already knew that."

She frowned. "I just took a drive out there. That's when I realized I needed to come find you. So, tell me Jim, why is she still there?"

He chose not to respond. In the years he'd known Mary Jane he had understood silence infuriated her. He suspected her two ex-husbands also discovered that. Neither of them lasted more than a year, and each time she asked the court to restore her maiden name.

She waited in vain, then reached into her purse. She unfolded a piece of paper and placed it on the counter.

"Perhaps you've seen the new zoning map. It was approved by the town six months ago. Look here, Jim. It clearly designates that section of town as residential. No business allowed. See? Especially not hers."

Yarrow squinted at the paper. "Hold on. I'm looking at the map's key, and it looks like most of that area is designated as both residential and agricultural. So she's fine, MJ. Don't worry about it."

He knew his response would raise her hackles.

"What do you mean fine? She's setting up a business. She can't run a business there. You need to stop it!"

"Nope. It's not a police matter."

"Excuse me?"

He listened to the tone of her voice. Was she flustered? He hoped she was.

"It's very much a police matter, Jim. Let me remind you about our town meeting three years ago. It was decided that police would be the ones to serve notices for zoning issues."

Yarrow shrugged. "Well then, start with zoning. They can decide if there's a violation. The police can take it from there. You could also start with the court. But I suspect you know your complaint would fail there. So, coming directly to the police is, what, your second choice? Maybe third?"

Rocco laughed, then caught Mary Jane's disapproving eye. He decided to collect empty Moxie bottles and move them to his back room.

"Jim Yarrow! You know exactly why the Bivens family was shut down a decade ago. And you know it's not a good thing that she's returned. Their whole business was illegal."

She waited.

His silence further stoked her anger. "It was a police matter in nineteen forty-one when they ordered the farm to be closed, right? That means it still is."

Yarrow gave Mary Jane an impatient look. Ever since they were teens, MJ had been insistent, entitled, and often unreasonable. He had long since reached his limit.

"I know you have enough legal knowledge to understand this, MJ. Becky is not her mother. It was Erin Bivens, not Becky, who was criminally charged, and who disappeared before she could be arrested. That property has changed owners over the years, and it was recently sold again. Becky herself bought it."

Mary Jane looked shocked. "Seriously? I wonder where she got the money. But still, she can't come back and reopen that business—or whatever you'd call her mother's illegal cesspool. This town has laws."

Rocco came out of the storeroom and walked behind his counter. He leaned against the back bar and listened.

Yarrow raised his voice a bit and tried to be blunt. "MJ, she can sell her farm products right there. She has all the right paperwork. There's nothing either of us can do. End of discussion."

Mary Jane crossed her arms and walked to the front window. She stood beside a three-level newspaper rack. *Boston Globe* on the top. *Lowell Sun* in the middle. *Portsmouth Herald* on the bottom. Their front pages displayed headlines about atomic bomb tests on Bikini Atoll and armistice talks in Korea.

Her voice caused other customers' heads to turn. "You know very well selling honey isn't what the farm is about, Jim. That's never been their main product."

Yarrow closed his eyes. "Okay, MJ. Let's say you're right. Let's say honey was just a small part of it ten years ago. But honey is all you'll find there today."

Mary Jane brooded. Then her expression changed. She turned and walked back. With a smile, she rested her hand on his arm.

"You know, Jim," she said softly, "you and I go way back. When did we go out on those dates? Freshman year, wasn't it?"

"Sounds about right. Two dates. That was enough." He looked straight ahead and scanned the menu board. The twenty-five-cent cheeseburger looked tasty.

"You know, it's too bad things didn't work out, Jim. You were fun. And you were so good on the football field."

"Thanks." He turned and held up a finger. "Hey Rocco? Check please."

"Just leave a nickel, Jim."

Mary Jane's expression turned to disappointment, then anger. "You know what? You always had a thing for Becky, didn't you? We all saw it."

"Jesus, MJ. How often did Becky even bother to come to school?"

She glared at him. "You know what you big oaf? Go home to your wife and kids. I'll talk to the mayor instead. The Riverbend Improvement Society works closely with him, and he knows we're trying to drag this three-stoplight town into the modern age. That new highway out there is our catalyst."

Yarrow laughed. "Sure, go talk to him. We elected a mayor who's only twenty-three years old. He got in because no one else wanted the job. So yeah, you can consult with a guy who was just thirteen when Erin's farm melted down."

Mary Jane oozed anger as she slid her arm into her purse strap. "Additional roads are being planned, Jim. If federal funding is approved, one of those new Interstate freeways is going to loop through here too. In a few years Riverbend will sit right at the intersection of two, maybe even three, major highways. This town's population is going to explode. Do you know what a bonanza that will be? New families are moving here already. Businesses too.

Rocco spoke up. "Come on MJ. Jim's brother died building that damn road."

"I know!" she snapped back. "Don't interrupt." She turned toward Yarrow and spoke so the full restaurant could hear.

"This growing town can't let Rebecca Bivens send the wrong message about what can be found here. It's taken a decade for us to live down that family's reputation. I won't let her reopen."

"What do you mean you won't *let* her?"

"I mean she won't be taking in her strays or promoting the whole "class conflict" mentality like her mother always pushed. I have too much invested in this town to watch that happen. You're a cop, Jim. Do your job."

As she stepped back, she refocused on Rocco. "And you. A prosperous town is good for your business too, or aren't you smart enough to see that?"

She turned and hurried toward the door. The bell clanged as she left, and Jim Yarrow shook his head and closed his eyes.

Chapter 3

Flourish

The New Hampshire portion of the Merrimack River gathers power and speed as the elevation drops. But as it reaches Massachusetts, it slows. The hills are shorter, and the river grows wide. In 1603 the first white settlers explored the river. Shortly thereafter, many indigenous peoples were pushed out, with European diseases further reducing their numbers.

Our Bend in the River, The Riverbend Historical Society, 1950

Rebecca Bivens worked hard to reestablish her farm.

In the first few days she only sold a few jars of honey, but the location was good. Steady traffic at the crossroads. People slowed down to look and sometimes they stopped. When they did, they usually made a purchase.

She decorated her table with wildflowers and decided to add another product. Strawberries.

Descendants of the farm's original strawberry plants still survived. When she was young, she helped Erin Bivens plant them. They were hidden from view behind a hedgerow but still received a perfect amount of sun.

Several peach and cherry trees also stood on the property. She expected the cherries to bear fruit by mid-summer.

Her fifth day of business was her first good one. She sold nineteen jars and late in the day, a local restaurant asked if she could supply four of her largest jars each week.

"I'm happy for the order," Becky said. "But that seems like a lot."

"You'd think so," the owner replied. "But we advertise honey tea on the menu, and we always offer honey toast with our breakfasts. I think just the smell of it spurs more orders."

Later that day, Becky drove to a farm co-op that sold plants and animals. She bought three chickens and a rooster, took them home, and let them run wild on the lot. For now, they could shelter under her truck at night. She hoped to build a basic chicken coop within a few weeks.

There was an old farm in her neighborhood that seemed neglected. She saw cucumbers, tomatoes, and yellow squash, but they grew in a garden filled with weeds. She decided to knock on the door and when an old man answered, she asked for permission to pick the vegetables. She offered to split whatever money she made.

"Huh," he said, then scratched his chin for a moment. "I guess they are just going to waste. So sure. Why not?"

Becky set up a second table using some old sawhorses and boards. There, she displayed the fresh produce, plus more bouquets of wildflowers. Realizing she could sell the flowers too, she placed them in water-filled mason jars and tied each with a red ribbon.

After the first week, cars rolled into her lot about every ten minutes. That seemed promising, and she knew the traffic would increase when the big road finally opened.

Every morning at sun-up she would rise, shake the dew off her plants, and pick the ripest strawberries. She had one Early Richmond cherry tree on her land that produced fruit before the others. She started offering a basket or two of cherries daily, which always disappeared before noon.

One day a farmer stopped by. At first, she thought he had come to check out the competition. Instead, he arrived with a business proposal.

"I have 30 cows," he said. We sell most of our milk to a wholesaler, but my wife likes to make butter and cheddar cheese. Vermont style."

"That sounds wonderful," Becky replied.

"Ayah. But we don't get any traffic down our road. I'm looking for a place where she can sell what she makes. Do you have any interest?"

"An interest … in offering her butter and cheese here? Yes, I'd like that. But I don't have a way to pay you upfront. And I have no way to keep it cold."

The farmer looked around. "Well, I guess I could spot you. We could see how it goes." He smiled as two cars arrived. "Tell you what, I have a big cooler that I ain't using. I suppose I could loan it to you. I got plenty of ice too. We always cut us a few big slabs from our pond and drag them into a cellar beneath the old barn. When you cover them with straw and sawdust, they usually last into the summer."

They talked a bit more and Becky agreed to his terms. She said she'd add a 30% markup to whatever she sold.

"I think we could do that. And if this test is successful, I'll be happy to restock the cooler every few days."

Her efforts to expand seemed to have an impact. A steady trickle of customers came and went. Soon she began selling green beans, herbs, and garlic, and making deals with other home gardeners. If they agreed to loan her their produce on speculation, she offered a generous split of the profits, while assuming very little debt or risk.

Yes indeed, she mused, *business is picking up.*

But she would not let the new products crowd out the glass jars of gold liquid. Those remained front and center, on their own table. The honey would remain the main focus and an important branding element for the Bivens Farm.

But her success meant she was starting to run short on honey. She needed more product. Every day she scanned classified ads in farm magazines and local newspapers. At last, she found what she was looking for.

The post was short and simple.

Honeybees for sale. Selling up to forty-five hives.

Most are eight frames deep. Make an offer.

That many hives would be a big leap forward and could keep her going for months. She wrote down the phone number and closed the stand for the day. At noon she drove her truck to the nearest payphone, with smoke puffing from the truck's increasingly noisy muffler every time she shifted.

On the third ring, a young woman answered. After a brief introduction, Becky asked about the hives.

"I'm getting rid of all of them," the girl explained. "My father died six weeks ago and, well, I need money. I'm probably going to sell most of his belongings."

Becky expressed her condolences.

"Thank you. I don't know nothin' about keeping bees," she said. "They were all his, and to be honest, they scare me."

They discussed price and Becky realized the girl had no idea what the value was for a working hive. So, she tried to explain.

"At different times of the year, hives can have different values. For example, if it's late fall, you won't get much for them. The season is over, and some hives won't survive the winter, especially if they've been moved and the bees feel out of sorts. Now in the early spring? A healthy hive becomes twice as valuable, especially if all the racks are full."

"I never knew that."

"So, for your hives," Becky continued, "we're at the start of summer. I'll need to look at them first, but I think this is what I might be able to do … "

She offered the girl a fair price and said she could collect the hives the next day. "First I need to make some modifications to my truck."

Transporting a beehive inside a vehicle could be dangerous. If any bees were to exit a hive, they could feel trapped and angry, and the driver would be trapped inside with them.

Becky drove to a second-hand store and bought a pair of tablecloths. Yellow oilcloth with red cherries in the center and flowers along the borders. She spent the evening hanging, tucking, and taping, effectively covering the opening between the driver's area and the back of the boxy truck.

The next morning, she rose early and drove out to meet the seller. The girl was waiting for her in the driveway.

"Are you Amy Maye?"

"Yes, I am. I hope you're Becky."

"Yup. Nice to meet you."

She could tell Amy was having a rough time. There were multiple patches on the girl's overalls. Her hair was clean but looked like it had never seen a sharpened pair of hair sheers.

"I'm guessing those are the hives?" Becky pointed.

Some were painted white. Others light gray. The dimensions varied, and Becky figured they had been constructed or purchased at different times.

"Would you like to go look?"

"I would! Will you come along with me? I'll probably need your help."

They went together into the field, but the closer they walked, the more hesitant Amy became. Becky walked ahead and offered words of encouragement.

"Watch. As we get close, they'll sense we're here. But don't worry. These hives look like they were well-maintained. Your father did his job, and the colonies are probably used to occasional visitors. The trick is to move slowly."

As she crept closer, she also moved slightly to the side of the first hive. "Here's something to remember—the worker bees come and go all day. So, try not to block their entrance. If you end up in their flight path, that may bother them. Just stay slightly to the side. Be gentle, calm, and deliberate. Keep moving slowly."

She reached the first wooden box and touched its top. "Be careful not to agitate them when you're near a hive. Don't act nervous or aggressive."

"So, I guess just be predictable?"

"Exactly. Try to remember how your father interacted with them."

Amy seemed surprised when Becky opened the top of the hive without wearing any protection. The buzzing increased, but she neither slowed nor hurried. The noise did not diminish. The bees were on guard and showed awareness of her presence, but they displayed no anger.

She held her hand above the open top and let it hover for a moment. When there was no reaction, she proceeded. Becky pinched one of the frames and slid it upward. She was pleased with what she saw. The colony looked healthy and productive. Several drops of honey fell to the ground. She slid the frame back into place, closed the top, and walked among the other hives. She opened five more and continued to be impressed by what she saw. All but one had a healthy buzzing sound.

Amy followed her through the colonies and Becky offered small lessons along the way.

"Whenever you open a hive, check to see if you smell something that's a bit like bananas. If you detect that, it's a pheromone. They release it as an alarm. If that hits your nose, just slowly back away."

Becky returned to her truck to suit-up in her full bee outfit. After a time, she convinced Amy to suit up in her father's outfit so she could actively help. Becky fired up her smoker but barely needed to use it. Pushing a two-wheel dolly, she slid the bottom edge under each hive and moved them one by one toward her truck. She lined up the first eight in the driveway. With Amy's help, she carefully lifted and loaded each box through the truck's rear door, taking care not to bump or tilt them. To take possession of all the hives, she realized she'd have to make several trips. She would not be able to open her farm stand today, but that was fine. It was a nice day for fieldwork.

When she drove back for her second load, she saw Amy standing under a tree and eating some strawberries. That made her wonder how much other food the girl had in the house.

After they loaded the next group of hives, Becky asked the teenager. "Would you like to see where I'm putting them?"

Amy shook her head no. "I don't want to be in the truck with them."

"It will be okay. We're safe up front." She showed her the tablecloth barrier. "And I think your dad would be pleased if he knew where they're ending up. I have a nice sunny field for them. Gradual downward slope. Lots of flowers and water nearby. It's a great place for bees."

It took some convincing, but Amy did climb in. As they rode together, Becky explained that she needed help on the farm. "I can see you're a good worker, and you're already braver around the bees than you were just an hour ago."

Amy smiled. "I guess I am. Maybe."

Back at the Bivens Farm, after they unloaded and hauled the buzzing boxes into the field, Becky extended an offer of employment. "And that includes a place to stay. Right over here," she pointed toward a flat spot on the edge of the field. "You can pitch a tent."

"Oh, thank you. But I have a house. At least for now."

"I understand. But do you plan to sell it?"

"I think so. I mean, I pretty much have to."

Becky expected that answer. "So, let me propose something. How about if you live here and rent your father's home to someone else?"

"I wouldn't even know how to do that."

"It's not hard. I can help you. If you rent your place, you could turn the house into a revenue stream rather than an expense. In fact, you will end up with two streams of income, one from the rent, and one from your job here."

Amy seemed to like the idea of getting out of the old house, making a little money, and having a new friend. She asked several more questions, and Becky could see she was interested.

"You know what?" Amy replied. "Maybe that would work. I guess we can try."

Becky knew this would be a good thing. Amy seemed smart. She could put her to work filling the honey jars and occasionally running the stand. Then Becky would have more time to do her accounting and grow the business.

As they went to retrieve the next batch of hives, Becky decided to share some personal history. "You know, my mother originally ran a farm on this property. She always said offering workers a free place to stay was the best way to make things work."

It took most of the afternoon, but they finally transported the last of the hives. Then Becky dropped Amy back at her house with a promise to pick her up the following morning. "Pack whatever you need to stay a few days. We'll work on getting you a tent, then maybe a trailer, and as for your house, I can help you write a newspaper ad to find a tenant."

On the way home Becky stopped at the top of a hill overlooking the river. It was Jim Yarrow, years ago, who inspired her to do that. During their short time together in high school, he had said, *whenever you're on a hilltop, stop to take in the view. It's a great place to think about where you are, and where you're trying to go.*

So, she stopped. And she looked. There was the big river down there, draining a watershed of over fifty thousand square miles, stretching all the way back to New Hampshire's White Mountains, and reaching out to the Atlantic.

Then she looked in a different direction. In the distance, she could see the dust from the road construction.

Ever closer, she thought. Her eyes traced the path the highway was slated to follow. Many trees had already been cleared. The construction would bring the big road right near her land.

This is good, she thought. *I'm glad I came back. I'll be ready.*

Chapter 4

The Distance

By the early 1800s, the industrial era of the Merrimack Valley had begun. Cities grew as they tapped into the river's waterpower. Textile mills soon dominated the shores. In New Hampshire, the key river cities were Concord, Manchester, and Nashua, while Massachusetts had Lowell, Lawrence, and Haverhill. Rafts of timber could also be floated downriver to meet an insatiable demand. Where the mouth of the river touched the Atlantic, Newburyport became a key shipbuilding city.

Scenes From a River, Peat Moss Press, 1949

When their shift is over, police officers feel a special relief when they walk through their front doors. It means they had the best kind of day. They made it home unscathed.

As a cop in a quiet New England town, Jim Yarrow seldom faced life-or-death choices. But he knew the nature of his job, and he knew he was vulnerable. Some random person passing through could be a killer, and all towns had unstable people or random domestic quarrels. He'd seen it all and, so far, he'd avoided the worst.

With a feeling of peace, he approached the safety of his home. The illusion held right up until he turned the doorknob.

Once inside he heard his two sons, Tommy and Curtis, screaming at each other. A red toy truck flew over his shoulder and struck a wall. He immediately scolded them, then stepped gingerly over a dozen scattered toys as he made his way toward the kitchen.

There, he found Linda standing at their white enameled stove, using one hand to stir a pot and the other to hold Bonnie, their sixteen-month-old daughter. Linda looked as beautiful as ever, but also disheveled. There was a milky vomit stain on her shoulder. Her hair was uncombed, and the breakfast dishes sat in the sink. They kissed, but he could tell she was upset. Not at him necessarily, but at the chaos.

Maybe she was a bit upset with him too. He had the privilege of exiting the home for nine hours every day. She did not.

"How was your day?" he asked.

"Fine." She thrust Bonnie into his arms. "I need to change my clothes. Can you stir this too?"

He did so, after giving Bonnie a quick cheek kiss. The contents of the pot smelled delicious. Beef stew, apparently. He could see chunks of onions, carrots, and peppers. Linda was an excellent cook and had been since he first met her.

He and Bonnie jabbered to each other for a while, then he put her down to toddle around on the kitchen floor. He pulled out a pot, put some rice on the stove, and let it simmer. When Linda returned, she insisted on resuming the cooking duties. Yarrow played with the kids on the living room floor, then lifted Bonnie into her playpen.

He walked to the big white sink and found dish soap behind the curtain that hung beneath the basin. Most of the pots and pans had been soaking and the dirty glasses were lined up along the yellow counter. Everything cleaned up with a minimal amount of scrubbing.

As he stacked the last plate in the drying rack, he said, "I stopped in to see Ma today. I was out in that part of town."

"It's nice that you try to see her every week. How was she?"

"Oh, you know. Feeling down. She's still coughing like crazy. I'm a little worried about that. And she still has a hard time with Will's death. She said the house feels empty there now. She starts to talk with him sometimes, then remembers he isn't there. She was a little teary-eyed when she told me."

"I can understand that. I feel so bad for her." Linda tasted the stew and declared it finished. "Has she been to the doctor about that cough? It could be walking pneumonia."

"She said she's gone twice."

The kids came into the kitchen asking about dinner and were immediately put to work. Despite the earlier chaos, the Yarrows fell into their evening routine. Curtis sloppily set the table. Tommy poured milk for everyone. Dad scooped the rice, and mom ladled the stew on top.

Then dinner.

Then clean up.

Soon, kids were in their jammies with their teeth brushed. If they got ready quickly, they were allowed to listen to the radio for half an hour before bed. The family owned a big floor-model Zenith because Yarrow liked the sound of its heavy speaker.

Bonnie seemed extra fussy, so once the radio was off, Yarrow rocked her to sleep while Linda put the boys to bed. Eventually, everything settled down and Bonnie was quiet in her crib.

He stood in the kitchen doorway while Linda headed toward the couch.

"Wine?" he asked.

"Absolutely."

As they sipped, they made the marriage version of small talk. Tommy and Curtis didn't have anyone to play with that day. Their school was out for the summer and the neighbor kids were already on vacation. Having no friends around made the boys extra keyed up, frustrated, and wild.

To complicate things, Bonnie was teething and often crying. Linda said she didn't have a chance to go grocery shopping like she planned.

"I need some relief, Jim. It's crazy. It just ..." she stroked the rim of her glass. "It goes on and on."

"I know honey. I wish I could come home at midday. Usually I can't, but I might be able to swap my patrol tomorrow."

"That's not what I meant. You know what I'm saying, Jim."

He looked at her, then at the big walnut radio in the corner. Its wide dial glowed, even when it was turned off.

"Look, Linda, I know what you want to do. But my work is here. All my friends are here. I grew up in this town."

"But I didn't." She looked like she wanted to wave her hands but instead, she placed one on his arm. "Jim, we've talked about this. My mom would love to help me during the day, but she lives in Freeport. If she wasn't eighty miles north all this would be easier."

She stopped talking and took a long sip of wine.

"And she still has no interest in moving here?"

"No, Jim. You always ask the same question. She can't afford to rent a place here, and neither of us wants her living in this house." She looked at him, though he avoided direct eye contact. "Besides, I'm not going to demand she move to Riverbend when I'm the one who moved away from home."

Yarrow took his own long sip, then studied the small bubbles near the edge of the glass. He chose his next words carefully. "When you moved here to be with me, you said it was exactly what you wanted to do. In fact, you were thrilled to get out of your old hometown. You said you loved Maine but not the empty gray winters. You longed for something different, and then you said you fell in love with our little town. I mean, I took you at your word."

She slowly nodded.

"But now you're asking the whole family to make a big change."

"I know I am. And I know how much this changes our plans and future. I do still like it here, Jim. But I think moving back to Freeport makes sense right now."

He shook his head. "Did your mother put you up to this?"

"Not really."

He raised an eyebrow and gave her a sidewise glance.

"Stop it. Like I said, it just makes sense."

He started to speak, but realized he was at a loss for words. Finally, he blurted out, "It's not easy to jump to another police position. You know that. Local cops tend to stay in their jobs for years and most towns don't have many openings."

She slid slightly closer to him. "Well, I've long said I'd love it if you found a different line of work. Every day, I watch you leave, and I wonder if this will be the day something happens to you. That's a real weight to carry and I wouldn't mind seeing it end."

There was a small pillow on the couch beside him and his eyes settled on its embroidered flowers. "Look Linda, I've always told you, you don't need to worry. This is a peaceful town. The last cop to be injured on the job slipped on ice. And that was five years ago. It's been twenty years since a Riverbend cop was killed on duty, and that was a car accident."

He felt her pull away a little.

"So, you think that automatically means you'll also be safe tomorrow? And the next day?" She looked dejected. They both grew quiet.

"You know, my uncle still owns that paper box factory in Brunswick. He's always looking for good workers. You know he'd help us out."

Jim closed his eyes. The idea of standing at a machine all day in a dusty factory burned a hole in his soul. He decided not to respond because he knew he would only sound angry.

They finished their wine. He offered to refill her glass, but she rose and kissed him goodnight.

"Just think about it, okay?"

"Sure. I'll think about it."

And he did sit and think for a while. *I don't want to leave here.* He thought. *I really don't. This is my whole life.*

Riverbend's downtown was postcard-perfect New England at its finest. Church steeples. A grassy lawn in front of the town hall and a white bandstand on the common. Nearly every day he ran into and greeted lifelong friends.

And he had a good job. He was proud of who he had become in this town.

Linda seemed proud too. But now she wanted a different life?

He turned his head and focused on their wedding picture on the mantel. They were happy at that moment. Linda was beautiful. And she was a good woman. He hated to see her flustered now.

Yarrow poured another drink—this time a whiskey— then walked through the kitchen and into a connected two-car garage. They'd built that addition the year before. The ice in his glass clinked as he walked across the concrete. With his paralyzed fingers it was a challenge to maintain a solid grip on a drink, so he switched the glass from his right hand to his left.

A set of unpainted pine stairs led to the floor above their garage. It was a large room and it remained unfinished. Once they had the time and money, they planned to turn the space into a big bedroom, a nice expansion from the original three-bedroom house. When it was ready, they would give their old room to Tommy. Then each child could have their own space.

Yarrow was proud of the big addition. But now, as he looked at the bare two-by-fours and exposed insulation, he wondered if their plan would ever come to pass.

The house sat atop a medium-sized hill with a steep drop-off and no trees on the downhill side. The view in that direction was stunning. After building the garage, the first thing they did was add a balcony. On warm nights he and Linda would often walk through the garage and have their wine out on that balcony.

He never told Linda, but a good hill was one of the main things he looked for when shopping for homes. There was something about being up high; it made his problems seem smaller and less troublesome.

From his perch, his gaze followed the river downstream. The night was clear. The moon was a bit past full. A few miles in the distance, he could barely discern where the land ended, and the ocean began. Out in that blackness, he could see distant lights. White. Red. Green. Those were cargo ships plying the waters east of Plum Island.

He sipped his drink. Allowed his eyes to adjust.

He tried to picture the place where the new highways would cross near Becky's property.

He wondered if one of the lights he saw in that area was her light. Then he remembered she didn't even have electricity. She was living rough.

For now, she was invisible. Alone in the dark and vulnerable.

So, he worried about her. And thought about her.

He stayed until his glass was empty.

Chapter 5

Taxing

The Merrimack Valley stretches over one hundred and fifteen miles and encompasses parts of sixty-eight New Hampshire and Massachusetts towns. The valley's evolution into a major industrial center started in the late 1600s. With ample waterpower, it became a major center for textile manufacturing. But many of the towns reached their economic pinnacle around World War I. After that, newer factories in other parts of America siphoned business away from the valley. In the 1930s one magazine referred to the area as a "depressed industrial desert." By the 1950s, the eastern end of the river, near the coast, saw a renewal. Road construction and suburban expansion took that part of the valley in a more prosperous direction, while the areas farther upstream would take decades to recover.

The Smith Guide to Industrial New England, 1989

Jim Yarrow followed his usual morning patrol route through the hills and fields near town. The hours had been uneventful, and he thought about returning to the station. But then something shiny caught his eye.

Nothing particularly troubling. Just a quick reflection in a fallow field. But that glimpse didn't sit right in his mind.

Was that a chrome bumper?

If that shiny blip was indeed a car, why was it pulled off the road and parked in a way that mostly hid it from view?

He downshifted, made a U-turn, and pulled into a rutted farm path. With hedgerows on either side, he rolled slowly, following the ruts away from the road for several yards. There, he found a Nash Ambassador parked behind some weeds. Two men stood in a nearby field. One was looking through a brass theodolite.

The lens of the surveyor's scope was trained on the meadow's far corner, where another man held an elevation rod. The man using the scope was staring so intently that he didn't notice the police car's arrival. He jumped a bit when Yarrow slammed the door.

"Afternoon!" Jim Yarrow called out. The man backed away from the scope and nodded. He held a map, which he quickly rolled and slid into a tube. The other man looked on from across the field. Yarrow motioned for him to join them and watched him walk, reluctantly, through the dirt and daisies.

"So, what are you gentlemen up to?"

They looked at each other before responding. "Just taking some measurements," said the man holding the tube.

"I see. And who are you working for?"

They looked at each other before answering. "We work for V.R.E. We're an engineering group out of Boston."

"Okay. Well, welcome to Riverbend." Yarrow pointed toward a farmhouse in the distance. "Did Ron Miller hire you? This is his property."

The men exchanged glances, then one replied, "I don't know."

"You don't know?"

"Not really. Our front office deals with the clients. We just do the work. This is the address they sent us to."

"I see. So, tell me again what it is you're doing?"

"Oh, measuring the size of the lot. Checking the elevation. Confirming all the lines and markers are where they're supposed to be. Then we pound in some stakes. You know, the usual surveying stuff."

Yarrow nodded. "And Mr. Miller knows you're here?"

They look at each other again. "I … I think so."

Yarrow stood for a while. The men avoided eye contact.

"So, I'll tell you what. I don't see any *no-trespassing* signs here. That means I can't immediately charge you with being here illegally. But I'm going to drive over and knock on Mr. Miller's door. If he answers, I'll ask him if he knows you're out here. If he says no, I'm going to head back here, and we will continue our chat."

He looked them in the eyes, switching back and forth. "Now, if you think you already know his answer, and if you think maybe he doesn't know you're out here, well, I wouldn't mind if you just packed up and disappeared while I'm over at the house. You'd be gone by the time I get back, and we won't have to have our little follow-up chat. I'll leave that up to you."

He returned to his cruiser and as he rolled back toward the road, he looked in his rear-view mirror. He saw them opening the Nash's big trunk.

At Ron Miller's house, the old man told Yarrow wasn't aware of anyone visiting his property.

"But, you know, I don't think it's the first time someone's been poking around out there. I've seen other cars and trucks. When I start to walk in their direction, they always drive away. I'm not sure what's going on."

Yarrow looked toward the field. "Well, if you think about it, their nosy nature makes sense. This is quite an enticing chunk of land you have here, Ron. As demand for houses goes up, I suspect some investors want to plan ahead, so they're ready to pounce with their offer."

Ron Miller just smiled. "Yeah, I know what I have here. And the land is still mine. I'll either keep it in the family or, if we decide to sell, I'll look for top dollar, just like everyone else."

Back in the village, Yarrow stopped by the town's zoning office, which was located near the back entrance of the town hall. A clerk sat at a tall metal counter. The name *Bob Dawkins* was engraved on his nameplate. Yarrow vaguely knew him from general town business, and he knew Bob had a son who was killed on Okinawa.

"Morning, Bob."

"Hi, um ... Jim, right?"

"That's me! Hey, do you mind if I look at any of the planning maps that show a detailed path for the proposed highways?"

Dawkins pointed toward a ten-level file at the back of the room. The stacked drawers were just the right size for maps and blueprints. "Help yourself, Jim. Police officers can come in here to examine any files they want. Heck, most of our files are open to anyone."

Yarrow read the labeling and eventually found the drawer and the map he wanted. Sure enough, the proposed path for the new road ran along the edge of Miller's property. Yarrow studied it for a minute, then called out.

"Hey, Bob? The town's been reworking a lot of the zoning, right? I guess because of all the new roads?"

"Ayuh."

"So—"

"Over on the big table. So many people want to see the new zoning proposals that I leave those maps out on display."

The three-by-five-foot sheets were so big that Yarrow had to lean over the table to see them. One of the first things he noticed was the town's proposed enlargement of what was presently a smaller commercial zone. The new plan would more than triple the size of the current commercial property in town, including one area that would be a mile long and a quarter-mile wide. It looked like most of Miller's property would soon be zoned commercial.

He let out a low whistle.

That land is really going to spike in value, he thought to himself. *That must be what's going on.*

The map also showed a proposed zoning change in the area surrounding Becky's property. Yarrow wasn't sure which lot number was hers, so he strolled to the filing cabinets where local copies of the deed records and property transfers. That file provided an easy way to check property tax information. When he pulled out the card for her property, he was puzzled by what he saw.

Becky's name was on the card. It confirmed that the ownership was transferred to her recently. But the address for where to send the tax bills was not hers. The card listed a post office box in a nearby town.

Yarrow walked to the window and held the card in the sunlight. The original address on the card had been erased, but it was still slightly visible. Yarrow recognized the faint number because he saw it painted on Becky's mailbox.

He ran his finger over the card. A Post Office box number was written in its place.

"Hey, Bob? Who's responsible for these cards?"

"All of us in this office can do updates. I mean, it's mostly Elenore, but she's been out for the past month." Bob dropped his voice to a whisper. "You know, woman problems."

"Yeah, yeah. Okay. Anyone else?"

"Jeez, Jim, people come in here all the time to look things up. I guess any visitor technically has access. They're not supposed to change anything, but we can't watch everyone."

He showed Bob the card. "Is this right? When the tax bills come due for this property, are they supposed to be sent to this P.O. Box?"

Bob looked closely. "Ha, Becky Bivens. That girl—"

Jim gave him a steely look.

"Okay. So, when I think about it, no. That address don't seem right at all. When she bought the property, I updated that card myself. I don't recall no post office box being part of it, especially not some address in Salisbury."

"Huh," Yarrow said.

"Huh is right. Someone changed it."

"Do you remember seeing any—"

Bob held up his hands. "We've been short-staffed, Jim. And people come and go every day. Like I said, anyone could have done that. Hell, she may have come in to update it herself."

Jim shook his head. He doubted Becky would have done that. That meant it was someone else, and he wasn't sure why.

He thanked Bob Dawkins and returned the card to the file drawer.

Out in the parking lot he sat in his police cruiser, trying to decide what to do. Then he grabbed the mic and checked in with the dispatcher.

"Tina? What else do we have going on today?"

"Not much. The stoplight's out over by Maple. But we already have someone directing traffic."

"Okay. I think I'm going to take a drive. I'm going to head over to the Salisbury post office. I need to check on something."

"Okey-dokey. We know where to find you. But's you'll be out of radio range after about 9 miles."

"Yeah, but I'll be quick."

He tried to formulate a plan. Maybe he could use his policeman's charm to persuade that town's postal clerk to tell him who owned box number 81563.

As he drove, Yarrow thought of something else that troubled him. All the towns near Riverbend were small. None of them would have enough PO boxes to have any numbers greater than four digits.

In less than an hour he had his answer. The woman at the post office was very nice. She answered his questions, and he never needed to ask for names. It turned out that PO box 81563 did not exist in Salisbury.

During his return trip, he mulled the issue over. It could be as simple as someone making a mistake, but that seemed unlikely, given that the old address was erased. This wasn't Yarrow's first time at smelling a rat. Maybe someone wanted Becky's tax bill sent to the wrong address. Maybe they wanted it to disappear into the void so that maybe, just maybe, it didn't get paid.

And if a tax bill remained unpaid for long enough, the property could be seized or auctioned.

It was a troublesome situation, and he would bring it to Becky's attention. But it was clear that some residents of Riverbend could be quite cutthroat, and she was already facing some underhanded activities.

Chapter 6

Inner Workings

Over three hundred and fifty species of bees live in New England. But only the genus Apis are considered true honeybees. The species did not exist in America until it was introduced during European migration. Once it was here it flourished, and its domain rapidly expanded.

Becky's Guide to Raising Bees

Sometimes, Becky had to remind herself, not everyone felt comfortable around bees. She had been a beekeeper for most of her life. So, she knew when to be nervous, and that was not very often.

Amy, on the other hand, was very nervous at the start. But as they worked together, she slowly relaxed. As they unloaded the last of the hives, Becky saw that Amy's fear had subsided.

She decided to show her new friend a few tricks of the trade.

"If you watch and listen, the bees will teach you what works. Just move slowly and gauge their reaction. If their buzzing grows louder or if their motion makes you nervous, go even slower. Sometimes I freeze in place and wait for them to calm down. Remember, if they sting you they'll die too, so most bees will avoid conflict if they can."

She popped the top of a hive. They moved closer and saw the bees move too, in a noticeable pattern.

"Just observe what they're doing and try to move along with that activity. Don't fight it." She slid a hand down into the box. "Slowly work your way in to do what you need to do. And when you open or close any part of the hive, be extra careful not to crush any bees. The group will sense if one of their own gets hurt and that can set them off. In fact, that's a key reason why keepers get stung."

Becky pulled a small paring knife from her pocket and showed it to Amy. "We'll get you one just like this. If you do get stung, try to scrape the edge of the knife along your skin right at that spot. If you act quickly, you can often squeeze out most of the venom. If a stinger was left behind, you might be able to scrape that out too. Do it right and you'll end up with a spot that feels more like a pinch and less like one painful long-lasting sting."

They worked for a few hours, enduring the sun and making their way through the hives, checking each one for problems. Becky showed Amy how water had penetrated the wood in some places. They found rot in a few small sections of four hives.

"These sections will be okay for a while, but I'll cut some wood and block those parts off from the inside. That will keep the bees in the better parts. Then, next time the hive is empty, we'll replace the rotted boards."

Then she showed Amy how to light an old Woodman's bee smoker. It was a simple tool—just a leather bellows attached to a tin cannister with a snout that looked like a stubby coffee pot.

They opened the top of the smoker, added some paper, then tossed in a handful of wood pellets. Becky lit a match and tossed that in too. She let things burn until a few pellets lit, then blew out the flame. She shut the lid and with a few puffs of the bellows the pellets smoldered, and a steady supply of smoke rose up.

"Try it."

She encouraged Amy to inject some smoke at the top of the hive.

"Smoke can help calm things down in the hive," Becky explained. "It does two things. First, the smoke can mask the bees' pheromone signals. That's how they warn of danger or signal other bees to attack. Second, when bees detect smoke near their hive, they think it could be a sign of fire. So, they start protecting the hive differently. Often, they retreat deeper into the box, away from the smoke. They want to protect their queen. Once we learn to predict their reactions to the smoke it gets easier for us to do our work."

She pointed to an inside corner of the hive. "See this? Sometimes you might have a group making preparations, just in case the colony needs to leave the hive. When they're doing that, they're more likely to ignore us."

Amy leaned in for a closer look. "What kind of preparations?"

"Well, they may start to consume honey, so they'll have extra energy, but not too much. Too much can slow them down and make them lethargic. Also, they may start signaling each other about intentions. They don't get far though, because once we take the smoke away the threat is gone and they return to normal."

Becky and Amy worked for another hour. They made their way through the hives and took notes on which ones were healthy and which ones needed more attention. After each inspection Amy assigned that hive a number, writing it on the hive's side with a big blue crayon.

They were almost finished when they opened a hive that had a different type of activity. Becky motioned for Amy to come look.

"See this queen? I think she's old and has some issues. This hive has fewer larvae. The workers are acting differently because of that. They're prepping some potential alternative queens. See these larger cells that look like saggy peanuts? Those are potential new queens. The whole hive is anticipating some changes."

Amy looked confused. "But doesn't the queen rule the hive? Doesn't she have a say in what they do?"

"Oh, she does. But hives are complicated communities. The worker bees may be followers, but their real loyalty is to the hive itself. They always work towards community survival and what is best for the group." She pointed to the center of the hive. "A healthy hive needs a healthy and productive queen. Their life cycle begins with eggs, and the workers are the first to notice if their queen is not producing them. It's a tough decision for the workers because they are loyal to her too. But the hive always comes first."

Becky applied a puff of smoke, then moved her finger closer.

"See here?" She pointed to the larva in some of the cells. "All bee larvae start out the same, meaning queens are raised from the same fertilized female eggs as the workers. A newly hatched larva, if it's female, is not yet a queen nor is it part of the worker caste. In reality, almost all of them will become workers, but they are all blank slates at the start. It's the existing workers who choose a potential new queen. Once chosen, that larva is exclusively fed what's known as royal jelly. The workers secrete it from the tops of their heads."

She saw Amy frown and added, "Yeah, I guess it is kind of gross."

Amy watched the workers as they tended to the larvae. "So, what's in that food?"

"I know royal jelly sounds fancy but it's just a variation of what all the bee larvae eat. But that royal version has ingredients that sort of flip a switch to turn on the reproductive system, so that larva becomes a queen."

Amy stared wide-eyed. "So, one of the worker bees' jobs is to raise the next generations of bees, including alternative queens?"

"Yes. And they often start with more than one. The first to emerge from that group of larvae will most likely be the new queen."

Becky pointed to the current queen of the hive. "Think about where that leaves her. Any potential new queen is a challenge to the established order. If the old queen senses she might be replaced, and if she's still healthy enough, she may patrol the area, seeking to destroy the new queen cells before they have a chance to emerge and grow."

"Wow. So what do the other potential queens think about each other?"

"Same issue. In fact, if the potential new queens hatch at the same time, they will fight to the death for control of the colony."

"That's kind of brutal."

"That's nature. That's a hive. The queen only reigns because the workers choose her, or at least they choose a few potential queens. Once there is a clear winner, that winner will reign supreme. It's only when her power declines that the colony seeks to replace her."

"Can she just leave?"

"Oh yes," Becky replied. "And often the hive will split because some of the workers remain loyal to their original queen. After a split, the departing bees swarm, looking for a new home."

"Where do they go?"

"Oh, wherever they can find a hole in a tree or a crack in a house. They just want a protected space where they can stay dry and with enough warmth to do their bee business. Often, when they first leave their hive, they land somewhere in the open, then send workers out in search of a better place. We should always keep an eye out for that. If we see a swarming colony, it's fairly easy to isolate the queen and just move her into another hive. The other bees will pick up the scent and follow her over the next few hours."

"I had no idea all that was going on in my father's hives."

Becky smiled as Amy watched the scurrying bees. "I guess every living being finds their special niche, and if they're successful, they evolve to take perfect advantage of that niche. If not, they move on. It doesn't matter if we're talking about humans, sharks, or bees. To thrive, we all have to find our place."

Amy watched the potential new queen cells for a while. She saw slight movements and realized the next generation was right in there, slowly growing. "I think we can learn a lot from a beehive," she said.

"Yes," Becky replied. "We certainly can."

Chapter 7

Exigency

In the 1950s, parent-child relationships were often characterized by greater parental authority and expectations of respect. As post-war family dynamics changed, both parents and grandparents often struggled to fit into the changing dynamics of modern households.

Social Expectations and How They Grew, Pan Art Press, 1955

Linda let out an exasperated sigh.

"Yes," she said into the phone. "I know mom. Come on, I know. Of course I'm trying."

She stopped and listened. The voice coming from the other end of the phone was angry and shrill. But it also carried hints of logic, and they made some sense to Linda. Those were dropped like ping pong balls to bounce around her mind.

She listened intently to her mom but frowned at one point. "Look, just stop it. You know I don't like it when you say things like that. Jim is a good man."

She'd been on the phone for ten minutes and still had not broached the subject that originally prompted her to call her mom. She had intended to ask if her mother could visit and maybe watch the kids overnight so that she and Jim could get away.

"Stop it mom. He works hard. Yes, I know I do too."

"You do know I love him, right? Yes, of course I love you too. And yes, I'll tell him that I'm upset that he hasn't—"

And just then, Yarrow walked in. He caught just the tail end of Linda's conversation. She looked embarrassed and walked down the hallway, dragging the phone cord with her.

He decided to go find the kids. He joined them on the floor as they played with blocks, and that's where he was when Linda returned. Sheepishly, she said "I know you heard that. And, you do know I love you, right?"

"Of course I do." He stood up and gave her a wink. "I can feel it."

"Thanks," she said, and she kissed his cheek.

"Later, when they were clearing the dishes from the table, she threw him a bit of a curveball.

"We're different, you and I, right?"

"Huh? I don't know. I mean, I guess we are." He gave her a pat on the shoulder, urging her to move to the side so he could get a new dish towel.

"But I've always felt our differences give us strength," she said. "We each bring something different, right?"

"Yeah. Probably true."

"So, that's all. I just wanted you to know that I see that. I feel it."

"Well, thanks, Honey. I can feel it too."

She shrugged. "You're calling me Honey now? You usually call me Sweetie."

Yarrow raised his eyebrows. He hadn't even noticed. "Well, yeah, I think both Honey and Sweetie seem to fit."

As they wiped down the counter, he asked her, "What prompted all this 'we're different' stuff? Of course we're different. I wouldn't fall in love with someone who's just the same as me."

"Why not? Would you get sick of yourself?"

"Yeah, probably."

Linda considered the question before she replied. "I know I've been pretty demanding lately, about wanting to move. And I guess I'm just reminding myself that we want different things. And I'm trying to understand that and maybe trying to accept it."

"I see. So does that mean you don't want to move anymore?"

"No. I'm not going to go that far."

As she reached to turn off the light, she could sense the ping-pong balls still bouncing in her mind. She wasn't happy about that. They were creating uncertainty and maybe a bit of resentment toward Jim. But she didn't want to share anything yet. She wasn't even sure what she wanted to say.

Chapter 8

What's Written

The North Shore of Massachusetts has at least six community graveyards established prior to 1630. Besides these formal graveyards, there are numerous private plots where isolated farm families buried their own dead and marked their graves with carved stones and tears.

The History of New England Graveyards, Willowtree Imprints, 1891

The Wednesday afternoon patrol was fairly routine for Jim Yarrow. He found a wandering dog near the edge of town. After checking his tags, he returned the pup to his home. An hour later he caught some twelve-year-old boys lighting firecrackers in a downtown alley. Their parents were called.

With little else to do, he drove around until he cruised past the town cemetery. There, he saw an old white truck parked just inside the gate. It was Leon's truck.

Excellent.

Whenever he ran into Leon Davis, he always stopped to talk. Like Yarrow and Rocco, Leon was a townie. They'd all known each other since grade school.

Once inside the gate he spotted Leon's big flatbed trailer, standing empty. Up the driveway was a Wain-Roy hydraulic backhoe, mounted on the rear of a Ford tractor. The machine sat next to a freshly dug grave. Yarrow parked his car and found Leon at the bottom of the hole, making a perfect rectangle with a flathead shovel. He saw rich and dark earth on all sides.

"Well look at you!" he called down. "At least one of us stays in shape."

Leon gave one last poke with the shovel then looked up. "Jim! Damn, now I have an audience. No more slacking."

Yarrow squatted near the edge. "Bah, you're fine. I'm on the clock too."

When they were teens, Yarrow and Leon used to smoke. He recalled that Leon liked Viceroys. Yarrow wished he had a cigarette to offer, but he gave up smoking when he became a dad.

"So, what are you up to?" Leon's voice called up from the hole.

"Not much. I just stopped by because I saw your truck. Nothing else to do. I guess we need a crime wave or something around here."

"If you're looking for something, I thought I heard firecrackers a while ago."

"Already taken care of. Those kids have been sent home."

Yarrow stood and surveyed the graveyard. Lush green grass in need of a mow. Newer headstones to the left. The older ones, mostly thin marble or slabs of slate, sat to the right. The oldest ones were carved with dates from the mid-1600s. He walked toward them for a closer view. Some had the classic New England look with arched tops and carvings below—often skulls with wings. The death's head was an old Puritan tradition he never really understood.

He made his way back to the grave as Leon was finishing up.

"Your truck has been out here a few times lately. Are you the main gravedigger now?"

"I think I am, at least for the last ten graves or so. You know me, Jim. Since I got out of the army, I just take whatever job I can get. Been doing it long enough that people seem to know me. I stay pretty busy."

Even though they were friends as kids, Yarrow and Leon lost track of each other by late high school. Leon struggled with classes and eventually dropped out. Then they both ended up overseas.

In recent years, with Yarrow constantly driving around town and Leon doing most of his work outside, they kept running into each other. That helped them get reacquainted. And they both had kids about the same age.

"So, who's grave is this, Leon?"

Leon hesitated.

"Old man Ashby maybe?" Yarrow wondered. "I know he died a few days ago."

"Um ... yeah. I think so."

Leon kept digging. He changed the subject, and they talked about the current high school football team, and how they might fare, come fall.

"They're not like our old team, eh Jim? Boy we were a force to be reckoned with. We almost won the playoffs."

"Oh yeah we did."

Leon tossed one last shovel of dirt out of the deep hole.

"And you! Top scorer of our final year. Well, it was the last year I was with the team. Remember? Then I dropped out."

"School just wasn't for you, Leon. And your last year on the team was a good one for me too because I had you knocking holes for me. I could practically walk right through them. You were the best offensive lineman we had, and it was tough on the whole team when you left."

Yarrow looked around as Leon worked. He noticed a card lying on the ground. When he picked it up, he could see the name of the person whose grave this was intended to be. It was a woman named Emma Giles.

That gave Yarrow an idea. For years he'd had a hunch about something, and he wanted to test his theory.

"Oh, here you go! Look at this card." He reached down and handed it to Leon. "See?" Yarrow continued. "Just like we thought."

Leon appeared to study it. "Yeah. Look at that, old man Ashby. Well, there you go."

Yarrow didn't speak for a moment. He wanted to carefully choose his next words. He waited until Leon was finished, and he gave him a hand as he climbed up out of the hole.

"So," Yarrow spoke as Leon was brushing the dirt off his pants. "I think I was wrong about what was written on the card Leon. But you ... agreed with me."

Leon avoided eye contact. Then he shrugged. "Don't matter who it is. I get paid by the job."

When they were younger, Yarrow knew Leon hated school. He didn't give much thought to what his issue might be. But part of Yarrow's police training was to understand unusual issues he might encounter, and that included dealing with people who might not be able to read.

His training had been minimal, but there was one word that stuck with him—that word was *dyslexia*. Since then, the more he learned about the condition, the more he thought of Leon.

"So, that card. When I handed it to you, were you able to read it?"

Leon shrugged. "Maybe some."

Yarrow thought for a moment. "You do have trouble reading. Come on Leon. You've had trouble with it since we were young."

"Nah. I can read a bit. I'm just not good at it. Short words? I do okay. Longer ones? Not so much. But it don't matter, Jim. I get by just fine."

Yarrow shook his head. "Jeez, a man deserves to know how to read Leon. Everyone deserves that."

Again, Leon just shrugged.

"Well. I could maybe try to teach you." Yarrow didn't say so, but he felt sorry for Leon. His father had spent more time with a bottle than with his children. And growing up, Leon spent more time on the streets than he ever did with books.

He had not intended to embarrass his friend, but he realized his offer had that effect. Leon just waved him off. "Look, don't worry about it, Jim. Okay? It ain't hurt me none. I'm always finding work and that means I'm doing just fine. Besides, everyone has their issues to deal with, right?" Then he looked Yarrow in the eye. "I mean, how's your hand?"

Yarrow snorted. "Oh, Jeez, cut me to the quick!" But he held up his hand and managed to wiggle three of the five fingers. "Feels mostly fine. See?"

"Okay. And does that old wound slow ya down much?"

"Hardly at all."

"So, there ya go. We all have problems. And we all have our own ways of working around them."

"You know, you're right. You win."

"Yup. Workarounds rule. You know, like that piece of metal you had some gunsmith screw onto the side of your .38 Police Special? I've seen how you rest your middle fingers there, and it helps you keep the pistol level, even with your distorted grip."

Yarrow frowned.

"You probably didn't even realize I saw it. But I did. It was last fall when we was shooting at those tin cans behind my house."

"Fine. You're right. And little workarounds like that do help. So anyway, I know of a guy who teaches reading in a special school—"

Leon interrupted. "Jim, I like ya but damn it. I don't need to take no courses. Let's drop it."

Yarrow nodded. And he dropped it.

As Leon packed up his truck they talked about other things. The weather. A wonderful new pulled pork recipe Leon's uncle sent him. And they talked about where some of their old teammates ended up.

They also talked about their mutual friend Eddie who was wounded in the Battle of the Bulge. He was still at a Boston Veterans hospital.

"Think he'll ever get out?"

Yarrow shook his head.

"Wow. Poor Eddie. I miss him."

A few minutes later they went their separate ways.

But Yarrow made a mental note to borrow some books from his contact at the special school. If nothing else, maybe he could encourage Leon to try to read more than just the short words.

Chapter 9

Futures

During World War II, beekeeping was declared an essential industry. Beeswax replaced petroleum for some types of waterproofing and honey replaced rationed sugar. Post-war, the government instituted price supports for honey production—to assure enough honeybees would remain available for crop pollination.

Synopsis from the U.S. Federal Agricultural Act of 1949

A sunny Saturday morning usually meant extra traffic on the road near Becky's farm. She expected the weekend to be particularly busy, and she pulled out all the stops—at least within the limits of her budget. New colorful tablecloths topped her folding tables. She made a larger sign and decorated it with yellow and gold balloons.

Even as the sun rose higher, a light and lingering fog hung within the river valley. The milky backdrop made the trees on the edge of the property look extra green and majestic.

The hives from Amy's farm turned out to be highly productive. Once they were in place for a few days Becky conducted a multi-hour harvest and ended up with over eighty jars of honey. Dozens of them sat on display at her center table. The other tables held baked goods, berries, honey-filled straws, and some hard candies. She made the candies by boiling down honey over an open fire and letting it caramelize. A separate table hosted items made by Amy and an old woman who lived down the road, including handmade beeswax tapers and silkscreened towels and shirts with images of bees and flowers.

Becky lifted her apron and wiped her hands as she watched a light-yellow Chrysler Imperial slow down and turn into her lot. As it cruised to a stop, she was struck by how the car's long sides looked like a shiny yellow wall. The vehicle was also equipped with something she'd heard about but never seen—power windows.

"I hear you have some top-notch honey for sale here," said the man behind the wheel. He looked like he was at least five years younger than her and he confidently wore the latest salt-and-pepper style sport coat and a fat green tie.

Becky recognized him immediately. "Why yes, Mayor Driscoll. I do indeed!"

"Excellent." He opened the door and stepped out. "I wasn't sure if you'd know who I am. I know you only recently returned to our town." He looked her in the eyes and smiled his neophyte politician's smile.

She looked back with a steady gaze. "I do try to know things, especially about the town where I live."

She also knew the young mayor was fresh out of college, rolling deep in family money, and looking for a career steppingstone. She knew some people viewed him as inexperienced and arrogant. But others seemed to view him simply as an adequate mayor. A common refrain was *Driscoll? He's okay, I guess.*

The mayor walked to the table and picked up a jar. "Now, what kind of honey is this? That's quite a dark jar."

Becky picked up a similar jar. "These come from a couple of hives that sit close to my neighbor's blueberry field. That can make the honey a little darker. Then I add a little blueberry juice to the mix. It gives it a very robust flavor. Try it on toast!"

He held the jar up to the light to study it. "Interesting! Very interesting indeed. Now, that's a fine-looking jar of honey. You know what? I'll take a bottle!"

"Certainly." She walked behind her table and opened her cash box. She hesitated for a moment, given that he was a government official. But she decided to proceed with her usual sales pitch. "Now, will you be paying cash, or do you want that on credit?"

Driscoll laughed. "You extend credit? Tell me about that."

"I'm sure you know how credit works."

"I do; I do. And I must be honest with you, Miss Bivens, I drove out here today because there's been some rumblings in the village about this produce stand. A few folks have raised concerns about the way credit is offered. I wanted to see it myself. But to be honest, I don't really understand what their objection is. Lots of businesses offer credit."

Becky nodded and awaited his decision.

"Okay, so … I think I will pay cash. You're a new business. I don't want to complicate things." Then he smiled a cordial smile. "This town needs all the new businesses we can get."

"Well, I do thank you kindly, Mayor, and I agree." She took his money and slid it into her cash box.

Then she handed him a second, smaller jar. Clover honey.

"Please feel free to take this sample too. It's one of my best sellers."

"Oh, I couldn't. People might think it's a bribe." He winked at her.

She found his over-confidence amusing and replied "Oh no. This is just the same deal that I'm offering everyone today. And you can consider it a favor—for a repeat customer. You know, your father used to buy honey from my mother."

The mayor looked surprised. "Oh. I … I didn't know that."

Becky put both jars in a bag, and as she handed it to him, she made a request. "Say, since you're here, could you drop a little hint to the highway department for me? I hate to trouble you, but I've noticed something."

"Oh?"

"Yes, as you can see, I have plenty of parking here. But it's a very tight turn into the driveway. People often don't slow down enough. They end up braking hard at the last second. The drivers behind them don't always pay attention, and I've heard squealing brakes and blaring horns a few times when people are caught off guard."

"Is that so?"

"Yes. So I'm wondering if, maybe, the shoulder here shouldn't be widened a bit. That would let people pull over a little earlier as they slow down, and they could get out of the way. Seems safer, no?"

He gave a half-nod. Noncommittal.

"Now, Mayor, I know you can't just add a real turning lane. That probably takes planning and hearings. But I'm wondering if, maybe, the town could dump a few loads of gravel to the shoulder here? I'm not looking for any favors for myself. I'm just trying to make things safer."

"I can't promise anything. But, sure, I'll mention it to the highway department."

"Well, thank you kindly again."

He turned to leave. But she called after him. "You know, Mayor, one more thing. I suspect the price of honey will go up over the summer. I hear tell there's a parasite that's been killing hives in Pennsylvania and New York. I worry that it might end up in Massachusetts too. That could mean less product. More demand."

Mayor Driscoll looked puzzled. "I see. Well, that's unfortunate."

"I'll tell you what. I will mark you down in my ledger. Two additional jars at the current price. Locked in. Like a stock future. When you want those jars, you just come and ask. That means you can buy your next jars at the current price."

He held up his bag. "I appreciate that. But this jar will last me at least a year. Maybe more."

"Oh, you don't have to actually come buy the jars if you don't want to. It's just a locked-in market price. If you prefer, you can trade that little contract to someone else. Maybe the value of it will have gone up in that time."

"Really? Huh."

"You just let me know when you want to collect."

"Oh. Well, okay. I guess."

Once back in his car, Mayor Driscoll placed his honey on the floor of the passenger side, then drove back toward home.

Honey futures? he thought to himself.

When it came to investing, he was quite familiar with the concept of stock futures. And he'd heard his father and friends brag about the money they made by trading agricultural commodities.

Then something occurred to him. An old memory from his childhood. He remembered his dad and friends talking about making investments years ago with Becky's mother Erin. They even joked about the ledger she kept. Then he remembered his dad and his mom fighting about something related to the farm. It was a heated discussion that went on for a few days, and his mom grew upset and quiet.

He didn't understand it back then. He still wasn't sure what it meant. But it worried him now. He looked at the bag on the floor. He looked in his rearview mirror as the farm disappeared behind him. He was both intrigued and a bit concerned about what he had just agreed to.

As he drove back down the road, he passed another car being driven by Mary Jane Danforth. He didn't see MJ slow as she passed the farm, nor did he see her expression change, first to surprise and then seething anger as she noticed the farm stand had expanded. And he didn't see her face change into a scowl when she saw Becky had added a new helper.

Chapter 10

Presence

In England, Puritans viewed loud pipe organs as the opposite religious piety. But New England was different. Large pipe organs became a focal point in town churches. Yet, as these behemoths aged, maintenance became a challenge. By the mid-twentieth century, some churches kept their big organs going, while others switched to cheaper electronic versions, often leaving the traditional pipes in place as show pieces.

The History of Church Organs in New England, Barbara Jones, 1949

It was nearly six in the evening when Jim Yarrow pulled into his driveway. Two books sat on his passenger seat. One was titled *Specific Dyslexia and Congenital Word-Blindness*. The other was a first-level phonics workbook. He'd borrowed both volumes from his friend, the reading teacher.

Inside the door he kissed Linda, pulled the books from under his arm and set them on the counter. She noticed and asked what they were for.

"Remember my old high school buddy, Leon Davis? I've probably mentioned him."

"Yeah. I know Leon."

"Well, funny story. I recently realized Leon has trouble reading. He's been good at hiding it. So, I guess I just want to help. And I think maybe I can."

Linda looked skeptical. But then she remembered some details about Leon. "Was he the one who lost both parents when he was in, like, third grade?"

"Yeah. He lost his mom to a stroke. It was tough on the whole family, especially his dad, who hit the bottle pretty hard. A few months later his dad was killed while driving drunk. So, that was doubly tough on Leon. He lived with an aunt after that. Didn't get much supervision."

Linda picked up one of the books and leafed through it. "Well, it's nice if you can help him. When are you going to meet with him?"

"Maybe tonight. He's working at the Congregational church. He said he's repairing one of the pipes on their big old organ. I figured I'd stop by."

"Can you wait until after the kids go to bed?"

"Of course."

They sat together at the kitchen table and made small talk about the day. Linda said Bonnie was in good spirits after a couple of grumpy days. Yarrow told her about a citation he gave to a seventeen-year-old he caught doing burnouts in the high school parking lot.

"He was driving his family's car. I don't think they'll be letting him borrow it for a while."

Linda rose and went to the big white O'Keefe & Merritt stove to stir a pot. "So, tell me. How is the search going?"

He looked confused. "What search?"

She took a long breath. "The search, Jim. For a job in Maine. You know, like we've been talking about? A job that would be somewhere near where we're moving. Remember?"

He did remember. But not quite the way she worded it. He had made no commitment to moving anytime soon.

"I made it clear, Linda. I'm happy in my current job. I know you want to move, and that could be a long-term plan. But—you keep trying to get us to drop everything immediately? Come on!"

"Come on where, Jim?"

He shook his head and picked up Bonnie, who had wandered into the kitchen.

"I'm serious. Come on where? You're a member of a small police department. There's the chief and, what, maybe seven officers? The chief isn't going anywhere. Even if you're a shoo-in for his job, it could be years before he leaves. We have three kids. We have clothes and braces and more to worry about. And God knows what else might be coming up."

"Your mother is putting you up to this, isn't she?"

"Stop it, Jim. And you also know I worry about what you might run into out there. I hate that I never really know if you'll come home or not."

He threw up his hands. "Jeez, Linda. I write maybe five tickets per week. I've never even had to draw my gun! Things are pretty darn low-risk here, and it's a nice steady paycheck."

They fed the kids. He tucked Bonnie into bed while Linda dealt with the boys. Then she said she was going to bed early to read. She dismissively waved and asked him to say hello to Leon for her.

He almost stayed home, but he knew that would change nothing for the evening. And he did want to help his friend. Leon didn't have a great childhood, and in some ways he was still paying for that.

Yarrow climbed into the family car and made the eight-minute drive to the Riverbend Congregational Church. There were four churches in town. This one, which sat on Church Street, the Catholic church on Oak Street, the Baptist church on Townline Road, and the Trinity Independent Christian Church—a more recent addition. Two years ago, it moved into an old school building on Hawthorne Lane.

He parked beside the building and walked to the front, admiring the big iron hinges on the old oak doors. The latch was unlocked, so he walked inside. From the floor above, he could hear loud metallic clanging sounds.

Up the hundred-year-old stairs he entered the nave. The interior was painted the same stark white found in most New England protestant churches. The layout was typical too. The preacher's pulpit. Behind that, the altar and seating for the choir.

The big organ and its wall of brass pipes loomed behind all. He spotted Leon removing one of the larger pipes and saw him struggle to balance it.

Jim didn't want to surprise him, so he called out. "Woah, woah! Let me help with that!" Leon still looked startled as Yarrow tossed his books into a pew and rushed forward. Together they lowered the brass tube to the ground, then lifted it to the table Leon had set up in an aisle.

"Wow, Jim! Thanks, and what are you doing here?"

"Checking up on you, that's what."

"Oh yeah? I've fixed seven of these pipes over the years. And you're just showing up now?"

"I guess I'm a little tardy."

"Thanks, but I think I'm doing just fine."

He watched Leon work for a moment, then asked, "Really? You've had to fix seven of these?"

Leon pointed to the pipe's base mount. "See there? These pipes are mostly brass. But when this thing was built, they skimped on the materials. They only used the nice shiny brass where the pipes could be seen. Here at the bases, and other places where parts of the pipes are hidden, they used tin instead. It probably saved the organ builders money up front. But it was a bad idea for the long haul. Where the two metals touch, they eventually corrode. So, when one of the pipes starts looking bad and coming loose, they call me in. I'm the patch-it-up man."

"Why don't they just replace all of the tin on all the pipes at the same time?"

"I've asked them that. But they're a church. They don't really have the budget."

Yarrow thought about showing Leon the books he brought along. But instead, he chose a different tactic. He'd just help him for now.

"So, what made you stop by?" Leon asked.

"I need your help with something. Figured if I can help you, then maybe you could help me. Here, let me hold this in place."

Leon shrugged. "All right. Guess that works for me. When I'm working alone, this place is kind of creepy-quiet anyway."

They worked on the pipe for over an hour, trimming away the corrosion and attaching a new strip of metal. Then they lifted it up. It was challenging to keep it vertical, but Leon said it was easier to slip into the base if it was fully upright. He was right. The bottom of the pipe dropped nicely into its hole atop the windchest. Yarrow held the big tube plumb while Leon attached three replacement screws. All were coated in paint to reduce rust. Then they stepped back to survey their work.

"Looks good Leon. Do you have to tune it too?"

"I have no idea how to do that. They have a guy coming in next week to tweak the tuning for the whole organ. That's why they wanted to get this fixed."

As they cleaned up, Leon asked Yarrow what his project was.

"Actually, I brought some books. I want to show them to you."

"What, you mean for reading? Damn it. I said I don't want you to worry about that."

"Come on, you can give me a few minutes. I mean, I just helped you for over an hour."

Leon shook his head. "You tricked me, Jim. You're goddamn relentless."

"I know. I'll tell you what. If we don't make progress in ten minutes, you can say I told you so. Then I'll go away."

Leon didn't say no, so Yarrow opened the first page. "Now if can you just look at this …"

He showed him an illustration. Then he wrote the word on a piece of paper. CAT.

"That's easy. I kind of know that one."

"Okay. Then that's our starting point. When you look at any word, don't look at just the individual letters. Look for groups. Groups of letters actually make a single sound. You said you can do okay with some short words. So, let's start there. Never mind CAT. What is this word right here?" Yarrow quickly wrote an *A* and a *T* on the paper.

Leon stared at it for several seconds. "AT," he said.

"Good. Good. See? You still remember some things from Miss Anderson's class. And what is this?" On a separate piece of paper, he drew a letter B. He asked Leon to pronounce it, and he did.

Jim then put the B and the AT closer together. "Read one. Then the other. It took a skeptical Leon a couple of seconds, but he read B and AT. Jim moved them closer still. "Now try that." Leon read the word BAT.

"Great!"

"I could do that years ago, Jim. Never got much farther than short words."

"That's because Miss Anderson never did her damn job with you, Leon. She was old, close to retirement, and she totally dropped the ball."

"You think?"

"Yes. A teacher's job is to keep at it until a student starts to learn, or they need to find someone else who can make that happen."

Yarrow continued the lesson, substituting other letters to make HAT, MAT, and SAT. Leon looked bored, but he got the pronunciation right for most of the words. Then Jim started introducing other letter combinations. When Leon read his first four-letter word, he looked stunned. Something had clicked.

That was the moment Yarrow knew his elementary school teachers had definitely missed their opportunity to do one-on-one work with Leon. To be fair, Leon was a tough nut back then. Maybe even stubborn. Poor performance was allowed to slide because the teachers were overtaxed with thirty kids in their classrooms.

After trying more words, Yarrow confirmed Leon had another issue. He was not able to consistently differentiate between lowercase b and d, no matter how many times he saw them. So for now, Jim only used uppercase letters.

Yarrow knew that decades before, researchers identified a condition they initially called *word blindness*. Eventually the condition was named dyslexia. He would need an expert to help Leon address his dyslexia. But for now, they were making some progress. So, he kept at it.

The phonetic approach seemed to help. Before they left the church, Yarrow made Leon promise to meet him at the town library the next Monday night.

As they parted he said, "Well, you got me, Jim. I didn't think I could do it, but I made some progress."

"Like I said, Leon, a man deserves to know how to read."

Chapter 11

Apiary

Beekeepers tend to have greater success if they maintain several hives at once. A place containing multiple bee hives is called an apiary. It comes from the Latin words apis, meaning bee and arium, meaning "place of."

Becky's Guide to Raising Bees (Unpublished)

Becky liked to give each hive plenty of room. With her latest additions, the apiary expanded to half the size of a football field. She wanted her colonies to settle in peacefully, so she only trimmed the grass away when a hive was first set in place. She would knock the tall grass down with grass whips, set the box in the middle of the cleared space, and monitor it for a few days. Once she was satisfied each group of bees had adjusted to their new location, she'd reduce her visits to once per week. Even though they might tolerate an occasional visitor, she knew bees preferred to be alone.

After making repairs to a hive late one morning she wandered across the field. There were some blackberry bushes along the eastern edge of the woods, and she noticed the fruit was starting to turn red. None of the berries had reached their fat black ripe stage yet, but she made a mental note to keep an eye on them. The first good fruit should come in just a day or two.

As she walked back toward the farm stand, she noticed movement in the distance. Up the road, she saw two young women walking in her direction. The day was cloudless, and the sun was hot. Her view was slightly distorted by waves of heat rising from the asphalt.

One of the women wore a knapsack. The other pulled a wagon. Becky walked toward the road and awaited their arrival.

As they entered the driveway, she could see they were quite disheveled. Dirty hair, worn shoes, and stained clothes. The things they carried were meager, and both looked nervous. Maybe even beaten down.

"Are ... are you Rebecca Bivens?" the taller of the two girls asked.

"I am."

They looked at each other. "We, um, I mean ... my friend and me, we're looking, you know, for work. We heard you might be looking for helpers or something? So, we came here. Anyway, um ... maybe yes?"

Becky wasn't sure what to say.

"We will do anything, you know? Just really anything." The girl looked down. It seemed like she had practiced her speech, but when it came time to deliver it, the words spilled forth in a graceless jumble.

Becky looked them over. "Who told you I might have work?"

The younger of the two girls started crying. "I told you she wouldn't! And now we've walked all this way."

The other girl placed an arm on her shoulder. "We knew it was a rumor. And we knew we'd be taking a chance." She looked into Becky's eyes. "We were living with an aunt on the other side of town. But we couldn't stay." She paused.

"You couldn't?"

"No. Because of her son. He was, you know ..." She looked away. "Anyway, we heard about you from an old woman at the gas station. That lady said she knew your mama. When she heard you were back in town, she thought you might do what your momma always did—to welcome girls who want to work. You know. Any work."

Then she bit her lip. She avoided Becky's gaze. As the seconds ticked on, the silence hung like a velvet rope between them.

"Never mind. I'm sorry, Ma'am. We shouldn't have bothered you."

Becky forced herself to smile. She wasn't ready for this. But she knew these types of visitors would eventually arrive. She had already made a commitment to herself about what the farm should become. That included making it a safe place for women like this.

She forced a smile. "Nonsense, dear. This is no bother. What are your names?"

The older one said her name was Agnes. The younger was Doris.

"Both of you, come with me. Let's sit in the shade." They walked across the warm gravel and settled on the grass beneath two maples. Fat branches stretched out, with shimmering leaves that displayed their silver undersides.

They talked for a while, then Becky went to her truck, grabbed three tin tumblers, and poured ice teas from a jug she kept in her cooler. Before exiting the truck, she leaned back against the wood counter, rubbed her forehead, and sighed. If it rained that afternoon, she had planned to work on the outline for her new *Guide to Raising Bees*. Lately she had been gathering many details and notes, and she'd written a rough introduction. One of her dreams was to someday publish it. She didn't know if she'd be able to do it, but she was trying to write a little each week.

But for this day, she would set the writing aside. These women needed a safe place.

She composed herself, exited the truck, and rejoined them in the shade.

"Here's the deal," she said. "If you want to stay here for a while, I will find some kind of work for you. You won't make much money. But it should be enough to buy some food and maybe a tent. In the meantime, I have some tarps you can use.

Once you get settled, I'll let you stay on the land for free—but that's only as long as you are doing some kind of work here."

She gave them an earnest, business-like look. "I will even help set you up so you can make money on your own. Like running your own little business."

"How does that work exactly?" the taller one asked.

"You can make something. Anything really. Candles, candies, hats, and gloves. Then you can sell your products at our produce stand. Or maybe you can offer some other service if you think that's easier. Like hemming skirts or cleaning houses. It's up to you. I won't ask questions."

They looked confused. Becky smiled at them. "It's easier than you think. Like I said, I'll show you how."

Chapter 12

Foothold

"God Almighty, in His most holy and wise providence, hath so disposed of the condition of mankind, as in all times—some must be rich, some poor, some high and eminent in power … others in subjection."

A Model of Christian Charity, Puritan leader John Winthrop, 1639

When Becky Bivens was young, she received a cryptic bit of advice from an old woman who lived on Erin's farm.

"Share what you will with the wind," the woman said. "When the wind moves over the hills, water, and forests, it touches all and takes from all."

In Becky's memory the woman was a mass of gray hair and flowing skirts; a spectral presence who fancied herself both poet and prophetess, though her efforts were mostly captured on tattered notebooks piled in the corners of her trailer.

But Becky still remembered the gray woman's musing on the wind and what it could carry.

"Pay attention to the wind, because it comes to know. It gathers from all and scatters that knowledge over distant landscapes. Breezes can carry the sweet promise of rain or hints of a distant fire. Sometimes the wind brings change. That may be a good thing," she said. "But, most assuredly, not always."

Those words ran through Becky's mind as she drove into town. She had blown in on the wind too, she supposed. And she likely brought changes that were not accepted by all.

It was Tuesday. That meant food bank day at the Trinity Independent Christian Church.

She parked near the old school building, which had been painted white to look more like a chapel, and followed a sidewalk around to the back. There, she found a basement door propped open with a rock. The words *Rock of Ages* were painted across its top.

She stepped inside and walked along a hallway of green wainscoting and iron coat hooks. Near the end of the corridor, a classroom had been converted to a food storage locker. She could see shelves full of canned goods, pasta, rice, and peanut butter.

A woman sitting at a table in the hallway waved hello. "Have you been here before?"

"Hello," Becky responded. "No, this is my first visit."

The woman offered a sheet of paper that listed everything available in the pantry. "We give out food to those in need. There's no charge, and there's no need to feel embarrassed. Every person goes through occasional hard times."

Becky smiled. "That's good to know. And thanks to all of you for doing this."

The woman brushed away the appreciation. "Give your thanks to the Lord and the people who donate. I'm just paid to sit at this table."

"Oh?"

"Yes. This position used to be handled by volunteers." Then the woman gave a little giggle. "But at some point they decided it was easier to pay me sixty-five cents per hour than to try to schedule a dozen unreliable volunteers."

She pointed toward the list. "Anyway, just look through this and tell me what you want. Every visitor gets to fill up a shopping bag."

Then her voice dropped a bit. "Actually, I was told this morning that we have more food than usual. So, if you also want to load up on flour and canned corn, you can have two bags. How does that sound?"

"That sounds wonderful," Becky responded. "I have several mouths to feed."

A small chain hung across the pantry door. The woman dropped it and walked inside.

"You'll have to stay in the hallway. They want me to be the only one in the room, so you can just call out what you want, and I'll grab it. "

As the woman popped open two paper bags, Becky named the things that interested her. "I'll take whatever rice you can spare. Some of that canned tuna fish. Oh, and maybe some spaghetti sauce." Her eyes scanned the shelves from outside the doorway. "Now let's see what else …"

In a few minutes the bags were full. The woman carried them out and set them on the table.

"There you are."

Becky thanked her graciously. "And I did want to ask; I'm wondering if you have enough to help me feed a larger group of people. I have a few women staying with me and I suspect more will be coming."

"Oh. I don't know. I'll probably have to ask the managers." She reached to pick up a clipboard.

"Now, you don't need to give us your name. But sometimes we do like to keep track. It helps us make sure the people who stop in here are doing all right, week to week. And you're always welcome to join our Sunday services."

Then the woman looked at her. Waiting. Pencil in hand.

Becky hesitated.

"First name is fine."

"Okay. Sure. I'm Becky."

The woman wrote it on the last line of the page, then she frowned a bit.

"Becky?"

"Yes."

"Huh." She wiped her brow. "As in Becky Bivens?"

Becky held the woman's gaze and slowly nodded.

The woman set the clipboard on the table. "Oh dear. Um … look. I'm afraid I'm going to have to ask … I'm sorry. I was told not to serve you." The woman looked embarrassed, but also a bit angry at herself for helping Becky.

"Just go please. You can take the bags that we've filled. They'll probably be mad about that, but I'm not going to take them back."

"Why would they be mad?"

The attendant looked confused. "Well, I don't really know the details. That's just that they don't like—"

Becky stared at her. "You seem like a good Christian woman. There must be a good reason for turning away the hungry and the meek."

The woman sat back down in her chair and closed her eyes. "Please don't say … look, the decision isn't mine. They just told me that the people who live on your farm are wicked by nature and an evil influence on people."

"Evil? I can assure you that we're not. We're just hungry. And some of us are living kind of rough."

"I'm sorry. Okay? I'm sorry."

Becky figured there must be other people somewhere in the church because the woman kept looking over her shoulder.

"Please take your food and go."

Becky bit her lip and carried her bags toward the door.

"Go with Christ," the woman called after her.

Becky turned around. "Oh, do you think He'll go with me? That's good. Because I'm pretty sure He's already left this building."

Becky blinked away some tears on her drive home. Her long-term goal was to make the farm self-sustaining, with no need for outside help. But she hadn't reached that point yet. And now it looked like any lift she hoped to find through charity would remain elusive.

So be it, she said to herself. *I can be resourceful, and so can the others.*

Chapter 13

Bonds

Matrimony; the high sea for which no compass has yet been invented.
Heinrich Heine, late 1700s, exact date unknown

The kids were in bed.

Jim and Linda escaped to their balcony, intent on enjoying their glasses of wine. Burgundy this time. Etched stemware glasses.

For a time, they just enjoyed the crickets and the night air. The air was just warm enough and slightly moist on an inland breeze.

"What a beautiful night," Yarrow noted.

"It is, isn't it? We're lucky to have this view." She motioned with her glass. "What do you think? Is that a tanker ship way out there?"

Yarrow squinted. It was miles away.

"Hum… well, see that second masthead light, a little forward? That usually means freighter. But not always."

"I like that you know that stuff." She smiled and clinked her glass against his. "But not always."

He chuckled and raised his middle finger.

"I know. And you know what else? I'm sorry that I've been such a bitch lately."

Yarrow raised his eyebrows. He'd heard the word a thousand times, but never from her.

"Come on. You're not a bitch. I mean…" He struggled to find his next words, and she burst out laughing.

"What I mean is, I know how you feel right now Linda. And I hate that we're pretty much at an impasse. We have too much of a good thing together to let something like this create a rift. I mean, it keeps gnawing at us."

"Gnawing, hum?"

"Am I wrong?"

She waved him off and took a long sip.

"Is this whole thing just the pressure of the kids?" he asked. "Because, we could do something. I don't know, hire a helper or a nanny or whatever people do."

"Come on Jim, like we have money for that."

"We could find it. Maybe give up other stuff."

She changed the subject and talked about the stars for a moment. She pointed to the Big Dipper. "And …" she looked around. "I've got nothing else. That's really the only one I know."

"Yeah, me too. Though sometimes I can find the North Star."

Again, they were silent. Eventually Linda took a long breath, then spoke. "Sometimes I feel like we had kids too quickly."

"What? Really?"

"Don't get me wrong. I love the little beans. But we moved here and then, boom! Kiddos. I feel like I never really had a chance to settle. You and I never built a solid friend group. I mean, you did, but those were your friends. Leon was always working, so I never got to know his wife, and Rocco? Well, he's just Rocco.

"Yeah, but what about Cathy and Lucille?"

"I'm not saying I haven't made friends. But I don't have anyone I feel super close to here, except for you."

He smiled.

"We had our first child within a year. Then two more. Who has time for anything else?"

"I guess I haven't thought of it like that. "

"I know you haven't."

He lifted his glass and looked through it toward the moonlight. "So, what if I agreed to watch the kids an evening or two every week? Or whatever. Maybe you can do other things."

"Do things with who? Other busy mothers?"

"I don't know. I just ..."

Linda stared into the night for a while, then said, "Maybe I could go back to work."

"No. That's ridiculous. I mean, that's fine if you want to. But don't feel like you need to."

"I'm just talking. Exploring ideas."

"Yeah, I get it. But how would you ever explain that to your mom?"

They both laughed and exchanged a couple of recent Barb stories. But then Yarrow stopped talking. He saw Linda stiffen a bit. He'd seen it before and understood that, even as she told her own stories, Linda could still be protective of her mom.

"I'll tell you what," he said. "How about if I invite some people over for a backyard barbecue or something like that? Maybe some folks from work, some neighbors, anyone we can think of."

"Well. Maybe. That might be nice."

They started to discuss other ideas, but suddenly they were interrupted by a dull thud. Then they heard Bonnie starting to cry.

"Oh, again? I can't believe she's already figured out how to climb out of her crib!" Linda stood up. "She's doing it, like, six weeks earlier than the boys."

"But she's still having trouble with her dismount," Yarrow added.

Linda took her wine glass and hurried toward Bonnie's room. Yarrow knew his daughter would need to be rocked back to sleep, and that meant the evening's conversation was probably over. But he made a mental note to try to do whatever he could to try to help Linda, and to make things right.

Then he refilled his glass and scanned the sky, searching for the North Star.

Chapter 14

Special Customers

Improvement societies first emerged in New England in the mid-19th century, with The Laurel Hill Association of Stockbridge, Massachusetts, leading the way. Their efforts were widely noticed, and soon other groups started to organize. In the decades since, coordinated local improvement efforts have flourished, but sometimes such groups can trigger riffs between those who focus on civic beauty versus those whose goal is economic development.

Echoes of Progress, Activism Press, 1968

The Riverbend Improvement Society was not the sort of organization Becky Bivens would join. Likewise, the RIS, as the members like to call it, would never invite someone like her to participate.

The RIS had no official government sponsorship or meeting place. They preferred to gather in private homes, and most often that was the home of Shannon Gates, the politically connected and outspoken wife of Dr. Andrew Gates.

Mary Jane arrived late to the Tuesday RIS meeting. She left her coat on the stairs and slipped into the home's large parlor. Besides the host, she saw gift shop owner Evie Shultz and old Mrs. Paquin from Elm Street. After her husband died, Mrs. Paquin became the sole owner of sixty acres of land adjacent to a new town park. Mary Jane offered to buy the property more than once, and she remained hopeful.

She also saw two people who were relatively new to the group, a middle-aged man who worked for a bank and a woman from the Riverbend Chamber of Commerce. Mary Jane hadn't bothered to learn their names the first time she saw them, but now she realized they might prove useful, so she would make a greater effort to get to know them.

There were a few other people near the back of the room, including Doug Grover, who owned the Main & Maple Apothecary. He was Mary Jane's ally on most issues.

She stood quietly in the doorway and listened to what Shannon was saying.

"… And that's why we're presenting our request for the new stoplight at the upcoming town meeting. Our latest traffic count at Main and Brandford Streets supports it. But most importantly, adding a light will slow people down as they come through town. That gives them a chance to notice all of our nice stores and restaurants downtown. And they can see the new flags and hanging plants we've installed on the lamp posts."

Everyone in the group nodded in agreement. A quick vote was taken, then Shannon moved on. "Okay, I see Mary Jane is finally here." She beamed a smile across the room to her friend. "Hey there MJ!"

"Hey there Shannon!" They greeted each other with a quick checkmark sign—made with their arms. That had been their personal greeting since they were on the Riverbend High School Cheerleading squad.

"Okay group, on to new business. Mary Jane says there's something she wants to talk about. Apparently, she drove by that property out at the corner of Route 110 and Coal Ferry." She groaned a bit. "You all know what I'm talking about."

There were sighs and nods about the room.

"Before she starts, let's remember the town has already proposed rezoning the area around that intersection, with a mind toward future development. You can come up and view it later on the town's new master plan." She pointed to a map sitting on an easel. "Now MJ, can you tell us what you saw?"

Mary Jane stepped confidently into the room.

"Thank you, Shannon. Yes, very happy to talk about it." She paused and dramatically prepared herself, like a preacher getting psyched for a sermon. She looked left and right. "I think many of you will remember what happened on that spot about a decade ago. How many of you remember the Bivens family?"

More than half of the group raised their hands.

"And you probably remember things didn't end so well. The mother of the family, if you can even call it a family, was named Erin Bivens and she was absolutely no good. Her daughter, Becky, was about eighteen when Erin's farm was shut down. I always believed Becky was mixed up in it too, but she was young—my age actually. Then the group left town quickly. Nothing was ever proven."

"What was their crime, exactly?" someone inquired.

"They were entertaining men for money!" A woman near the back shouted. Laughter and groans filled the room.

Mary Jane held up a hand and waited for quiet. "Yes. They allegedly were doing that. But it was never proven and our attorney told me we should always say 'allegedly'." She paused again for dramatic effect. "But there was more to it than that." All eyes focused on her and she savored the attention.

"In case you don't know the full story, they were extending credit on their books, then allowing people to trade those credits back and forth. It was all terribly complicated. I didn't understand it then, and frankly, I still don't. But it was an effective way to mask their money transfers."

She looked around. "I'm sorry to say some of the men living in Riverbend and the surrounding towns took advantage of what that farm had to offer. Erin was quite adept at disguising the cash payments by calling them investments."

There were more nods, yet the room was strangely quiet. Since many townsfolk had family or friends who got caught up in the Bivens system, there was lingering embarrassment and some didn't want to talk about it.

After the awkward silence, someone spoke.

"I do remember," said Evie Shultz. "It was the state police and the courts, the ended up shutting them down, right?"

"That's right. The husband of the head of the PTA was caught visiting the farm. That's when things started to collapse, especially when some other prominent men were named."

There were more murmurs in the room. One woman said she worked as a nurse back then. "I won't name names," she half whispered, "but I remember treating some of the farm girls with penicillin."

Mary Jane gave a look of disgust, then brought the discussion back to the main topic. "So, I will say this tonight. Nothing good can come from allowing the Bivens Farm to start up again. Don't tell me she's only selling honey, because that's how it started last time too. We all know where that went. For goodness' sake, she hasn't even changed the name."

"Okay," said one of the men, "but for now, there's nothing illegal, right?"

"I'm sorry, what?"

"I understand what happened in the past, but she isn't doing anything illegal right now."

"Isn't she?"

The man blinked. "Do you know something we don't?"

Mary Jane looked exasperated. "Her whole family is unethical and unhealthy. We don't need her kind around here, especially when the town is trying to develop our new commercial districts, including that area. And keep in mind Erin would often make pleas to both the town and the county." Her voice started to sound a lot like the sneer she was making. "She was always asking for help—food or medicine for her workers. Like we owed them something. Well. Guess what? Senator Joe McCarthy and others in Washington have already warned us about the dangers of creeping socialism, and that's exactly what

Erin represented. Looking for handouts while camping and squatting is exactly how these leftist groups get their foothold."

Most people in the room responded with blank stares. Eventually Evie spoke.

"So, ten years ago, do you know if any of the women working on the old farm were married?"

Mary Jane looked flustered. She had hoped it would be easy to leverage the country's current political climate to put pressure on Becky. All other questions were just a distraction.

"No, none of them were married. At least I don't think so. And as my momma used to say, never trust a group of women who try to build all of their alliances without men."

"What does that mean exactly?"

Mary Jane waved him off.

"Look," she continued. "In this town, we all know families are the foundation around which solid societies can be built."

Mary Jane knew Shannon kept a bible on her bookshelf, so she walked over, found it, and held the book high. "Can't we all agree the family unit, and this book right here, are the rocks that make us all capable and strong?"

She saw many nods around the room and knew she had hit a nerve. These were solid church-going folks. Good citizens.

"We and our families," she continued, "exert a refining and ennobling influence here. We can't let our influence decline because of the other people who show up."

She used her hand with the bible to point toward the zoning map. "This town is growing. Think of it as us being rewarded because of who we are. Many more good people are hoping to move here. It's safe and we can be very supportive of the right people."

Then she held up a finger. "But …" She stopped and let the word linger in the air for a moment. "But … we all know, when growth happens, it can go either way. Just look at the shadier parts of Boston. Growth can also lead to slums. Then crime. Things need to be managed correctly."

When she saw some smiles she knew she had them.

"But anyway, I know Shannon asked me to tell you what I saw at the farm. I think you'll be shocked. I parked my car around the corner and snuck through the woods. I saw a lot of beehives, and I do mean, *a lot*. I think she's been buying them from others and moving them here. It looks like she's quickly building up the business."

"So?" said the man who was now clearly miffed. "Isn't that how business works?"

Mary Jane looked angry too. "It's a problem because it isn't a normal business. It's some sort of commune."

Mary Jane knew the people raising objections were newer transplants to the town. They didn't know the full history.

"Look, let me give a brief summary. Erin Bivens showed up in our town in about 1935. Remember those years? The American economy was on a big downward slope. People had already started calling it The Great Depression."

Mary Jane became animated in her movements, making sure she kept the full group's attention. "When Erin moved into that lot the crossroads weren't even paved yet. She was far enough outside of town that nobody paid her much attention. When she started selling honey, most of the customers were her neighbors. I'm not sure when she started taking in wanderers, but times were tough. People were losing their homes and Hoovervilles were popping up all over the country. So, her farm didn't seem that unusual when it started."

She looked at the faces. They seemed to be following her story, so she continued.

"But things got worse when the Essex County almshouses and poorhouses started to fail. Then Suffolk County too. Suddenly more people needed a place to live and some of those people found their way to Erin Bivens. And she let them stay."

Mary Jane gave a sly look. "Then people noticed it was mostly women living out there. And the number of cars visiting from other towns increased, especially in the evenings. Special customers, if you will. Erin found herself in a different and more profitable business."

She let that sink in. She knew she had dropped just enough sordid details to hold people's attention. So, she switched to explaining Erin's complicated ledgers, her loans, and other money-shuffling activities.

She finished with details on undercover police officers visiting the farm. Arrests were made and during the follow-up investigation, a dead rat was discovered in a trash pile.

"That rat gave the town the excuse to clear Erin and her crew off the property immediately. Then they started drawing up criminal charges."

She looked around the room and was happy to see some smiles.

"And then she was gone. For over ten years the family hasn't been here and there was no need to worry about that empty lot. Grass even started to grow through the gravel."

She looked down and spoke softly. "But now one of them is back. We can't allow it. Justice was served once. We need to do it again."

Some of the people shuffled uneasily. But no one disagreed.

Chapter 15

Deviant

In the late 1800s, a common way to handle homelessness, mental issues, and eldercare was to establish a "town farm." Indigent residents were expected to find a sense of purpose and self-sufficiency there through farm work. By the 1930s, these local relief efforts were often poorly managed and unreliable. The farms were replaced by state and federal government programs, but some residents were simply cut loose, with no other opportunities.

The Darker Corners of New England, Salem Wonderland Imprints, 1950

Jim Yarrow fell into a new routine. Two mornings each week, he met with Leon for twenty minutes to practice reading. Often they sat in a booth at the far end of Rocco's grill. He cut a deal of sorts with Linda to get this extra time. Any day he left early to meet with Leon, he came home after work and cooked dinner for the family.

Though Leon had been reluctant at the start, he eventually grew excited as he saw the progress he was making. He told Yarrow about the signs and billboards he could read. "I still have trouble with long words and some letters," he said. "But I'm getting there."

"Look," Yarrow admitted. "I know these books are dull. *Sally has a new dress. Jack likes his dog.* Who the hell cares? But you know what? When I hear you read them, it's rewarding to me too."

When the breakfast crowd started to trickle in, their lessons usually ended.

But there was one remaining challenge. Yarrow would have to look for advice on how to deal with the dyslexia. In the meantime, he wanted to give his student the confidence to keep trying.

When Leon left, Rocco poured Yarrow a fresh cup of coffee.

He took a long slip, closed his eyes, then set the cup down. "Excellent, Rocco. As always. Now, do share with me your daily wisdom."

Rocco waved him off. "No philosophy today. I'm busy cooking eggs."

"Come on. You have a degree in philosophy, right? I demand wisdom!"

Rocco just laughed. He stood at his big grill that took up a third of the back counter. Above it was a backsplash and a large stainless steel fan. A metal fleur-de-lis was bolted onto the front of the fan housing. It was an artifact from the previous owner, who returned to Quebec after selling the building to Rocco.

"You know, I probably ended up running this diner *because* of that philosophy degree," Rocco said as he cracked eggs. "I guess I was finding inner peace and all that." He dropped a pile of hashbrowns on the grill. "And I guess I do find that here. So, that's your wisdom for the day."

Aloof and blunt as Rocco could be, he was one of the brightest people Yarrow knew. Rocco was like a small-town oracle. At the counter, their conversations could slowly unfold. Sometimes other people joined in, invited or not. Such was the give-and-take of a small-town diner.

Rocco followed up with another question. "How are Linda and the kids?"

"They're all doing well. Linda started a vegetable garden. And the boys found a new friend in the neighborhood, and now the kid is over at our house all the time."

"You have to love summer, huh?"

When they had a private moment, Yarrow lowered his voice. "I also talked to Becky late yesterday. It was an interesting chat."

Rocco used his ever-present cloth to wipe up a spill. "I'm sure anytime you talk with Becky it's interesting. She lives a remarkably different life."

Yarrow agreed. "Do you know what she told me? She said displaced women have been showing up at her farm. Her mother allowed it, so I guess people still look there."

"Does she take them in?"

"I think so. She lets them stay like migrant workers. But if too many come, she can't help all of them."

"Nope."

"She said someone who's coming soon is a widow with two kids."

"You know, Veterans' Administration may help widows and families, but unmarried women with dubious claims usually get ignored. And good luck if they're immigrants lacking birth certificates."

"Yeah," said Yarrow. "A few days ago, Becky asked if I could help her find other resources. Government social services. Private charities, whatever. I made some inquiries, but didn't find much at all. Those places start asking questions I can't answer."

Rocco was sympathetic. "But I guess they have to keep trying."

"Yeah, but there's a problem. Becky's visitors don't have official addresses. The farm doesn't even have a building. Becky isn't able to help them get past the first hurdle."

"No help from the town?"

"Totally useless."

Rocco kept talking as he wrote down a customer's order. "Yeah, well, New England has a tradition for how they treat vagrants. Towns just 'warn them out.'"

Yarrow looked confused.

"Used to be common. Towns could just tell people to leave. Point them down the road and then they become the next town's problem." Rocco shook his head. "Look, I admire what she's trying to do. But it's not sustainable. She needs to work with someone with better facilities and deeper pockets."

Yarrow knew Rocco was right. He looked out the front window. A swath of the river was visible between two buildings, and he watched a large private yacht chug by.

He emptied the last of his coffee and spoke. "You know, Rocco, you and I are both veterans. So, what really hits home with me is the kids. I'm pretty sure they're the sons and daughters of soldiers and sailors and, goddamn it, I don't like seeing them abandoned."

Rocco gathered some dirty plates. "Yeah, and for some of the fathers who didn't make it back? Their reward is to see their kids branded as illegitimate."

"Thank you for your service, hum?"

"There's another issue too, Jim. Maybe some of those guys came back, but not all the way. And I think you know what I mean."

Yarrow drummed the counter with the fingers of his good hand. "I mean, that happened to all of us, right? At least a little. The first year I was back, all I wanted to do was to keep to myself."

"Me too, I guess. I think we were trying to understand what happened. Like what the hell did we just go through?"

"Yeah."

"But after a while, you push through it. You try to forget."

Rocco corrected him. "We won't forget. We just come to terms with it."

Rocco served another customer. Yarrow's voice dropped low. "You saw some of the worst of it. I know that."

"I didn't see combat like you, Jim."

"That's not what I'm talking about."

Rocco shrugged.

"Is that what lead to your philosophy degree?"

Rocco looked at the floor. "Yeah. In a way."

Someone asked for change, then Roco waited until he and Yarow were alone again. "Look, I've told you some of this before, but I'm not sure I told you the bulk of it." He took a deep breath. "By mid-forty-five I thought I 'd gotten off easy. Our destroyer was always on the outer edges of the major sea battles. But as things were wrapping up, they sent us into Japan. First, we went into the Seto Inland Sea, and then we anchored at the port of Hiroshima. We transported some of the first occupation forces. When some of those guys returned to the ship, they were wide-eyed and silent. After a few days, it was my turn to go ashore."

"It's all right Rocco. You don't need to—"

But he continued. "It took me a long time to sort through my thoughts, Jim. So now I've just got to say it. You're absolutely right. I did see things. Some pretty dark shit. Buildings in ruins. Burned people walking aimlessly as their skin and bandages peeled away. Frozen shadows on the ground. And the smell. My God, the smell." He shook his head. "Anyway, back to what you said. Yeah that whole experience eventually made me decide to study philosophy. I thought it might help me make sense of everything. It didn't, but I can find some level of peace now. And here at work, I guess I find it by serving others."

He took a deep breath, then added. "You've probably noticed I always have music on a record player or a radio in here. I think it occupies my mind. Keeps the other thoughts away, you know?"

They were both silent for a while, one looking at his cup and the other looking toward the windows, where Rocco's name appeared backward on the glass.

Yarrow decided to change the subject. "Do you carry honey here Rocco?"

Rocco gave him an annoyed look. "For toast and tea, yeah. But you're drinking coffee."

"You know what I mean. Do you carry the good stuff? Fresh? Local jars, like Becky's?" He laughed. "Do you even dare?"

Rocco held up his hand. "I know where this is going, Jim. Don't ask me to choose sides."

"No, no. Not my intention. Just wondering if you take your honey supply seriously."

Rocco reached beneath the counter and pulled out a jar. He set it down with the label facing Yarrow. "Is this what you want to see? There you go. Straight out of Bivens' Farm."

"All right then. Excellent choice. 'Best honey for your money!'"

"Yeah. It is pretty tasty."

"So then tell me, my friend, why hide the jar? Why does doing business with Becky trigger such anger in some people?"

"Don't know. Maybe they just don't like honey?"

"I'm serious. She's a local business, licensed and everything. Yet she stokes anger."

"It's the history of the place, Jim. You certainly know that."

"Not buying it. We don't do multi-generational damnation in this country."

Rocco went to take a new customer's order. The bell over the door clanged twice while he was gone.

"Okay, Jim," he said as he returned. "Truth be told? I don't think their anger is related to any legal issue. It's deeper. The Improvement Society's just coming up with different arguments to mask that."

Yarrow listened, sipped, and waited.

"Look. The way I see it, every town needs a Becky Bivens. She fills a niche. People are stubbornly hierarchical creatures. That includes both men and women, but let's start with the women, since they make up about eighty percent of that stupid RIS group."

"Go on. I'm listening."

"Okay. So, someone like Becky? She gives the others someone to look down on. When you have a group whose stated purpose is to improve a town, you have to think, 'in contrast to what?' The people at the top want to separate themselves from the bottom dwellers so they can blame that group for anything bad. Having a common enemy gives them an example of what they think the town should move away from."

"Really? What are we, still in high school?"

"It's very much like that! High school is just a practice run. Having a common foe builds group cohesion and the person who seems most different from them—becomes the easiest target." He chuckled slightly. "Well that, and Mary Jane is always looking for property to develop, and I'm sure that farm looks attractive to her."

Yarrow looked dejected.

"Anyway, people like Mary Jane may claim to be tolerant. They may even support some charities. But if the have-nots start looking for too much … those RIS people will find ways to cast out the outliers."

"Huh. I guess that really is what some of them are. Outliers. But Becky doesn't seem to fit that mold anymore. I'd say she's succeeding, not failing."

"Right," Rocco replied. "And that's also a problem. They've already labeled her as some dangerous, wicked *other*. They can't let someone who was once beneath them suddenly start winning at the game."

"Okay. I can see that. But we live on a big river. Every river town from here to New Hampshire has their waterfront riffraff to deal with."

"Yes. But the riffraff usually stays riffraff. But by finding success, Becky Bivens is actually upending a system that once successfully kept her at the bottom." Rocco held up a finger, like a professor explaining a tough subject. "Now, you might think bootstrapping your way upwards is the great American dream, right? Hard work leads to success."

"Of course."

"Well, sometimes that's just a load of horseshit. If we don't like people, we just want them to fail. That's how to stay on top. And some people get very angry when an expected failure doesn't happen."

Yarrow frowned. Then, some level of acceptance creeped in, which Rocco must have noticed.

"When you think about it, Jim, the most successful citizens of Riverbend had multiple reasons to want Erin to fail ten years ago. The women at the farm seemed deviant in multiple ways. Born out of wedlock, tempting the town's men, running a questionable business that was tough to monitor. Erin's success became her own undoing."

Yarrow breathed deeply. "And now? Do you think Becky is becoming too successful?"

"Her growth happened awfully quickly, no?"

"I guess so. But what I mean is, do you think they're committing a crime out there?"

"Jesus, Jim. How would I know?"

"Well, is there anything illegal about the way she's keeping her books or selling those damn honey options?"

Rocco scratched his chin. "My guess is that she's not following any rules related to common financial practices or accounting. If she was audited, I suspect she'd fail."

"Yeah." Yarrow agreed. "Unfortunately, I think you're right."

Rocco continued to tidy up, and then he spoke again. "In many ways, what Erin did was similar to a typical stock market. They both offer options and futures, right? They offer contracts for goods and services that will be delivered later."

"Yeah," Yarrow agreed. "But she's not really following the rich people's rules, is she?"

"No. She deviated from the norm and that brings trouble."

"So … deviant?" Yarrow laughed.

"As the word is classically defined? Yes. Deviant."

Yarrow smiled and lifted his cup for a toast. "All right then, here's to the deviants! Sometimes the world needs them."

Chapter 16

Boston

In the late 1800s, multiple social reform movements were launched to address the paradox of ongoing poverty at a time when the American economy was increasingly productive and prosperous. In the 1890s, a group of prominent Bostonians founded the New England Kitchen, which sought to teach poor families how to obtain inexpensive, clean and healthy food. Other kitchens followed suit, including many that were open to everyone.

Soup Kitchens as a Social Reform Movement, Paulist Pages 1947

By July, the path through Becky's property slowly became the well-worn center of their community.

Becky followed it every day as it skirted the meadow and meandered downhill toward the river. Evening dew cooled her ankles, and the songs of crickets and katydids guided her steps.

One evening she moved slowly. Deliberately. Rehearsing her words. She wanted to be prepared for when she reached the spot where tents and makeshift lean-tos stood in a circle. As she arrived, she caught a whiff of smoke. The campers were cooking something on a makeshift spit. It looked like a Muskrat. From the river. Skinned and basted with oil, honey, and pepper.

"Hello," she said to the group. The women looked up and nodded. A few waved. They seemed genuinely happy to see her, and why not? They were sleeping here for free, thanks to her.

But Becky didn't intend for her visit to be social. She came to talk. She hoped they would listen.

She carried a basket of fresh peaches and stood for a bit near the edge of the campfire glow. Dancing yellow light faded to gray. When there was a lull in the conversation, she stepped into the brighter light and placed the basket on the ground.

"If any of you are hungry, please help yourselves."

Several women immediately hopped up. When quiet descended again, Becky decided to speak. "That looks like a wonderful dinner on the fire. Who caught that?"

Doris, the youngest girl in the group, shyly raised her hand.

Becky offered praise. "You must be quite nimble to snag a muskrat. I know, because I used to catch them myself."

"Would you eat them?" Doris asked.

"Sometimes."

Another girl spoke up. "You can have some if you'd like."

"Oh, thank you so much Agnes. But no." Becky moved closer and sat on the ground near the fire. "I just wanted to come and talk. Please, continue whatever you were doing."

Agnes pulled the cooked muskrat off the fire and set the charred wooden stick across a pair of rocks. She waved her hand back and forth to cool the meat.

Becky knew her arrival stalled their conversation. So, she waited. As the talk resumed, it focused on whether the distant hoots they heard came from a Great Horned or a Barred Owl. Then there was a discussion of whether the speed of a cricket's chirp could be used to gage the air temperature. She listened for a while, and when the time seemed right, she spoke again.

"I wanted you all to know, I'm planning to take a drive tomorrow. I'm heading down to Boston and I'm hoping several of you might come with me." All faces turned toward her. She saw a mix of curiosity and skepticism. Besides Amy, Agnes, and Doris there were several other women who had trickled in. Then Becky noticed someone she had not yet met. There was a baby asleep at her feet and a boy of about two sitting beside her.

Becky tried to smile. "Now, the trip won't be all that comfortable. It's about 45 miles each way. We'll hit stop-and-go traffic as we get closer to the city, and you'll have to ride in the back part of my truck. There are minimal places to sit there and only some small windows on the rear doors." She saw some frowns and realized she needed to make the idea sound a bit more enticing. "But it would be a chance to get out. You'll get a meal there and you can see something besides this farm."

She looked from face to face. "What do you think?"

They were all silent for a moment. Then Amy asked, "Why are you going there? And why do you want us to come?"

Becky hesitated. Then she decided to be honest. "Well, right now, I want to make sure all of you are taken care of. If things were going great for you, I don't think any of you would have ended up here." She swallowed hard but hid her growing anxiety. "So, you are all welcome to stay here, but right now I don't have much food to offer you and I probably won't until next week."

She gestured toward their evening meal. "And I hate to see that all you have to eat is muskrat."

"It's actually not so bad," Agnes countered.

Becky looked at each of her guests, watching the yellow light dance across each face. The breeze was picking up and she could hear leaves blowing across the field.

"But we're all struggling. So, here's what I'm thinking." She leaned forward and made her pitch. "There are free soup kitchens in Boston, including a large one in an alley near Scollay Square. I ate there myself a couple of years ago. They serve a lot of people, so I'm sure they won't complain if we arrive as a group. We could eat, and if we're lucky, they may have some leftover food we can take home."

"I don't know," Agnes replied. "I've been to Scollay Square. That's not a nice area at all, especially for women."

Becky wasn't going to sugar coat things. "You are quite right. That square is full of crime, vagrants, and prostitutes. The city has talked about leveling the whole area, including dozens of those old run-down buildings. The fact that it's a sad neighborhood is likely why the kitchen is located there."

She looked at them and gave them a moment. No one spoke against the idea.

"So, my plan is that we all stay together. We park the truck and walk into the building together." She stood as she added, "And hopefully we'll all get fed."

"Maybe," Agnes said. "But I'm also okay just working with Doris to catch and cook things right here."

But Amy, who had been thrust into the role of senior resident, offered the first support for the idea. "I don't want to have to catch everything we eat. And I do like the idea of getting a good full meal. So, yes. I'll go with you."

Reluctantly, a few of the other women agreed. "Yeah, why not?" one of them said. "I haven't been into Boston for a few years."

Becky looked happy. "All right then. I'll try to time our visit so we can hopefully get both lunch and dinner while we're there. Let's plan to leave at eleven."

Then she bid them goodnight.

The following morning the women finished their farm chores then several of them climbed into the bakery truck. As the engine roared to life, Becky noticed the muffler was getting louder.

Amy sat in the front passenger seat and tried her best to read a map.

"I think we should head east for a few miles first, then turn south at Route One." She flipped the map over and looked flustered. "I guess we'll figure it out from there."

Because of the truck's interior modifications, Becky couldn't see the back area from the driver's seat. But she knew at least two women were sitting on her makeshift bed while others sat on the floor. As she drove she could hear them talking and laughing, and at one point she heard them singing. The trip might end up being a fun time for all.

For the next hour they drove through a series of towns. Saugus, Revere, Chelsea, then into Charlestown and along the edge of Cambridge. Brick buildings and copulas seemed to be everywhere. They saw trolly tracks in the middle of streets, plus churches, markets, and pubs. The marquee at the Central Square Theatre advertised *The Day the Earth Stood Still.*

Traffic slowed to a crawl as they crossed the Charles River and pushed into Boston.

The old truck's engine started to overheat, but Becky kept things slow and steady. Amy called out their turns and they edged through the area around North Station, then they zig-zagged through side streets to reach Scollay Square.

Buildings looked much rougher in the square. Corrugated tin nailed over broken doors and smashed windows on upper floors. Uncollected trash was strewn across empty lots.

Men stood in doorways with hands in their pockets and cigarettes dangling from their lips. Some wore their fedoras pulled down to their eyebrows. "Around here, most business isn't conducted in the stores," Becky mused.

With Amy's help, she found the correct alley. They turned left just past The Old Howard Theatre with its blinking lights and burlesque shows posters.

Parking was prohibited in the alley itself, but right behind the kitchen there were two spaces marked for deliveries only. She hoped her bakery truck would look like it belonged there.

A few minutes before one they walked into the big dining room. It was functional, but minimalist to an extreme. The walls were stark white, and a cafeteria-style serving line stood at the far end. Just a dozen people were pushing their trays along the food line. At least fifty rough-looking men and women sat eating at the long rows of folding tables. No tablecloths. Not a single decoration on the walls.

No one greeted them, so they claimed one of the open tables and sat down. Becky slipped into the kitchen and found a woman who appeared to be in charge. The woman looked to be about fifty years old. She was tired and hassled, and walked the brown-tiled floor, barking orders to the cooks and serving crews. Becky knew she should approach cautiously.

"Are you the director here?"

The woman barely looked her way. "I am—as much as this chaos can be directed."

Becky pointed through the door toward her group. "I've brought a few women with me. We're hoping to eat. Is that alright?"

The woman shrugged, again barely acknowledging her. "We don't turn people away. If they want to eat, just join the line."

"Thank you so much for that. That will mean a lot to them. And to me."

The director slowly turned toward her and Becky thought maybe she had won her over. She could tell the woman wasn't used to being thanked. She likely spent her days doling help out into an endless void, where both providers and recipients had grown numb to the process.

"Line's short right now dear, so go. Tell your girls to grab some milk or water. Coffee too, if they want." Then she looked Becky up and down. "So, what is your story? And theirs?"

Becky's response was demure. Respectful. "I drove in from a small farm. North of here. The women all live there. Most want to work, but I don't have much to offer them. That's why we came here. To get them fed, and maybe to find out what else may be available to them in the city."

"I see." The director looked skeptical but asked several more questions. She sought information about the women's races, ages, religions, number of children, and more. Becky was surprised at the level of detail and the director noted her skepticism.

"Look, I ask these questions because there are different services available, and the help you get can depend on who you are. For example, if a woman is Catholic, I'll refer her to the Sisters of Charity. If she's negro, I'll refer them to Boston's

League of Women for Community Service. And if any of your entourage has children, I can refer them to the Boston Children's Aid Association. They're a good group, and they are the fastest at providing help for a family. But I always warn everyone first—that association will investigate the heck out of a mother, and they have government authorization to take kids away immediately if they think the parent isn't treating them well. So, any women I send there should be aware that's a possibility and they should plan accordingly."

Becky thanked her. "I appreciate the honesty. But can I ask another question? You only mentioned private charities. Is there also government help? Would any of these women be able to apply?"

The director rolled her eyes. "Well, dear, let me say this. That will only happen if your women can wait a good long time. Government social programs in Boston have way, much to deal with and their funding is abysmal. Just think about all they're dealing with right now. Thanks to the Displaced Persons Act and the War Brides Act, there are people still arriving from the hardest-hit parts of Europe. There are women who left marriages because their husbands were different men when they came home from war. And now we have more political unrest that's driving people out of Cuba, and Haitians fleeing their island and coming here because there are rumblings of yet another revolution in their country."

She stopped and looked at Becky. "So, you see dear? The government-funded social services are overwhelmed right now. There's a long line, and the chances of your friends getting help from anything other than a private charity is minimal."

Becky wanted to push harder for help, but she didn't want to alienate the one person who could at least offer them a meal.

"I see. Well, thank you again, and I appreciate the information."

While her group ate their lunch, Becky asked for directions and walked four blocks to an office of an Episcopal charity. There, she was told they lacked the resources to offer assistance to her whole group. But the church said they might be able to help at least a couple of the women. But they insisted on receiving a formal application from each woman and warned their intake process could take a few days.

"Also, each participant must commit to a three-month education program. And they will need to bring identification papers."

Becky knew that would be a problem. She just said thank you, grabbed a few blank forms and walked out.

Feeling dejected, she made her way back to the kitchen. When she re-entered the big room, she suddenly smiled. There was Amy, sitting at a table with several boxes of leftovers. "They gave two more meals to each of us!" she said with joy.

Becky helped Amy load the boxes into the back of the truck. After they climbed in, the director came out and approached Becky.

"I'm sorry we couldn't do more for you."

Becky just stared through the windshield. A light rain was starting to fall. "Where I live, people keep arriving," she said. "I honestly don't know what to do."

"I know. That happens here too."

Becky gripped the big steering wheel. "There are always people who fall through the cracks. Other people, like you and I, try to keep that from happening. But we can't do it alone."

"No, dear. We can't. But we do try."

Becky wasn't sure she should say more. But she felt compelled. "There are other alternatives that are of dubious legality. You and I both know that. But sometimes people, especially women, well, they do what they have to do."

The director said nothing. She just nodded slightly, gave Becky a pat on her shoulder, then turned away.

As the other women climbed aboard, one woman named Carla hesitated. She walked to the driver's window, baby in her arms, and said, "I'm going to stay here in Boston, I think."

Becky figured the girl couldn't be a day older than eighteen. "Okay. But why?"

"I was talking to a man when we were eating. He joined us at our table when you were gone. He said he has a place nearby. He seemed nice, and said I can stay there. He said his daughter can watch my baby during the day and he thinks he has work for me."

Becky closed her eyes. "No. Absolutely do *not* do that, Carla. He's not going to help you. Not the way you think."

"But he is! He said he's helped a lot of girls. And he has a lot of friends who are looking to hire temporary workers."

"Carla, please just listen!"

But the girl turned and walked away.

"Carla? Carla!"

One of the other women jumped out and rushed to stop her. But a stiff arm came up and Carla hurried on, disappearing around the corner.

The rain fell harder. Becky shook her head and rolled up the window. The other women settled down in the back.

She put the truck in gear and turned up the heat as they navigated their way back out of the city. Again, they passed a sea of gray fedoras. Again, they weaved through streets of brick, awnings, litter-filled gutters, and blinking neon.

As they reached Route One, someone in the back finally spoke.

"What now?"

It took Becky a few moments to respond. "Now … we explore other options. I've already told some of you that if you want to stay on the farm, you can set up your own businesses. We can find a way to make sure you get paid. So, I guess we can focus on that."

"What kind of business?"

Becky didn't reply. She just stared at her white knuckles on the steering wheel and listened to the rhythm of the windshield wipers.

Chapter 17

What We Carry

At the end of World War II, some military men found it challenging to return to civilian life. The nation's divorce rate more than doubled between 1940 and 1945. The booming economy and new legislation gave veterans some support and provided access to education, home purchases, and the "American Dream." But the pressure of social change and equal opportunities proved daunting to some.

1950 Federal Report on How Veterans Have Adjusted

Jim Yarrow had just flipped on his siren and was starting to accelerate when his radio crackled for a second time. He picked up the mic.

"Yarrow here."

He listened.

"Ten-four. So, no response needed?"

"No," said Tina. "Now Mrs. Edwards is saying she doesn't have any trespassers. It was just a neighbor boy. He accidentally let his family cat escape and he was trying to catch it."

Yarrow chuckled, then uttered another quick "ten-four."

In a way he was disappointed. He hadn't had an interesting complaint to investigate for days. He was looking forward to finding out who might be intruding in Mrs. Edward's backyard.

He could picture his own kids doing the same thing, and it made him smile. He really did love his little town, and the comfort of living here with Linda and the kids. It reminded him again that he didn't want that to change.

With no place else to go, he fell back into his usual patrol routine. Eventually he turned onto the higher road that let him drive along the small hills above the water. And that road would also take him by the Bivens Farm.

He wondered if he'd see her.

The answer came quickly. There was a woman he didn't recognize tending the produce stand. A little farther on, he saw another woman walking on the side of the road. He squinted.

Yes, it was Becky.

She carried two wire baskets—the kind milkmen use to carry glass bottles. But, instead of milk, she had several jars of honey tucked into the slots; enough to make for a fairly heavy load.

What in the world is she doing? Yarrow thought to himself.

He slowed the big cruiser and pulled up beside her. "Well, hello there," he called out. "Not using your truck?"

She flashed him that elvish grin. It gave him a certain feeling and he mentally reprimanded himself.

"The truck won't start," Becky replied. "Sometimes it has trouble after the rain. But I promised the Blanchard General Store I'd deliver these jars." She lifted one of the baskets. The amber liquid seemed to glow in the sun. "They've agreed to stock some of our honey. It will be in a rack by the checkout."

He was happy for her. "That's wonderful Becky. I'm impressed."

She stood back and looked at him. Then she raised her eyebrows. Inviting. Unrelenting.

He looked away and chuckled a bit. "Darn it, Becky. You know I'm only supposed to use this car for police or town business."

"I understand. You do what you must." She started to take a step down the road, then she gave him one of her winks.

He stared at the road ahead. "Look. I guess I can't let you walk with that heavy load either. And I suppose you're sort of … I don't know. Blocking traffic?"

She shrugged. "Maybe."

He laughed, mostly at himself. "Okay, just get in."

She struggled to open the heavy door, then slid into the seat beside him. Legs first. Visible seam up the back of her stocking.

They rode in silence for a minute. She seemed to grow restless at the tension and decided to speak first.

"So, how is your day?"

He kept his hands at ten o'clock and two o'clock on the wheel. Eyes front. "Good. Good day, thanks."

More silence. Yarrow forced himself to continue. "Um, kind of quiet so far. I guess not much happens around here."

"I suppose not." She shifted the baskets, placing them together on the floor by her feet. "But there must be folks around somewhere getting into mischief. You know, like you and your friends back in the day?"

He laughed. "God, I hope not."

"Oh, I remember you guys. Especially Matt Dickenson. Good Lord, you two would raise some hell. Sneaking beers into the basketball game. Parties in that field out past the Mill Pond, remember? And how about all of you jumping into the river over at the old Rocks Village bridge? That was a big drop. I thought all of you were crazy."

For Yarrow it was a good memory.

"You know what I recently discovered?" he said. "The middle of that bridge is just past the Riverbend town line. It's outside our police jurisdiction. And the town on the other side never cared much about what was going on out there. That's probably why we always got away with swimming and drinking out there. No one wanted to investigate."

Becky recalled a few other incidents where Yarrow and his friends got into mischief. They both laughed and reminisced. Then her voice took on a somber tone.

"I also remember when your dad died, Jim. That was a surprise, though I never knew the details."

"Yeah, well, it was liver cancer. It took him in just eight months. That was tough to watch. And, yeah, I probably got a bit wilder after that. Doing things like those bridge dives. Drinking."

She gave his hand a pat.

"But now?" she said, "Goodness, what a job you have. All dignified. Wearing a uniform. Respectable family man. But even during your wild days, you seemed like a guy who was destined to settle down some day." She patted his hand. "I always had confidence in you."

He bit his lip. "Thanks. You were always supportive, Becky. Even back then. Too bad we never got to spend much time together. We had, what, a couple of months? Then boom. You were gone."

She looked at the road ahead. White lines came toward them like tiny daggers. "That's true. Then I was gone. And I guess that was it. I mean, for us."

That part was not a happy memory for Yarrow. When the farm was shut down, he was angry for months. In some ways he still was.

There was something else he needed to say. He was hesitant to broach the subject but felt like he had to get it out. He tapped the wheel with his fingers.

"You know, when my friends and I heard the police were at your mom's farm, we all piled into an old Rambler wagon. It belonged to Matt's dad. But the road was blocked off. They wouldn't let us drive close to the farm. We ended up watching from that hill across the road. I tried to walk through that field to find you, but they turned me away at the driveway. I tried going through the woods too. But ... same thing."

She pursed her lips and continued to look at the road.

"Later on, I heard they only allowed you and your mom to leave with one box each. They seized everything else. I thought that was petty of them."

"Yeah." She reached down to adjust a clanking jar. "That was a tough day. We lost most of what we had."

More silence. Yarrow decided to say his piece.

"So, you need to tell me Becky. How come you never came back? I mean, you and me, we had something together. It was brief, but we both felt it. Yet, after that day, I never saw you again. I never heard from you. I had no idea where you were. I wanted to know if you were okay."

She finally looked at him. He knew she could see the hurt in his eyes. He didn't care. He wanted her to see it.

"I'm sorry, Jim."

He remained silent.

He sensed she wanted to grasp his hand. But instead, her fingers went in the other direction, to the arm rest on the door. She rubbed it absentmindedly.

"I … I don't know how to explain it. I felt so stigmatized when we ran away. I felt shame. I guess that was because of who we were, and what we did. I always tried to deal with things by acting like some kind of ice queen. I wanted people to think nothing bothered me. But that day, things hit hard. It ruined us, Jim. Erin's crimes were exposed. Everything the whole group was doing was uncovered, and it all happened in such an embarrassing way. The ridicule was intense. Some people who gathered to watch our eviction made sure to make their condescending comments loud enough that we could hear."

He listened to her, and then it was his turn to talk.

He downshifted as they approached a hill. "I understand. But to never come back at all? To never contact me? No phone or letter? You knew how I felt about you. But you just disappeared." He shook his head. The next words spilled out before he had a chance to stop them.

"You broke my heart, Becky."

She dabbed at her eyes and turned her head away, looking at the passing trees. "I knew how you felt about me. And yes, that's how I felt about you too. But I didn't know how you would feel after … everything. I guess I thought you'd hate me. I was something tainted. Accused of being a criminal." She sniffed a little. "There was a lot you didn't know about me then."

Yarrow waited for a moment, then spoke slowly. "Not everyone was your enemy that day Becky. Your mom actually did have some supporters, and they weren't just the people who invested with her. Some folks admired the way she took in those who needed help."

She searched for a tissue in the pockets of her dress but came up empty. He handed her a napkin.

"Maybe. But most people didn't admire us at all," she said while wiping her eyes. "And I guess that was the problem. We split the town. We managed to take some of the money with us. But Erin also purposely left some behind. But some of that just disappeared into nothing. I think the police pocketed half of what they found."

She balled up the napkin and held it in her hand.

Yarrow drove on. "You said you felt tainted. Is that because of what all the girls were doing?"

She nodded.

He turned to look at her. "Including you?"

He saw tears in her eyes again. "Yes, Jim. Including me."

He squeezed the thin steering wheel and closed his eyes. But he was driving, so he forced them back open. Up ahead, the store's driveway was approaching. He flipped the turn signal.

As they slowed, he asked another question. "So once you left, Becky, where did you go?"

"We drove north. We spent the first night near Kennebunkport, at a friend of Erin's who lived near the shipyards. I stayed with Erin for a while as we made our way north, trying to put some distance between us and Riverbend. We wanted to stay unnoticed. But, without a business to run, Erin and I didn't really have a way to work together. We eventually split up."

Her wording troubled Yarrow. "You keep saying Erin. You mean your mom, right?"

She shrugged.

Yarrow was puzzled. Then doubt crept in. He tried not to sound demanding with his next words, but he knew impatience was seeping into his voice. "So, why do you call her Erin instead of Mom? And why the shrug?"

She hung her head a bit, then looked at him.

"Oh, Jim. I don't want to get into this. I have honey to deliver."

"Just … please Becky. Tell me. You owe me this much."

She clasped her hands tightly together, like she was praying for a reprieve. "What, Jim? What do you want to hear? That things were even worse than you thought? That she wasn't really my mother? Okay. Enough years have passed now. There you go. She was not."

Yarrow felt strange. Like the temperature inside the car suddenly dropped. He shivered a bit. "Erin wasn't your mother? But you were the Bivens family, right?" He stared out the windshield without really seeing anything. "So, is your name even Bivens?"

"That much is true actually. Bivens has always been my legal name. Mom, or we'll just call her Erin now, registered my birth when I was born. She listed me as hers, even though I was not. So, on paper at least, she's always been my mom."

"Well, then who was—"

"My real mom? I never knew her. Nor my father. My real mother was one of Erin's workers. She was an underage vagrant who lived on the property after running away from the Lawrence Poor Farm. She did what some girls do to get by. When I was born, she panicked. She left the farm and she left me, as soon as she could stand upright."

"Wow."

Becky nodded. "Erin didn't want to bring me to an orphanage. There would be too many questions about where I came from and why women were living with her. So, she just told people I was hers. I was kind of raised communally by the residents. I've always been thankful she didn't just throw me in the river."

Yarrow watched Becky quake a little. He wasn't sure how many people knew her full story. He suspected he was one of the few to hear it. He turned the key and killed the engine.

"Okay. So, she wasn't your mom. But you lived there from the start. When did Erin put you to work? I mean, not just doing chores, but working as ..." He realized the nature of his question and his voice trailed off.

"You want me to be honest?"

"Yes. I mean, I think I do."

"I was fifteen, Jim. There. Are you happy?"

He was not at all happy. His hands flew upward in a motion of disgust and anger. "Jesus Christ Becky! Are you kidding me?"

He watched her pick up her honey carrier and climb from the car.

"I'm not saying any more. And you don't have to wait."

"I'll wait."

A few minutes later she exited the store without the honey baskets. She walked toward the road rather than the police car. He watched her pass, shook his head, and pulled up next to her.

"Come on Becky. Get in. I wasn't judging you. Not at all."

She crossed her arms and looked at the asphalt. She kept walking.

"It's at least two miles Becky. Let me drive you. I promise I won't ask any more questions."

She looked up the road, stopped, then looked at the ground again. "You promise?"

"Yes!"

She kept looking down as she climbed in. They drove half the way in silence. Then Yarrow grew tired of the tension. Despite his promise, his next words just spilled out.

"I mean … I mean … " He made a fist with his good hand and banged the steering wheel. "My God Becky! She started you in that sort of work when you were fifteen? What the hell?" he said through gritted teeth. "If I ever find Erin."

"Don't find her," she turned and pointed at him. Her tone surprised him because he had never once seen her angry.

"Why?"

"Because I'm asking you not to. For all I know, Erin is dead now. I don't want anyone looking for her. If you try, I'll refuse to share any details with anyone. I will not participate." She slumped back into the seat. "Just let it go."

He stewed for a while. "I just … I didn't know, Becky. I wish I had. I would have helped somehow."

She looked at the police patch on his blue sleeve. Then at the scars on his hand. She realized how committed he was to keeping the peace, whatever that peace was supposed to be in a place that always supported a certain status quo.

"I know you would have helped if you could have. You're a good man, Jim." She placed her hand on his arm, then slid her fingers down to gently hold his battered palm. He let her hand stay. They watched the houses passing. Fences and farms. Places where families lived, but not families like hers.

She let go. "So now, it's my turn to ask you a question. How did you and Linda meet?" She bit her lip a bit after she asked.

He paused and looked down at his hand before answering.

"Oh jeez, Becky. It's not that interesting, really." He quickly told the story about how they both worked at Hampton Beach. He talked about their first few dates.

Becky listened, then asked, "But why did you like her?"

"What? I don't know. I mean, she was nice. She was cute. She laughed at my jokes."

"That's good. But it could apply to a lot of the girls at the beach, I'd guess."

He shrugged.

"I don't want to pry. But if you want to share, I'd really like to know."

She saw him fidget. He was silent for nearly a minute, but she waited.

"I liked spending more and more time with her. And talking. She seemed to sense my feelings. Then one day she said something that caught me off guard. She said I didn't have to be broken."

He retreated back to silence. She continued to wait.

"Okay, I know that sounds funny. And I certainly didn't feel broken at all. In fact, when I came home from Europe, I felt strong. I felt alive. I was a survivor, and that was a fine thing to be after walking through Hell. But inside, I felt different. Most of us did."

When they arrived back at the farm, he turned the car off. Then they sat. Neither of them seemed to want to part.

Yarrow spoke again. "I don't know how to describe it, but when you spend months at a time in a bloody kill-or-be-killed mode you end up living this strange and terrible life. You use violence to stay alive, and you accept that. Then it all ends. You reemerge and you're expected to suddenly be different. And you're not sure if the war was the real world, or if this is." He waved his hand toward the road and fields.

"But, anyway, when we were in combat, we were strong. And competent. We were killers. When we came back stateside we found our old places and we just hovered there for a while, trying to let the normal seep back in. Everything else, we kept hidden." He stopped. He started to bite his fingernail, then stopped himself.

"But that hidden angry part of me didn't quite go away. It started to seep out. You know, maybe I'd be annoyed by some scene in a movie, or some stupid thing someone said in a bar. Or sometimes it was the opposite. I might be sad and sympathetic if I saw a wounded vet trying to swim. I'd rush over." He shook his head. "The roller coaster of feelings just went on and on. So, I guess that's why I fell in love with Linda. She saw the jumble of light and darkness in me. I'm not sure how because when I came back, I was a closed book. Not even Ma or Will could pry any details out of me. But Linda focused right in on the real original me beneath it all. And she knew the rest could be soothed."

He turned to look at her. "So, why did I fall in love with Linda? Because she was there for me, Becky. She helped bring me back home."

Becky dabbed at her eyes, then looked toward her bee hives. "She was there, and I was not."

Yarrow nodded. He decided it was time to move the conversation in a different direction. "So anyway, the way you all got kicked off the farm back in forty-one? That made me mad. When I saw it happen, that was actually the first time I thought about joining the police department. I wondered if I might have been able to intervene if I was a cop. I was young, but even then, I knew what they were doing was wrong."

"That's a nice thought, to know you joined the police out of good intentions. A lot of cops join for far different reasons."

He watched her climb from the car.

"One more thing Becky," he called after her. "If I find out anyone underage is working at your farm, I'll shut you down too. I hate to be that blunt, but I'll protect them in a way I could never do for you when we were younger."

She leaned back through the car window and gave him an earnest look. "You don't need to worry, Jim. I lived that life. And I know I could never force that existence on any other underage girl."

As he watched her walk toward her produce stand, he decided to believe her.

Chapter 18

Colony

A healthy hive needs three types of adult bees—the workers, the drones, and a queen. They focus on nest building, food collection, and brood rearing. Each member has specific tasks, but the full colony's coordinated efforts are crucial for survival and reproduction. Individual honeybees cannot survive without the colony's support.

Becky's Guide to Raising Bees

When Mary Jane needed something, she often would invite people to join her for a nice breakfast.

Because she needed to persuade several people outside of her usual improvement society, she booked a reservation at the nicest restaurant in town. There, she would present her case for why they should coordinate their efforts to oppose the Bivens Farm.

The La Belle Du Palm was quite upscale compared to other places in town. Instead of heavy ceramic coffee cups and paper napkins, the Palm served from crystal water glasses and fine linen. Their most popular breakfast entrée was Croques Meurice.

During their first course, which included a drizzle of vanilla bean yogurt, Mary Jane tried to explain to some of the town's most influential people why they should be worried about Becky.

"You all remember what happened. I know you do."

"Of course we do. But opposition can be risky," said Eldred Jacobs, a local attorney. "I don't disagree with you, but I'm sure you're aware—you could face a lawsuit if you interfere with her business."

Mary Jane politely disagreed. "I think there are far greater risks if we decide to do nothing."

There was mild agreement around the table, plus plenty of speculation. But none of the attendees wanted to make a commitment to aggressively force the honey farm to close.

"Don't get us wrong," Jacobs added, "we'll continue to keep an eye on the place. But at the moment, I think you're being premature."

Mary Jane sat and stewed. Then something dawned on her. She was the only person at the table who grew up in Riverbend. The rest of them came later and only heard the stories from others. None had family members who were caught up in the scandal. None felt the public embarrassment and shame.

They talked some more, but as the breakfast wound down, she realized her effort had been wasted. A different strategy was needed.

"Thank you all for your time," she said coolly. "I guess Becky's return worries me more than the rest of you."

"It's not that we aren't worried Mary Jane," said Eldred Jacobs as he stood to leave. "It's that we see a need for discretion and proper timing."

After leaving the Palm, Mary Jane drove directly to the oldest and most reliable financial institution in town—the First National Bank of Riverbend. She entered with a flourish, looking for immediate attention.

"I'm sorry," said the woman behind the counter. "The president doesn't often meet with customers. But I could refer you to one of our customer serv—"

"No, I need to see Theodore Markley, and I need to see him immediately."

"Yes but—"

"Only him. And please don't waste your time arguing."

The woman eventually threw up her hands and relented.

As Mary Jane walked into his office, it was obvious the portly Ted Markley was not thrilled to see her. He listened but doodled on his green blotter and tugged at the end of his white moustache. When she finished outlining her concerns, Markley made it clear he was tired and miffed.

"I won't confirm who we loan money to, MJ. You know that's a private matter."

Mary Jane tapped her finger on the surface of his walnut desk. "You don't need to confirm anything, Ted. I know she got her mortgage here. I inherited some family stock in this bank, and I see all the reports. But that doesn't even matter."

Her eyes were accusatory, and she spoke in a low voice. "I know the bank's policy is that women always need a male cosigner, especially if that woman is unmarried. So tell me, who signed for her?"

He said nothing.

"Never mind. I already checked. There's no other name, Ted. Someone let her glide right through."

"If you say so."

"Then let's just talk risk. If Becky's business fails, or criminal activities happen out there, you will have egg on your face."

Markley shook his head.

"Face reality, Ted," she said in a bitter voice. "The bank could lose money here."

Markley slipped his sleek executive pen back into its holder. Mary Jane's gaze remained unrelenting. Finally, he looked directly at her.

"I understand your concerns. But this bank provides loans to many dozens of small businesses. It's part of our charter and we're proud to do our part to keep this town growing. We only make loans when it makes business sense. That means solid down-payment money, good credit, and a decent business plan. That's all it takes." He leaned back in his chair. "And the loan you're so concerned about? It wasn't very big. If we ever had to foreclose, which we won't, it wouldn't even cause a blip on our books. In fact, if we had to repossess, the property's already gone up in value."

"It's still an unnecessary risk, Ted."

He placed his fingertips together. "I shouldn't even bother to argue with you. But I guess I will. You know what's essential to the world's food supply, MJ? Bees that can help pollinate crops. And that means bees are also important to our local food supply. This bank has made loans to multiple farms in the area. They harvest corn. Wheat. Apples. Peaches. Heck, there's even a big flower farm about six miles from here. They sell to all the local florists. Some of those farms have already made lease arrangements with Becky to drop off one or two of her hives. They were glad to have the bees there for a week during pollination season." Markley chuckled. "I'll bet you didn't even know loaning her hives for pollination was a secondary income source for her."

Mary Jane avoided eye contact. But she could hear his chair squeak as he leaned forward. He rested his elbows on his desk. "I'm going to be blunt. I'm glad to have this business in town. She has the only bee yard within twenty miles. I'm glad she's finding a bit of success and I'm glad this bank can be part of it."

She glared at him. "And you really think there's that much money to be made from honey?"

"The money she makes out there is inconsequential. Last year some farmers actually complained to me about how challenging it was to get proper pollination on their crops. So that's our real investment here—she offers something my other customers need. Right now, she's paying her mortgage and I think she'll probably expand. Heck, I may even loan her more money to replace that wreck of a truck she's driving!"

"Well, I just think—"

He interrupted. "Look, I need to cut this off. I don't understand your personal issue with this woman. But it's none of my business. And frankly MJ, you don't own a big enough chunk of this bank to make me want to change my mind."

Mary Jane sat and stewed. After a moment, she confided. "You know, Ted, there's a reason my family doesn't own a larger percentage of this bank. I think maybe I should tell you about that."

She stood and closed his office door. When she returned to her chair, she took a moment to compose herself.

"Let me level with you. About ten years ago, before you moved to Riverbend and took this job, my family was the majority owner of the other big bank in town. It was ours for three generations. I'm sure you know some of this story already."

She stopped for a moment to make sure he was listening.

"Unfortunately, my father was a weak-minded fool. Under his management, the bank ran into trouble. A large part of that trouble involved Becky's mom."

"He was being foolish, you say?"

"My dad's weakness, frankly, was that damn farm and all the adventures he could find out there." Mary Jane shook her head and attempted to inject some drama into her voice. "I mean, with all those different people living there."

Ted Markley just closed his eyes and listened.

"My parents had been divorced for a while, and my dad started buying his produce from Erin. At least, that's what he did at first. But then he developed a taste for honey, if you know what I mean."

"I'm not sure I do."

"I'm quite certain you do, Ted. But let me be blunt. Becky's mother had a few girls working for her. The colony made its money because those girls did all sorts of work on the side. Massages of course, and many things beyond that. Their reputation spread and more customers appeared. People started to notice."

"I see. I'm assuming the police eventually got involved?"

"It wasn't that easy. Erin put a lot of thought into how to structure things, and she kept herself isolated from most activities. She was shrewd and made sure she never directly handled the money. From the mid-1930s until 1941, Erin Bivens managed a strange exchange system."

"Yes. I'm aware of the basics of what she offered."

"Then you also understand how my father and others discovered her system could be used as an alternative form of currency. People, almost always men, bought and sold futures contracts in order to build up credit on her books. Then they could spend that credit anyway they wanted."

"Spend it with the farm workers, you mean? The women who worked there."

"Yes. Becky's mom ran the place like a casino; the house took half of each transaction. As the value of the futures increased, late comers had to buy in at a higher price. But most visitors didn't balk and the price. Their costs went up, but they still got what they wanted, in a way that proved very tough to trace."

"That just sounds like she was using a token system instead of cash," Ted noted. "That's still against the law, especially if her ledger served as the token registry."

"Yes. But by the end, even the local banks were investing money with Erin, because they saw the investment gains. When they saw the value of the futures contracts going up they got dollar signs in their eyes. They feared missing out."

"But once the banks got involved—"

"Yup. That's where Erin made a mistake. Early individual investors weren't necessarily seeking a profit. They were using the system to hide their tawdry fun. But banks? They expect accurate accounting and real returns."

"Of course they did."

"As new money flowed in, Erin used some to pay off early investors. That's also illegal."

"Sounds a bit like that 1920s scheme in Boston by Charles Ponzi. People eventually figured out what he was doing."

"Yes. My parents were divorced and my father started spending more time at the farm. He kept investing more money. He even moved funds over from his more solid investments. I'm sure it was quite a glorious time for him and his overly horny friends."

Markley chuckled.

"But it was all too much, Ted. The town investigated and immediately called state officials. In a matter of days, things collapsed. My father's selfish investments disappeared. That's when most of Erin's workers fled."

"And no one went after her?"

"People certainly looked for her. But some of those involved just wanted things to quiet down. They just wanted to take a settlement because some of the money was left."

"Really?"

"Yes. Strangely, Erin took just half of what she accumulated. She left a note. It was her peace offering, of sorts."

"Interesting."

"Now, my father did hope for more, because he was the largest investor. He hired private investigators. They eventually tracked down one of the older girls. She claimed she had gone straight. She was putting herself through college. Unfortunately, she had no idea what happened to Erin and Becky. And that's the last we heard from any of them. Until Becky showed up again."

She stopped and took a deep breath. "Given the loss and humiliation my family endured, I think you can see why I'm bitter towards her."

"I understand. So, what happened to your father?"

"The bank's board of directors let him go as the head of operations. His finances never recovered, but we survived. And, because of the stupid amount of money he invested, our bank had difficulty remaining solvent. That's when this bank, right where we're sitting now, offered to buy us out. Dimes on the dollar. The percentage of the other bank that my family still controlled ended up blended into this bank. That's how I came to own roughly seven percent of your First National Bank of Riverbend."

They talked for five more minutes, but Mary Jane had shared the relevant details. Ted thanked her, but stressed that Becky was a different person, and deserved to start her business with a clean slate.

"If you have evidence that Becky is doing anything illegal now, or if she was criminally involved in her mother's old dealings, you'll have to bring it to the police or the courts."

Mary Jane shook her head. "If I had that proof, I'd have filed suit by now." She pointed at him. "But you know I'm right."

As she rose to leave she added, "I do have to say Ted, I think Becky's biggest skill is being a seductress. She presents herself as a businesswoman, or a purveyor of charity. She's able to get others to help her because she pretends to be some wonderful and caring Madonna who looks out for the forgotten masses. It's really quite a talent."

"I see."

As she adjusted her coat, she said, "I was the straight-A student in school Ted. Becky, when she bothered to attend, received mostly Ds. She's not as smart as she likes to think she is."

"Maybe she's a different kind of smart, MJ."

"You think so?" Mary Jane walked to his office door, then looked back. "I'm just going to say it, Ted. Don't you or any of your buddies let yourselves get seduced."

Chapter 19

The Talk

By 1950, as new global threats emerged, the United States became the world's strongest economy, largely due to its postwar economic base. But demographic shifts and labor demands led to more Americans moving toward coastal areas, where the larger manufacturing and defense plants were located.

Baystar's Global Economic Report, 1951

The kids were finally tucked into bed. Yarrow had just settled into his favorite chair with a new copy of *Look* magazine when Linda came up behind him. She kissed him on the top of his head and asked him to join her on the porch.

He felt a moment of dread. Whenever they thought the kids might overhear them, they took their conversations to their porch. And he knew Linda had talked to her mom earlier in the evening.

This time she carried no glasses and no wine. They sat facing each other in white wicker chairs. Shell-shaped backs and bamboo print cushions.

Linda began with small talk about her day, but her sentences seemed clipped. Almost practiced.

"So, anyway," she finally said. "We need to talk."

Jim nodded. "I thought that's what we're doing." He placed his hands on the arms of the chair and prepared himself.

"I think you know why."

Yarrow looked to the side for a moment. He saw her reflection in a window. She was quite graceful, with a housewife's wholesomeness. He could see she was looking directly at him, so he turned back. "I guess I do know. It's pretty clear. You want to move to Maine, and I'm happy with where we live now. I've told you; I really like this town. I guess I like Maine too. But mostly in the summer. I have no friends there, Linda. And I don't want to be there year-round. So … that's it. We both feel strongly about our choices, and here we are."

She stewed for a moment, then stood and walked to a window. Once again, he saw her reflection. He tried, to no avail, to make eye contact with it.

"Look Jim, I won't insist that you work at my uncle's box factory. I know that's not for you. But there are other types of work. Obviously, there are other police forces you can join, if that's really what you must do. I just thought you would be looking into that by now. Or looking for any other job."

"I did look into police jobs," he replied. "More than once. And one thing I've learned, by talking to other towns, is that there are many guys out there looking for police jobs. A lot of veterans who were MPs or who saw a little combat think becoming a cop is the perfect thing for them." He sighed. "Hell, that's exactly the reason I joined the force. Having experience in the military police moves you to the front of the line. Towns are flooded with applications and most departments try to hire local guys first."

"I just find it concerning, Jim, that you've made no progress."

"Come on, you know I've been trying, Linda." He could hear resentment creeping into his voice. He tried to calm down. "I sent inquiry letters to six different towns in Maine. That's every town surrounding where your mom lives. I've kept you informed. Jeez, I even left carbon copies on the counter, so you'd see what I was doing."

"I know. But … it's just …" She turned to look at him. "What about other things? What about being a security guard? I could ask my uncle about whether the facto—"

"I'm not going to be a damn security guard Linda!"

"I'm just saying … try to branch out a bit."

They sat in silence for a few minutes. Linda finally spoke. "You know, I've been talking to my mom and sister.

Yarrow closed his eyes.

"Just to get things started, I can live with one of them, temporarily. Then, once you're able to transfer up there, we can keep living with them while we're house-hunting."

"Yeah. Live with your mother." He shook his head. "Come on, Linda. I don't want you to move out. We're a family. I don't want the kids to be away from me! So, I'll keep trying to find a new job on some another force. But neither of us should transfer up there until we have all of our ducks in a row."

Linda waved her hands dismissively. "I don't think you're making the effort."

"It takes time!" He returned her icy stare with one of his own.

"Jim, don't look at me like that."

He immediately felt guilty. He loved her and didn't mean to telegraph resentment.

"How long will it be?" she asked. "A year? Two? Let's just go there now and you can do your searches from there. Right?"

"That makes no sense, Linda. I look much more hirable if I'm already working and looking to transfer. I don't want to apply as some unemployed guy who used to be a cop." Yarrow realized he was raising his voice again. He paused and looked at the ceiling. "And keep in mind, I'm a bit of a cripple." He held up his hand. "My chief was willing to overlook that. I don't know if others will do the same."

The pressure from Linda had become unrelenting. It bothered him that she wouldn't acknowledge the bitter pill he was trying to swallow. If she was going to push him, then he was going to push back a bit.

"Linda, do you remember where we met?"

"Of course I do. Don't be silly."

"I remember too. Hampton Beach. I was walking on the boardwalk with my friends. You and some other girls were waiting in line. I can't remember what for."

"It was ice cream. At Howard Johnson's."

"Yes. That's right. We stopped and talked with your group. We both had summer jobs at the beach. I was just back from the war after VE Day. I didn't know what I wanted to do. But I did know I needed to unwind and spend some time at the shore. I found a cheap room for the season and was hired as a ticket taker at the Casino Ballroom. And you were a waitress at one of the tea rooms, right?"

"That's right."

After our first encounter, we kept running into each other. Once, I was sitting on one of the boardwalk benches. You accused me of sitting in your seat."

Linda laughed. "You knew I was kidding."

"I did. And it made me laugh. We ended up walking and talking that evening. Up and down the boardwalk in front of the stores and bars. Then we walked to the water and put our feet in."

"It was cold."

"Numbingly cold, if I remember."

Linda smiled. "The second time we met up, we ended up talking until it was quite late. All the shops were closed."

"Yes. And do you remember our nickname for Hampton Beach?"

"We called it our neutral territory."

"Right. So, you do remember."

She squinched up her face. "How could I not? I grew up in Maine. You grew up in Massachusetts. That made New Hampshire a neutral halfway point."

Then it was Linda's turn to look away. "That was a great summer, wasn't it?"

"It was. And as the summer went on, we spent more and more time together. I was always honest about how I wanted to settle down. I wanted it to be somewhere right along the Merrimack River. Somewhere like—well, right about where we are right now. And you said you liked that idea. You were even excited. We talked about whether we were more likely to find good jobs here or in Maine. We even talked about which place would be better for kids, should we ever get that serious. You told me your dad was a lobsterman, and you didn't want your own kids to follow him into that life."

Linda nodded.

"We knew, by the end of the summer, that it was more than just a summer romance. As we left our neutral territory, we agreed to reconnect within a couple of weeks. And we did."

"Yes."

And that's when you told me you wanted to live in Massachusetts. After visiting here, you said this town, with the river curving around it, was quite charming. You wanted us to live here. So, we made it happen. We built a life around that decision. And now you want to unplug from that? And at a nearly impossible speed?" He wanted to say more. But it just came out as a sigh.

Linda pursed her lips, then whispered. "That was all before we had kids. I guess I didn't know how much I would miss being near family and having their help. I just didn't, Jim."

He rubbed his chin. His conflict was deep. "Look, I'm not ruling out a move. You know I've been looking for work. But to insist we depart immediately? Telling me I should abandon everything we've worked for here, in order to move to an even smaller town, for less pay? That seems like chopping ourselves off at the knees."

They both looked at the porch's painted wooden floor. Glossy grey. Scuffed in a few places by the wheels of toy cars.

"I understand how you feel, Jim. But, honestly, you know how I feel too."

They chatted for several more minutes. But they knew their impasse was deep. Best to retreat to their neutral corners.

Linda rose and kissed his cheek. "Let's talk in the morning."

He sat alone for a while, arms resting on raised ridges of wicker. He thought about pouring a drink and walking to the balcony again. But he wasn't in the mood. He didn't want to find himself looking in the direction of the farm.

So, he just sat. And he wondered.

Chapter 20

Recruiting

Early New Englanders viewed religious and social history as fully intertwined, with Puritans establishing religious control over both church and local governance. After a century, their control faded, but their influence remained, and it could be seen for centuries in the downtown church steeples and the faces and attitudes of the people.

Puritan Echoes, Riverfront Press, 1948

The Riverbend Congregational Church sat on the east side of town, atop a slight knoll. That's where the sidewalks narrowed, then gave way to dirt paths. It was a white chapel with an impressive steeple and tall windows. Its side yard held thin slate gravestones. Chunks of granite marked the corners of family plots. Mary Jane Danforth's ancestors were founding members, and three were buried in the churchyard.

For generations, the Danforths were a pious, proud, and prosperous family. They used their church ties to help others, and occasionally to help themselves.

With nowhere else to turn, Mary Jane decided to take her case to the church. But she needed to proceed diplomatically. First, she would raise a few red flags. She'd make people feel uneasy. Troubled.

Then, she would covertly inquire about what people thought of Becky's business. Once she identified others who didn't trust the farm, she could decide how to leverage their misgivings.

She started with the woman's council. At their monthly meetings the women, mostly mothers and grandmothers, gathered for tea, ice cream, and gossip. On the appropriate evening, Mary Jane hung her coat in the building's long hallway and joined other women in the lower parish hall.

Get the mothers on your side, she said to herself. *The others will follow.*

She said hello to four women at a round table. Two of them stood to greet her. "Mary Jane! How are you?"

"Oh please," she said, "don't get up. Sit."

Polite hugs, then talk of children and relatives.

"But to answer your question, I'm doing well, thank you so much!" Mary Jane said as she sat down. "I mean, as well as can be expected."

That response drew their attention. One of the women asked what she meant.

"Well, I'm just so upset about what I'm seeing out on the edge of town! You know, out there just past Route 110? My goodness, it's got me so worried!"

"Why, whatever do you mean?" The question came from one of the older women. Mary Jane knew she was the mother of one of her old classmates.

She took the time to explain the situation to the group. They sipped their tea and listened. Her speech ended with plenty of details on what had happened in 1941.

"And that's when the whole rotten group of them just up and ran away!" she explained. "Scattered like roaches! And you know how those kinds of people can be. No addresses or bank accounts. Very difficult to find them. And that means they were never brought to justice."

The women at the table looked deeply concerned. Most knew the basics of the story, but this was the first time they realized history could be repeating itself. Mary Jane saw embers of doubt and worry taking hold. She just needed to fan them to life.

She avoided making highly charged statements and kept her accusations vague while making her own feelings known. She was happy when one of the women expressed concern for her son and husband.

"I just hope someone will do something," the other woman said while clutching her hand to her breast. "My God, I can't believe they haven't shut them down already!"

Most of the women knew Mary Jane, and they respected her. She quickly wrapped up her conversation, then moved from table to table, catching up on other news, asking about mutual friends, then planting another seed of panic before moving on.

Buzz buzz ... something is happening out at that farm.

Worry worry ... could it be similar to what happened before?

Whisper whisper ... someone should do something.

The following Sunday, she continued the conversations after the church service. She made sure to always mention what a strong temptation the farm presented.

"Oh, and rats," she said. "How could there not be rats?

Over the next week she sought out families of those who invested and lost money with Erin. She knew many of them still felt anger in the wake of the collapse. She made sure to stir those feelings yet again.

Next, she encouraged parents to talk to their kids, to warn them of the dangers they might face at the farm. Her real goal was to encourage others to become carriers of her message. It was an effective way to burn worry and concern into their minds. Within two weeks, she felt like she'd been able to fan her embers into flames.

Then she set her sights on a different meeting.

The church's teen youth group always gathered on Thursday nights. That week they were tasked with cleaning up the Sunday school classrooms, which they did. Reluctantly.

Mary Jane saw this was an opportune time to deliver her message to the teens. But she mostly wanted to talk with the boys. She asked the youth group coordinators to split the girls and the boys, sending them to clean separate rooms. Mary Jane then met with Shannon Gates and Evie Shultz in front of the church.

"Are we ready?" Shannon asked.

"Oh yes," Mary Jane replied. "I believe the parents of most of those boys have already talked to them. And a couple of boys are aware their families lost money. I think we can leverage that."

"Yes indeed," said Evie.

Mary Jane smiled. "All right then. Let's see what we can get started." They made their way through the kitchen entrance, then on toward the classroom wing, where they could hear the boys working.

Chapter 21

To Be the Queen

Once a colony of honeybees has filled roughly eighty percent of a hive's available frames, it's time to give them room to expand. Just place another deep box on top with additional frames. Make openings between the boxes and the bees naturally want to migrate upward. They'll quickly start filling the extra frames. The result is a larger, more productive hive, including more workers.

Becky's Guide to Raising Bees

Becky usually preferred to inspect her hives in the early afternoon. That's when most of the worker bees and drones were away from the colony. But she had missed her afternoon rounds. By early evening the air had turned cool, and since cool air tended to slow the bees, Becky decided to conduct a rare early evening visit.

She recruited Amy to help her, along with two other women. They walked the rows and pulled the tops away from the boxes, adding a puff of smoke each time. Then they slowly slid individual frames out of the boxes—looking for potential problems.

They had been consistent with their hive maintenance. Any trouble was addressed immediately, so they knew they were unlikely to find any serious issues during this inspection.

In one case they discovered a new queen being born. The hive was showing signs of splitting. "This is good," Becky explained. "It's a regular part of the growth when a hive is strong."

They carefully moved the old queen to a new frame and placed that frame in an empty hive, adding a few handfuls of other bees to keep her company. "We'll see how many others from the old hive migrate to the new location," Becky said. "I think more than half of them will move over the next two days."

The work greatly impressed the new girls and they were full of questions.

Amy asked Becky if she remembered the first time they worked together, transferring the hives that once belonged to Amy's father.

"Of course. That was just a little over a month ago."

"And remember when I said I thought we can learn a lot from bee colonies? You agreed with me."

"Yes. I do remember that."

"Well, when I see all the workers who have come to this farm since then, and how you've managed to keep everything organized, I'm starting to see the connection. I think you're like the queen bee here. You really make things—"

Becky interrupted her. "Let me stop you there. I'm not the queen bee here. Not at all. For one thing, I run this farm in a way that queen bees would not."

"Really?"

"Think about it." She paused to set the hive's top back in place. Then she moved on to the next box. "The queen is the mother of all bees in the colony, right? That's certainly not me. The people here come from many places. They weren't born here. Also, the queen is, by far, the dominant bee in a hive, right? Does that sound like me? I prefer to let people find their own path. And if anyone threatens us, I'm barely able to stand up to them. I'd say I lack the power of a queen."

"I don't think that's true."

"Also, you've probably noticed I can barely find enough work to keep our residents busy. I'd say we're not an efficiently run colony."

She opened the lid of the next box and looked inside. Everything seemed fine.

"Finally," she added, "in a beehive, the other bees will follow and protect the queen. I'm not sure I have that level of support from everyone here. We are all just waiting, doing what we have to do to survive."

That upset Amy, and she said, "Of course you have our support! Or at least you should. I can see you're trying to help us all. The others know it too."

Amy also could sense Becky was feeling discouraged. She tried to find a different way to cheer her mentor's mood.

"Remember when you told me that any female in a colony can be chosen to become the queen? You also said none of them can seek the title, and if chosen, none can deny it. The decision happens before the queen ever hatches. That means the queen has the leadership role thrust upon her."

Becky had to laugh. "Okay. Very clever."

"I'm serious. A queen has her important role to play and when I look at a bee colony, I see a group that instinctively understands the value of working together. The workers, drones, and queens all have their roles and tasks, just like you said. Each is essential for the colony's survival." Feeling embarrassed, Amy softened a bit. "Anyway, I guess that's all I'm saying. We all have a place here, and you are the one who keeps this colony functioning."

Becky remained quite reluctant to accept queen bee status. Her voice took on a serious tone. "You know, Amy, in a real hive, it's the worker bees who handle all the decision-making. The queen's main job is to produce offspring. And look at me, I don't even have any children."

Amy lifted her hands. "We're all your children here."

Becky brushed her fingers through her hair and looked toward the river. "Well, one more thing. In bee hives, it's the workers who rule, and usually that's by consensus. Remember when I mentioned how the workers decide if a new queen is needed? Well, that's not at all what we will have here. I'm unlikely to accept a worker rebellion if the group tries to remove me from my own property."

Amy laughed. "You know that would never happen." Her objection inspired the other two girls to laugh too.

Becky was quiet as they moved from hive to hive. Then she spoke again. "There are other differences too. If the hive splits, workers go out in search of alternative homes. If there's more than one potential new place, the bees may visit each contender. Then they decide, as a group, which place is the best. Again, that's not what we have here. Meager as it is, I've bet my future on this location. If half of the workers suddenly decide to move, I won't be leaving with them."

Amy seemed to search for more words. She still liked the queen bee metaphor because it made sense in her eyes. "Since I've come here, I've watched how bees live communally. I admire the way their efforts mesh. When my father died, I found myself alone and I became overwhelmed by all the things I didn't know how to do. Then when I joined this farm, I could see how much better it is to have a bigger group of people to do the work. As part of a group, I can thrive."

As they opened the top of the last hive, Amy proudly pointed toward the middle of the buzzing mass. "If you watch them closely, you can see none of the bees have any sense of self-esteem or vanity. They just have their sense of being. Each works diligently at whatever their task may be. Most of them will only live for a few weeks."

Becky looked into the hive. "I agree. It really is remarkable to watch. I don't mean to discredit the way you feel, Amy. I've seen the same things when I look into a hive."

"Okay, then I'll just add, I also admire the way a hive works together to defend against outside forces, sometimes even sacrificing themselves. I admire how they plan together for the hive's future, even though many of them won't be around to see it. I think that's real altruism." Then she grinned. "And I think that's the first time I used that word since I learned it in school."

"It's too bad altruism is such a rare commodity in our world," Becky said.

When they finished, Becky stood and brushed dirt from her hands. Then she extinguished the burning embers of her smoker.

"I have to say Amy, there's another reason I want to avoid being queen. The workers of a colony eventually must replace their queen. Sometimes she ends up weakened with age, with nothing left to do. And in the end, if she doesn't leave, the others may kill her." She placed her hand on Amy's shoulder. "So, there you go. Don't try force me into the role of the queen. It comes with too far much baggage for my comfort."

Chapter 22

The Other

No one can take the place of a mother, yet somehow a mother can take the place of all others.

Old Irish Saying

On the Yarrow's kitchen wall there hung a tapestry.

"Variety is the spice of life."

That phrase was one of the more common kitchen decorations in America, with versions available at places like Woolworths and Grants.

But in reality, the family didn't experience much variety. Their lives had become enjoyable, predictable, and maybe a bit bland.

On a typical day it was dinner by six thirty, then dishes done and kids in their jammies before eight. Then maybe a little time in front of the radio as mom made everyone lunches for the following day.

Then bedtime for the kids, followed by bedtime for mom and dad.

"I love you," Linda said when they climbed into bed. She leaned over for a kiss.

"I love you too."

They both had magazines to read, *McCall's* for her *and The Saturday Evening Post* for him. She tore out a page that had five different Jello recipes and set it on her night stand. He muttered something about the war in Korea getting bogged down ever since Truman fired General MacArthur several weeks before.

Then after five minutes, Yarow noticed Linda had grown quiet and had not turned another page. She stared straight ahead with little movement.

"Lost in thought?" he asked.

She blinked. "Oh. Yes, I guess so. Just thinking about the old days. You know, summers at the beach. Going to the dance halls."

"You miss that?"

"Well, I'm not saying I want it back. I do like being a mom. But it's okay to miss it, right?"

"Of course. I miss the old days too. Hell, I even miss some things about the Army. When we weren't getting shot at, it could be fun hanging out with a bunch of crazy guys who were all my age."

"Exactly. So, I guess I was thinking about those times. And I was also thinking about that silly show on the radio called *Queen for a Day*."

Yarrow scoffed. "I hate that show. I feel like they're exploiting those poor women."

"They kind of are. But sometimes it's nice to see at least one of them get a reward."

"I guess so. Did anyone interesting win this time?"

"Yeah. A woman who was a widow. Her son had a heart condition, and she was worried about losing her apartment because of all her bills. So, when she won the applause meter thing, they did the usual. The announcer described how they wrapped her in a robe and gave her presents."

"I suppose that could be satisfying. But also, kind of sad."

"That is exactly the way it seemed."

"So, is that what sparked your feelings? Thinking about the old days and maybe feeling like you want to escape?"

"No. Come on, Jim."

"Or maybe you want to be queen for a while?"

"Certainly not that way."

"Good. Because you're already the queen here." He gave her knee a little pat through the blanket.

"Thanks. But I'd be happier if I could just be a better mom."

Yarrow dropped his magazine onto his lap. "You're a fantastic mom. What are you talking about?"

She gave him a sheepish look.

"All right, what did Barb say to you today?"

"Nothing. It's just, I don't feel like I'll ever be as good a mother as she was."

"Stop that. She had two kids. You have three, and much closer together, and I'd say you're handling it like a champ."

Linda said thanks. But her gaze was distant.

"You know what? Every time you talk to her, she's critical. She does nothing but correct you. It's all I can do to keep from telling her off."

"Please don't."

"I won't. But that's only out of deference to you. You know I really want to, and you know she deserves it."

He could tell his strong words hurt Linda a bit. She could be quite protective of her mom, even though she'd occasionally admit he was right about her.

He decided to diffuse things with a little humor. "So, if you don't want to be queen for a day, does that mean I get to be king?"

"Oh, jeez. Maybe."

"Ooo. And do my subjects have to do what I say?"

She gave his hand a pat. "Maybe tomorrow night dear. At the moment, this subject has a lot of decisions to make."

Once the lights were off, Yarrow stared at the ceiling. He tended to worry whenever Linda said she was trying to make a decision, especially if he wasn't part of the process.

Chapter 23

The Push

People seek order in their lives, and they seek to belong. If you place a hundred people in a room and tell them all to walk randomly, eventually some of them will start walking in a set pattern. Soon, others will follow. Many people simply like being shown what to do, and they may take comfort in not having to think. It's easier for them to be part of the herd.

The History of Mob Mentalities, Oxbridge University Press, 1946

For the boys in the church, cleaning classrooms was not their idea of fun. With little supervision, they soon descended into rowdiness.

When Mary Jane and friends walked into the room, they discovered a six-foot stack of hymnals on the floor. One group of boys threw erasers at the stack while others tried to block the shots. They all looked guilty and quickly disassembled the stack, but they soon realized they weren't in trouble.

Mary Jane spoke first. "I guess you boys have had enough cleaning for the night?"

"Definitely."

"Then how about if we all get a snack?"

The boys agreed and hurried down the long hallway. Mary Jane hung back and whispered to Shannon, "This may be easier than we think."

"They're already pretty wound up," Shannon said. "And I know their parents have warned them about the farm, so the place is already tainted in their eyes. It might be fairly easy to plant your idea."

"That's good to hear."

"But, please MJ, our names can't be connected to this. I mean, mine certainly can't."

"We should be able to stay out of it. We'll stoke the anger, but the boys will think the idea was their own."

Once they reached the church's kitchen, the women raided the cupboards for sugar cookies. They also found lemonade in the refrigerator. The boys and the church ladies gathered around the central counter to enjoy their feast, standing atop red and white linoleum and leaning against the white-tiled counters. Mary Jane started by talking about the weather. Then she broached her subject by asking the boys if sugar or honey was the best sweetener for cookies. Most voted for sugar.

But since honey was mentioned, she slyly turned the conversation to the Bivens Farm. As if on cue, the other women rolled their eyes and casually mocked Becky Bivens.

Mary Jane asked the boys what they thought about the farm.

The oldest boy was happy to respond. "My dad said if that camp keeps growing out there, property values could drop for the whole town."

"I think that's a great observation," Shannon agreed.

"I heard they've been stealing from people," said another boy. Mary Jane hadn't heard that, but she still nodded enthusiastically. Then others chimed in.

"My aunt said the people are dangerous."

"I hear they're all gypsies."

She let other comments flow, the added, "It's definitely an illegal encampment. And you're right about property values. That could even affect the value of what you all inherit years from now."

The boys started to look worried and had more questions. Eventually Mary Jane held her hand up and asked for quiet.

She knew it was time to channel their anger into something more than noise. But Shannon spoke first, hastily upping the ante. "Apparently, there's also a young child who's gone missing, and people are saying the folks on that farm had something to do with that."

Mary Jane deftly followed Shannon's lead, making up her own addition. "That's fascinating, because I've heard they may have conducted child sacrifices out there. It's completely ungodly, and it's gotten out of hand."

"Those poor babies," Shannon echoed.

The other women looked at each other nervously. Wondering if Mary Jane and Shannon had gone too far. But they did nothing to stop them.

"Well, boys," MJ continued. "I'm sure it's surprising to hear some of the moms talk this way. But you're old enough now. And really, we just want to make sure everyone stays safe. That includes all the people you know here at church, or at your school. We need to look out for your younger sisters and brothers too, my God."

The boys looked at each other. The oldest one spoke. "I mean, we're here, and can help protect our families, right guys?"

The others nodded in agreement. Mary Jane smiled, knowing she had planted the seed. "Just be careful," she said.

As the conversation continued, the boys started to open up about what they thought of the farm. At some point it became a bragging match about which of them could do more to keep things safe.

Then one of the younger boys asked about the bees.

"Yeah, well I'm not scared of those!" said another.

Shannon and Mary Jane exchanged glances, acknowledging their apparent success.

When the time seemed right, Mary Jane made one more strategic comment. "You know, it's too bad someone doesn't do something to get rid of those hives. I'll bet Becky and her troublemakers would run away after that. We'd all be better off."

"Well, whoever helps get rid of them," Shannon added. "They'll need to get in and out quickly, when it's dark. But I tell you, those brave people, whoever they are, would be big heroes."

After the gathering broke up, several of the boys lingered in the church parking lot. Some waited for their parents to pick them up, while others—old enough to have licenses—would drive themselves.

Soon their number dwindled to just six. There were five seniors, Rob Lewis, Mitch Wilson, Tylor Campbell, and Colin Evans, and one younger boy; a freshman named Jack Webster. His family moved to town just a few weeks before.

They leaned against the cars and Rob reached into his coat. He pulled out a pack of Lucky Strikes. He offered them to the others and everyone but young Jack grabbed a smoke.

"You know," Rob said as he flicked his lighter, "the moms in there tonight were full of crap."

The lighter was passed hand-to-hand down the line.

"Yeah," said Tylor. "All complaints. No real action." He took a long drag then blew a smoke ring toward a streetlight. "I'll tell you; our families are just a bunch of yokels."

"Ayuh," Colin agreed.

"I don't really understand what's happening out there," young Jack said. "Anyone got the dope on that?"

The others laughed.

"Aw, you know," someone chimed in.

"Yeah," Rob replied, "we all know what's up. But don't you think it's lame those women in there didn't mention the dirty stuff? They just hinted at things. And come on, child sacrifices and a missing baby? If that really happened, holy moly, it would have been all over the news."

"Well, they're just panicking," Rob replied. "Got to protect their precious kids, ya know?"

The other boys hooted.

Rob raised his hands like a preacher. "How about it! Do you all feel protected?"

"I feel like we should do something," said Tylor.

A few boys boasted about what they could do to fix the problem. Then they agreed that what they really should do was to drive out to have a look for themselves.

They all piled into Rob's big 1948 Mercury, which he purchased at a big discount after the first owner smashed it up. Rob's uncle let him rebuild it in his garage.

"So are you coming too, Jack?"

Young Jack Webster shrugged, then nodded. They told him to sit in the back seat, in the middle.

The boys shouted questions to each other over the noise of the motor.

"Are we going to just drive by? Or stop?"

"We'll at least slow down."

"Are the girls there at night? Will we see any of them?"

"They're always there, stupid. They live there."

"What about the bees, do they fly at night?"

"Come on, pipe down guys," Mitch interrupted. "You do know those girls are the real reason our moms are worried, right? They're afraid those women will corrupt their sons or something."

"Shit, that sounds good to me. Bring it on!" Tylor shouted.

Someone punched him in the arm.

"I don't think it's just the girls," Rob added as he coaxed the steering wheel into a turn. "The part about the property values is probably true. They're worried about the trashiness."

The boys grew silent. None considered themselves wealthy, but they knew their families were comfortable. They also knew their houses represented the biggest chunk of their families' worth. Any perceived threat to that investment was cause for alarm.

They approached the farm from the south and parked a hundred yards away. They sat in the car, looking toward the big field. They saw flickering lanterns and candles in the distance. The hives were set apart and in the moonlight they looked like rows of bluish-white cubes.

"What was it Miss Danforth said?" Tylor asked. "That the bees are the only reason the farm is here? Well, there they are."

No one responded. Rob shut off the car and climbed out. "Let's just go look."

The others climbed out too, but hesitated.

"I'm not going closer."

"Well, I am," Rob boasted. He walked a few feet into the field.

The other boys looked at each other. "Thought we were just coming to look," said Jack.

"And that's what we're doing."

"Yeah, but … maybe we should go look at that produce stand first?"

But the group ended up moving together toward the field. And they listened.

"Wow. You can hear them buzzing even from here."

"So, they're not sleeping?"

Rob held up a finger. The group was silent for a moment, then he said "Huh. Not all the hives are buzzing. Just a couple."

As they walked into the first row, they started to feel safer. None of the bees were out of their hives. In hushed tones they started exchanging boasts and dares. By the time they reached the middle of the field they had more confidence.

"There must be sixty or more hive boxes here. That's like … a huge number." Rob tapped his finger against one. The buzzing increased slightly, then slowed. "That would make more honey than they could ever sell here at their farm stand."

He tapped again, rocking the hive slightly.

"Do it Rob, push it over!" one boy called out.

"That will just make them mad," he replied.

"Maybe," said Tylor. "But it would still be pretty funny. Besides, bees don't fly at night, right?"

Rob grinned. "Let's do it. This place deserves it." He crept up to the hive and gave it a mighty shove. As it hit the ground, the stacked boxes separated and one broke apart. At first, nothing happened. Seconds later the buzzing grew shrill and urgent. Small angry shadows slid through openings, looking to defend their colony.

The bees circled blindly in the low light, but the buzzing kept ramping up—in a terrifying way. The boys were caught off guard. Suddenly they could feel the bees bouncing off their shoulders and coming toward their faces.

"I think they can see well enough!" someone shouted.

A few started to scream. In their haste, the teens bumped into each other. They stumbled and ran for their lives. The commotion triggered activity in other hives. More bees came spilling out, aimless at first, then joining the chase. The boys saw their path out of the field, but it had filled with a cloud of buzzing dark dots.

While some of the boys panicked, Rob tried to stay cool, shouting instructions as he swatted bees away from his face. "This way. Back to the car, and let's tip some other hives as we go. Move it!"

The boys ran. Each time they passed a hive they stretched out their arms, tipping whatever they could reach. Occasional stings happened, eliciting screams from one boy, then another. Their shouts caused panic, but they managed to stay together. Nearly everyone was stung at least once.

At the rear of the group was the ninth grader Jack Webster. He didn't care about tipping over boxes. He just wanted to get away. His legs pumped and his heart pounded. But as he ran, one of the hives fell directly in his path. In the dim light he stumbled against it, tripping hard and crashing to the ground.

He landed right next to a crack where angry bees rushed out. As he struggled to rise, a dark buzzing wave descended over him.

He could hear the other boys ahead of him. In the distance headlights appeared on the road.

"Let's move it, Jack! We need to get out of here."

He tried and was stung again and again as he staggered to his feet. He fought the pain and tried to call out to the others, but everyone was shouting, and no one heard his panicked plea. He limped forward, but after several seconds he felt his eyelids swell. His lungs suddenly tightened like his chest was trapped in a vise. Then his heart started to race, and his throat felt dry and full of straw.

"Guys?" Jack coughed as he bent over. He placed his hands on his knees, trying to catch his breath. Instead, he vomited. More stings came as the bees caught up to him. His hands rose to his face. He felt welts and burning sores. He slumped forward, falling toward a ground that no longer seemed to be there. When he finally smacked into the earth he heaved again, and continued heaving until his stomach went dry and his world went dark.

Chapter 24

Aftermath

If a hive is destroyed, there may not be enough bees for a colony to start again. But if a living queen is still present, and if there are enough worker bees, they may swarm and try to find a new home. Even if the queen is dead, caretaker bees may be able to find a safe place. If they move quickly, and if they're able to create an emergency queen cell, a new queen may emerge, and the hive may live on.

Becky's Guide to Raising Bees

Yarrow was reaching to turn off his kitchen light when his phone rang. He stared in the direction of the noise. *Who the hell is calling at this time of night?*

Hoping the sound hadn't disturbed the sleeping kids, he quickly lifted the receiver. At the other end of the line was the town's central police dispatch.

"Jim?"

"Yeah?"

"Can we pull you into something tonight? We have a situation." It wasn't Tina calling this time. It was the night dispatcher. Yarrow didn't know her very well.

He hesitated. "I guess so. What's up?"

"Something happened out at the Bivens Farm. We need some back-up."

The words caught him off guard. "I'm sorry, what? What do you mean 'something happened?'"

"I'm waiting for a full report. But there's been some vandalism. Mostly smashed hives. A bunch of kids got stung and when they took off, apparently one of them got left behind. It's a mess. Some of the kids came home with multiple bee stings and their parents brought them to the hospital. That's when their whole story came out. So, while the one kid is still missing, he may just be hiding in the woods."

"Oh boy," he said with exasperation. "What do you need me to do?"

"Can you drive out to the farm? Nate and Ed are out there trying to take a report. But some of the parents showed up and they're all up in arms. Having an extra badge out there would be good. Pronto."

Yarrow closed his eyes. "Wow. Okay, I'll head there right now."

He left a note for Linda then picked up his hat, gun, and badge.

Once he arrived at the farm he immediately started assisting his colleagues. Nate and Ed, both corporals in the Riverbend Police Department, were trying to calm three sets of parents. They all demanded the police do something, though they couldn't say exactly what that should be.

Nate asked for their names, and said they wouldn't charge anyone yet. "Look, everyone please just go home. Let the police conduct our investigation. We'll call you."

After some grumbling and vague condemnation of the farm, the parents returned to their cars. Yarrow wanted to look for Becky, but first he wanted to see the damage for himself.

It was past midnight when the trio of officers pressed the buttons on their big flashlights and walked toward the field. "All right," said Yarrow. "Let's see what we have here."

Chapter 25

Nature's Commodity

Early in New England's history, the economy was cash poor. Silver, copper, and scarce gold coins were used as legal tender, while some private banks issued their own paper notes. But currency reputations were not always trusted. To bridge the gap, local economies often relied on trade, and sometimes credit. New Englanders became skilled at keeping written accounts of their investments and any money they were owed.

This History of Trade in New England, The Filbert Independent, 1942

When she heard commotion in her fields, Becky bounded out of bed. She dressed, but after hearing shouts of anger, she elected to remain within the metal cocoon of her truck. She stood back from the windows and tried to see what was happening without anyone seeing her.

When a knock came at her door, it was still dark. A voice outside announced the arrival of the police. She opened her door slightly and found herself looking at an officer she'd never seen before.

"Are you Miss Becky Bivens?"

Her back stiffened. She remained silent for a moment, then nodded.

"I am."

"We've been walking the length of your property ma'am. I'm afraid there's been some damage."

She took a deep breath. "I did hear noises. I knew something was happening. What did you find?"

"Can you say what you heard during the last hour or so?"

"Some banging. Voices. People running. But I'm parked away from the field. I couldn't tell what was going on."

"Please step outside ma'am."

Becky hesitated, then complied.

"We found broken pieces from several beehives," the officer said. "It looks like some vandals came through the field, tipped them over, then ran. Some of your bees got loose too."

"Oh no ..."

"Yes, and we have a missing boy too. He didn't come home last night. We think he may still be here."

Becky folded her arms. "If the other boys ran, why do you think one boy is still here?"

"We've talked with his mother on the phone. She's been calling around looking for him. She's a widow and doesn't have a car."

"And?"

" Some of the boys ended up in the hospital and they admitted they lost track of the youngest when they were here. Heard him yelling but couldn't see him."

The cop turned his head and looked over his shoulder. "We're walking through the farm now, looking for him."

Becky was dismayed. She grabbed a sweater from a hook near the door. A moment later she spotted Jim Yarrow walking out of the woods. She headed in his direction, then broke into a run as she got closer.

"Jim? Oh, thank God. What's this about?"

He shook his head. "You'd better come with us Becky."

A hint of light pushed into the east as they walked toward the top of a small berm. As the whole field came into view, Becky's hands went to her cheeks, then they covered her mouth as she stifled a scream. Along the center rows of the hives, nearly every box was tipped over. Fourteen in all. Several of them had broken open. Even in the dim light she could see honey oozing out.

In the beam of the officers' flashlights, she saw circling clouds of confused bees.

Yarrow held her arm. "The first time we searched the area we didn't find anyone. But a few minutes ago, as things got lighter, we spotted a pair of shoes sticking out over the edge of that small gully."

Becky sprinted toward the spot. Yarrow and the other officers followed. Becky stopped when she saw a boy lying face up. His face and hands were ghostly white. The body was in a contorted position, with dozens of bumps on his cheeks and hands.

"Oh no …"

"We figure he's been dead for a few hours. Coroner is on his way to confirm it. I'm … I'm so sorry, Becky."

The rest of the morning was a blur for her. Dawn fully broke with its usual misty optimism, but it was not a feeling she shared. Her mind kept drifting back to the dead boy. She felt sorry for him. Who was he and why was he in her field? From the marks on the body, she knew it was the bee stings that killed him.

Her bees.

She could not get the boy out of her mind. But she couldn't do anything. The police closed off the field and told her to wait near her truck. That was frustrating too because she needed to set her hives upright. If she worked quickly, she might coax some colonies back home. As she waited she was losing honey. It was just seeping into the ground, and some colonies would be so traumatized they'd swarm away.

Once the police and the coroner finished their investigations, local firefighters carried the boy's body toward a waiting van. As they traversed the uneven ground, a car pulled up and a distraught woman climbed out of the passenger side. She spotted the stretcher and ran toward it.

That's when the wailing started. The tone and the despair made Becky shudder. It was all so sad. And so unnecessary. She watched a grieving mother hug the lifeless body.

The firemen resumed their transport, and the mother walked beside them, holding her boy's hand. When she spotted Becky, her expression changed. Sorrow turned to outrage.

"You!"

She released the boy's hand and her fingers coiled into a fist. She rushed toward Becky.

Yarrow moved fast, placing himself between the two. "Hold on." With lightning speed, he caught the woman's arm while it was in mid-swing.

"You!" the mother growled again. Her anger grew as Yarrow held her back.

"I know you caused this! You don't belong here. You brought the devil with you when you came, and now you've cost my son his life!" She fell to her knees and let the bitterness pour forth. "My sweet boy is gone, and you did this!"

Yarrow kept hold of her shirt collar as she stayed on her knees, still flailing her arms. But it was half-hearted. "We just moved here, but I've already heard the stories. This town was rid of you! Why did you come back?" She burst into tears as she realized she would get no revenge that day. She leaned forward, hands on the dew-coated grass. "This town was rid of your family," she cried. "Why did you come back?"

Chapter 26

But …

Besides splitting and swarming, bees may leave a hive for another reason. It's called absconding. That's when issues such as overcrowding, damage, or lack of forage may cause the whole colony to depart. Even a recently settled swarm may abscond. That can happen if they are not happy in their new home, or just because they don't feel any long-term connection to a place.

Becky's Guide to Raising Bees

Later that morning, Yarrow stood with Becky as they watched the last of the emergency vehicles pull away. A newspaper reporter stopped at the farm, but Becky waved off his request for an interview. Yarrow referred him to the police station. "Just ask for the official report," he said. "It should be available by this afternoon."

Several women from the encampment watched from a distance. Yarrow sat with Becky at her picnic table. When they had a moment, he asked, "Are you okay?"

She shrugged. "I guess I am. But that was a terrible thing to see. And for the boy to die that way. From all those stings." She shuddered.

"You're near bees all the time. I'm glad that's never happened to you."

"But it wouldn't," she said with a shaking voice. "Bees really have to be angry for them to attack." She looked at the field and the sprawling mess. "But I guess anger is an appropriate response when their homes are toppled."

She looked back toward Yarrow. "What will happen now?"

"With the bees?"

"No, Jim, with the police. With the investigation. I mean, will I be in trouble?"

He looked puzzled. "I can't see how. The boy was the trespasser. All of them were intruding here and being vandals. I don't know what they would charge you with, and if they try, you should be cleared quickly. I mean …" Then he hesitated.

"I feel like there's a 'but' looming there, Jim."

He nodded. "But, when someone is already looking for reasons to shut you down, they may try to focus on any issue they can find." He raised his eyebrows. "And this? This could be a big one."

She closed her eyes. "I know. And I feel bad. I don't even know why those boys were here."

Yarrow put his hand on her shoulder. "I'm going to go out on a limb. I'm going to say none of them really know either. They are all young and looking for adventure. I'm pretty certain they were easy to manipulate."

Yarrow and Becky continued to talk as they walked to one of the tipped hives. They approached slowly, then carefully pushed it back upright. He stepped back when the buzzing grew louder, which made Becky laugh.

"Look, don't worry about this. I have plenty of help here. My workers and I can handle the cleanup."

"Yeah. About that. How many girls are living here now?"

Becky had to count to herself. "I'm not exactly sure. Besides the ones living at the far end of the field, there are a couple of tents in the woods and one more down by the water. Probably around twenty in total."

"Wow."

Yarrow drove to the station, talked to the chief for a few minutes, the settled in to write his report. He wanted to take his time and make sure he didn't miss any details. Becky spent the rest of the day using her bee smoker and restoring the hives, sliding frames back into place and returning scoops of bees to their appropriate homes. A few of the girls joined in, including Amy Maye, who had become quite fearless when dealing with the buzzing nests.

I need to keep busy," Amy said. "I have to occupy my mind, I guess, because I keep thinking about that poor boy."

For the badly broken hives, Becky recruited two women to construct very rudimentary boxes. Then she moved the queens and some of the broken frames into the alternative spaces. She hoped they would quickly reestablish the colonies. Later on, she could build better hives and install legitimate full frames.

Once they finished lifting the hives, Becky scooped honey from the ground—as best she could. She knew it was ruined now, but it was still useful. Honey was a good fertilizer. Carrying puddles of goo in a dustpan, she made several trips to her flower garden. There, she also replanted several Black-eyed Susans that were knocked loose by the marauding teens.

Amy stood to one side. She and two of the new women watched Becky as she worked. Then they joined her, squatting and pushing the roots of the flowers back into the dirt.

"Look at you. You're amazing."

Becky remained stoic. "Thank you, Amy. But no. Not amazing. I just keep going. I don't know if that makes me strong, or just stubborn."

Amy wiped her hands on her dungarees. "I don't mean just these flowers. I mean, look at everything. You helped restore all those broken hives and you didn't get a single sting. I think many of these colonies will survive. And I have no doubt those flowers will take root and grow again."

One of the other women, Etta, spoke up. "She's right. I feel like I'm watching Mother Nature herself."

Becky waved them away. "Enough of that."

"And this place," Etta continued. "You took me in and all these other women. Making sure we can live and work here. I have to say, I don't understand why the townies criticize you. They should be doing nothing but singing your praises."

Becky also brushed the soil from her hands. "I don't ever expect the people of this town to sing my praises. I know I'm not the kind of person they admire."

"Then I want to know why that is," Amy shot back.

Becky lifted her hands, as if grasping for a way to explain. "Well, think about it. These people are quite happy living in their beautiful river town. In their minds, prosperity means being more exclusive. I try to be inclusive, and that's pretty much the opposite of their goal. So that's it. We'll never be part of their club."

Amy thought for a moment. "But things are changing, right? Not everyone needs to follow their mold."

"Easy to say, Amy."

"What I mean is, who cares what they want? There are so many new people moving to town now, and I don't think any of them much care about this farm—unless someone has already bent their ear and tried to convince them the place is evil, like they did with Jack's mother. Before all of this, the average person in town probably wasn't thinking at all about either you or that Mary Jane Danforth person.

Becky smiled. "I like your attitude, Amy. But ..." She looked at their hill and camp. "This is going to make people think about us now. And to some, we're in their way. We're trash that needs to be removed."

She looked toward the village. It seemed far away now, like another world. "They're the lucky ones, those people in town. They already have what the women here can only hope to achieve. Yet, I can see they want even more. And that means we must make do with even less."

Amy had a bitter look. Downturned mouth, furrowed brows, and narrowed eyes. Becky sensed her anger and disappointment.

"They're angry because of what some women do here, right?"

"I never ask what people are doing, Amy."

"But—"

"Okay. Yes. I'm sure that's a big part of it." Becky returned to working on her flowers and pressing roots into the ground. "The people of this town are welcome to help us find other work if they want. Lord knows I keep asking them. But help never comes. So, we do what we must."

Amy was not easily stymied. "Okay. But. If 'what the girls do' is the biggest issue people have with the farm … those activities will continue to taint everyone's view of us."

Becky gave Amy a sideways glance.

"So, could that part stop at least? I mean, come on Becky. You know what's going on. Can't you stop it?"

Becky said no. "The women who live here all have their own spaces, shabby as they are. I can't feed them all. I can't pay them all. But they still need to live, and I am happy to shelter them. That's what I offer, but I don't control them. Nor do I want to."

Amy started to turn away. Then she turned back. She did not like challenging the woman who had helped her so much. But she also saw the level of hatred pointed their way and worried it could bring them down.

She risked one more question.

"You track the payments and spending here, right? You move credits to different columns in that ledger of yours. Your transaction records include the honey options, right?"

"Yes."

"So, doesn't your accounting make you an accomplice?"

Becky just smiled. "I'm just a beekeeper who's been forced into the role of bookkeeper." She gave her a straightforward look. "The world is just a commodities market, Amy. Just like the honey itself."

Becky saw Amy's puzzled look.

Etta leaned close to Amy. "Come on," she whispered. "Becky's being nice to us. Don't keep going on about it."

But Amy shushed her. "First, tell me what you mean by that, Becky."

"Commodities? Okay." Her voice took on a more pragmatic tone. "One lesson that was drilled into me by Erin is that we live in an investment-driven society. It's pretty much forced on us. We may not like it, but none of us will ever change it." Then she grinned. "It may surprise you to hear this, but I'm not fighting it. If we're going to live with good old American capitalism, there's no reason we can't also play the game."

Becky held Amy's gaze and tried to make things crystal clear to her. "If someone's investment here grows, that's because we made their investment worthwhile. And if it grows, shouldn't these women, the ones who also took a risk be able to profit from that? And should they not be entitled to spend those gains any way they want?"

"I guess so. I mean—"

"I know that you read the newspapers, Amy. But here's what I've seen. After the war, all around the world, the industrial base of many countries was wiped out. Now, six years later, they're still trying to recover. Here in America we lost men, but we lost very little infrastructure. We still have our factories, our farms, and our highways. That's why our economy has been booming. We're one of the few places that still makes and sells what the rest of the world needs. But the boom times didn't come for everyone. People may say they want unfettered business, but they mostly want that for themselves. It's not all-inclusive."

"I realize the deck is stacked against us," Amy said, dropping her gaze in resignation.

"Yes. So, we have to find our own ways to succeed."

In that moment, Amy realized there was a certain ruthlessness to Becky—hardened by time and circumstance. But Amy couldn't condemn Becky for it. In a way, she admired it.

The conversation stopped when they saw two new arrivals coming up the driveway. They were disheveled-looking girls toting their belongings in dirty pillowcases.

"Oh no," Becky whispered. Then she went to welcome them.

The woman with darker, more matted hair spoke first. "We're looking for work. And for a place to stay. We heard maybe we can find that here?"

Becky introduced herself, then said, "Well, I'll tell you this. Around this farm, there's always a place for those who know how to work." She smiled. "And we are especially interested in those who know how to be creative."

Chapter 27

Inside the Empty

In nineteen forty-six, the divorce rate in the U.S. spiked, reaching its highest level ever. There were over four divorces for every thousand people. The jump was triggered by increasingly liberal divorce attitudes and by the return of soldiers who were away too long, and who came back as different men. By 1951 the anomaly was over, and the number of divorces fell back to their previous level.

A Statistical View of American Couples, Colbert Research Inc. 1952

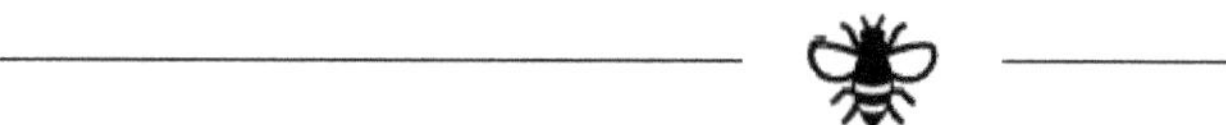

Yarrow had been up all night, dealing with death and senseless vandalism. By the time he came home he felt drained and weary. He decided it was his worst night since he returned from Europe.

As he locked the front door, all he wanted to do was sleep. But his eyes focused on a pair of salt and pepper shakers on the kitchen table. They were milky glass in color with silver tops and blue sailboats printed on their fronts.

The middle of the table was not where the shakers usually stood. Between them was a white envelope. He picked it up and saw his name on the front. Before opening it, he called out to his wife.

"Linda?"

He walked to the bottom of the stairs and called again. "Linda?"

There was no answer. No noise at all came from upstairs. He sat on the couch and tore open the note.

Dear Jim, it started.

"Shit!" he said aloud.

He looked at the ceiling for a moment. During his time in the army, he'd seen plenty of men receive these types of letters. He never expected to get one himself.

He started reading again.

Dear Jim,

The kids and I have gone to visit my mother and sister. I'm not sure when, or if, we are coming back.

He shook his head.

Please wait a day or so to call me. I need time to settle, and to make some decisions. You probably need time too.

I hope that we can talk in two days, and then you will come to see us. After that, I hope you will start to make real plans to join us here. I'm sorry to do this so suddenly, but I really hope you can make the effort to hold our family together.

Yarrow rubbed his eyes. He couldn't believe this was happening.

Even though you asked your dispatcher to call me, even though she told me you'd been looped into some investigation, I was still worried. And I realized living here in Riverbend was becoming too overwhelming for me. I can no longer stay, especially with my constant fear for your safety. But if I'm honest, my real reason for leaving is this: There was little progress being made toward our move to Maine. So, I had to take the first step.

Again, I really hope you will decide to join us. I look forward to talking soon.

Fondly,

Linda

Yarrow dropped the letter onto the coffee table and stared across the room.

"'Fondly?' Really Linda? Just 'Fondly?'"

She left with no warning. No discussion. He couldn't believe she just took their kids to another state. Could she legally do that? He was a cop, and it bothered him that he wasn't sure.

Should he contact an attorney? He couldn't decide on that either.

Damn it, I don't want my marriage to end.

He thought again about hiring an attorney, but would that end up pushing things over the edge? Alienate the kids? But maybe she was already talking to a lawyer? It would be foolish not to do the same.

In his mind, Linda was resorting to blackmail. If he wanted to be with his kids, he'd have to follow her up there like a desperate puppy.

He was so tired from the long night. All he wanted to do was sleep. But he knew sleep wouldn't come. He ended up pacing the floor, looking out the windows, and drumming his fingers on furniture.

After a couple of hours, he realized his every thought—every consideration—brought him right back to one reality. He had been blindsided, and he did not know what the hell he should do.

Chapter 28

The Choosing

The New England Home for Little Wanderers was established in 1865 to assist orphaned and homeless children after the Civil War. The home also played a role in the controversial Orphan Train movement which, from 1854 to 1929, relocated two hundred thousand children from the eastern states to the Midwest. Opinions were split on whether this was good for the children or whether eastern cities were simply using orphan trains to dodge any responsibility for the children.

A Bright New Day for Children's Charities, 1931

Jim Yarrow didn't sleep. When he slipped into Rocco's Grill the next morning, his eyes drooped, and he dragged a cloud of anger and dejection in his wake. Rocco immediately sensed something was wrong. That was confirmed when Yarrow made no comment about the bell above the door.

"Morning, Jim. I've seen you look better."

Yarrow picked up a menu—also out of character for him. Then he set it back down without reading a word. "It's been a terrible morning, Rocco. I feel numb."

"This have anything to do with last night's commotion out at Becky's place? People in here have been talking about it all morning."

Yarrow scratched at a small cigarette burn on the countertop. "Well, the problem at the farm is how things started. Then it got even worse. Linda left me. Sometime during the night."

"I'm sorry. What?"

He explained the full situation to Rocco.

"Jesus, I had no idea things were headed that way. I'm really sorry, Jim."

"Yeah, well, you know how it goes."

"I guess I don't. Did you see it coming?"

"No. I mean, things weren't all wine and roses. But what marriage is?"

"So you had hints?" Rocco raised his eyebrows.

"Maybe. Just didn't think it was that bad." Then he abruptly stopped, like he didn't want to say another word until he'd had more time to think. Instead, he turned the conversation back to the commotion at the farm.

"It was just a bunch of kids out there, Rocco. They were being shitty little vandals, tipping over her hives. But then one of them ended up dead. Stung to death."

Rocco let out a low whistle. "Wow. My God. Who?"

"Young teen named Jack Webster. I'll tell you, Rocco, that was a sad thing to see."

Rocco replied in a hushed tone. "That kid? I can picture him. He came here to eat a couple of times with his mom. Seemed like a happy kid. A little shy but smart. Wow, that's tough for them."

Yarrow sat and stewed. "Yeah. He may have been young, but he was hanging out with some older troublemakers. He got the short end of it. All of those kids come from nice families, but that didn't stop them from getting into a bad shade of mischief. Anyway, when the mom showed up she confronted Becky. And things sort of went to hell."

"Hold on. Her kid was with a group of punks causing damage, but the mom blamed Becky?" Rocco made change for a customer from his cash register. "Well, maybe that's natural when you lose someone—to blame someone else."

"I've seen it before."

Rocco stacked glasses and filled his saltshakers as they talked. "So, what kind of damage did they do?"

"Becky's still assessing. A bunch of hives were broken. But she's really good with those bees. She'll probably lose some and save some. Maybe even most of them."

"That's good. I hope the police throw the book at those kids."

"We'll see. Some people are already pushing for things to go the other way."

"Jeez. Don't tell me."

"Yup. Claiming the boys were trying to protect the town from the farm's corrupting influence, or some similar garbage. I suspect they'll keep floating different theories until they find one that sticks. I've seen this scapegoating bullshit before. It was pretty common during the war."

"None of that has happened yet, Jim. Hopefully it won't."

He plopped a glass of water in front of Yarrow, who took a sip.

"Well, you've always had more faith in people than I do."

Rocco said nothing. He just offered a sympathetic ear.

"I'm wondering, Rocco, why is there no damn acceptance of her?"

"Why do you care so much, Jim?"

Yarrow looked away, hesitated, then elected not to respond. Instead, he continued his question. "I mean, look what she does! She takes people in. She gives them work. Gives them hope. That's a good thing."

Rocco took a deep breath. "Well, normally it would be. And if it was someone other than Becky providing the services, like maybe an established church or charity, the townspeople would be boasting about the wonderful help being provided. They might even donate more money and pat themselves on the back. But Becky is an outlier. Still a deviant, right? We've already talked about that. She doesn't fit, and that's always been her challenge."

Yarrow just stared. Not in anger, but in bewilderment.

A large truck drove by outside, noisy enough to rattle the windows. Rocco waited for the commotion to subside. "You know it's true. When you think of the people aligned against her, it tells a different story. Mary Jane's family is front and center of the wealthy, long-term residents of Riverbend. So, when any sort of charity work is needed, what does that group do?"

"Nothing?"

"Actually, no. They reinforce the status quo of the town by only choosing status quo solutions. That means the long-established churches or big-name charities funded by wealthy families."

"But those places barely help."

"Oh, agreed. It's definitely just barely. And when those institutions do provide help, it often comes with caveats."

"Like what?"

"Like, if you need a meal, it might come with religious lectures or hymns. If an orphanage helps kids, they'll only be placed with good Christian families. You know the drill. They offer help that supports the existing structure of the community. For that group, even with charitable acts, any deviation from tradition is frowned upon."

Yarrow looked skeptical. But he understood what Rocco meant. "Okay, so you said, 'on one side.' What's the other side?"

Rocco seemed hesitant to say more. But he and Yarrow were friends, and he knew he should continue. "Okay, now this is just my opinion, Jim. But aligned with the other side, I think you'll find folks who would also like to provide help. In fact, they would provide a wide range of social services if they could. And this other group is strongly opposed to the idea that help should only come through religions or philanthropies. They believe those traditional organizations are too-often aligned with special interests. Make sense?"

"Not yet."

"Well, this other side believes services to poor people should not rely on the whims of donations and charities. They believe help should mainly come through government-funded efforts, where everyone pays a small share. That can be a great equalizer. Their approach is non-religious and non-partisan. In their minds, it's the government that should provide housing when it's needed. It's the government that should offer free schools, free health clinics. All of that."

"So, basically socialism."

"Yes."

Yarrow seemed to wave the idea away. "That's very utopian. But we both know that's not going to happen, Rocco."

"Probably not. But that's their dream. Now, let's think about the two sides we just defined. One side is pushing to have only well-entrenched, conservatively aligned, and woefully underfunded charities handle everything. The other side is pushing for government assistance that's also woefully underfunded and understaffed. The two sides remain incompatible, and neither can possibly fill the gap."

Rocco noticed Yarrow's water glass was empty, so he gave it a quick fill. Then he mentally rehearsed his next words.

"So, here's where things fall apart. Becky remains an outlier because she doesn't fit into either of those groups. She has no wealth or influence. She's not well-connected and doesn't support the status quo. Thus, she isn't someone the conservative charities want to help. In fact, they outright reject her because they don't want someone like her gaining any power."

"I guess we've already seen that happening."

"Exactly. Yet at the same time, Becky's approach also doesn't mesh with the other side either. The socialists or the Boston left-wingers? She doesn't dovetail with them at all."

"You don't think so?"

"No. Those folks have a utopian worldview that pushes for, you know, broad social equality and egalitarianism. But that's not her either. She's well aware of the shortcomings of a totally socialist approach. Becky, and her mother before her, have long sought help from both sides, yet they've been given almost nothing. The end result is that her orientation has migrated to something that falls in between the groups. Something more libertarian, I guess, but with her own flavor. She believes in private ownership and investing, and also free choice. She wants her people to have the opportunity to earn a living in any way they can, without being told that what they do is unacceptable."

Yarrow took a long sip of coffee. "I hadn't thought of it that way. But then, most people don't look at everything through a philosopher's lens like you do. "

Rocco shrugged.

"But I understand your point. And being an outlier from multiple groups must seem discouraging. But Becky seldom seems discouraged. Well, at least not until last night."

"Yeah."

"But you're overthinking it, Rocco. I'd say the people on the farm are just looking to survive."

"Whether she realizes it or not, Becky is growing a potential new empire, albeit a tiny one. The people who invest with her are beholden to a monetary system that she alone controls. Both sides see it. Both feel threatened by it. She's become like one of the 'enemies within' that Joe McCarthy keeps warning us about." Rocco placed his palms on the counter and leaned close. "I think her system evolved accidentally. But if she can avoid proper audits, it ends up being brilliant. When existing systems break down, someone like Becky always tends to emerge."

Yarrow smirked. "Go on."

"We both know neither the wealthy nor the leftists can deliver on even a fraction of what they claim. Philanthropy is an exercise in power that only the wealthy can enjoy, so they use it sparingly. Meanwhile, socialism is like a wheel that never gets greased. It just carries more and more weight until it breaks."

"The poor can always go into the military. Like we did."

"Great! Everyone can enlist and get their teeth fixed. But I think that's why some people, like Becky, simply choose to walk a different path."

"You make it all sound so corrupt."

"Her?"

"No, the two sides. Left and right."

"They *are* corrupt. But that's what we have. Embrace the strict status quo, and get your meager reward, or follow the left's social agenda, and also get a meager reward."

Rocco tossed his cleaning cloth toward the sink. "Anyway, that's what I see happening. But what the hell do I know?"

"So where does that leave things? Just an eternal stalemate?"

"Yeah. Neither side fully wins or loses, and life goes on."

"I don't like it. That means Becky's people have to borrow or steal to get by."

"Or, it leads to something like her convoluted ledger. But she can't be too successful with it, or both sides will see her progress, declare it illegal, and they'll shut her down. Like I said several days ago, Jim, she's an outlier. A deviant, and her success could lead to her own failure."

"I understand, Rocco. And I think you're right."

Yarrow stood and turned to leave as Rocco offered one more thought. "You know, Jim, it's interesting that Becky chose bees as her way to make a living. Bees are not something you can really domesticate. They don't depend on anyone for their food or shelter. Sure, if someone provides a nice dry box they're willing to live in it. But they only do that because it's convenient. They can be quite happy in the wild. They don't need you to maintain their hive or take their honey. They don't need people at all."

Yarrow didn't look back but said, "Yeah, and if the going gets tough, they can abandon the hive. I know that much."

Chapter 29

Options

Tourism got an early start in New England. It took hold in the nineteenth century, and rapidly evolved, thanks to an expanding network of coaches, steamships and railroads. Tourism further expanded as wealthier families gained more time to spend at leisure. New Hampshire, with its mountains, lakes, and proximity to Boston became a favorite destination during hot summers.

The Economics of New England Tourism, 1953

Mayor Driscoll rose early and was on the road by seven. That was a good thing. On Fridays, summer traffic could clog the routes that wound through Massachusetts' North Shore. Seasonal traffic jams on the older two-lane coastal roads had become one of the catalysts for new highway construction.

Driscoll was headed north to a relative's summer home on Governor's Island on Lake Winnipesauke. He decided it would be nice to bring a gift for his aunt and uncle. Maybe some fresh fruit and maybe a jar of honey too. That meant a stop at the Bivens Farm. He also wanted to view the aftermath of the vandalism.

As he pulled in, Becky saw him and waved. There were three other customers at the tables. *A decent number of patrons for an early morning,* Driscoll thought.

He saw a set of makeshift shelves. Atop the shelves were multiple wood baskets. Quarts and pecks. They held blueberries, peaches, early pears, and more. He made his selections and also grabbed a watermelon from a big bin. He brought everything to Becky's check-out area, which had expanded from a single table to a long awning-covered counter. As usual, an array of honey jars stood near the cash box.

Becky stepped forward.

"Hello Mayor."

"Hello Becky."

He studied her for a moment, and she held her head high under his gaze.

"I'm on my way to New Hampshire." He struggled to find appropriate words. "I ... um, I hope you're doing okay. I was sorry to hear about the vandalism that happened here."

"Thank you. But it's already cleaned up."

"And, goodness, that poor boy."

"Yes," she said, "that was such a tragedy. Two of our workers left this morning. I think the attack troubled them."

Driscoll nodded. "I imagine it did. But then, you're not really licensed for tenants."

"Officially, they're squatters. But I don't have the heart to kick them out."

"I see. So how many do you have living and working here now?"

"Oh, a few. They come and go."

He looked toward the fields. He could see at least seven tents, plus some kind of lean-to in the woods. He made a mental note of the number but said nothing.

"Oh, and I'll take some honey too. Your largest jar, please."

"Sure thing. Clover? Cranberry blossom? Wildflower?"

"Oh. I don't know."

As they spoke, two women from the field set their baskets aside and strolled over to join them. It was a humid morning, and they both wore halter tops. Yellow for one. Pink gingham for the other—her blue shorts had trim on the bottom that matched the halter.

"We've had many compliments on the cranberry blossom," Becky explained. "And it can be hard to find."

"Okay then. Let's try that."

He held out his money, but she asked him to wait. She reached beneath the counter and pulled out her ledger. The two women came closer, one on either side of Becky. They smiled at Driscoll and followed up with probing stares.

"Now let's see." Becky flipped through the pages and ran her finger down a column. "So, it looks like the honey futures I gave you several weeks ago are now worth, goodness, nearly three hundred and seventeen dollars! Isn't that wonderful?"

Driscoll looked stunned. "Wait. What? How can that be?"

One of the women moved around Becky and walked toward him. The other placed her hands on the counter. She leaned forward, flirtation and cleavage riding with her.

"Girls, this is the mayor of our town."

The woman in gingham nodded and smiled. "Very pleased to meet you mayor. My, you certainly are a young and good-looking politician. Is there anything else you need?"

He felt flattered, but only for a moment. Then he felt defensive. She looked predatory. And hungry.

"Now girls, the mayor is on his way to New Hampshire. Perhaps we shouldn't keep him."

They both backed away. But lingered.

"Is that right Mayor?" Becky asked. "Are you in a rush today?"

"Oh. Yes, yes. I definitely am."

She looked back at her ledger. "Now, usually we don't allow people to spend their earnings just on the produce. But for you? I think we can make an exception. I'll even give you the honey at cost." She looked up. "Then next time, we can talk about how you might want to cash in those other options."

Driscoll quickly held up his hand. "No, no. I don't want any special privilege. Here. Just … take my cash."

He paid quickly and gathered his items. As he walked toward his car, one of the women called to him. "Stop in again Mayor! Any time. We'll be here."

He started his car, but before putting it into gear, he looked in the rearview mirror. "What the hell just happened?" he muttered to himself.

At the counter, the three women stood within whispering distance.

"Tread lightly there, girls," Becky admonished. "I'm not sure how he might react."

"But we should try, no?" said the woman in the yellow top. "We could use some political connections."

"Of course," Becky agreed. "But let's be careful not to push him the other way. We don't want him to turn against us. Let's see if he returns. We'll know more if he does."

As Mayor Driscoll reached the lot's exit, another car was pulling in. He recognized the driver. She was one of the clerks from the town hall. She rolled down her window and signaled for him to pull alongside her.

"Heading to your relatives? In New Hampshire?"

"Yup, I'm on my way. I stopped here to pick up a few things." He held up the honey jar and fruit, as if to prove he was only there to shop.

"I wanted to ask; did you talk to anyone at the town hall this morning?"

"No," the mayor replied. "I didn't go in today."

She leaned out her car window, scanning to see if anyone was within earshot. "Well, the mother of the boy who died here is talking to the police chief about whether they can charge Becky criminally. I guess Mary Jane Danforth paid her a visit and got her all riled up."

Driscoll shook his head. "What? Becky was the victim. It was those kids who were out of line."

"I know. Everyone else knows it too. But MJ and her friends are saying things like 'unsafe conditions,' 'attractive nuisance,' and 'threat to the town's wellbeing.' So when I saw you, I wanted to flag you down. I thought you should know."

"Wow," he said with exasperation.

He thanked her and drove on. He turned his radio off and continued north in silence. Eventually he turned northwest. He didn't touch the knobs until he made it through Manchester and Concord. He stared straight ahead until saw the White Mountains in the distance. He kept mulling things over, and realized he lacked the experience to handle issues that could turn so ugly so quickly.

Chapter 30

Motorola

In 1948, just 1% of US households owned a television. By 1955, that number grew to seventy five percent, making TVs the fastest growing consumer product of the era. Having an antenna on one's roof became a new kind of status symbol.

Broadcast Empires, All Media Press, 1960

Yarrow donned his favorite gabardine coat and climbed into his car.

It was Wednesday, his day off, and that made it a perfect day to see go see his kids. The night before he made arrangements with Linda and now he was excited to be on his way.

As he drove through downtown, he saw a printed banner in the window of Abe Lewin's Department store. It read "August Outdoor Sale!"

The morning traffic was light mid-week and he made good time up the coast. Offshore, the sun hung in the sky like a fat pearl.

After crossing into New Hampshire, he merged onto a four-lane highway that led to Maine.

In time he rolled into Freeport and found the right street. He heard a screen door slam as he turned into the driveway.

"Daddy! Daddy!"

Curtis ran down the path first, with Tommy close behind. Little Bonnie stood inside the door and waved. Linda was nowhere to be seen.

"Hey champs." He lifted one, then the other. "Good to see you!" They already felt heavier than he remembered. Their hugs felt earnest and loving. He missed that so much.

As he made his way toward the house, Tommy started chattering first. "Remember what you said Dad? Right? You remember?"

"Humm, let's see, what did I say? Was it … that we would … walk around the block?"

"No!"

"Humm … that we would … eat a peanut butter sandwich?"

"No! Dad! Come on, you said you'd take us to see a television."

"Oh, that! Right! But you don't really want to do that, do you?"

"Yes! Yes, we do!"

He laughed and didn't let on that he was just as excited. He had not seen a television set in twelve years. In 1939 he and his friends made it their mission to visit the World's Fair. One day they skipped school and took a train to New York City. They strolled through Flushing Meadows and at some point they wandered into the RCA Television Pavilion. They made their way through the displays and stared in wonder.

TV was something that was always *coming soon*. But in the pavilion that day, they saw the real thing for themselves. There was an amazing array of small screens and moving images. Newscasts. Movies. A guide said the signals were broadcast from a tall building in Manhattan. As curious teens, they were enthralled, and once they saw the glowing tubes, they assumed they'd be able to own televisions within a few years. But the war delayed that plan, and it took even longer for large cities to offer video broadcasts.

Today, it was the kids' turn to be enthralled. He carried the boys up the front steps and onto the porch. As he put them down, they quickly pulled him inside. There, he picked up Bonnie for a welcomed hug, then called out to Linda. On the second call she looked around the corner from the kitchen.

"Hi," she said. "Have them home before six, okay? And just be aware that Bonnie will get grumpy in the afternoon. She still likes her naps."

"Okay. And, um, hello?"

Linda just waved and disappeared back into the kitchen. She shouted from there. "They're all excited. They said you're planning to take them to see some TVs?"

"Yeah. They're supposed to have a few on display at Sears this week."

"Okay. Sounds like fun."

And that was that.

The boys pushed each other as they climbed into the car. Both wanted to sit in the front seat. Yarrow made them sit in the back. "Bonnie is going to be up front with me."

He retrieved a metal car seat from Linda's mother's Pontiac and moved it to his car. It was made from bent chrome tubes with a vinyl seat slung in the middle. Another pair of tubes slid over the back of the car seat. He loaded Bonnie and secured her with a thin strap that buckled over her lap. Then they headed south.

"We're going to Sears, right Dad? The big one in Portland?"

Yarrow smiled. It was time to explain some things to them—like a dad.

"The stores around here don't offer televisions yet. That's because no stations are broadcasting in Maine or New Hampshire. That might happen soon, but right now there are just two TV stations anywhere around here, and they're both in Boston."

"Woah, are we driving to Boston?"

"No. We don't need to go that far."

Over the next few minutes he explained that TV signals only reach about 50 miles from their broadcast tower. "The farther a TV is from a signal, the worse the video looks. From here we can't see a signal at all."

"So where are we going?"

"We're heading to a store in Salem, Massachusetts. I saw their advertisement in the Boston Globe. They're hosting a traveling exhibition of televisions. They'll be at the store for a few days, and Salem is close enough to Boston to pick up the broadcast signals."

For the next hour the boys were full of questions about what makes TVs work, how the pictures and sounds travel through the air, and when they might have a television of their own. Eventually, they drove into Salem and spotted the building for Sears, Roebuck & Company. It had started as a smaller downtown store, then expanded twice by taking over some neighboring stores. Because of this, it lacked a large parking lot. He found a space on another street about a block away.

"It's probably a good thing we're here in the middle of the week," Yarrow said. "Even on a Wednesday, this place looks crowded."

"A lot of people want to see the TVs, huh dad?" Tommy said.

"I guess so. People are curious."

The boys ran down the sidewalk, past a Rexall Drugstore and a newsstand with piles of that day's papers.

When they entered Sears, a woman with a blue nametag said the TVs were near the back of the store. Yarrow nodded and realized they wanted everyone to walk past their other product displays to get to the main attraction.

When Tommy and Curtis caught sight of the screens, they took off running. Yarrow walked more slowly, carrying Bonnie on his shoulders.

The boys sat on the floor right in front of the largest TV. The screen was about thirteen inches—larger than the ones he'd seen in New York. He placed Bonnie on the floor between her brothers. Then he stood behind them, marveling at the moving images. After a minute, a salesman approached.

"Pretty incredible, hum? That's the future right there."

"Yeah," Yarrow agreed. "And it's been the future for … how many years now?"

The salesman chuckled. "You're right, besides all the other delays, for the salesmen it's been a chicken and egg thing. People wouldn't buy TVs if no one was broadcasting, and investors didn't want to launch new TV stations when no one owned a TV. But it's finally happening. There's already WBZ and WNAC in Boston. As you can see, we're showing both of those stations here. Where are you from?"

"Riverbend."

"Where's that? I don't know the local towns. I'm out of the Sears headquarters in Chicago."

"Really? You came in from Chicago?"

"Yup. On a multistate tour, we're taking these displays to stores in a dozen cities. It helps us drum up interest. We'll do three stores around Boston, then we'll head to Albany and work our way back toward Illinois."

Yarrow gestured over his shoulder. "My town is about thirty miles north and a little west of here."

"Thirty miles farther north? That's out of range for the Boston signals. Salem is already close to the limit."

"Yeah. And too bad. I kind of like that one." Yarrow pointed toward a model with a Mahogany case. Nice bright screen. It had dials on the front and tan speaker cloth on the sides.

"Excellent unit. Motorola 14k1, sitting in the Ts88 chassis. I especially like the reddish wood."

"How much would that run?"

"Currently? Four hundred and sixty-nine dollars."

"Wow. I guess I couldn't afford one anyway."

"Well, you picked out the highest priced one. The Philco brand is a bit cheaper, and as more people buy, I expect prices will drop."

The salesman went to talk to other customers and Yarrow let his kids linger for an hour. They watched most of *The Howdy Doody Show*, followed by *Amos 'n' Andy*.

He told his kids the Amos 'n' Andy show was based on an older radio show. Yarrow didn't mention that the original show used white actors pretending to be black. He was pleased to see the TV version used actual black actors—Spencer Williams and Alvin Childress. He remembered Williams from an old Buster Keaton movie.

A woman next to Yarrow leaned over and whispered, "I remember the radio show."

"Yeah," he replied. "I read that several radio shows are being adapted for television. Quick and easy, I suppose, and they already have a loyal audience."

As they talked, a commercial came on the screen. A cartoon beaver sang the praises of Ipana Toothpaste.

When the show was over, it was tough to pull the kids away, but he managed. As they walked toward the front entrance, he saw something he'd never seen before. The store had a working TV camera. A sign called it a closed-circuit TV. The camera, about the size of his army footlocker, sat on a rolling tripod. People could step in front and see themselves on a nearby screen. The boys had great fun looking at themselves and running in and out of the camera view. Bonnie just danced and pointed at herself on the TV.

As they drove toward home, Jim Yarrow fielded endless questions from the boys.

"How does the TV screen work?"

"How do broadcasts work?"

"Do tiny pictures just fly through the air?"

He explained things as best he could, talking about cathode ray tubes and other things he remembered from his visit to the RCA pavilion. He knew they wouldn't fully understand. He didn't understand it himself.

At ten minutes past six Yarrow rolled into Freeport and cruised to his mother-in-law's house. Linda came to the door immediately and called for the kids to come inside. Then she walked to his car.

"They were supposed to be back by six, Jim."

"I know. We hit some traffic on the way home."

"Traffic? Where were you coming from?"

"Sears."

"How much could that slow you down? It's not that far away."

"Yeah, well, the TV event was at a different Sears. The kids loved it. They even got to walk in front of a camera."

"That sounds fun. Which store?"

"We drove to Salem."

"What? You went to New Hampshire?"

"Um ... Salem Massachusetts, actually."

Linda looked shocked. Then angry. "Hold on, Jim. You took the kids out of state without asking me first? Two states even? You can't do that."

He turned and looked her directly in the eyes. "Yeah, Linda, I guess I did do that. Just like you took them two states away too—without asking me first."

She dismissed him with a wave of her hand and walked away.

But her comment angered him. "And you know what the difference is Linda? I brought them back. Right? But you know what I haven't seen? You—bringing our kids back home."

The screen door slammed as she went inside.

Slamming seemed like the right response. He slammed the car into reverse, then slammed it into first gear as he reached the street. He accelerated and pointed the car south, toward home.

His home. Their home, goddamn it.

Riverbend.

Chapter 31

Bone Yard

The Merrimack River was once filled with salmon and sturgeon. But pollution grew and water flows changed during the industrial revolution. Some fish populations dwindled. By the mid-1800s the river became the realm of sailing vessels, including many lumber schooners that came downriver from the north.

Macky's Merrimack Sailing History, 1939

When displaced women arrived at the Bivens Farm, some came with tents or worn trailers. But others were destitute. They arrived with little more than one set of clothes and worried faces.

Two new women arrived with children in tow, and similar stories. Their boyfriends died during the war, one by a grenade during the Battle of the Bulge, the other on a merchant ship sunk by a German U-boat. Lacking legal marriages, they had no veterans' assistance.

Becky had space to offer, but little actual shelter. She was working on a way to fix that. She'd been scanning the classified ads and found something that might prove useful. She circled the ad, and on Saturday morning she made sure each worker knew their assigned chores, then she climbed into her truck.

Eventually she made her way to River Road, which ran near the Merrimack. The last leg of her trip took her down a dirt road that ran toward the water. She passed marinas and industrial sites and eventually spotted the address she wanted.

The sign said *Durgin's Salvage Yard*. As she pulled in, she spotted a pair of dilapidated mobile homes. Those were what she came to see. She parked near an old sign, now rusted and faded with age, which read *"Scrap Brass Wanted, Let's Lick Hitler."*

She circled the trailers, looking at all sides, then underneath. They were rougher than she expected. As she stood on her tiptoes, looking in a window, a man emerged from a gray Quonset hut at the yard's edge.

"Just hauled those here a few days ago!" he shouted. "Are you interested?"

She nodded slightly. "Thought I was. But there's more rust than I was expecting. Especially underneath."

"Bah, that's mostly cosmetic. The shells are painted aluminum and the steel frame underneath is mostly protected from the rain, so not that bad."

"Where did you get them?"

He opened the door and bid her to step inside.

She hesitated.

"During the war they were extra housing at the East Point Military Reservation. You know, down in Nahant? I got them at an auction."

"Interesting," she replied. "Hard to believe they're still liquidating stuff six years after the war."

"Oh, it will go on for a time, believe me."

"How much are you asking?"

"Four hundred apiece. Firm."

Becky's heart sank. She had nowhere near that much money. "Seems expensive, since they both need work."

"Understood. But the price is firm."

She wondered if she could make a deal. She decided to risk visiting the inside of each trailer. Both had the remnants of a kitchen, though they lacked appliances or cabinets. She had hoped to use them as housing for her workers, but as she tallied the amount she'd have to invest, the numbers didn't work.

"I could do two fifty apiece," she said.

He waved her off. "The metal alone is worth that much! I'd just scrap it."

"That's all I have to offer."

"No can do."

She tried other tactics, including offering honey futures from her farm. But the junkyard owner didn't know what she was talking about and refused to budge.

As she drove away, she was already considering another plan.

During her drive she passed a marine salvage yard. It looked like they were using cranes and hooks to pull old boats apart. She remembered seeing sorting piles; reclaimed steel in one, wood to another, bronze and brass fittings in a third.

What really caught her eye was the hull of an old schooner. It must have been towed there for its final cannibalization. It had become a rare thing to see a big schooner this far upriver.

The wrecking yard's front gate was open, so she drove in and zigged down close to the water. There was the old hull, still floating and tied to a dock. It sat well away from the yard's big cranes. She was immediately surprised by the length of the ship, or what remained of it. It was over sixty feet long at the waterline. Substantially longer at the deck. She climbed onto a pile of pallets to view the topside. The masts were gone and there were scars on the deck planks where other equipment had been removed. But the decking itself looked decent. All the boards were still there with heavy calk lines between them, probably cotton ropes soaked in pitch.

There was a slightly raised cabin area and sealable hatches fore and aft.

She stood for several minutes, looking and thinking. Then she walked to a barn. Inside, she found a man processing a pile of invoices. He gave her a gap-toothed smile.

"Well good morning, pretty lady!"

She gathered her composure. "Good morning. I'm hoping to learn more about the hull of that old schooner out there."

"That big one? I guess it's been here about two years."

"Is it for sale?"

"Everything is for sale."

"Can I see the inside?"

He let out a long exhale. "Now, why would you want that old tub? It would cost so much to restore it that any sane person would rather buy a new ship."

"I'm not looking to sail it. I live near the river."

She didn't want to let on that it would be used to house some of her workers. Thinking fast, she said, "I'm just looking for something I can use for a while, for storage."

"Well, I don't know. I was just planning to cut it up and sell the steel. It's worth a fair amount just for that."

Until that day, Becky never thought about the value of scrap metal. Then she heard about it twice in the same morning.

"What would that be worth?"

"Hundreds. Probably more."

"How long would it take you to cut it up?"

He laughed. "Many hours and a lot of torch work. I guess that's why I haven't tackled it yet."

She walked to the window and looked out at the ship. "What do you think it's worth, for insurance?"

"What? I don't know. I don't keep it insured."

"But doesn't your whole yard have insurance? You know, for fires or theft, or whatever."

"For general business loss? Yeah. What are you getting at lady?"

She walked back to his desk. "What if I offered you a way to get some money out of the hull where you wouldn't have to cut it up. And you might make more from the insurance than you would otherwise."

Becky knew it was risky to make such an offer. He could refuse and report her to the police. But she had long dealt with people who lived and worked near the river. It was a hard and sometimes shady life. Dock workers. Boat rats. Mechanics.

Riggers. Most were just looking to make money. So, she played her hunch.

"Go on. I'm listening."

"I'll explain my idea. But first I want to see how much of the original ship still exists inside that hull."

Chapter 32

Hive Minds

New England counties and towns built so-called poor farms or homes to address the needs of destitute citizens. These houses often required labor and were also used to provide housing for those with serious health and mental issues. Residents were referred to as "inmates" or "the indigent." The rise of Social Security and other welfare efforts led to the end of the poor farm era.

The Rise and Fall of New England Poor Houses, 1950

"I don't know, guys. I just don't know."

Yarrow sat with Rocco and Leon on the bar side of Rocco's Grill. That area was always less crowded than the breakfast and lunch side. Rocco did little to advertise his alcohol sales. He used the bar area more as his own private joint. Anyone else who wandered in was welcome, but they would not be part of Rocco's circle of townies.

"What is it you don't know, Jim?"

"I'm thinking of the people in town who are staunchly against the Bivens Farm. I guess I understand their concerns. But why is shutting the place down the only solution they offer?"

Rocco said nothing. He just listened.

"I'll bet a lot of them couldn't even tell you why they think she's a problem, Yarrow continued. "They just parrot the words of others. That's mental laziness in my book."

He looked at Rocco and Leon for some sign of concurrence but found none. "What? No agreement? Come on! There are people here who still admire and support her, right? Anyone with a brain can see she's helping people while others ignore them."

"Yeah," said Leon. "I guess I shouldn't worry if she gives people help and a place to live."

Rocco held up a finger. "Okay. So, let's talk about that. Becky encourages the women who live with her to do what, exactly?"

Yarrow frowned. "I guess that's a bit of a mystery."

"Come on, Jim. Is it?"

"No, you come on. Like everyone else, you're making assumptions. She is an entrepreneur. She encourages others to be entrepreneurs."

"Okay. But her attitude is decidedly amoral."

"So what? Yarrow replied. "The women there have total freedom. They can sell … I don't know, the carrots they grow maybe? Or pottery, or candy, or—"

"Their bodies?"

Yarrow hesitated, then pushed on. "Well, they do that in Nevada, right? And Amsterdam! Come on guys, when we were in the service we saw it everywhere."

"Yeah, but those were desperate times," Leon admonished.

"But it's always desperate times for someone, right? People choose how to deal with their challenges."

"And you're an officer of the law, Jim?" Leon said.

"Oh, piss off."

"You make her approach sound so simple," Rocco added. "Gosh, maybe even wholesome!"

Yarrow looked at one, then the other. "Come on you two."

Then he sighed. "Look, I know it's not simple. That's the challenge. That's why I started this whole conversation by saying 'I don't know.'"

"Okay. And I'll ask you again. What don't you know?"

Yarrow rubbed his forehead. "Okay, is it right for a girl to sell her body? I don't know. Is it completely wrong? I don't know. Not being a woman, I don't think I should be the one to judge." Then his voice took on a more somber tone. "I do understand it's *not* something any of those women *want* to do.

I'm sure it's not their first, second, or even tenth choice of how to earn money."

He looked at them again. Rocco and Leon stared back. "Come on guys," he continued, "if we lived in a town that actually took care of its people, none of those women would be doing what they're doing. But this community makes no effort. Instead, they try to chase the undesirables away."

"That's for sure," said Leon.

Yarrow's expression turned grim. "And none of us has the power to change that. So, what is the alternative? Do we block them from doing what little they can? Do we force square pegs into round holes by saying their help can only come through religious or government charities?"

"I don't know."

Yarrow slapped the bar. "Exactly! That's what I've been saying. Yet, we have two sides squaring off and trying to decide who's right and this whole thing just hurts my brain."

Rocco laughed. Then his expression changed, like a chess player who just discovered an exploitable opening. "You know, when you see these kinds of fights, it's never just because the other group exists. You have to follow the money to find the cause. So, who benefits when there's a conflict?"

"Probably a lot of people."

"But let's look at the main players. Becky and her little country coven benefit from what they sell. You can debate what their products are, but they fill a weird local business niche. The people who visit the farm aren't the ones who object to her."

"Okay."

"Second, there are other local people who have invested in her honey futures. For now, they're making a good return. Setting the morality of the issue aside, we can say they get some benefit too."

"Fair enough."

"So again, they aren't the one's looking to shut down the farm. Now, let's look at the women themselves. Where do they spend the money they make? They rarely venture downtown. But they do spend money at the Blanchard store and that new plaza on the outskirts of town. They use the laundromat there too. So, it's a small win for those businesses."

"All right," Yarrow responded. "So, you're saying none of those people are trying to force Becky out."

"Exactly. But we also have this fourth group, with folks like Mary Jane, who are doing all the complaining. They're the town's old money. Well-entrenched business interests. They see no benefit in allowing her to expand. She's potential competition and her farm represents a temptation to husbands, sons, and relatives." He thought for a moment, then added, "And Mary Jane comes from a family of real estate developers. So having that piece of property go up for sale might be attractive for them too."

Yarrow shrugged. "I hear what you're saying. Yeah, the property is attractive. But as for them worrying that Becky is growing her business and influence from out there? Come on. She isn't looking for power. That's not her thing. She just wants to live. She wants her people to live."

"Fair enough, Jim. But she wants at least enough influence to get her people the things they need. She's sought help, been turned down repeatedly, and she's explored other opportunities. So, her solution was to resurrect the ridiculous honey futures thing her mother invented."

"Yeah, that's not helping things," Yarrow admitted, while inside he winced a bit at hearing Erin referred to as Becky's mother.

"But it's a model Becky understands. She doesn't necessarily want to be an outlier. But she learned her tricks from other outliers."

Yarrow rubbed his forehead. "I ... I know you're right." He stared at the bottles on the backbar. Lights beneath the glass shelves gave the liquids a warm and colorful glow.

"And keep in mind, Jim," Leon added. "MJ has that family score she wants to settle."

Just then a group entered and walked toward a back table. Yarrow was glad to see them, but Rocco seemed ambivalent. He forced a smile and went to take their orders. Leon leaned in and whispered to Yarrow. "So, are you thinking Riverbend has reached some critical point for the Becky issue?

Yarrow reluctantly answered. "Yeah. I suppose it's coming. Every week the construction guys from the new road get their paychecks and spend the money locally. That's new money coming in, and I've seen it being spent at that new plaza and at Becky's farm. The old guard isn't happy because they're not seeing a cut."

"Yeah," Leon agreed.

"Mary Jane's instinct is to snuff the competition. There is no 'live and let live' with her."

As Rocco returned to the counter, Yarrow let out a deep breath. "I guess we're all just waiting to see what's next."

Leon drained the last of his drink. "Jim," he said, "I don't know much about these things. But people say it's just a big scheme."

"I don't know. I hope not."

"So maybe Becky can fend off Mary Jane. But there are other things that could bring down the farm. You're a cop, Jim. You're protecting something that could blow up in your face."

"I know Leon."

"I'm sure you also see that Mary Jane will keep trying to light the fuse."

Chapter 33

Strange Currency

By the 1950s, nearly two thirds of American households collected trading stamps. The stamps were awarded by retail establishments based on the amount of money spent. The companies issuing the stamps operated retail centers where stamps could be exchanged for consumer goods. The legality of trading stamps was challenged multiple times, but the trade remained active until the 1970s, when it was replaced by other promotional programs.

Alternative Currencies, Interpretive Press, 1976

A light rain fell as Mayor Driscoll walked along Main Street. His footsteps made a damp echo that changed in tone each time he passed a recessed doorway. Eventually he reached the entrance of Rocco's Grill. The big windows were fogged from the heat inside.

The bell chimed and he slid into a seat at the counter.

"Not many people here, eh?"

"It's early," Rocco replied. "But you're here Mayor. Anxious to get started with the town's business?"

Driscoll waited for his coffee and took a sip. "Let's say I'm doing research before I go to the town hall. Let's say I'm trying to understand something."

Rocco studied the mayor's face. The young politician looked troubled.

"Go on."

"Okay. But first, let me opine a bit. There are people in this town who claim they've never seen you outside of this building. They say you're one of the wisest people in town, but this, right here, is your sanctuary. And you seldom leave. So, if I want wisdom I have to come here."

Rocco laughed. "Well, that's just silly. I live upstairs, and I'm out of the building quite often. Just yesterday I drove my truck to Tate's Garage. But if someone wants to talk? Yeah, I'm usually here. And I try to have an open ear."

Driscoll looked down at the counter.

"What is this all about?" Rocco could see the politician pushing past his own reluctance.

"I have a little problem that I'd like to run by you. But it's confidential."

"If it's town business, I don't want to be dragged into it."

"No, no. It's personal. I mean, it has the potential to affect other things. But for now, it's just me."

"Legal? Or Illegal?"

"I don't know. That's part of the problem."

"I'm not a lawyer, Mayor."

"I know. I'll talk to one if needed. But not yet."

Rocco set up another pot of coffee and hit the brew button. "You know what? I like ya, kid. You're the youngest mayor in this town's history, and you're pretty damn green." He saw Driscoll frown, but he continued. "I'm sorry, but it's true. Yet, you seem to have a lot on the ball. So, what the heck. If you need advice, I'm game."

Driscoll set down his cup. "Do you happen to own any of Becky's so-called honey futures?"

"Hell no. Wouldn't touch 'em."

"Well, I guess I did touch 'em. I own some."

"You do?"

"Yeah. Two futures contracts. I don't even know what that means. At the start she said they could be exchanged for two jars of honey. I thought that was fine. But the value has grown and just now I'm understanding that buying jars of honey is not really what the futures are meant for."

"Nope." Rocco shook his head. "Okay Mayor, how long have you had them?"

"I think it was the first week, right after she opened."

Rocco gave a satisfied nod. "At least you're in good shape on that front. From what I understand, if you got in early you now have something worth a lot more than that."

Driscoll spoke through gritted teeth. "Yeah, that's what's confusing me. And she just sort of handed them to me. I didn't even buy them."

Rocco dried some juice glasses with a towel. "Well, maybe that's a good thing. Did she know who you were at the time? Meaning, that you're the mayor?"

"Yeah, she knew."

"Ahh. So, Arnie … mind if I call you Arnie?"

"No problem at all Rocco."

"My guess is she purposely gave them to you because she wanted you to be part of it. Having the mayor's name in her books gives her some legitimacy. And if things start going bad, you might be reluctant to support any investigation."

Driscoll took a deep breath. "That's my concern. I talked about it with one of my uncles when I was in New Hampshire. He raised that red flag immediately." He shook his head. "So stupid of me to accept them. I should have said no."

Rocco nodded. "Probably so. But you didn't know. Politics is dirtier than you thought, eh?"

"Yeah. I just thought she was offering some marketing promotion. You know, like coupons or Green Stamps."

"It's more dubious than either of those."

Driscoll wiped his brow, almost in slow motion. "I'm not even sure how it works, or if it's even legal."

"Look, kid, I can't say either. But let's be honest, it's probably not."

Rocco spent the next several minutes explaining how commodities markets work, and how futures play a part. He slid packets of sugar around to explain how the growth or decline of investments can happen. Then he slipped a glass over one of the sugar piles and moved it in front of the mayor.

"Let's pretend that's one ton of sugar. Let's say you just signed a contract that allows you to buy it later at a set price. So there it is. Reserved for you. But you don't have to actually take delivery of the sugar. You can sell that contract at any time. If the price of sugar goes up, you make a profit, even though you never touched it."

"Okay."

"Becky's system is similar, with the prices boosted by ongoing demand for services. No one is actually buying honey with them. Whatever the service is, it can be collected at some time in the future. The buyers are looking for other services. So, will the shady nature of those services make it likely her market will collapse? That remains to be seen."

"But it probably will. Eventually."

"Good possibility. But it depends on how smart she is. Commodities markets can go on for years. They can grow to the point where what seemed like a big problem at the start ends up being just a tiny bit of pollution within the larger investment pool. If she reaches that point, people won't care about her suspicious start. Look around. Does anyone care that this building was a speakeasy back when it was built?"

"I get your point."

"Becky seems smarter than her mother Erin. Smart enough to get the local mayor locked in early in the game."

The reality stung and Driscoll lowered his head. "I'm fucked, aren't I?"

Rocco was non-committal. "The way I see it kid, no one is fucked until the fucking takes place. So, stay quiet and keep this to yourself."

Chapter 34

Of Kindness

In the year nineteen hundred, the life expectancy of a New England woman was 46.3 years. By 1950, that rose to 71.1 years. Improvements to local sanitation, healthcare, housing, and education all played a part.

Trends and Anomalies in Adult Mortality, Health Directions Press, 1957

It was cloudy and cool the day Ma Yarrow died.

Feeling tired and weak, she entered the hospital on a Friday. They discovered a relapse in her infection and put her on antibiotics. But things grew worse, and by Sunday she was gone.

Sepsis they said.

But Yarrow knew the truth. Ever since Will's death, his mom had become melancholy and quiet. The loss piled on top of her other grief. The death of her husband ten years before. Her boy Jim returning from the war with a permanent wound. Things seemed to hit Ma hard.

He knew his mother had long felt the call of the abyss and Will's death just pushed her over. He had visited her every week, but he watched as Ma Yarrow closed up inside. She lamented the unfairness of a world that, in her words, "keeps trying to take my family."

He tried calling Linda to tell her. But her mother answered.

"Hi Claudia. Is Linda there?"

"No, Jim."

"Do you know when she'll be back?"

"I don't."

He'd hoped to talk to his wife directly. He wanted her to bring the kids down for the funeral.

"Listen, Claudia, I'm calling because of Ma. She, um ... she died yesterday." He paused while Claudia extended perfunctory condolences. "Yeah. Thanks. So, could you tell Linda? Yeah, and please ask her to tell the kids. They all loved Ma."

Claudia's response was short. "I'll make sure Linda knows."

He said thanks and shared details on the funeral.

Calls from Linda had become infrequent and she recently postponed one of the kids' scheduled visits. But he was hopeful everyone would join him for the service.

He went alone to meet with the undertaker. He selected a casket; tasteful and not too expensive, just like Ma would have wanted. He made arrangements for the church service and talked to friends and family. Then he waited for the moment to arrive.

The morning of the funeral he received a call from Linda. She said she decided not to come. Her mom didn't think the boys should be subjected to a funeral. "And there's so much uncertainty between us right now, Jim."

"Uncertainty," he replied. "I see." He pleaded with her because he wanted his family to be with him. But she insisted the time wasn't right.

"But my Aunt Shelia is heading to the North Shore next week. Maybe I can ask her to bring the boys along. They can spend a night at your house."

He didn't like to hear that phrase. *Your house.*

He wiped away a tear and hung up the phone. He missed his family, and not just the kids. He felt the absence of his wife. Will and Ma too. For the first time in a long time, he felt completely alone.

The church service went well. The crowd wasn't huge because several of Ma's friends had moved away or already passed. But the minister knew Ma for years and shared several stories. People laughed. Yarrow started to feel better. He knew his mother had had a good life. Raised two boys. Loved her grandkids.

As the people rose to leave, he saw the silhouette of a woman slip out the rear door.

He stood at the entrance shaking hands and talking with each person. With the exception of a few cousins, Yarrow didn't know most of the attendees. But he was grateful for their support. Twenty-four people came along to the grave site for the final goodbyes.

As he stood near the casket, listening to the minister's words, a light rain started to fall. That's when the reality of his situation started to wash over him. An ominous emptiness. So much lost and no real certainty anymore.

As the rain ran down his cheeks, he felt a presence beside him. It was a woman, dressed in black. He turned his head and there was Becky. She was dressed in a way that kept people from recognizing her. Long grey scarf over her hair. Coat buttoned tight around her neck and oversized dark glasses that probably made it difficult to see on a dark rainy day.

Inwardly, he chuckled. He appreciated her support, and he appreciated that she didn't want to trigger any gossip, especially since his wife wasn't there. He reached for her hand. But she took a step back and looked straight ahead.

Of course! It was a reckless gesture on his part. He understood.

But she did give him a slight sideways glance. He couldn't see her eyes, but he could tell she gave him one of her classic winks.

The minister finished his prayer and the crowd filtered away. Yarrow collected pats on his back. Whispers of friendship. Offers of "anything we can do." He wished he could properly grip each person's hand. But he made up for it by using both of his hands for each handshake.

Becky sat in a grey car, which she must have borrowed. When the crowd was finally gone, he joined her.

"Thank you for coming, Becky. I wasn't expecting it. But you know what? I needed it. You helped get me through this."

"Of course I came. Why wouldn't I? I didn't know your mother for very long, Jim. But I did know her."

Yarrow looked puzzled. "I didn't realize that. In high school we weren't together long enough for me to bring you home."

Becky placed her hand on his shoulder. "When I was very young, before Erin's business started to grow, we struggled. Whenever your church offered free meals, we came."

"Usually Thursdays, right? I remember working in the kitchen as a kid."

"So that's how I knew her. Some of the church women were quite grumpy. They didn't like the young kids running around. But your mother was always kind to me. I still remember that. She was kind to every person she met. Even back then, people just called her Ma Yarrow."

"Yeah," Jim smiled. "They sure did."

"There was one winter day when I only had a light sweater. I felt quite cold when we arrived and I shivered by the kitchen stove, trying to get warm. Ma found a coat in the lost and found box and she told me to wear it. After we ate, I tried to return it. But she insisted I keep it. I wore that coat until I outgrew it."

She brushed Yarrow's hair from his forehead. "So yes, Jim. I remember your mother. And as I grew older, I came to know you too—from afar at first. I watched you at school sometimes. I already had a good feeling about you before we became friends. I saw some of Ma's kindness reflected in you. Little things. Like picking up someone's dropped book or stopping a bully."

He blushed.

"It seems that my first impression of you was quite correct. And that includes when you were a teen, walking with your friends down our hill and pretending not to look at us girls. That also includes you as a man and as a police officer. You come from good people Jim, and you still hold that in you."

"I think you mean what's left of my people." He looked at the graves of his father, Will, and now Ma. Then he remembered the space at his side, where Linda should have stood.

"What's left now is you, Jim. And some of us are very glad you're here."

Chapter 35

Payment Due

When a leaky boat starts to list, and if the owner can't fix that list, a savvy scrapper knows it's time to make an offer. The first offer is seldom accepted, but the scrapper is willing to wait. The boat's list will grow worse. Owners eventually will take what they can get. That's how a scrapper stays in business, by seeking boats nearing the end of their lives, then stripping them of everything that might be valuable.

The Lives of Riverfront Workers, Sand Crab Publishers, 1948

Becky was opening her stand for the day when a grey pickup arrived at the farm. It was a forty-eight Chevy, split windshield and fat vertical bars across the grill. To her, the grill looked like a smile with chrome teeth.

She immediately recognized the man who stepped out. It was the owner of the scrap yard where she found the old boat hull. After their first meeting, he agreed to work with her, but he knew that meant making questionable insurance claims, so he wanted to set certain rules.

First, he said Becky could not return to his office. If a fake accident was arranged to send the ship her way, he didn't want anyone to associate Becky with his business.

Second, he refused to rely on a potential insurance payout. There was too much risk. He insisted on getting some of the money up front. As he climbed from his truck, Becky assumed he had come to collect it.

"Hello," Becky called out as he approached.

"Hello again."

She knew he was wary of her scheme. But he had avoided cutting up the ship for two years and was anxious to explore an alternative.

"Have you come to finalize our deal?" she asked.

"I think maybe that can happen. But we have many details to work out." He looked around. Turned away from the road. She could tell he was nervous about being seen. "For starters, I'll need at least a few hundred dollars up front."

Becky shook her head. "I told you I don't have that."

"I know. I know. But I came to see what you do have. To trade, to swap, or whatever."

Becky smiled. When they first met, she had shared details about her business and the honey futures. She also shared the phone number of one of her most trusted customers, a used car dealer from two towns over. That man had become a true believer in her system because he found his own spin on it. He discovered he could continuously buy and sell futures to others, walking away with a small profit each time. The car dealer also believed having more participants join the system meant more profit for early investors. So, he had no problem convincing others to join.

"Did you have a chance to talk to Don?"

"I did," he replied. "And I learned quite a bit about your honey farm here."

"I'm glad."

"Don was a good salesman for you."

She moved some of the jars on a table, purposely bumping a metal box, which caused a clanging sound that echoed down the hill. A moment later, she saw some heads poke out of tents.

Becky pulled out her ledger and showed him a list of the people who'd bought into the honey system. The columns stretched across multiple pages, listing the entry and exit prices for various investors. She started to tell him more about the process, but he was distracted. His eyes were drawn to a couple of women walking up the path. They wore flannel shirts in the morning chill but left them unbuttoned.

When her visitor asked about how difficult it might be to spend his credits at the farm, she knew she had him.

Don the car dealer had indeed been a good salesman.

Eventually they came to terms. Thirteen futures contracts, plus about $100 in cash. She didn't tell him, but she would have been willing to go higher.

"So, let's get this paperwork out of the way," he said. "I can tell you this; my real name is not going to be entered in your ledger." He pulled out a license and put it on the table.

"Whose name is this?" she asked.

He grinned. "When I was in the war, I did some buying, selling, and trading on the side. I learned it was much safer to use an alias. Back stateside, that's one of the first things I did. The name on this license is a man who doesn't exist. I carefully crafted his correspondence and paper trails until I had enough documentation to make him seem real. And now, let's just say this name is a person who also does business on occasion."

Becky used the fake name to label his entry in the ledger.

"Glad we could reach an agreement," he said. "I'll come back and collect when I can." He looked at the women standing behind the table. Then he looked at Becky. "Don't cross me lady, that's all I can say. You can trust me as a partner in this little deal. But do not ever cross me."

He folded his contract and placed it in his shirt pocket.

"For now," he said, "I'm washing my hands of this. If you get caught, I had nothing to do with it. I'll say you stole it. If you actually manage to float that hull down here and if you can hide it, I'll be collecting a fairly basic insurance payment. And I'll be damn glad to avoid the effort of cutting it up."

"Understood."

"Finally, I'm not just going to untie it and set it to drift. You need to come at night. You need to be the one to take it, and you decide where it goes. All responsibility is yours once it's off-dock."

She looked uneasy. "I had hoped you could help me tow it with that little tug of yours. I don't have a boat.

"Won't be me. We can kill the deal right now if you want."

Becky shook her head no.

"All right then. I do promise the boat will be empty. When you pick your night, just send me some kind of message and I'll be sure no one is around. Once the hull is gone, I'll wait about twelve hours to report it. That's what I can offer."

"Okay," Becky replied. "That's the deal."

He jumped back in his truck and sped away.

She turned to the other women. "Sorry, girls. I guess we didn't need you this time."

One of them shrugged. "That's okay. He'll be back. They always come back."

Chapter 36

Harbor Lights

Throughout history, it has been common for large rivers with natural deep-water harbors to become inland ports. Often ports evolved as far upstream as large ships could safely navigate. The towns that grew around these ports often became thriving centers of commerce.

New England Upriver, Founders Light Publishing, 1949

Evening rush hour, such as it was in Riverbend, was over. The number of cars driving past Becky's farm slowed to a trickle. That's how she knew it was time to pack up.

It had been an average day. She sold a decent amount of honey and fruit. But it wasn't a great day either.

Just typical.

In a strange way, average days were the ones that weighed most heavily on Becky. When business was good, she felt good because things seemed successful and growing. When business was bad, she felt bad. But slow business also lit a fire under her. She'd become fixated on improvements, trying new things, and getting her business back on track.

But an average day? Those made her uncomfortable. How was she supposed to react? Average days seemed like a compromise. She feared the comfort of routine might hinder her progress.

She started wearing stylish dresses while working. That helped make her more noticeable among the other farm stands in the area. Most other owners were classic farmers with overalls and straw hats. But Becky wanted to set a different tone.

She scavenged Salvation Army stores and thrift boutiques. She had an eagle eye for designer outfits and low prices. On rare occasions she could find Christian Dior, Claire McCardell, and even more rarely her favorite—Norman Hartnell.

That day she wore one of her favorite new/old outfits, a swing skirt with a lilac pattern at the lower edges. Yellow fitted blouse with white and purple trim. And always an accent scarf. Dark green this time.

As she finished her work she heard a car, and when she turned to look, she saw him.

Jim.

He wasn't in his police car. Today he was dressed in his civvies and driving his family car.

The evening hours approached. He glided to a stop next to her table, wearing a friendly grin and dark aviator glasses.

"That truck of yours still giving you problems?"

She looked back quizzically. "Um, yes."

"I brought my tools. Mind if I take a look?"

"Oh, that's nice of you, Jim. But you don't have to do that."

"I know I don't. But I want to. You need your truck for business. And I don't want you to keep walking on that busy road."

"I think you're overestimating how often I need to restock the stores."

It was his turn to wink. "Let's just get you a working truck."

She folded a collapsible table and wiped her hands on a rag. "Suit yourself. It's parked about halfway down the hill."

Yarrow drove along the bumpy trail and stopped near the bakery truck. He pulled a canvas bag of tools from his back seat. The first thing he tried was to jump the battery. He started his car and let it cross-charge with the truck for a few minutes. But when he turned the truck's key, there was nothing but a click. That meant the power from his battery was doing nothing to help turn the other starter motor.

Next, he used a Hoyt electrical meter to check the connections and wires. With his arm hanging into the engine compartment, he found it tough to manipulate the probe with the fingers on his bad hand. He felt a growing frustration, but had learned to channel that feeling into slowing down and thinking creatively. He kept at it, picking up a stick and holding it in his mouth at one point to support the meter's wire.

He suspected the problem was either a bad alternator or a faulty solenoid. Within minutes, he narrowed it down to the solenoid. Sure enough, when he pulled it, he could see it was badly corroded.

He looked around for Becky, but didn't see her. What he did see was the sun dropping lower in the sky, with a pink frame of clouds around its edges. It was a beautiful evening.

There was a small Sears Auto Center about four miles away. That might still be open. But as he examined the solenoid, he realized it was an unusual size. Becky's truck was an older specialized vehicle, and that could mean odd and tough-to-find parts. He decided to wait until the next day. He would drive over to Parkway Auto, the largest parts store in the area. They stocked just about everything.

He was wrapping up the wires from his tester when Becky appeared, holding a bottle of wine and two glasses.

"I appreciate you doing this, Jim. Can I make a peace offering?"

"We weren't fighting, were we?"

"No. But I feel that I may have stepped over a line by visiting you in the graveyard. I don't think either of us felt comfortable."

"Nonsense. You came when others didn't. I was grateful."

"Well, good. So, a little wine then? Maybe by the water?"

He nodded. "Sure. Let me put my stuff in the car."

Becky poured two glasses. Stemware. A bit fancier than what Yarrow expected out in a field, but that fit her whimsical nature. With glasses in hand, they strolled toward the river.

Golden hour. Soft yellow light clung to the branches like syrup. The day's last bees flew past, heading back to the hives. They saw butterflies too, but compared to the bees, their destinations seemed aimless.

Yarrow realized this was his first time walking the full length of the path since his high school days. It looked the same, except for the missing shack. "You know," he said, "when my friends and I came here to swim, they always kept an eye out for the other girls, but I always looked for you."

"I know."

He turned to look at her. She winked.

The surface of the Merrimack was mirror-still. A mallard swam away from shore, splitting the quiet water into a perfect V.

Yarrow paused and slowly turned in a circle, taking it all in and remembering why he so loved this modest stretch of sand.

Becky slipped out of her shoes and hiked up the lower part of her dress. With the hem above her knees, she waded toward a fallen tree. She sat on its arched trunk and let her feet dangle in the water.

Yarrow had a brief flashback. He remembered watching her here, more than ten years before. In fact, that was the day when they first made …

He tried to push that thought from his mind, but there she was—patting the top of the log and beckoning him to come sit beside her.

"We don't need to stay long," she said. "We'll just drink our wine. I know you need to get home."

He laughed. "You know that I don't."

Yarrow took off his shoes, rolled up his pantlegs and joined her. He left a foot of space between them as he sat. They watched a group of water skippers treading atop the water, their feet making impossibly tiny dents in the surface.

"Speaking of home ... there's not much for me to go home to right now. You know Linda is gone. She wouldn't even come to the funeral."

"I noticed."

"I don't know if she's coming back, Becky." He stretched his foot and kicked the water. "I was planning to sign Tommy and Curtis up for some stuff at the town rec center. But I guess that's not going to happen. It feels so strange."

Becky saw the pain in his eyes. "I'm sorry, Jim. I know your kids mean the world to you." She gave him a pat on his knee. "And that's a pretty tough word you just said. *If.*"

He looked at her quizzically.

"What I mean is, that's a word that makes things confusing for you. *If* she comes back. *If* you can figure out where things stand. I think *if* is a word that leaves you in limbo."

"Yeah."

He drained the wine from his glass. Across the river there was a patch of lily pads. He fixed his gaze on the yellow blooms atop the floating green leaves.

Shadows from the trees started to lengthen. The air moved, the water moved, and the sun dimmed. He realized how infrequently he took time to just sit like this and watch the motion of the earth.

Becky looked up at the bluish-orange sky. "A few clouds can help make the best sunsets, don't you think? That's the sort of thing I think about when I'm out here all alone. A sunset on a clear day just isn't as interesting. But add some clouds? They give the sky personality. Every angle provides a different hue."

Yarrow looked up. The clouds really were beautiful, and her way of describing them made him appreciate them even more. He was glad to be here. Woods and water. Red and orange bleeding out into a darkening sky.

Even Monet with his palette and brushes would have found it daunting to capture the water, the lilies, and the majesty of the valley.

As he pointed toward a dramatic smear of colors, Becky looked at his hand.

"Does it still hurt?"

"What?"

"Your hand. Where you were shot."

He looked at his palm. "Not really. Not often."

He felt like she was searching for what she wanted to say. Finally, she spoke.

"So many people killed in that terrible war. So many people wounded. It was heartbreaking."

"Everyone hates war. It just happens sometimes."

"Why?"

"It's complicated."

They sat quietly, watching fish nibble at the surface bugs. Then Becky spoke again.

"I'd already left town when you went off to the war. Do you remember how the newspapers used to list wounded and dead soldiers by town? I would always read the names. I guess that seems morbid now. But on the home front, that's what we did. We all scanned the lists and felt sad when there was someone we knew."

"Ma told me the same thing."

"When I saw your name, Jim, my heart sank. I tried to find more information, but I couldn't. Then a month later I saw your photo in one of the papers. You were still in Europe, standing with a bunch of other wounded soldiers in some hospital hallway. You looked fine except for your hand, which was splinted and wrapped in a bandage. It's strange to say this, since you were hurt, but seeing that it was only your hand was a big relief to me."

In the dim light, the yellow flower on the lily pads had faded to grey. "It's okay. Thank you for caring."

"But I'm sure it wasn't easy for you. Trauma like that can linger."

He shrugged. "You know what's funny? I felt guilty for a long time. Isn't that stupid? When that photo was taken, I was standing next to guys who were missing limbs. One lost an eye and had shrapnel in his brain. My wound seemed so minimal compared to others. Sometimes I'd just hide it. I put my Purple Heart in a drawer and kept my hand in my pocket."

He looked at his hand. "I mean, if you're going to lose the use of a couple of fingers, the two in the middle are probably the best ones to lose."

"But it's your right hand."

"Yeah, but I can function. I can scratch my nose. Hold my pistol."

She took hold of his hand again. "I hope you don't still feel like you need to hide it, Jim. Be proud of all you did."

"I feel different about it now. When I look at the scar, it's become part of who I am. I made a choice, and I know I fought on the right side."

She opened his palm and looked closer. "Do you want to tell me how it happened? You don't have to."

He looked toward the lily pads once again, but they were barely visible now. "It's silly to dwell on it."

"But since I asked …"

He laughed. "Oh, all right. Since you asked. We landed near Anzio in January 1944. And at first, we surprised them. Very little resistance. A few shots came our way and there was a Luftwaffe strafing run, but we chased that plane off with just rifle fire. Shockingly, that was all we saw for the day. Some of our first patrols made it 10 miles inland without seeing much in the way of Italian or German troops. But our damn brass? They didn't want to keep going. They told us to dig in while we waited for more troops. But all that did was give the Krauts and the Eyeties a chance to get organized and to advance toward us. We should have been the ones marching—toward Rome. Instead, we ended up sitting in mud holes, getting shot at and shelled. It went on for months."

She gripped his hand tighter. "That must have been terrifying."

"Well, it was. But you know what's funny? When you're in a situation where you're terrified every day, it just becomes background noise. Your main goals are staying alive, advancing your position, and killing the enemy. I know that's blunt. But it's that simple."

She softly stroked the dimpled scar where the bullet hole had been.

"So anyway, the Italians were firing a bunch of their Brixia mortars at us. Cheap but deadly. They would blast one part of a trench, then their riflemen would pick off the wounded guys as they'd try to climb out. One of those wounded soldiers staggered toward my trench. He fell in front, bleeding and looking like hell. When I reached up to pull him to safety, some bastard shot me right through my hand. It hurt and burned. But it also made me angry. So, I stayed low and used my other hand. I slid it under him like a snake. Just grabbed his clothes and yanked him toward our hole, then into it."

"Did you save him?"

"You know, I'm not even sure. In the fog of it all, I never looked at his name tag. Someone else dragged him toward the rear while a medic bandaged my hand. There were a lot of wounded to haul away that day, so I just walked to the rear on my own."

"I'd like to think you did save him. And I hope he made it home."

"Me too. But who knows? Anyway, because several guys saw me grab him under fire, and because earlier in the day I'd also shot an advancing Italian soldier, the U.S. Army decided to give me a Bronze Star. I didn't even want to look at it at first. I put it in the same drawer as the Purple Heart. But after a few years, I did start to feel some pride in it. Now I keep both medals on a bookshelf in the den."

"What do you think when you look at them now?"

He thought about the question. "Pride, like I said. But I also wonder why. Why did I have to go through that? Why the hell did any of us boys end up there? Why were we killing each other? I mean, I know all the political reasons. I know the fascists had to be stopped. But I was barely nineteen when I joined, just twenty-one when I got to Anzio. I killed guys who were my same age. I still think of them. None of us started the war. None of us should have been there. Conflicts are driven by the greed of people who aren't fighting."

"You all answered the call, Jim. The world was at war and good people stepped up."

He tried to be stoic. "Don't get me wrong. I'm damn proud of stepping up, and I think I was a decent soldier. But I look at the other side too. The fascists cared little about sending their own boys into the meat grinder. They glossed over death by calling it glory. Then we had to do the same."

"There's no shame in feeling sympathy for an enemy too."

"Yeah. Not the leaders, but the men. Because I understood how they'd been duped. Is that strange? There they were trying to kill us, and a part of me very much hated them, but I knew their naivety was what allowed them to be sucked in. They heard the Nazi propaganda. Others heard the garbage coming out of the Royal Italian Army. It hypnotized them into thinking, *wow, this is the cause I want to fight for.* And the shitshow kept growing."

He slipped his bad hand under his good one. "Millions of people lost. Millions of walking wounded—and all it did was bring us back here, to the same normal lives we were living before any of it happened."

"Don't be too jaded, Jim. You helped make the world a better place."

"Maybe for a while. But greed always comes back. Greed takes over like a plague."

"Are you including this town?"

"Of course. Callous disregard isn't limited to wars. My brother died because some construction company didn't care about safety."

"It's all too much sometimes."

He tried to force a smile. "Thank you for understanding. And I know you've seen your own tragedies."

She patted his arm. "I still say you should be proud."

"Anyway, to finish the story, when my hand was healed enough, I went back to active duty. For the rest of my time in Europe I was assigned to the military police. That was the first time in two years that I was away from the front lines. I mostly yelled at drunken soldiers and tried to convince them to just stagger back to the base."

She leaned into him.

"That's how I ended up becoming a cop when I came home. A few months of military police work gave me a leg up at a time when a lot of guys coming home hoped to snag a government job."

"I'm glad they chose you. You deserved it."

They sat in silence for the rest of the sunset, until Becky held up a finger.

"Listen."

It took him a moment to hear what she was hearing. It was music. Drifting out from between the trees on the far bank of the river. Woven harmonies backed by distant band music.

"Do you recognize it?"

"Yes," he replied. "Sammy Kaye, right? *Harbor Lights.*"

The music came from an old house that was little more than a fishing camp. Electricity only reached that isolated road a few years before. For Yarrow, it was strange to see lights there because in his youth, that part of the river was always dark.

"They must have their radio out on the porch."

"Yes. Such a beautiful night for it."

As the music played Becky slipped off the log and stood ankle deep in the water. Then she twirled. Her lilac skirt flared like a bell flower. When she stopped, it dropped, soaking its hem. There was a strange and smooth syncopation to the music, and she kept moving along with it. He watched her try to find the rhythm and when she did, she seemed to lose herself in it. Eyes closed. Smiling and swaying.

"We never danced in high school, did we, Jim?"

He shook his head. "I don't think so. Did you even come to any of the dances?"

She extended her hand. He wanted to refuse, yet in the scent of the evening and the haze of the wine he found himself rising to join her. He dragged his feet through the water and tried to remember what to do.

They held hands and moved together in the shallow water. Rock step. Triple. In his memory, he was a better dancer. Maybe several years of bouncing in jeeps and cop cars had muted his sense of rhythm and motion.

The music stopped. They stood for several moments. Facing each other. Staring into each other's eyes, then away. He felt the spell break and he quickly dropped her hand and stepped back.

"I'm sorry Becky. I just … I don't know."

"I understand. You have a lot to think about."

With hands in his pockets, he walked to the riverbank. A nearly full moon was rising over the trees, brightening the valley again.

"I don't want my family to break up, Becky. I can't walk away from that. Not yet."

She rubbed his back for a second, then picked up the glasses and the nearly empty bottle. "Thank you for dancing with me. I haven't done that in a long time, and it felt good. Let's go back up."

They stepped onto the sand, then walked to a grassy spot to don their shoes. He walked behind her as they ascended the path.

Back at the bakery truck, he showed her the corroded solenoid and shared his plan to find a replacement. She thanked him then walked with him to his car.

"So, do you think you'll follow Linda? Will you move to Maine?"

"I don't know. I've been driving up to visit the kids on my days off. I also talk with them on the phone when Linda allows it. But to be honest, there's no job for me there, and no friends or other family. For me, it would be nothing but compromise." He thought for a moment then added, "And probably lingering discontent."

After he climbed behind the wheel, she leaned into the window.

"Well, between you and me, your wife is being foolish. In you, she found something remarkable. I think she should see that. And she should cherish it."

"Thank you, Becky."

She tousled his hair and added, "If it's any consolation, you're the best thing I ever lost."

He started the car and quickly drove away. He knew staying even another minute would make it harder to leave.

He drove in that direction of the coast, just to see the full moon over the Atlantic. He pulled over in a place where a shore road skirted the top of a sandy knoll. As his eyes adjusted, he could see the white crests of small waves. He listened to the low roar. And as always, there were lights out on the water.

He closed his eyes. He knew he was far different than the people on those boats. He was not a sailor and he felt no prevailing wind to set his direction. But it didn't matter. For now, he was a ship drifting into uncharted waters, with a sail that remained tightly furled.

Chapter 37

Temporary Tug

The least expensive way to dismantle an old metal ship is to run it aground at high tide. When the tide recedes, torches can be used to cut off the bow. As high tide returns, the stern of the boat will float slightly and what's left can be winched farther ashore. Each tide cycle, some parts of the ship can be chunked away, until even the stern is no more.

A Scrappers Guide to Beating the System, Pigstone Press, 1955

Leon Davis wrapped a rope around his hands and leaned back, pulling hard.

His plan was to borrow an old river dory, but it sat several feet above the high-tide line. Black gunwales and blue lapstrake on the sides. It was heavier than he expected.

With a bit of effort, he pulled it loose and dragged it over the sand. Straining and puffing as he reached the water's edge. He stopped to catch his breath, then hauled it over rocks and into the river.

He had longstanding permission from a friend to use the old workboat whenever he needed. Tonight he needed it, but he kept silent about his mission.

Of all the odd jobs Leon took in recent years, this would be the most challenging. Highly physical. Dangerous. But it would make him some quick money. Plus, he was helping Becky.

The mission started when Becky and Amy showed up at his door. They had an audacious plan to move an old hull by towing or pushing it with a smaller boat. They said they wanted to hire him, but insisted he couldn't tell anyone. They also said the operation would not take place until a good-size storm came through the area. And it might be dangerous.

That's when he learned they were planning to commit a bit of insurance fraud.

"Waiting for a storm allows us to use that as a cover story," Becky said. "Hopefully it will look like the hull just blew loose from its dock."

Leon nearly declined the offer. But when he heard the ship would be used for housing people at the farm, he relented and agreed to help.

But it did concern him a bit that Becky asked him not to mention anything to Jim Yarrow.

He almost said no again when he learned about the size of the hull. His borrowed dory measured barely eighteen feet, and its outboard motor packed a measly thirty-five horsepower. But he eventually decided to do the job simply because he wanted to see if he could pull it off.

He brought a stack of tires with him. Once his borrowed boat was in the water, he lashed six tires to the bow, three to each side. They'd act as bumpers if he had to nudge the big hull in various directions.

It took four pulls to start the outboard, then he accelerated away from the bank and into the current. The motor seemed strong enough, pushing the dory upstream at a decent pace. He was determined to *complete the mission*. That phrase was drilled into him during his army years. A soldier on a mission was expected to complete it.

Besides, people downstream would be waiting. They would intercept the ship and pull it toward land.

Sheets of rain washed over him as he approached the dock. He guided the craft on a nearby bank, killing the motor and tipping it up at the last moment. As the hull made contact with sand he stepped out, sloshing through water that felt surprisingly warm.

He secured the dory and did a quick survey of the ship. The rudder was gone. He immediately started scratching his chin.

Without the stabilizing effect of a rudder, it would be much harder to tow the hull in a straight line. It could fishtail dangerously. He'd have to rethink his plan.

Also, he saw no fenders or padding along the starboard side. Usually, some kind of bumper would be there to protect the ship against the dock. He figured everything was removed that day by the boat yard. The hull was only attached to the pier with two ropes.

Wow, he thought. *How do I even get started?*

The bow of the ship was so close to shore that there was no room to get his boat in there. He brought a towing cable with him, but was already forming another plan in his head.

Leon walked up and down the dock, examining the hull from multiple angles.

Maybe I can leave the stern line attached until I have things lined up.

And that's what he did. He untied the bow and gave it a mighty shove. Between his muscle and the downstream flow, the bow slowly pivoted outward, until the ship was parallel to the shore, facing downstream and attached only by its stern line.

He ran back to the dory, started his motor and left it idling, then ran back to the dock.

He cast off the stern line and watched the hull slowly float free. It started moving with the current. No pilot. No rudder. Heading downstream. Thousands of pounds of floating steel with no control.

And there it goes. Oh, my God, this is insane.

He felt a moment of panic, then tried to calm himself. So far, the old ship was doing what he wanted it to.

Racing back to his dory, he jumped in and accelerated until he came alongside the hull. He nudged it a bit. The impact made a loud clunk, but the big hull barely moved. He nudged it again, harder this time. Through sustained contact and small accelerations, he managed to adjust the ship's trajectory.

Okay, he thought, *I can steer it a little. That's good. Just … keep things slow.*

As the ship started to pick up speed, he accelerated ahead of it. Then he cut his speed and let the front edge of the bow touch the stern of his boat, off-center and away from the propeller. The impact gave him a good jolt. He fought to keep his smaller boat straight. He shifted into neutral as they touched again. Once he had sustained contact he shifted into reverse. The effect on the heavy hull was … basically nothing. With so much weight behind him, reversing his motor had little effect.

He increased the throttle. The prop thrust increased. In a minute, he could feel a slight slowing.

Okay. This might work. Take your time, take your time, he told himself.

But he knew he was coming to a large bend in the river, and that would be the most challenging part of the trip.

He slowed the heavy hull as best he could, then pulled free and let the bow drift past him. He again touched the side, pressing near the waterline and urging it to stay near the center of the river. The rain let up and he could see the river ahead. He noted the spot where the Merrimack made a fifty-degree curve back north within just a few hundred yards.

The hull loomed beside him like a tall metal wall. With his bow to the ship's side, he fully accelerated. The old schooner barely turned, so he let the dory slide closer to the bow, then he pushed again.

Ever so slowly both boats turned. As he entered the bend, he was confident he could navigate the turn.

What he didn't realize was the river narrowed a bit, and the strength of the current would suddenly increase. Even as he successfully navigated the curve, his speed was increasing and he realized he was coming out of the turn much too fast. He ended up oversteering.

Again, he tried to slow things down by moving to the front of the hull, allowing contact and again reversing his engine. But the looming weight pushed too hard. His prop was small, and he had nothing resembling a brake.

Out of the darkness, a shape emerged in front of him. He strained to see what it was. He realized he was heading toward a dock.

What the hell? How close to the shore am I?

The dock extended over thirty feet from the bank. A new-looking sailboat was tied there, and its pulpit extended four feet past where the dock ended.

Leon had less than one hundred feet to adjust the trajectory. He tried to brush the water out of his eyes, then he tightened his grip on the wet throttle. He could barely see, but he knew he was closing in fast.

With no other options, he raced the motor, pulled ahead of the hull, then quickly turned about. He throttled directly toward its bow and purposely hit it, slightly to the side. He hoped to slow it and to turn the craft but his impact had little effect, other than jostling his own boat. But he backed off and tried again and again, accelerating and hammering the ship each time. His heart raced and he worried about being crushed, but he could detect slight corrections with each bump.

The dock was getting closer. Fifty feet, forty feet, thirty—he was full throttle now and just pushing.

Fuck, fuck, fuck! he said to himself.

The clouds opened up again, spilling more rain. With the water pouring over his face, he could barely see.

Leon could tell his dory and the hull would miss the dock by mere inches. But the sailboat's extended pulpit was a different story.

His boat fit under it. The steel hull did not. With a clang, it caught the sailboat's bow rail, along with its anchor mount, which was right at the tip of the pulpit.

The impact jerked the sailboat toward its dock, issuing a loud thud. Leon watched helplessly as the impact ripped off the boat's rail, along with the forestay, then the stemhead, anchor, and chocks. Some of the parts plopped into the water.

The hull was pulled slightly sideways as they passed, but then it yanked free.

Damn! Oh, Goddamn it!

For the next few moments, he worked in a heart-pounding panic. The sailboat's rail was dangling from the hull, so he zoomed over to grab it. He pulled it away and let it sink. He then worked feverishly to straighten their course.

Accelerating. Tapping. Again, and again. Changing sides. By making some heavy-handed adjustments he was able to get the bow pointed downstream again. Then he rubbed the water from his eyes, took several long breaths and calmed his nerves. He knew that was the worst of the trip. The smaller bends in the river would be nothing after this one.

Okay, okay. Got a feel for it now. Insurance, he thought. *The sailboat owner can claim insurance, right? Hold it together Leon.* He continued the navigation. A little push to port. Another push to starboard. Progress.

He kept the hull on track for another fifteen minutes and as the rain let up a bit, he found himself approaching the sandy riverbank behind Becky's farm.

That afternoon, three of her workers had cut down several trees. He could see them lying beside the bank. Next to them he saw some movement. Becky promised to wear a white jacket to make her easier to spot.

He picked up his flashlight and blinked it twice. On the shore, a light blinked back. He heard a tractor start.

He had been told to look for a canoe. And there it was.

It moved out ahead of him. Leon didn't know who was paddling, but he knew the canoe was supposed to carry a cable out from shore. The other end was attached to the borrowed tractor.

Their plan was to boost the hull's downstream momentum while pulling it hard toward the shore. The tractor would keep pulling as long as it could.

As the hull moved closer to the canoe, he could see a woman holding the end of the cable. A large metal clip was attached. She was wearing shorts and a tank top and her eyes looked terrified as the hull came toward her. But slowly, she stood and prepared for impact.

Leon's instinct was to try to help her snap the cable in place. But he had his own job to do, and that was to help make the hull go as fast as possible and to force it toward the shore.

He nudged the bow one last time, then moved astern. His final contact with the ship came with a bump. Then he accelerated and pushed for the final run.

He knew the canoe would be grazed by the rushing ship. That was part of the plan.

I hope that woman is athletic, Leon thought to himself. *Boy, I sure hope she is.*

He heard a slight yelp as the hull struck the canoe. He couldn't see her, but he heard banging and scraping up front.

"You okay? Did you get it?" he shouted.

He could barely hear her as she shouted back, "I'm hanging on the bow! I grabbed that front cleat thing!"

"Yes! Right there! Clip it on! Fast!"

He saw the canoe float past. It was upside down.

"Do it!"

"I'm trying!" she shouted.

After a few tense moments, he heard a metallic clink. Someone on the shore cheered and there was a splash. A moment later he spotted her in the water, swimming toward shore.

Leon accelerated the outboard to full bore. He felt the hull pick up its pace, thanks to the current, the push of his boat, and the pull of the tractor.

He could hear the tractor roar at the base of the hill. It moved forward, keeping the cable tight, and revving more as it started to climb the slope.

Son of a bitch, he thought. *We may just pull this off.*

It was satisfying to feel the ship's speed rushing along now. In fact, they were gaining impressive momentum.

The impact on the bank came with an intense crunching sound, and the ping of denting metal. He kept pushing until his momentum waned, then he peeled away. By that time over half of the ship was up on shore.

As he drifted past, he saw the tractor continue its hill-climb. The hull, moving slower now, slipped up and then mostly over the bank. The tractor wheels dug in and the engine groaned for another thirty seconds. The big tires threw dirt down the hill. Eventually its front wheels lifted off the ground. Whoever was driving it cut the engine, and everything came to a stop.

Leon could hear cheers behind him.

In the end, most of the ship ended up well onto the bank, with only about four feet still hanging over the high tide line.

Leon leaned back in his seat and let the rain wash over his face. He just wanted to float and bask for a minute. He couldn't believe they did it. They had some scares and damage along the way, but *wow*. They did it.

Behind him, the people on the shore dragged the trees up and onto the hull. They laid them so their big crowns dangled over the transom. Then they piled on more branches, shrubs and leaves. The rain helped press the dripping mess into place.

In a matter of minutes, the ship was fully camouflaged. It just looked like a big fallen tree, knocked over by the storm.

Leon turned about and headed back upstream. He surveyed the work and gave a wry smile. On-shore, a flashlight beam pointed in his direction. A voice called out, "Thank you!"

He recognized it as Becky's. He stood, illuminated by the beam of her light, and gave a cartoonish salute. Then headed back to where he had picked up the dory.

Leon knew the owner of the damaged sailboat would discover the missing pieces in the morning. He'd probably report it. But people were likely to assume the harm was the result of the storm and maybe the empty drifting hull that had apparently broken away from the salvage yard.

If Becky could keep the hull well-hidden on the riverbank, people would assume it had drifted out to the ocean. There might be a cursory search, but he was pretty sure no one really wanted it back.

Leon smiled all the way home. If he ever had grandkids, this would definitely be one of his best grandpa stories.

Chapter 38

Reward

Over one hundred fifty thousand Quonset huts were manufactured during World War II. They came in a variety of sizes and were distributed around the world. Most were constructed from galvanized steel. The American version was first used at Quonset Point, Rhode Island, giving the huts their name. After the war, thousands were sold as surplus.

The Logistics and the Aftermath of WW II, Barley Field Press, 1948

Leon Davis was always a bit shy when it came to asking for money. Even when he knew he'd done a great job, he hesitated. It was just a personal quirk. He came to collect from Becky but lingered near the edge of the parking lot as she talked with a customer.

When she saw him, she gave him a bright smile and beckoned him toward the counter. She opened her cash box and paid him what he was owed. She also handed him some honey futures in a sealed envelope.

"I'm so sorry I couldn't get this to you the night you delivered the ship," she said. "But things were a bit chaotic."

"No problem. That was an amazing night."

He pocketed everything without counting it. He trusted her.

"That trip had its scary moments," Leon admitted. "But we got it here, eh?"

"You're the one who got it here, Leon. Thank you for that. The hull already has two residents. They built nice little bunks and some boxes to hold their things. More people will live there soon."

"That's nice." He lowered his voice a bit. "Any repercussions yet?"

"None." Her voice also dropped to a whisper. "I saw a couple of boats cruising slowly, like they might have been looking for it, and a police patrol boat has been poking around. But so far, no one has spotted the ship beneath all those branches."

"That's actually hilarious. I'm so glad it worked out." He turned to leave, but Becky called after him.

"By the way, Leon. I have another job for you, if you'd like."

"Uh oh."

"Don't worry. It's nothing as wild this time. I need something assembled. "Do you see those big, curved sheets of metal over there?"

"The ones with the ridges?"

"Yup. I bought an old Quonset hut. It was disassembled and moved here."

"How about that." He walked over and picked up a piece.

She walked over as Leon was lining up a second piece.

"You've got it right. The pieces overlap and bolt together, and they're all labeled with chalk."

"Oh, I've seen plenty of them," he said. "They're really simple to put together."

"Well, I'd like to offer you three honey futures to assemble it. The toughest part will probably be moving all the pieces down the hill."

"I don't see any end pieces."

"No ... those weren't included. And that's probably why it didn't cost much. I figure we can just attach boards and tarps to the ends. It will end up being half tube and half tent."

Leon walked around the pile and examined the pieces.

"What will you use it for?"

"Just more living space. I'm trying to get folks out of the smaller tents before summer ends."

Leon exhaled slowly. "I mean, yeah. I can assemble it. Glad too. But it's not going to be a comfortable place for anyone to live. There's zero insulation."

"I know. But it would keep people dry. I have old pallets to use as a floor. We'll add a kerosene stove at some point."

Over the next three evenings Leon came to the farm with a younger man. He introduced him as Isaac, his cousin. The boy's eyes grew wide as he looked at the whole scene; the river, the bees, and the women. But Leon kept Isaac on-task. They chose a spot that was barely visible from the road and dragged the pieces down the hill. They started bolting the hut together one metal rib at a time. When they lifted up the first rib it formed a tall arch, twelve feet high in the middle. They temporarily propped it up with long branches.

Eventually they fastened three ribs together. That improved stability and they continued to attach other additional ribs.

As they worked, some of the women came to watch. They brought drinks and fruit to share. Becky arrived too. When Leon had a moment, she pulled him aside.

"Look at Isaac," she whispered. "I think your cousin is enamored."

"Oh, he definitely is. I'm going to have to hustle him right out of here."

"He's fine," she said. "Let him stay."

As they lifted the last of the steel ribs into place, one of the girls lit a bonfire. Within minutes, others appeared with tin platters containing skewers of cut-up rabbit, peppers, lemons, and onions. More residents emerged from tents and trailers, toting lawn chairs and crates. They ate in a big circle around the fire. Wine bottles and gallons of beer were passed from hand to hand.

Someone with an old fiddle started to play.

Eventually the dinner ended, but the drinking and singing continued.

Becky sat near the edge of the circle, taking it all in. For weeks, a fledgling community had been forming here. Now, with the arrival of the ship's hull and the construction of the big metal hut, it seemed like the start of a new chapter for the farm. A small village was taking root. It was a community with rough edges, but with residents who valued it.

Becky wondered if Leon and Issac would spend any of their honey futures before leaving. She didn't really care. It was just nice to see everyone having a wonderful evening.

But, now what? she thought to herself. *If we keep growing, our space will quickly fill.*

She rose and tossed another log onto the fire, then looked toward the road that brought them to her.

I wish they'd stop coming. But I don't think they will.

She rubbed her forehead and forced the thought from her mind. For tonight, she would try to relax and listen to the music.

Chapter 39

Drifting

At Low Tide, the Merrimack River delta is dendric at its mouth. Separate streams carry freshwater into the ocean. But as the tide rises, those bird foot-style patterns disappear. Waves flatten sand, and the end of the river becomes a single uninterrupted triangle of water for a few hours.

Rivers and Deltas, Shoreline Books, 1948

Yarrow felt a certain level of guilt. He could admit that much to himself.

At the cop-shop, his usual days off were Tuesdays and Wednesdays, and on one of those days he usually tried to visit Tommy, Curtis, and Bonnie in Maine. They had just enrolled in school in Freeport, so he started picking them up later in the day, and they'd go someplace fun. Maybe candlepin bowling or mini golf. Then they'd go shopping, because they always needed something.

Then he would drop them off, exchange a few tense words with Linda's mother, and head home to Riverbend.

But one Tuesday the boys had a Cub Scout sleepover, and Linda wanted to take Bonnie to see one of her aunts.

So, he would be on his own.

As he sipped his morning coffee, he told himself he shouldn't feel guilty. He wasn't the one who canceled the visit. But other things gnawed at him. The grapevine of family friends told him Linda had visited an attorney. That didn't necessarily mean divorce was pending, but it wasn't good.

Maybe he also had a second source of guilt. When Becky heard he wasn't traveling to Maine, she invited him to spend the day at the farm. She needed his help for a couple of things. It would be a hot day, so she told him to bring some shorts for a dip in the river.

As a married man, he should have vowed to keep his distance.

But what is my marriage now? he thought. *And where is it? Still here in this house? Up in Maine, keeping its distance? Or is it nowhere?* His eyes went to the pair of brass hooks where he and Linda hung their keys. Her hook was empty.

After several minutes, he stood and grabbed his keys from the other hook.

Compared to his police cruiser, the family car felt smaller and more maneuverable. He could see the Merrimack as he drove to the farm. The water was silvery and clear. There were no recent storms to give it a milky brown tint. And the water looked warm. He didn't have to touch it to know. When it was cold, the river had a disquieting steel-gray look to it. Today was the opposite. It looked shiny, light, and inviting.

He noticed two things when he arrived. The shoulder of the road had been widened considerably with gravel. It was wide enough now to have a nice turning lane. And the tables were void of honey. The farm stand appeared to be closed for the day.

He found Becky behind her truck. There was a new picnic table and she was stringing ropes above it to hang a tarp.

"Wow. Every time I visit this place it looks more like a home."

She looked down from her step ladder and winked. "Well, then you should stop by more often."

He extended his hand and helped her step down. As she wiped her hands on her apron, she said, "I'm glad you came. I wasn't sure if you would."

"Well, I wasn't sure either. But here I am."

She showed him her progress. She paid some concrete workers to pour footings for a new building. She unrolled a set of blueprints. "I can't afford to build this building yet, and it's pretty rudimentary—just twenty-four by thirty-six feet." She pointed to the details. "Only five windows and two doors. But I'm excited about it."

She explained that she wanted to live in part of it, if she could find the money for a small kitchen and bathroom. "Of course, I'll also have to drill a well. And septic. It all gets so expensive. But this is my start. Once it's framed in it will be the first house I've lived in for quite a while!"

Yarrow studied the drawings. "I hope it happens Becky. You deserve it. You've been bathing with river water for far too long."

She placed a hand on his shoulder. "Thank you. I hope so too. I feel like everything is so tentative now. A lot of people are trying to stymie us."

The plans reminded Yarrow of a smaller version of the simple ranch houses being built around the country. Most were occupied by veterans and their young families.

"I think you're doing fine, Becky. The law is still on your side for now, so don't let Mary Jane and her hellions get you down."

She folded the blueprints and put them away. "Does that mean you're on my side too, Jim? I guess you're also the law."

"Yeah. In a limited way," he admitted. "And I'm cheering for you."

She then showed him something she found at the town dump. It was a faded red, white, and blue sign that once marked the site of a Works Progress Administration project.

"Ha. I remember those WPA signs," Yarrow said. "They used to hang wherever there was a government-funded project. I'll bet that hung near one of the sewer plants built around here in the thirties."

"Maybe. I just wanted to save the sign. When I was seventeen, I sometimes worked at a WPA sewing room. We made army pants. That was the first time I took a job outside of Erin's farm."

She invited him to sit at the table, to chat and share some tea. But instead, he asked about the chores she wanted him to tackle. It turned out to be a simple list. A leg on one of her produce display tables had cracked. He swapped in a new one. There was a brush pile that had grown too big, so he started a bonfire and tossed in branches, one at a time.

He noticed some metal fence posts had gone rusty, so he gave them new coats of grey paint. Then he hung Becky's WPA sign.

It grew hot by late morning, so he returned to his car and changed into a pair of old shorts. Circle-S cut-offs, gone to fringe at the bottom.

She met him as he walked back and asked him to come with her down by the water. They could cool off in the shade and she claimed a surprise waited for him on the bank.

As they approached the water, she asked if he remembered their first date. "Or at least it was our first time together."

"I'm not sure which date would be considered our first."

"Well, what do you think?"

He considered the question. "The first time we did anything together? That was probably when a group of us seniors skipped school. It was steaming hot, and we bought some big black inner tubes from McGreevy's service station. We blew them up with his air hose and carried them to the river."

"Yes," Becky said. "That's exactly the time I was thinking of. I'm glad you remembered!"

He saw she had piled some things near the end of the path. That's when he noticed the black inflated tubes, just like the ones from ten years before.

"Oh wow. I can't believe this."

Between the two large tubes there was a smaller one. All three were tied together. The smaller tube held an old, insulated milk box.

"Interesting. You're bringing milk?" he asked.

"No, that's our lunch. Plus, a six-pack of beer."

He laughed. "Wow, this really is like high school. I love it. Where did you get this stuff?"

"The tubes came from that Atlantic station down the road. I picked up the sandwiches and beer from Blanchard's store. And the milk box? That's mine. We get milk delivered."

Yarrow dove into the river to cool off. He glided under water, stroking three times and rising thirty feet from shore. He could feel a tug from the river's current, but it was easy to swim against it.

As he treaded water, Becky pushed the tubes out into the shallows then stripped off her thigh-length terrycloth coverup. She wore a tight two-piece Jantzen bathing suit, orange with no shoulder straps. It fit her perfectly. Their feet sank into the dark river muck. That made it challenging to climb aboard, but they managed, awkwardly kicking and settling into the tubes.

Using their hands, they paddled toward the main part of the river. They found a stronger current and relaxed as it moved them downstream.

"We're a little past high tide," Yarrow said. "The river will speed up as it empties. We'll need to be careful not to drift too far."

"Oh, we actually have a destination," Becky countered. "This morning, I followed Amy and we left her dad's old car near the mouth of the river. That means we can drift all the way to the ocean."

"What? The coast is at least seven miles from here."

"Yes, but the river is moving at, what, maybe two to three miles per hour? That means we'll get there in three hours.

Probably less." As if to quiet him, she held up a can opener attached to a string.

"You brought a church key!"

"Of course."

She rummaged through the milk box, found two cans of Narragansett, and punched fat triangles through the tin tops. She handed him a cold one and said, "Let's enjoy the ride."

They talked and drifted in the sun until it got too hot, then they paddled toward shady areas. Sometimes they would slip into the water to feel the refreshing temperature change on their skin.

And sometimes they drifted in silence. During one quiet time, a curious fish nibbled Yarrow's toe.

"I think this is the most relaxed I've been in weeks," he confided.

"Good. That's what we're here for."

He wondered how Becky, a woman with so little, could make him feel welcome, appreciated, and carefree. It was like discovering she had a superpower that she previously kept hidden.

"You see that spot over there?" she asked. "Where the land against the water is sort of low and flat?"

"Between those trees?"

"Yeah. When I was a child an old woman told me an Agawam tribal village stood there until the early seventeen hundreds. Then they were pushed out. People still find arrowheads there, and broken pottery."

"Where did the tribe go?"

"I don't know. Mostly dead or assimilated, I think."

Yarrow reflected on that for a moment. "You know, it bothers me that neither of us knows for sure. Whole generations of people lived around us. First natives, and then European settlers. But we only know a handful of the stories. One group arrives and replaces another. People get pushed out. And we're mostly left with footnotes."

"I guess most people just fade into obscurity. We don't know their journeys."

"Some of those choices probably still affect us," Yarrow said. "But the memory of how things happened? That gets lost."

As the river started to widen, they felt the current slow. They drifted past small islands and long docks that stretched from shore toward deeper water.

Slowly Becky and Yarrow drifted toward the salt marshes of Salisbury. There, the water grew wider still. Sometime during their third beer, they started talking about the old days. High school. The people they knew. The sense of freedom.

As their inner tube raft moved, it would slowly spin, allowing them to take in the full grandeur of the river and the low valley. Clear water against brilliant-green hills. As they moved east, those hills continued to flatten out into marshland.

"You know, Jim," Becky broke their silence, "after Erin and I left, but when things started to get better for me, I should have come to find you. I know it, and I'm so sorry I didn't."

He nodded. "Yes, you should have."

She gave his hand a squeeze. "I think I was waiting. In my mind, I needed to rehearse how I would approach you. But in a matter of weeks, the war was underway. Everything changed. Men were called up and women were in demand for work. From then on, no one asked me any questions. That's when I finally felt free. I was recruited to run a machine in a copper wire factory for a month. Then I found work at the big shipyard—the Bath Iron Works. They actually recruited me to be a welder. Can you believe that?"

"I'd loved to have seen you do that."

"It was a short stint. They were trying to finish two new destroyers every month and they were desperate for workers. But the girls who were bigger and stronger than me were better at welding, and when the bosses learned I could type, they moved me over to office work. The pay was okay, so I stayed. And I learned a lot about how businesses operate. That's what gave me enough confidence to start my own."

"I see."

She shifted a bit on her inner tube, so she could look at him. "When I did finally come back to Riverbend, I kept a low profile and only talked to a few people. I looked for you, and was told you had gone off to college."

"I didn't stay."

"I came back a second time too. Maybe ten months later. I was determined to find you, but then I learned you had been drafted like so many others. No one knew how to contact you and I didn't dare approach your family. So, I left. And then I just worried. Pretty much everyone was worried back then about their friends and family."

Yarrow lay back, face up, staring at the clouds.

"So, that's all I can say, Jim. Circumstance separated us. The war changed things, then passing years separated us even more. By the time I heard you were back, I also learned you were engaged. So, I stayed away. I knew I had to."

Slowly and in silence, the current carried them eastward. They passed beneath the bridge near Newburyport, then Coffin Point, and the south edge of Salisbury.

They emerged into the broad delta. He reached again for her hand and they stayed that way, fingers locked, floating, twirling, and watching the sun move across the sky. The wide river was ending its long journey. They used their hands and feet to angle their tubes toward the back side of Plum Island.

Spotting a sandy area on the bay side, they kicked and paddled toward it, cutting a diagonal path across the current. It took a while, and when they finally climbed onto the beach, the sun was approaching the horizon with yellow intent. They tied the inner tubes to a log and sat beneath the scrubby beach pines.

The delta area at the mouth of the Merrimack was often busy. But it was a weekday evening. No other soul was in view, and they enjoyed a private and splendid isolation.

Both were quiet, just drinking in the view, until Becky reached up to stroke his hair. She softly asked him a question, which he couldn't quite hear. When he leaned closer, he felt her lips brush his.

The touch was soft, but to him it felt electric. Memories came rushing back. The taste of her. The way he once felt about her. The anger and abandonment, now forgiven. And then there was his current loneliness. An absent wife and the strange, untethered feeling that settled over him in the mornings and evenings.

Then she kissed him again.

He responded and allowed himself to get lost in it. He reached up and held the back of her head, hastening the next kiss. And the next one too. For that moment, everything around them seemed to stand still. Only they, together, were moving.

In that unwinding moment, a series of images ran through his head. He was back in high school. Then fighting in the army. Then he felt like he was falling … falling. Until he realized he was indeed falling. With her. Toward the sand.

In the waning light, he found her just as he remembered. But different too. Passionate. Playful. More confident now. Experienced. Even wanton.

All of that was good.

As he kissed her, he could see the moonlight reflected off both of her lips. And in between those lips, for a moment, he thought he saw the depths of the universe. Just a glimpse, but endless, and timeless.

There on the sand, they lost themselves to the moment. And their embrace lasted, in various ways, until the last light was gone and the stars emerged. In time, they settled, caught their breath, and he lay beside her. She sat up a bit, hugging her knees. Face turned upward toward the moon. And in that light, he saw her slowly smile. She closed her eyes and took a deep breath of the salty air.

"This is wonderful," Becky said. "This is eternal, even if we aren't."

A few minutes later she rose and waded into the water. She dove forward then swam back.

Yarrow watched her emerge from the bay, bluish moonlight clinging to her skin.

"My God you're beautiful," he said. "And look at that, I guess the water was cold?"

She playfully pushed him over, then climbed a small dune.

She stood there, looking lustrous, even primitive, as she slowly scanned the horizon.

He continued to watch. Then asked, "What are you doing?"

"I'm trying to figure out where I parked the car."

He laughed at her reply.

Eventually they dressed, gathered their things, then walked, dragging the innertubes, toward where she thought the car would be. They had to wade through thigh-high water at one point, but they found the parking lot about five hundred yards away.

He drove and she leaned against him. There was minimal conversation as they headed toward Riverbend. But the silence didn't seem awkward. He accepted it as something comfortable and profound. There was reassurance in just being together. He wasn't sure why he felt that way. But then he realized—what he was feeling was simple satisfaction.

Chapter 40

Fury

Some beekeepers will swear their bees recognize them, while others say they've never had that experience. Recent studies at leading New England universities indicate bees are indeed capable of remembering some things and recognizing some features. But more studies are needed.

Proceedings of the Eastern Apiary Society, Q2, 1958

They kept their group small, this offshoot of the Riverbend Improvement Society. Just four people, with an unspoken understanding that their plans were controversial. But Mary Jane was angry and she picked this core group because she knew they too were angry.

The others waited at a picnic table in the town park. They turned to acknowledge her as she approached.

"Thank you all for coming," she said. "I believe we all have similar thoughts about recent events. Obviously, what's going on isn't acceptable."

"No, it certainly is not," said Shannon Gates.

Mary Jane didn't sit. She stood at the end of the table and passed a handful of photos to the person closest to her. "Please, take a look at these and pass them down. They were taken three days ago and as you can see, there are even more tents now. Two more trailers too. Seems like a lot of people want to join Becky Bivens' little Hooverville. We've filed our complaints, the town has taken no action, and I fear it may already be too late."

She stood tall and looked at the others. "We need ideas, people, and we need action."

"This is really a town issue, MJ," said Shannon. "And you're right. We aren't getting their support."

Mary Jane raised her eyebrows. "Obviously, we haven't found the right approach. Last time, I think we ended up complicating things by sending boys to do such an important job."

The others grumbled their agreement, but one of the men said, "One of those boys died MJ. I mean, at least have a little respect."

Mary Jane shot him an icy look. "It would be better to think of him like a fallen soldier. Isn't that fair? Soldiers get sent to fight all the time, and sometimes they die. That's just the cost."

The man turned his head to the side, like he'd been hit by a stiff wind. "Jesus," he said as he stood up. He said nothing more and walked back toward his car.

"Okay, fine." Mary Jane called after him. "I guess we can see where your loyalties lie."

Then she continued. "And now, because of what happened, somehow we are the ones under scrutiny. It's so unfair."

"Definitely not fair to us," said Doug Grover, who closed his drug store to attend the meeting. "I thought we were making progress. I believe at least a few people now blame Becky for what happened."

"Yes. But she's slippery. I'd say more people seem to be leaning the other way. They're pointing at us." Mary Jane looked around the room. "This simply cannot stand."

Shannon held up a finger. "Before we rush forward too quickly, I see a potential problem. If we manage to close the farm, those residents will have no place to live. They may end up drifting into town like a swarm. Then we'll be dealing with that too, and even more townsfolk will be mad at us."

For the next few minutes, multiple ideas were floated. They discussed the merits of lawsuits, Health Department inspections, and zoning. But every idea triggered follow-up questions and potential negative consequences. Whenever the group seemed non-committal, Mary Jane raised her voice and stressed the threat the farm represented.

"MJ," said Doug Grover, "the big problem is that boy's death. The spotlight turned toward us because we're the ones who have been so vocal. So if anything else happens, the police, the town, the judges—everyone will look at us! The additional scrutiny could be risky."

The group sat in silence until Shannon made a suggestion. "Why don't we just go talk to Becky?"

Mary Jane made a gasp of disgust. But others seemed to think the idea was plausible.

"It's not a terrible idea. Come on, at least we should try. Right?" said Grover.

"And say what to her?" Mary Jane sneered. "That we think she should stop everything? What do you think she'll say? 'Oh gosh, you're right? I'll shut down immediately?'"

"Well …" said Grover.

She shook her head. "You all are clueless. She won't cooperate, because we're well beyond that point."

But others wanted to try, and after further haggling they found themselves riding in Shannon's Pontiac Streamliner. The big V8 purred as they drove toward the outskirts of town until they found their way blocked by sawhorses and signs.

"What is this?" Shannon looked confused.

"Road closed again?" Mary Jane scowled. "I am so damn sick of all the road construction going on in this town."

They could see a portion of the road ahead was being widened. A double lane of asphalt was being laid down. The detour signs sent them a mile out of their way.

"Ridiculous!" Mary Jane sputtered. "We're wasting time."

She folded her arms and stared out the window as they drove. She had no interest in finding common ground with Becky, but she knew she would have to play along.

It was nearly noon when they arrived at the farm. The sky was brooding. Tall grey clouds lingered, but rain was holding off for now.

Someone else was minding the stand, so they walked to Becky's truck but found it empty. Shannon pointed to the Quonset hut down the hill. "What's this? Now she's adding more buildings?"

They made their way toward the hut. The ends were sealed off with tarps, rope, and wood. They didn't see a door, so they knocked on the metal side. Footsteps could be heard inside, but no one answered. They knocked again and heard a voice.

"Who is it? Who's out there?"

"Is that Becky?" Shannon called out. "We'd like to talk with you!"

They heard no response.

Mary Jane stood behind the others, her simmering anger stoked by many things, including Becky, Erin, the women on the farm, the dusty road construction … even her own foolish father.

"I know she's in there," MJ hissed.

"Becky? We're a few people from the Riverbend Improvement Society," Shannon continued. "We just want to meet with you for a bit. Could you step out?"

A few moments passed when no one spoke, then they heard, "No, thank you."

Shannon tried again. "Look, if we could—"

Before she could finish, a golf ball-sized rock flew past them and clanked against the side of the hut. The others jumped and turned. They saw Mary Jane picking up another rock. Again, she threw it hard against the building.

"You get out here right now, Becky," she shouted. "Do you understand? Just get out—"

"MJ, what in the—" Shannon grabbed her friend and tried to pull her away.

Mary Jane shook her off. "Stop it. She needs to come out here and she needs to talk to us. I'm sick of all of you taking this hands-off approach."

A noise came from behind the hut. They heard a tarp being brushed aside followed by footsteps running away.

Mary Jane raced around the hut, picking up another rock. Shannon tried to catch up while the rest of the group laughed.

Becky ran toward her aviary. Mary Jane hurled the rock and it struck Becky on the shoulder. She flinched a bit but kept running. She only stopped when she reached the middle of her hives. The group closed in but stopped when they got to the first row of hives. Mary Jane pointed at Becky. "This is your last warning, bee girl. Do you hear me?"

The commotion and movement caused a stir in the apiary. Bees in the closest hives exited. The buzz grew louder as more bees emerged. A cloud of them swirled around Becky. But she stood still, staring at the other women. She held her head high. Even though she ran at first, she now projected a cool confidence as she waited amidst her hives.

"You people need to leave me alone!" she shouted. "And you need to leave everyone who lives here alone."

The other women backed away. Mary Jane stood as close as she dared, but her confidence waned as she eyed the swirling bees.

"All of you, just leave!" Becky shouted. "Now!"

Mary Jane gave Becky one last angry look. Then she turned and walked away.

"Did you see those bees around her?" she whispered as she walked past the others. "Was she directing them? I think she was. What is she, some sort of a witch?"

"The bees just don't consider her a threat, MJ."

Shannon placed a hand on Mary Jane's shoulder, but she brushed it away.

As they exited the field, they noticed a line of women from the farm. Many of them carried farm tools and sticks, and they walked in their direction. The visitors panicked and rushed to their car. Shannon accelerated back onto the road, looking in her rear-view mirror.

"Did you see that? Did you see it?" Mary Jane demanded. "Those women. They had weapons, right? We came there to talk and those women carried weapons and threatened us!"

There were murmurs of agreement.

"But you threw rocks at her, MJ. Did you think the others weren't going to defend her?"

But Mary Jane repeated her claim. "They outright threatened us!"

Shannon relaxed a bit as they drove. She steered the car toward the village. "Well," she said, "whatever happened back there, we know that place has become a force to be reckoned with. This is no longer about asking them nicely to leave. This has become more complicated."

"Actually," Mary Jane corrected, "it may have just become easier for us. We need to file a complaint. Pure and simple, and we need to do it quickly. We'll tell the town our side of the story before they do. We went out there to talk and they picked up weapons against us."

She looked at Shannon. "Why don't you drive us directly to the police station? I want to file an official complaint. And with any luck, we can even do it through her friend, Jim Yarrow."

Mary Jane stared out the window and laughed in a way that prompted uneasy looks from the others.

"Yeah, let's see how Jim likes that!"

Chapter 41

Pheromones and Fabrications

Colonists in Massachusetts established a legal code in 1641 to outline what they deemed capital crimes. "Idolatry" was the first crime they defined. The second was "witchcraft." The Massachusetts body of laws said witches who consult with spirits should be put to death. In 1957 the General Court of Massachusetts issued an apology to the descendants of some of those executed witches.

Long-term Impact of the Salem Witch Trials, Familiar Spirit Press, 1961

Yarrow heard Tina's voice on his police radio. "Looks like something happened again out at the Bivens farm."

He scowled before answering the call. "Ten-four. Details?"

"There's a group of angry people at the town hall. They want to meet you." She hesitated, then added, "They specifically asked for you."

"Me? Why?"

"They want to file a complaint."

He felt a moment of dread, wondering how much anyone knew about his relationship with Becky. "I'm sorry, why would they only want to talk to me?"

"Something about harassment and intimidation."

"Wait Tina … what?"

"I don't know what happened, Jim. They're probably trying to get out in front of something. Just meet with them." Then she added, "I'll definitely want to hear the story afterward."

He asked a few more questions, and when he learned it was the members of the Improvement Society, he found himself driving slower. He knew whatever trouble they had with Becky would cause him even more headaches.

As he approached, he deduced the reason they asked to meet at the town hall. Mary Jane likely wanted to make it look like weight of the town government was behind them.

"Hello Officer Yarrow," Shannon called as he stepped from his car. "Do you want to join us inside?"

"Actually, I can't. I need to stay near my radio in case I get a call."

Both Shannon and Mary Jane looked miffed.

Mary Jane stepped forward. "We want to file a report, Jim. We were threatened by a group of women out at the Bivens farm. They followed us with sticks and farm tools. It was pretty scary."

"Really?"

"Absolutely."

"Well, that does sound scary. Did this happen on the farm property? Or off?"

The members of the group looked at each other.

"We were returning to our cars," Shannon replied.

"So, on the property?"

"Yes."

"Okay." Yarrow took out his notebook. "So where were you when these women threatened you?"

They hesitated and exchanged more looks.

"I'll have to interview the folks at the farm too, so it's best to be as honest and detailed as you can."

"We were out in the field, Jim. Near the beehives."

"I see. Just so I understand the setting, were you near the edge or the middle?"

"Closer to the middle."

"I see." He made a few scribbles. "So, it sounds like you were past the signs that say only employees of the farm can enter the apiary? That's the field with all the hives."

Shannon started to answer, but Mary Jane interrupted. "I don't know about any signs. If they're there, we didn't see them."

"Okay. Well, if you go out there again, you can look for them. They stand right next to the no trespassing signs."

There was silence. Yarrow started to close his notebook, but Mary Jane stepped forward.

"You need to take our statement. And you need to arrest Becky Bivens. We demand it."

Yarrow shrugged. "Arresting her could be an option. I guess we'll see. Now, tell me what she did. Did she threaten you? Brandish a weapon?"

"No," Shannon volunteered. "Like we said, it was her workers. It happened while we were walking back toward the road. But she directed the workers. I mean, she had some sort of control."

"Okay. What did she say?"

"I feel like you aren't taking this seriously, Jim! Do we need to talk to another officer?"

"I don't know. Do you want to? I can ask them to send someone else. I'm not sure who's available this evening."

The group huddled together. Yarrow could only hear murmurs as they talked. But he did hear someone suggest dropping their complaint.

When Mary Jane turned back toward him. He saw that she was seething.

"I don't know what's going on with you Jim, but I know we were threatened out there. And there was something even worse. It was what she did with the bees. It was the strangest thing. They swarmed around her, yet they weren't attacking her. It was like she had them under some spell. Then they swarmed toward us in a threatening way. It was creepy. She's a dangerous woman."

"They weren't swarming," Yarrow said.

"What? They most certainly were too."

"No, no. Wrong word. Swarming is when a group of bees leave a hive together, looking for a new place to live. I learned that from Becky. What you saw was a group of bees that sensed danger. They came out to protect themselves and their hives."

"Damn it, I don't care what word you use, Jim. She was directing them."

"Huh. Well, if they didn't attack her, but seemed wary of you, they must have sensed a threat. I'll bet they were releasing pheromones and stoking each other up. I just learned about that recently too. It's their own warning system."

"For God's sake, Jim."

He looked back and forth between Mary Jane and Shannon. "Were you threatening them? Or maybe threatening Becky?"

"We most certainly were not threatening anyone. They just decided to attack, and we think it's strange they didn't attack her."

"Okay. Let's go back to the beginning. Why were you all at the farm?"

"We wanted to talk with her."

"And she ran out to the middle of the apiary? Then her workers gathered nearby?" He frowned and gave them an inquisitive look. "You know, I'm getting the feeling maybe she didn't want to talk."

Mary Jane pointed at him and uttered a string of swear words. He just closed his notebook.

The town hall stood near a busy part of Main Street, and people in the village heard the commotion. Soon a dozen people leaned on a nearby fence, watching and listening. When Mary Jane saw them, her demeanor changed. Yarrow had stymied her efforts, but she could play to the audience instead. She started talking louder and making broad gestures.

"I don't care what you say, Officer Yarrow. Becky Bivens was most assuredly directing those bees. We all saw it. I'm starting to think she may be some kind of a witch. She's learned how to harness the power of those bees and she sicced them on us. I'll bet she sent them after that Webster boy too. She is in league with the devil and a huge menace to this town!"

Yarrow let her rant but took no additional notes. Mary Jane didn't even notice. Her new goal was to warn the local citizens about mysterious behavior and strange dangers.

When she was through her audience left and he motioned for Mary Jane to accompany him back to his cruiser. He was angry but tried not to show it. He kept his voice even and businesslike.

"What are you doing MJ? Claiming she has some special power? Be careful with that. It could make you look ridiculous. And it's disrespectful to the Webster boy and his family."

"I'm not worried, Jim."

"I know you don't even believe what you're saying. Witchcraft? Controlling the bees? That's not like you. What the hell?"

She spoke quietly, through clenched teeth. "It doesn't matter what I believe. What matters is what others believe. What matters is what they talk about. You saw them listening. A few will believe it. They'll talk and others will parrot their words."

He climbed into his car and cranked down the window. "Then what? Are you planning to go full Joan of Arc on her?" His voice grew louder, despite his efforts to control it.

"Confused and frightened people can be quite useful, Jim. Churches and kings taught us that. If we get some scared people on our side and we can force the Bivens plague from our town."

"You're dispic—"

"Stop, Jim," she interrupted. "I am so disappointed you chose to support that woman. You were born here. We are your people. We have the political influence in this town, not them." Then she whispered, "I have it on good authority you're on thin ice as far as keeping your job."

"You know nothing."

He started to shift the car, then stopped. "She hasn't broken any laws you know. But you? You lie every time your lips move."

"And you're blind. She's already in deep trouble. Running scams. Allowing women to sell themselves. Accounting fraud. My God, she's broken so many laws I can't count them. And you're guilty by association."

Yarrow halted the conversation there. He didn't agree with Mary Jane, but he knew some of what she said was true. He had failed to be discreet.

He muttered to himself and slapped the shift through its gears as he drove away. *Witchcraft? That's the story you want to push? You can just go to hell, MJ.*

Chapter 42

Alliances

Some well-established families seem to yearn for a bygone era—when churches and social groups supported and sheltered society's weakest members. But that era was a myth. Those charities could never be that generous. Demand always outstripped supply and distribution was politically manipulated.

Where Charities Fail, First Grace Press, 1968

Infuriated by his confrontation with Mary Jane, Yarrow drove aimlessly for the rest of his shift. Sometimes, that's what cops do—they just cruise and wait for the next call.

He paid minimal attention to the buildings that rolled past. He knew standing up to Mary Jane could make things worse. She craved a confrontation and knew an open confrontation would draw public scrutiny.

And that was his dilemma. Silence wasn't working but fighting back carried even larger risks.

When his shift ended, he drove to the farm and found Becky working in the field. He waved as he walked toward her. She leaned on her rake.

"Hey stranger," she said.

"Hi. Um …" He paused there. He came ready to vent about his encounter with the Improvement Society, but he realized he and Becky hadn't really talked since they made love on that delta sandbar.

"I was worried you were avoiding me."

"No, no. Of course not."

She smiled at him. "Good."

"I'm glad it happened Becky. I really am. I think we both needed that."

She gave him a wink.

"And I came because I heard about what happened when MJ and her supporters came out to confront you," he said. "Hopefully nothing got tipped over this time?"

"Not this time."

She was cleaning out an abandoned hive. He helped her rake up a bushel full of dirty honeycomb and dead bees. They dumped it in the high grass below the field. As he worked, she noticed his preoccupation and simmering anger.

"I take it someone tried to rope you in again?"

"Huh? Oh." He looked sheepish. "Yes. It was all the RIS people. I was asked to arrest you. But I think I headed it off."

She looked stoic. "I'm sure you tried. But no. They're not going to stop. I'll just have to stay calm and try not to take their bait."

"That will be tough."

"Perhaps. But I'm in a better position than I was a few weeks ago. In many people's eyes, I run a legitimate business. The farm stand is always open and busy. People see our brand in stores and diners. Some people don't look beyond that." She smiled at him. "Also, I keep myself fairly isolated from what the residents are doing. Trying to blame everything on me could be more challenging than they think."

They checked other hives, then went to the tent where the honey jars were filled. Inside was a workbench and a pegboard with a variety of honey-scraping tools. An old photo of Franklin Roosevelt was pinned with a thumbtack.

He helped her pour unfiltered honey into a funnel-like sieve that screened out any lingering wax and dirt. Then he slid jars underneath, watching each one fill. When the oozing honey reached the top, he'd swap in other bottles. The task was slow, steady, and surprisingly satisfying.

"I'm not sure you can stay isolated," Yarrow warned. "I learned something scary about MJ today. We already know she's a liar, but if her people can't win, she has no problem creating even bigger lies. Like, bigger than I've ever heard from her. Her crew will tell wild stories, hoping each lie will bring a few more people over to their side."

"What did you hear?"

He told her about Mary Jane's town hall rant and how she accused Becky of being a witch and having the ability to make bees bend to her will.

Becky laughed at the idea but Yarrow felt she was ignoring an oncoming train and found her reticence concerning.

"I think you should at least get a court order against MJ. Keep her away. Maybe you can even sue her for libel."

Becky took his hands in hers, holding them tight with dirty and sticky fingers.

"Oh, Jim, you make it sound so easy. But do you know what would happen if I filed a lawsuit? It would shine a spotlight into places that frankly, I don't want people to see."

"Really? Why not?"

She gave him a puzzled look, then looked away. "I think you know."

"The way you do your accounting? Or your history?"

"Such as it's known."

He had his ideas. But he chose to remain silent about that and waited for her to explain. Instead, she changed the subject.

"I will say this; if I'm asked, I will tell people I have no actual concept of what a witch is or what one supposedly does. But the fact that I even need to deny such claims is bizarre."

"Agreed. But they want to push you. Maybe you should go on offense rather than playing defense."

She tapped the sieve and let the final bit of honey trickle through. Yarrow filled it again.

"In their eyes, I'm not even a traditional farmer. When they see me living mostly outside and spending my time immersed in these fields and trees, it confounds them. When they see me giving shelter to the very women they seek to shame and exclude? That baffles them too. This place seems wicked to them, and I know I will continue to be the type of person that worries them."

Yarrow could tell Becky was speaking from a deeply personal place. Her actions were the essence of how she lived her life.

She grasped a newly filled jar and held it high. "Look at this wonder! Why would anyone *not* want to spend their time in nature? Why not be someone who nurtures creatures and people? They're all building their empires, yet they have no interest in understanding the ways of plants and seeds. I prefer to nurture. But to them that somehow makes me someone to be feared."

Yarrow saw tears forming in her eyes. He hugged her and listened. They eventually ran out of jars and allowed the filtered honey to pour into steel buckets.

"I just feel that's why all of us are here," she continued. "We all live in this incredible place and time, and some of us just need …" She stopped and leaned against the table. It was the first time Yarrow ever thought she seemed weary and beaten.

"I don't know what to say, Becky."

"I am just a human being on this earth. I'm part of it. Living it, just like every other plant and animal we see. I try to treat people and things as important pieces of a much greater whole. And doesn't that make the world a better and healthier place? I think it does, and that's the difference between Mary Jane and me."

He helped her lift five gallons of filtered honey up to the tabletop. They covered it with tin foil.

"I don't think Mary Jane is even capable of understanding your point of view. It's a foreign concept. To her, everything is about winning, and that means others must lose."

Becky started to clean up. "In her case, it's also about revenge."

He stayed with her for a few hours, then headed home after midnight.

People like Mary Jane don't just want to be in charge, he concluded. *They want to be the ultimate authority as to whether someone like Becky can even exist.*

As he pulled into his driveway, he thought about where he was. He thought of Salem, and its witch trials.

Back then, it was easy to label someone you didn't like as a witch. Then they could be eliminated.

They don't sell the truth, he thought as he climbed from his car. *They sell a myth of their own making, and then the myth becomes a weapon.*

Chapter 43

Where We stand

Convex mirrors emerged along with the expansion of glass blowing during Europe's Renaissance period. These mirrors became popular throughout the continent and then migrated west across the Atlantic. English colonists seemed to fancy them, while some French settlers called them "L'Oeil du sorcier," or "The Sorcerer's Eye."

Teaching Glass to Curve, GH Press, 1934

With no family around, Yarrow found himself returning to old habits, including one from his bachelor days. He gulped down his morning cornflakes while leaning over his kitchen sink. But mostly, he took his breakfasts at Rocco's grill. It was a nice way to start the day. Sometimes Leon stopped by.

Yarrow slid onto his usual stool next to Leon and uttered his usual question. "Tell me today's wisdom Rocco."

"No wisdom today, Jim. But maybe you can get some from Becky? I hear she's a witch."

"Siccing those bees on people," Leon added. "Now that's a talent."

"How about you both pipe down with that."

Rocco grinned as he carried plates of bacon and eggs to one of the tables.

When Rocco was gone, Yarrow asked Leon how his reading was progressing.

"You know, it's a little bit better each week. I gave you a lot of grief when you wanted to teach me. But I'm glad of where I am now. Makes life easier in a lot of ways."

"That makes me happy to hear, Leon. But I'm also afraid I can't offer you much more. You've reached the end of my skills for teaching, which were meager to begin with."

"It's okay. I'm spending more time at the library now. I think that's my next step; to learn there."

Rocco returned with a somber look. "Okay, you want wisdom? Here you go. I know you've been angry about the way people treat Becky. But I don't think Becky gives much thought at all to the people who oppose her. She's faced opposition her whole life. To her, those people are just temporary annoyances. Like gnats."

"I am going to push back on that one. I've seen her upset. To tears even. It all affects her."

"Oh, no doubt. But it's like when someone taps on one of her bee hives. The reaction is genuine but short-lived. There's some buzzing. But then things settle down. The minor annoyance has passed."

"Huh."

"The next time you see her, I bet she won't even mention it. It's people like MJ who live in a fog of anger and resentment, not Becky." He stopped to stack a few juice glasses. "But, hey. That's today's limited wisdom."

Yarrow leaned back. "I certainly hope she's paying more attention than that. The people allied against her will take advantage if she stops being vigilant."

Rocco shook his head. "You've gotten too close, Jim. You know that. Your relationship is affecting what you see."

"Nope."

"Jim, come on," Leon added. "Like hell it's not affecting you. You're spending a lot of time with her out there. Your wife is gone. We're not idiots."

He shrugged.

"I do admire what she does," Leon added. I do like that she helps so many people. But she's a powder keg, and you're right on top of it."

"Whatever."

"You have feelings for her," Rocco said.

"I do."

"Come on. Don't brush it off. Let's explore it."

"Oh, God. I'm leaving." Leon asked.

"Stay put," said Yarrow. "I think maybe we'll hear another Rocco parable? We both usually love those."

Rocco held up a finger. "Maybe you find some of them fun. But I'm not sure if you're going to like this one."

Yarrow looked skeptical. Then curious.

"You know, Jim, I've been trying to picture what you actually see when you look at Becky. As opposed to what others see. Especially someone like MJ."

"Go on."

Leon chuckled. "You know, given the jobs she's hired me for, and what I've seen, I know what I think of her."

They both looked at him. "What's that? Yarrow asked cooly.

"I see a woman who's trying. Against long odds. My parents had their problems, and I still consider them honest, even if they had to steal an occasional loaf of bread or a gallon of milk."

"Yeah. I'd agree," Yarrow said.

Rocco held up a finger. "And I'm going to say I don't think it's possible for us to gain a clear picture of Becky. There is no single way to view her."

Yarrow rolled his eyes.

"Stick with me here. I've been thinking of a silly metaphor, but I think it's appropriate."

"You think too much."

"Stick with me here. Let's picture a convex mirror. You know, like those round ones people hang in their foyers? Often, with lights or candles hanging on either side."

"My grandmother had one of those," Leon recalled.

"The mirrors are convex in the front because that helps reflect and disperse the light."

"Yeah, I know what they look like."

"Anyway, if you stand directly in front of one of those mirrors the reflection looks somewhat normal. There's a bit of a fisheye look and distortion around the edges, but what you see when you stand in front still makes sense."

"I'm with you so far."

"Now think about how the view changes if you move to one side. Looking from that angle, the distortion increases. Now most of us understand the mirror's shape is what causes the distortion. But for others, when they stand to the left or the right, the reflection they see looks wrong to them. They don't like it."

"Okay," said Yarrow. But he was not sure where the tale was headed.

"So, let's think about their reaction. The mirror is designed for a specific purpose, so the problem isn't the mirror. It's their viewpoint. Moving back to the middle could give them a less distorted view of the reflection, but some people are incapable of moving or adjusting. They prefer to stand to the far left or far right and then blame the mirror for giving them a skewed perspective."

"Why?"

"Lots of reasons. Maybe one particular spot is the place where they've always stood. Maybe it's where their friends and family stand. For whatever reason, they stay where they are, and they blame the mirror. They feel like everything it reflects is wrong."

Yarrow laughed. "Why don't they just walk away?"

"Exactly! Why don't they? Why should they even care about the reflection? Why should they care about Becky? Because some people become obsessed with the distorted views they have. If things don't look right from where they stand, they never think their own views might be the problem. Coming back to the center is never even considered."

Yarrow thought about it. "Okay. Interesting take. And people can have wildly different views. So, some see her as a savior, others as a threat."

Rocco was silent for a moment. "Yes." He held up a finger. "But."

"But … what?"

"Sticking with this overburdened little metaphor, I wasn't actually thinking of Becky as being a reflection in the mirror. I was thinking of her as the mirror itself. What you see in her says more about you than it does about her."

"Umm ..."

"Let's keep going." Rocco leaned forward again. His voice dropped to a whisper. "People who stand on the right see a woman who threatens the status quo. In their minds, everything she does affects their businesses, their property values, or their banks. In her, they see a threat to everything they define as progress."

Leon nodded. Yarrow just rubbed his chin.

"If you move even farther to the right, the view of Becky distorts even more. If you're extremely financially conservative, the people she's helping look parasitic. If you're deeply religious, she looks like a sinner. You may even see her as someone who could lure your children toward hell. She represents sex and gambling and every vice people crave."

Yarrow raised his eyebrows. "I don't think so."

"Hold on. Now, let's go back to the center, and this time we move to the left instead. Just a little to the left at first. From there, Becky might look like someone who's helping women, but it may seem like she's exploiting them too. After all, she does make money from their labor. And some may feel she's ignoring the dangers and humiliation that comes with the sorts of 'services' her tenants offer."

Yarrow and Leon looked at each other. Leon's look was half smirk and half acknowledgement.

"Now," Rocco continued, "move even farther left? You'd think Becky would look great from there, right? But instead, to some on the left, Becky looks like someone who complicates and threatens the social safety nets leftists have been trying to build for generations. I mean all the things the left has pushed for. Unions. Work hour limits. Minimum wages. Welfare. She isn't part of those efforts. To some, she may even look like one of those company towns where employees are required to live in the town. To those people, Becky is more like an anarchist than a savior. Some may even see her as a laissez-faire capitalist."

"Or God knows what else," Leon added.

"Exactly. It's the eye of the beholder. So, since you asked earlier, I guess my parable is that, left or right, up or down, when people look at the distorted mirror-that-is-Becky Bivens, what they see depends almost entirely on where they're already standing. Their preconceived notions about what's right, wrong, or acceptable can have a huge impact on how they react to her."

"I think you're saying none of those views should be considered the single, correct one?" Leon asked.

"Exactly. She remains inscrutable."

"Okay. So …" Yarrow started to say something. But his voice trailed off.

"So, what's the answer? I don't know, Jim. I really don't. But we've heard you singing the 'I don't know' refrain too, right? Today, none of us are any closer to an answer."

"Huh."

Leon gave Yarrow a pat on the shoulder. "I think what Rocco is saying is this. No one sees the real Becky, Jim. Probably not even you."

Chapter 44

Rain on the Roof

Do not let contempt move into your home. If it does, one of you will need to leave.

Tales of the Esherwood, Pigmart Press, 1880

On most Sunday evenings, Yarrow talked to his kids by phone. They liked to chat about all that was new in their lives.

His daughter Bonnie was too young to carry on a full conversation. But she would say little heart-melting things. He would ask questions and encourage her. He heard about …

New tooth. Red slippers. Funny doggie.

She would blurt out answers with a toddler's logic, and it made him laugh. And that made him miss the kids even more.

Sometimes Curtis and Tommy would tell him about the pick-up baseball games they'd play with neighbor boys. They'd also ask him when they could come home.

"You all can come home any time you want," he said. "And I wish you would."

That answer didn't sit well with Linda.

One evening, after he said good night to the kids, Linda took the receiver. He heard some muffled words being exchanged between her and her mother.

"I am. I know! Yes, right now. Jeez."

She asked him to hang on. He heard footsteps and pictured her mother's phone. The bulky black Western Electric unit was mounted on the kitchen wall, with a ringer box mounted below. There was a curly cord that could stretch long enough to allow her to take the hand set to another room. He heard a door close.

"Hi," she said.

"Hi, Linda. How are you?"

There was a long hesitation. "I'm well. And you, Jim?"

He hesitated too. "I'm ... I'm doing okay Linda. It's always nice talking to the kids."

They made small talk for a bit, and then she dropped her bomb. She was giving him a deadline of one month to move up to Maine. Then she was planning to file for divorce.

"My God, Linda, so soon? Is that really what you want?"

"No, Jim. It's not."

"I don't either. So why do it? No one is asking for this."

He pleaded and argued. He said divorce didn't make sense. But he also didn't want to move, and he sure as hell didn't want to live with her mother. At some point he heard Linda having another muffled conversation. After that, their call ended with raised voices and angry words.

But Linda got in one last dig. "You know, Jim, I don't think you should come up here for your next visit. It's not a good time." Then she hung up.

After the call, Yarrow paced for a long time. If he went to bed he knew he would never sleep.

Even though Linda left the door open, ever so slightly, for reconciliation, there was a troubling finality to her words. Clearly, he was being blocked from having any influence on the major decision of where the family should live.

He went to the sink and poured himself a big glass of water.

He found it troubling that her ultimatum came so soon, especially since he always updated her on his job applications. He even told her about a potential patrolman's job that might open up just twenty miles from her mom. But they couldn't hire him until another officer retired, and that would be nine months.

Yarrow wandered through his house in a dumbfounded state. He sat at his kitchen table. He made himself something to eat but barely touched it.

Eventually he put his robe on over his clothes, poured himself a stiff drink and started to walk through the garage to his best thinking place—the balcony.

But he never made it. Still wearing his robe, he found himself climbing into his car. Drink in hand, he drove with no clear destination. When it started to rain, he turned on the windshield wipers and kept going. Before he knew it, his car was on the road that led to Becky's place.

He turned his lights off before entering the lot. He also killed the engine, allowing the car to coast to a stop. Then he sat. He watched raindrops as they danced and gathered until they ran down the glass. The world outside grew blurred and abstract. Dark clouds blocked the stars.

He wasn't sure why he was there. Now he had to choose what to do next.

After several minutes, he decided to turn around and head home. But at that moment he saw a shape approaching. The rain and dim light made it difficult to see.

There was a tap. Becky's blurred face appeared at his window. He hesitated, then rolled it down.

"I heard someone pull in. I saw your car."

He nodded.

"Are you all right?"

He started to nod again, but then he shook his head. "Things aren't good. I talked with Linda."

"Can I get in?"

"Let me come out." He stepped into the rain and stood beside the car.

"I must look comical in this robe." He suddenly felt like he didn't know what to do with his hands. Then Becky embraced him. He slowly lifted his arms to hug her.

"You're all tense, Jim. I can feel it." They just stood together, and let the drops run down their faces.

"Come with me."

She took his hand and led him to the bakery truck. They climbed through the rusty back door and he sat on one of the stools at her built-in table. Becky poured water from a big jug into a tea kettle and lit the burner on her camp stove.

He told her about his phone call with Linda and her threat of divorce. He lamented the finality of her words, then hesitantly admitted his intense feeling of failure. He tried to describe it. "It's like floating in Limbo. Nothing has actually ended. Yet, everything feels like it's eroding."

When the water boiled, she made two cups of tea and settled on the other stool.

He spoke honestly with her and admitted to still feeling a sense of love for Linda. "I am so glad to have reconnected with you Becky. I carried you in my heart and mind for a long time. But I can't just shut off what I feel for Linda. She had become my anchor here. And I do sense there is still some level of love reflecting back from her.

"Has that diminished?" Becky asked.

"I think it's still there, but it's been cut to pieces and scattered. It's a jigsaw puzzle of a relationship now, and I can't make the pieces fit."

She reached over and patted his hand.

"I don't know what to do Becky. And I don't want to hurt you either."

"I know, Jim. You're in a difficult place."

He tried to speculate on what might come next. But the words fell short. Too much remained unknowable. He stopped talking and looked at the truck's interior. It was so small, yet she seemed so happy here. Her bed sat to one side, like a coiled snake he knew he should avoid.

With nothing left to say, he decided words could just go to hell for a while.

Things grew quiet between them. They just stared at each other. Eye contact. Pursed lips.

"You need to give a lot of thought to what you want to do. This is your life, Jim, and your crossroads. I know there's an anguish that comes from having to choose."

"Yes."

"And any choice will have its lasting scars."

He looked at the floor. "I know that too."

Then he looked up at her.

He took her by the hand and led her to the bed. The kissing started before they fell. Because their clothes were wet from the rain, they had to pause to help each other peel off the clinging layers.

The embrace, when they returned to it, was welcoming. And ravenous. He had assumed their encounter at the river would be a one-off thing. But now things were different. In each other, they found something that was both old and new. And growing.

Her bed, primitive as it was, was large enough, and soft enough for two. It let them disappear into each other. The tapping of the rain on the metal roof became part of a rhythm. And into that, they settled.

Chapter 45

What We Pretend to Be

"The way officers support and enforce the law varies too greatly from town to town or state to state. I've looked, but I have never found any level of universal functioning across police systems. I have respect for individual, fearless, and honest officers. But the system as a whole is too easy to corrupt and incredibly challenging to fix."

Post-retirement letters between Officer Ralph Michaels and Officer Roland Freberg, 1959

They lay in bed and watched the sky grow brighter out the truck windows.

In time the rain softened. Birds announced dawn's arrival and hints of pink appeared through the truck's back windows. Becky leaned on her elbow and slowly drew a finger through Yarrow's chest hair. He closed his eyes. Her touch felt genuine and honest.

Eventually he smiled and she whispered, "Ah, you're awake."

"Kind of hard to sleep with you doing that."

She kissed him, jumped out of bed, and walked naked to her stove. Their morning coffee would be primitive and strong. She lit the flame under a pan of water and scooped in the grounds.

As he watched, Yarrow realized Becky was no longer as rail thin as she seemed just weeks ago. She looked healthier now. She looked good.

He said so, but with a wave of her hand, she dismissed his comment.

"Fine," he responded. "I'm just telling you what I see."

"When I look at you, do you know what I see?"

"Uh-oh."

"Don't worry. It's good. I see a man with integrity and compassion. And I truly mean that. You've certainly helped me. You protect the town and before this, you were a soldier. You've always been a man who can see what needs to be done, and then you do it. That's the mark of good character."

He considered her words. "Maybe you're giving me too much credit. Look at me. Still married, yet here I am, lying in your bed." He stared at the ceiling. "All I did was fall off the fidelity wagon."

"Nonsense." She reached to stroke his hair. "You've lost family members. You're separated now and that was not your choice. You're separated from your kids too. Again, not by your choice. So here, right now, you're lonely, stressed, and in need of a friend. Despite all that, you still get up and go to work every day. Give yourself some credit."

He looked at her. "Thank you."

"You're welcome. But you may feel differently when I say one more thing."

A moment later she was next to him on the bed, lying on her back. He could feel her warmth beside him. "A person's character becomes their destiny," she said. "That's not my saying. It's from some Greek philosopher. It was also used on a Marine recruitment poster."

"It probably worked."

"So, let me say this, Jim: I worry about your destiny."

"You do? How so?"

"Partially because of your job. You're a good man. Always try to do what's right. But as a police officer, you have a job that can take its toll."

"This is Riverbend, Becky. It's not Boston or New York. I see maybe two stressful things per year."

She glanced at him. He knew that look, and the intensity behind her eyes.

"I'm talking about who you work for. I'm talking about the long-term repercussions."

"Not sure I'm following."

"You represent the law and all the power behind it. This is a nice town, where most people feel safe and successful. They're all remarkably similar to each other. You represent and enforce the power of this place and the inclinations of its people."

He blinked. "I guess you're not wrong."

"Like a lot of towns, Riverbend is built around a certain status quo. Minimal accommodation is made for anyone who seems different. As the law, you enforce that whether you realize it or not."

He frowned but didn't interrupt.

"When people lack inclusion, they try to look for it elsewhere. But that's a challenge. So, I guess I'm their safety net for now."

He rolled to face her. "That's what you think? That I'm enabling bad treatment of people? Come on Becky." He wasn't happy with her assessment. But he also knew he'd never considered it from that perspective.

"I just want you to think about it. That's all. In larger cities, the police become much more jaded. Sometimes even ruthless. Their support for the entrenched powers is more obvious and they do their job efficiently."

"I don't think that's—"

"Working here in Riverbend, you've been able to play the good guy for a long time. You help old ladies and catch dogs. You take accident reports. It gives you a sense of virtue. But that won't last as this town grows. So anyway, that's why I worry about your destiny. In the future, your choices may become starker."

He said nothing. But he did put his arm around her.

As she cuddled up, she added, "Even good cops support the established rule, Jim. That's part of enforcement. But it can't ever be fair to all. Last night we talked about the mental and physical scars that can come from one's choices. Well, being a cop could create some lasting ones."

He gave her a pat on the shoulder. "You don't need to be concerned. And I know you work hard to help people and stoke change. To be honest, I think I've helped you get away with a lot."

"You have, Jim. But it can't always be so."

He kissed her forehead. "There's nothing to worry about yet. Believe it or not, I do still know the difference between right and wrong."

"Perhaps. But the choice may not always be as obvious as you think."

Then she lowered her head and let it rest on his shoulder.

Chapter 46

Required Myths

Shared myths can serve as a society's "common knowledge." The myths represent something people want to be true. Anyone who seeks acceptance by a group may first need to embrace their myths.

When Myths Start to Matter, Parallax Publishing, 1969

Yarrow was about to start his shift when the chief called him into his office. He took a seat across from his desk as the boss slowly closed the door.

"Am I in trouble?"

There was silence for several seconds, then the chief looked Yarrow in the eyes.

"Not exactly. But, let me cut right to it. Are you familiar with a group called Riverbend Improvement Society?"

"Oh, Jesus. They've made sure that everyone in town is familiar with them."

"Usually, I try not to pay too much attention to these amateur citizen's groups. I have enough trouble keeping track of all the official government agencies."

"Did they file some sort of complaint?"

"No, but they keep asking me to meet with them. I'm at a loss as to how to respond."

"Maybe you don't have to respond?"

The chief laughed. "I think it would be highly prudent, so I called you in here to get your advice. But first, let me share something with you. Some folks in that group seem particularly angry with you. Maybe we should make that part of today's chat."

"Sorry if it's causing you concern."

The chief dismissed the comment. "Look, someone in town is always pissed off at one of our officers, and sometimes they're mad at the whole department. We deal with it." He tapped a dog-eared manila folder on his desk. From what I've seen, you've played it by the book so far with this group. I mean, you should have taken their statement about that so-called attack at the farm, even though we both know their claim was garbage. But let's table that. There's something else I want to understand."

The chief toyed with his pen, then got to the point. "I guess what I'm looking for is to learn more about the main players. Let's start with Mary Jane Danforth and Becky Bivens. Each one seems to intensely dislike the other. From what I hear, you know both of them."

"I do."

"So, lay it out for me."

Yarrow crossed his arms and leaned back. "How far back do you want me to go?"

"Hell, I don't know. Enough so things make sense?"

Yarrow gave a brief history, including how they'd all known each other since high school. He mentioned how Mary Jane was always manipulative, even to the point of flirting with people to get her way. He talked about briefly dating Becky back in the day, then explained how she disappeared, and how the collapse of MJ's family-owned savings bank triggered her long-term hatred of the Bivens family.

The chief listened intently, then held up a finger. "All of that is useful to hear. Especially the part about the bank. Mary Jane has been a major thorn in my side, so that explains a lot. But I think you're sidestepping important points. So, let me be blunt."

"Okay."

"Is Becky committing any sort of crimes out there?"

"Crimes sir?"

"Don't dance around the issue, Seargent. I'm talking theft, prostitution, financial issues, anything."

"Her personally? I don't think so."

"I mean anything at all, by anyone."

Yarrow bit his lip and thought for a moment. "Frankly, I don't know sir. As for financial stuff, some people believe she's managing a legitimate pool of investments, while others say her transactions are suspicious. If you want a financial crimes investigation, our department isn't equipped for that. That would be one for the county boys and the courts."

"Fair enough. And if the complaints continue, I do plan to seek help from the county or state. So far I haven't seen enough to take that step." Then the chief shifted his voice to a more serious tone. "But what about the other complaints, Jim? What about prostitution?"

Yarrow shrugged. "Like I said, I don't know. For Becky? No. I don't know much about the other girls."

"Don't you?"

Yarrow looked away for a bit, then looked back. "How old are you now, Chief?"

"What the hell does that have to do with anything?"

"Just humor me for a minute."

The chief looked impatient. "I guess I'm about ten years older than you."

"Okay, then you certainly remember the camps full of unemployed people that happened during the Great Depression. Bums, hobos, wanderers. People who didn't have a home tended to gather in places where no one bothered them. Those were never nice places. There were always criminal elements there, and people did shady things to survive."

"Of course I remember. You couldn't miss them."

"We like to think Hoovervilles are part of the past. That's partially true. American businesses have done well since the end of the war. Most of the old encampments have faded away. But down-and-out people still exist in this country, and they still need places to live."

"Yeah," the chief replied, "and I know Becky is letting people camp there. And that's a problem. We get calls every week demanding that we go out and shag every single camper out of those tents and huts."

"You haven't done that though."

"No. And here's why. Since it's mostly women and children, her shanty town is unique. Busting that place up, without giving the residents someplace else to go, would spark a nasty controversy. I'm talking front page of the Boston papers. So, that's one reason we're waiting."

"Well, thank you for that."

"But you know shutting them down could happen at some point."

"I understand."

The boss started fidgeting with his pen again.

"So, is that why you wanted to talk with me, Chief?"

"Partially. But like I said, these pretentious Riverbend Improvement Society folks have asked to meet with me. I'm not sure I should."

"I can understand your reluctance."

"That's why I'm going to send you instead."

Yarrow threw up his hands. "What? Come on Chief, don't throw me to those crazies. They already don't like me. They think I'm a supporter of Becky's."

"Are you?"

Yarrow rubbed his forehead. "I support her efforts to help people. The other stuff? Um … I don't know."

The chief could see Yarrow was struggling. So he interrupted. "Look. I'm asking you to do this because I think you might be able to have a positive impact. And I think you could help diffuse the tension."

"I appreciate the vote of confidence, Chief. But I'd have the opposite effect. I'd just make things more complica—"

The chief cut him off. "Enough. Just tell them I've appointed you as our police liaison to the group. Go listen to their concerns. Feel free to mention whatever good or bad things you can think of about the farm. I'm sure they'll argue with you, and that's how you'll learn what they think and what they all plan to do. Let's meet after that. Have a report ready."

Yarrow rose to leave. "Fine," he said.

"One more thing Yarrow."

"Hum?"

"What's really going on with you and Becky? Enlighten me."

"I'm a married man, Chief."

The chief chuckled. "Okay, let's leave it for now. Why don't you make those details part of your report?"

"Like hell I will."

Back at his desk, Yarrow decided to reach out to Shannon Gates. He didn't feel like talking to Mary Jane and Shannon seemed more rational.

She answered on the third ring and was startled to learn they would not be meeting with the chief.

"Okay," Shannon said. "If that's the way it must be. We'd like to meet this afternoon if possible. Let's meet on that hill across the street from the farm."

"Why there?"

"It's Mary Jane's idea. We can get a broader view from there and point to what we see."

That made him uneasy, but he agreed.

He hung up and planned his approach. *If I meet with them alone, I'll be at a disadvantage. I should bring some support.*

Calling Rocco's Grill during the day was always a bit of a gamble. If it was noisy, no one could hear the phone. But he let it chime a dozen times. Rocco eventually picked it up.

"Hey, Rocco. Are you working alone today? Or is that new waitress there?"

"Peggy is here. Why?"

"I need your help for a little mission." He explained why he wanted Rocco to tag along, and asked if he could find Leon too.

"Sure, Jim. Happy to go with you."

"Thanks. You guys won't be there in any official capacity. You're just, I don't know, observers or something."

"That's fine. But we both know you're not going to diffuse a damn thing. They only want to hear their own voices."

"I know, Rocco. But I've been asked to try. I'm just treating this as a fact-finding exercise."

They all met on the hilltop and Yarrow immediately sensed there would be trouble. As he, Rocco, and Leon approached, Mary Jane greeted them cooly. "So, I see you brought your little posse, she said." There were no handshakes. No smiles. Everyone with her just glared at them.

"So," Yarrow kicked things off, "you wanted to meet?"

"We wanted to meet with the police chief. Not you."

"Well, let's start with me. We can go from there."

Mary Jane looked at him with disdain, then pointed at the camp. "I don't understand why those people down there have not been charged with threatening us, Jim. That was a dangerous situation. Just look down there. Her thug girls were lined up along that field, ready to attack. We barely got away. Yet, your department is ignoring what happened."

"Okay."

"Honestly, Jim, I'd go over your head to the mayor, but he's as useless as the rest of you."

He looked at his friends, then faced her.

"So, here's the thing, Mary Jane … let's put the Becky discussion on hold for a moment. Let's talk about your visit. If I arrest anyone, it's going to be you. You were the ones who came to the farm, where you harassed people and made threats. You threw a rock for God's sake."

She looked taken aback. "I don't think you understand, Jim. We are not the ones in the wrong here. We are on the right side of things. End of story."

"You've made your feelings quite clear." He rubbed his forehead. "Look, you wanted to meet out here. So, let's keep talking. Just don't lie to me."

Mary Jane pointed to a different spot. "See all the stuff that's there now? Those structures don't conform to zoning laws. There's sewage just running down the hillside."

"I don't see any sewage."

"You know it's there, Jim. Where else would it go? The brothel-like behavior is obvious too. Our organization has the absolute moral and legal high ground here, and she does not."

Yarrow looked at the camp. "Moral? I'd say no. Legal? That remains to be seen."

"And that flippant response is why I asked for your chief. But I guess you can be the carrier of our message. This is the last time we'll complain to the police department. Within a week we will be filing a lawsuit to ask for a cease-and-desist order, and to ask for an investigation of your department."

Then she smiled at him. "So, if you plan to do something, do it soon. Tell your friends at the encampment they can all pack up and run away now. Or they can wait for things to go bad."

Yarrow gritted his teeth. "Tell me, MJ, where do you want these women to go?"

She looked genuinely confused. "I don't care. Just not here."

"Don't you understand? Some of those women don't speak our language or have any documentation. They came here as refugees, often from countries whose records were destroyed. And what about the American mothers who were never able to get married because the fathers never came home from war?"

A man's voice came from the rear of the group. "They should have thought of that before they got knocked up!"

Mary Jane dismissed Yarrow's comments. "Those women can get welfare help in Boston. Or Portsmouth. They need to go to a city, Jim. No one needs to bring those services out here to Riverbend."

"But this is where those people are."

"And they shouldn't be here." She emphasized her next words with a staccato rhythm. "It's. Not. Our. Problem! Only one person is trying to make it our problem, and that's Becky."

She pointed in a different direction. "Now, see over there? See the dust and the bulldozers? That's our future. Faster connections to Boston, Maine, and the whole rest of the country. We are blessed with a wonderful opportunity, but only if we shepherd things in the right way. Otherwise, we'll end up looking like the worst parts of Boston."

"I don't think that's how it works," said Rocco, weighing in for the first time.

"Yeah, thanks for your opinion, Mr. breakfast cook." Then she pointed her finger. "All of you need to understand that some people create their own personal hellholes wherever they go. You've seen rough neighborhoods, Jim. As any town gets larger, the rough places get rougher and larger. That's when you move people along. You can't give the rough places a chance to form."

Then Shannon weighed in. "Jim, I know you think you're protecting these people. But it's a place of sin. Do you really want to be known for endorsing that?"

"I'm not endorsing anything. I just want them to be able—"

"Of course you're helping support it," Mary Jane interrupted. "And it looks like you're having a good old time in the process."

Yarrow didn't like to raise his voice. But he couldn't help it. "So that's your whole plan? Label everyone a sinner or a criminal so you can cast them out? You feel good about that?" He started to step forward, but Leon held onto his arm.

Mary Jane stepped back nervously.

"And, since you brought up sin, Shannon, let's talk bible quotes. What does that book say about feeding the hungry? Or bearing one another's burdens? Do those verses not matter?"

Rocco stepped up to stand next to his friend. Leon did the same.

Mary Jane gave him a stern look that suddenly made her look ten years older. "You can't charm your way past the fact that there are some absolutes in this world, Jim. And what's happening at the farm is absolutely wrong. Your loyalties clearly lie with that woman, not with Riverbend."

Yarrow turned his back and walked away. Rocco decided to speak.

"MJ, do you know what town sits less than 30 miles from here?"

She didn't answer.

"That would be Salem, MJ. You know—the place where some self-righteous townsfolk launched their famous witch hunt in the 1690s?"

"This isn't relevant Rocco, and I'll thank you to—"

"Hold on. The whole thing in Salem started when some marginalized women were accused of witchcraft. They didn't fit well into the fabric of the town. Some were scorned because of the men they married. Some were scorned for not attending church, or for trying to control their own finances. The real issue was that they were different and not aligned with the dominant family in town. The witchcraft accusation was an easy tool to punish them for not fitting into the dominant mold."

"You are out of line."

"Am I? I have to tell you MJ, I hear a lot of echoes of Salem in your damn words. And I see you leaning on the word 'sinful' like it's a crutch."

"I call it sinful because that's exactly what it is, Mr. Rocco."

They all knew the conversation was over. Both groups departed in haste.

Once he and his friends were clear of the group, Yarrow shook his head. "That didn't go well. Screw them."

"Yup."

"Remember what I was saying earlier, Jim?" Rocco asked. "We are required to buy into and believe their myths. If not, we're called evil too."

"Yeah," Leon agreed. "And if their group gets big enough, they get to say what's right or wrong and everyone else has to play along."

Chapter 47

Town Meeting

In many New England Towns, a town meeting allows eligible residents to directly participate in a process that determines their town's governance. This differs from representative town meetings, where elected representatives hold most decision-making power.

New England Politics and Traditions, Merrimack Leadership Forum, 1960

The door at the back of the meeting hall gave a long and low squeak. Heads turned and the room grew quiet.

Jim Yarrow, sitting halfway up the center aisle, didn't need to turn. He knew who entered. He knew her by her footsteps. Murmurs spread like the wake of a boat as Becky walked past. That made him smile. He knew she would face a hostile crowd. He also knew she would meet their noise with determination and confidence.

Bivens Farm was not officially on the town meeting's agenda. But the rules said any citizen could rise to speak. New issues could be debated. The RIS made it clear they planned to raise their concerns during the meeting, and Becky came to participate.

She looked straight ahead as she reached the front row, where the seats were reserved for those who intended to speak. So far, she was the only one to sit there. The wooden chairs were uncomfortable, rickety, and over one hundred years old. But she sat quietly, unintimidated by the many eyes pointed toward her.

A minute later, the selectmen, town clerk, and the moderator who would run the meeting, filed in and took their seats. They talked quietly and waved to folks they knew. Then the gavel banged.

"I'd like to call this meeting to order," said the moderator, who also was the owner of a local grocery store. He looked at his notes and said, "The first order of business is a proposed change to the local zoning laws, parcel B28, north of Clarins Road."

Yarrow could see what the moderator was doing. If the meeting jumped right to the Bivens Farm discussion, tempers might flare. The meeting might spin out of control. Instead, by dealing with some mundane issues first, the moderator and the Select Board members could take the edge off and set a tone of moderation. At some point they would slowly ease into the meeting's most volatile issue.

The zoning discussion slowly grew more animated. Some people expressed support for a new commercial district near Clarins Road. Others lamented how the new construction meant the loss of the Riverbend they loved and remembered. The item was tabled until the next meeting.

Next on the agenda was the town budget. That conversation droned on for forty-five minutes and several people left the building.

Finally, an hour into the proceedings, the moment arrived.

"So, next ..." The moderator paused and took a deep breath, "this is the point in the town meeting where citizens can rise to speak. I know there is a group that wants to raise their concerns about the Bivens honey farm. And I see the owner Rebecca Bivens has joined us here tonight, so I'm sure she can answer your questions."

More murmurs filled the room.

"Order please!" The moderator gave a scowl, as if to drive home the serious nature of the gathering. "Before we go on, I must stress the following. No criminal or civil charges have been filed related to the things we will discuss here. I was told by the police chief an hour ago that no charges are pending." He looked around the room, nearly daring someone to disagree. "There is no supposition of guilt, but we do recognize the Improvement Society's request to speak."

He stopped to look at the crowd. "Also, anyone who speaks tonight should only talk about their own direct experiences with the farm. We don't need to hear second-hand comments like 'my neighbor said' or 'according to Joe Dokes.' If those people have a story to tell, they should be here themselves."

Yarrow saw a few people in the room nod. Most of the others just stared at the moderator or Becky.

"Also, please direct your questions and comments to me, not to each other."

He asked if there were any questions. Seeing none, he proceeded.

"All right. First, Miss Bivens, I appreciate you joining us tonight. Is there anything you would like to say as an introduction?"

She shook her head. "I see no reason to."

He nodded. "Okay then, it looks like the first person on the list is Elenore O'Day. Mrs. O'Day, can you stand?"

A fifty-year-old woman rose and nervously looked about the room.

"Go on," said the moderator.

"I ... I just want to say," Elenore began, "I don't think it's a good thing to have the Bivens Farm open again. I remember the last time it was here. I heard there were illegal activities too. So, you know, I just don't want it to be open. Let's close it."

The chairman nodded. "Okay. And?"

Mrs. O'Day shook her head. "That's all. I think I speak for, you know, a lot of people when I say I want you to close it. Thank you." Then she sat down.

The chairman rubbed his forehead, then addressed the crowd. "Once again, I will remind everyone that we are looking for specific issues, not opinions. And I'd like to stress that you should only share your personal experiences and that you are not speaking for others."

"Next up … Mr. Groveland?"

An elderly man near the middle of the room rose to speak. "Most of you know me. I used to be an accountant." He straightened a bit and stood taller. "Ayah, had my business on Main Street for thirty-five years. And I've been a deacon at the Congregational church for almost as long." All eyes in the room were now focused on him.

"I'm not here today to complain about the farm. I have no problem with someone making an honest living by selling honey or whatever. But as an accountant, what I'm most concerned about is the way Miss Bivens takes in money for her so-called honey futures. She collects that money as an investment and allows it to increase in value. But it's not clear how that happens and there is no government oversight. At least not what we've heard. So, my request is that I'd like to hear some details. Does anyone review Miss Bivens' books?"

The chairman gestured for her to respond. Becky didn't rise. She looked over her shoulder. "I'm not sure who you mean. There are people in my organization who review them. Yes."

"I mean are they reviewed by a professional? Does a CPA approve the books and are taxes filed?"

"I haven't been in business very long. So, no. None of that has happened yet."

"But you intend to?"

"I will do what all businesses are required to do, and that includes filing taxes and following our laws."

As Mr. Groveland sat down, a low grumble snaked through the crown. "That's a lie," someone called out.

"Order!" bellowed the chairman. "Everyone should address the chair and not the room." He called the next name; Mary Jane's friend, Shannon Gates. She sat near the front of the room, right behind Becky.

Shannon stood slowly and turned to face the crowd. Her back was toward Becky, effectively blocking her from the others.

"I think you all know me and you know the wonderful group I belong to. The Riverbend Improvement Society. We have been working so hard at the RIS to make this town a better place. I'm proud to say we're succeeding. You've seen the flower boxes on Main Street. We helped get sponsors for that. And we helped plant the shrubs in front of the school. Also, anyone who wants to contribute to help repair the bandstand on the common is welcome to do so."

Someone clapped and Shannon gave a satisfied smile.

"But some of you also know the Bivens Farm has become one of our biggest concerns. Rather than helping improve the town, that farm is pulling us in quite the opposite direction. Not only was a young boy tragically killed out there, but we also see people from other towns coming to visit that farm for the wrong reasons. Frankly, that place is giving Riverbend a reputation that will do nothing but hurt us.

Becky turned in her chair and watched the back of Shannon's head.

"My other concern," Shannon continued, "is with the farm property itself. There appears to be quite a tent and trailer camp growing there, full of migrants and hobos. And, for some reason, most of the camp residents are women. I'll leave you all to speculate why. Each week more people arrive. And most seem happy to live in squalor."

The moderator interrupted. "I do ask that we refrain from speculation and insults."

Shannon smiled and continued. "I won't be judgmental. I'll just say there are no real bathrooms on that site, other than temporary outhouses. There does not appear to be any heat so I'm not sure what they do on cold nights. And when winter comes? That should be interesting." She paused to watch the impact of her words.

"It's basically an unsustainable mess, and the town needs to do something about it." As she looked around, she lifted her nose into the air. "So, I'll reiterate. That encampment sends the wrong message about our town. You don't see this sort of thing happening in Newburyport, or Rockport, or Ipswich. In fact, the closest thing I can think of would be those camps that popped up after the hurricane of 1938. But even those were temporary."

Shannon dropped her voice to a whisper. "The mess out at that farm has no end-date that I can see. So, we are asking the town to do something and I'll be interested in hearing Rebecca Bivens speak about these issues.

Shannon sat down. A woman beside her gave her hand a soft pat.

Slowly, Becky rose and faced a chorus of whispers. She looked past them.

"I understand the concern," she said. "If I was in your shoes, I might even share those concerns. But I'm not in your shoes. At the moment my concerns are much more basic and frankly much more desperate."

It was her turn to pause and drive home her point.

"You talk about the danger my farm presents because a boy died there? I worry about vandalism that damages my farm and my livelihood. You talk about the town's status and property values? Well, here's what I worry about. I worry about food."

Her eyes drifted back and forth, between Mary Jane and Shannon. "I worry about shelter and the safety of the small community that's taken root at my place." She took a few steps toward the center of the room. "And I worry about the coming winter. You see, our community stands much closer to the edge of poverty and despair than most of you will ever know."

She scanned the faces, seeking a connection. Some people stared back while others looked away. "That's why I have great sympathy for the women who find their way to my farm. If they are willing to work, I always try to find a place for them. Some are simply migrant workers who will be gone in the fall. Others are young—recently released from orphanages because they turned eighteen. They don't know what to do or where to go. Some others are war widows. Many have no real experience in the world and no family."

She detected a few sympathetic looks in the room, but fewer than she hoped.

"I'd love to find a more permanent place for all of them. My farm should never be more than their temporary waypoint. I want their journey to take them toward something better." She turned her gaze toward the board members. "Who among you can help make that happen? Anyone?" She scanned the room, but she already knew no hands would raise. "Whenever I ask these questions, it's common that no one has answers. The lack of answers is the very reason our tent encampment exists."

She cast her eyes downward, nodded, and sat in her chair.

There was a moment of silence, then Mary Jane Danforth asked to speak.

"You all saw how Miss Bivens quickly turned our questions into a different discussion. She made it about the world's haves versus have-nots. So, let's bring the focus back to what's really going on out there. How many of you have shopped at Becky's farm? Have you noticed that, when you buy any products there, it's mostly just the men who are offered a chance to buy her so-called honey options? I'd like to ask the women in here, have those options ever been offered to you?"

No one spoke up.

"We do make an occasional offer," Becky said. "If we sense interest."

Nervous laughter filled the room.

Mary Jane looked disgusted and walked to the front of the room. "For some reason, her honey options always appreciate in value! Isn't that amazing? Have any of you ever seen a stock option that only goes up? But here, new money is always coming in. Word gets around. Demand goes up. That drives the price up. Isn't that a wonderful scheme?"

Mary Jane saw understanding nods but also looks of bewilderment. "Okay," she continued, "let's think. What is available out there for a man who has extra money to spend? Just honey? Just fruits and vegetables? We all know what's going on there, but the activity is hidden under layers of tent fabric and deceit."

Yarrow closed his eyes. He knew Mary Jane's posturing was just theatrics. But it would have an impact.

"Miss Danforth," the chairman stepped in, "can I remind you this meeting is about facts, not conjecture?"

"I understand. But I would not say it if it wasn't true. My son's friends were whispering about the arrangement in our living room last week. They didn't think any adults were listening. Apparently several young men from the football team went there, and they had—"

"Enough!"

"Okay. Anyway," Mary Jane continued. "Miss Bivens can dress it up any way she wants. But, somehow, she's managed to successfully build her little confidence game and its associated perversions. And she's done it all without even building a house on the site."

A few folks in the crowd cheered. The chairman banged his gavel and Yarrow looked at his feet. He wasn't sure how Becky could possibly respond.

"Miss Bivens?"

Becky rose again and turned to the crowd. Her eyes looked puffy.

"On my property, I have workers. When they work for me, I pay them to do farm chores, and that's all they do. They mainly help raise bees and package honey. They also pick and pack fruit, tend the garden, and manage the sales counter. If they don't work, they can't stay.

Just as Mary Jane had done, she moved front and center in the hall. "So, I think what you might be asking is what some of the farm residents do in their private time. And in their private spaces. My answer to that is, I don't know."

She again looked around at the faces. "People like to think we focus on illegal activities. But that's absurd. Some women sell artwork. One of them built a wood-fired oven so she could bake and sell bread and cookies. Others will wash your car. For goodness' sake, I don't have full insight into what every woman on the farm does on their own time. That's not my business."

Yarrow chuckled to himself as protests erupted near the back of the room, but Becky lifted her hand and waited for quiet.

"Most of the women on my farm ended up there for one reason. Because they need help, and they sought that from me. But let's be honest, they would take help from anyone who could provide it. So, the question is, why did they come to me and not to you?"

She smiled; hands upraised like a preacher.

"Because I was willing to help. But they still need your help too. I can't provide work and assistance for all. So that's my question, who here can help take care of them, so they don't need to work on the farm anymore? Someone? Anyone?"

The room grew silent. Becky paced.

"Can someone take even one of these destitute women under their wing? Can you maybe let them stay at your place instead of mine?"

She waited. No one spoke up.

"When people don't help, they will do what they can to survive. So, are your concerns really about what they sell? Or is your real issue that you want them to move along and not live in Riverbend at all?"

"That's not our concern," Mary Jane said as she jumped to her feet. The gavel banged and the moderator again educated the crowd on the formalities of the town meeting. Then he officially recognized Mary Jane.

"Like I was saying, this isn't our problem, and it's not supposed to be. There are government programs for these things. There are charities and churches, and anyone who wants to help should donate to those places." She held her head high as she added, "Places like that are run by the *right* people. Instead, we're letting people wallow in filth and decadence at that camp. We don't deserve to have another Bivens business in town."

Half the crowd cheered. Some rose and clapped. The moderator raised his hand and waited for quiet.

Becky raised her hand and was recognized again.

"Charity does seem like an option. But is it really? Most of these women don't qualify for help. They don't have a set address. The Aid for Dependent Children office requires an investigation before they provide money, and some of these women know they won't pass because of their current living conditions, missing birth certificates, and more. Some could lose their children at the whim of an inspector. They fear that most of all. And we haven't even discussed issues with language, race, and much more."

"Again, not our problem," someone in the crowd shouted.

Becky stood tall. She carefully chose her next words. "That's convenient, isn't it? But ever since I was a child, here's what I've experienced. People like to say charity is available. But let's not pretend this country has a level of charity that's even close to what's needed. It helps some. It misses many others."

The moderator chimed in after picking up on the undercurrent of anger in the crowd. "I do have to say Miss Bivens, some people seem disappointed with the defiance they hear in your responses. The goal of a town meeting is to air issues and work toward some common ground."

For the first time during the meeting, Yarrow raised his hand. The chair recognized him, and he stood to speak.

"Mr. Chairman, I'm a town police officer. But tonight, I'm just here as a local citizen, and I want to say I don't see Becky Bivens as being defiant. She's answering your questions. You just aren't happy with the answers."

He saw other town employees and board members cast angry looks his way. He immediately realized, as a town employee himself, he had just publicly chosen a side in a deeply political matter. He wasn't wearing his uniform and he had the right to speak. But what he did was heavily frowned upon.

He sat down, crossed his arms, and leaned back in his seat. He'd support Becky, but he had to be judicious. If opinions turned against both of them, they could both suffer and the odds of the farm succeeding would diminish.

Becky would have to win this on her own. He was confident she could.

She searched for sympathetic eyes. Then she remembered something Yarrow had shared with her. It was Rocco's metaphor about the mirror, and where people stand. She decided to borrow from that as she spoke.

"I am a woman who, somehow, has found herself stuck between two strong-willed entities. On one side, you have successful people in this town. And here's what I hear them say: That every person should be able to pull themselves up by their own bootstraps. I suppose that's not impossible. But those same people set limits on how that can be done. They control what kind of bootstraps are available. They only employ certain people. They control how money is doled out. They set rules on where the poor can live. The bootstraps aren't long enough for most people to reach, yet they make marginalized people feel like failures when they can't find something to latch onto."

Becky walked to the left, subtly implying she was now addressing the other side of the issue.

"On the other hand, when I visit places like Boston, or Lowell, or Portsmouth, I encounter a much different group of people. There, I've met outspoken socialists and labor leaders. You know, the very people Senator Joe McCarthy has been warning us about. In cities, I meet true believers who still support Roosevelt's New Deal of fifteen years ago. They want organizations like the WPA and the CCC to be brought back and expanded. They believe the government, including town and city governments, should be the ones who provide most of the help and opportunities for disenfranchised citizens.

The very words socialism and New Deal made several people in the audience groan.

Becky held a finger in the air. "Hold on. Before you object, I think you'll be interested in what I'll say next. To the big city 'socialists,' the idea of women living in tents and struggling to survive is an abomination. I must admit, I agree with them. No one should end up like this. A place like my camp should not need to exist."

Several people in the crowd looked confused. Becky held her arms open, as if searching, even begging, for a solution.

"Here's the problem. Left-leaning groups talk a good game, but they lack anything close to the funding they need. They just hope it will appear someday. And while we wait, some leftists stymie the Laissez-faire efforts of people like me. They say our approach is counter-productive to the heavily subsidized society they want to build."

She shrugged. "And that's what I mean when I say I'm a woman stuck between two entities. No charity can provide for the needs of all. No government agency can fund the level of social services the world needs. Now, do I wish they could? Yes. Very much."

"Communist!" someone shouted. The gavel banged. Becky continued without hesitation.

"Even though neither side can provide, they both demand that my alternative should not be allowed. Yes, I understand my system is flawed. But it fills the gap. I have people at my place who need to eat—right now. They need shelter—right now. At least I've found a way to provide it. So, this is my dilemma, kind citizens of Riverbend."

Then Becky did something unusual for her. She raised her voice.

"Some people in this town just want us to go away because we don't fit either of their agendas."

Mary Jane shifted noisily in her seat and crossed her arms.

"Don't claim you're helping!" someone shouted from the back of the room. "What I see at your farm is moral decadence. That's why you're not wanted."

Again, the chairman banged his gavel.

Becky remained stoic. Determined. "I understand your concern. The idea that women can sell their services, whatever those services may be, is something to which you object. It might be surprising to hear that I agree. No woman wants to choose that life. No woman should be forced to make such a tough decision."

Her voice dropped to a whisper. "But what if they've already fallen to that point? What if all of us, left or right, rich or poor, have abandoned them to the point that they have no other choice?" She paced. Her arms waved. "At my farm, they can stay alive. Do you want to leave them with nothing?"

Yarrow could see her passion. He hoped others could too.

Becky continued. "Taking everything away is what we're talking about, right? Two minutes ago, I asked who among you could help these women. Not one of you stepped forward. I said many who seek shelter at my farm don't qualify for government help, nor charity. But again, no one stepped forward to offer food, or housing, or … anything. The people who live in my fields seem grateful that I offer what little I can. They understand they have become pawns between factions that will never agree."

Becky looked at Mary Jane, then looked away when she felt tears flowing to her eyes. "You want bootstraps? My people can't even afford boots!"

She scanned the faces in the crowd. "I'm just asking that you don't become oblivious to the plight of others, and don't you dare pretend that you have the moral high ground." She let out a heavy sigh. "Just, just let us be."

Mary Jane asked to be recognized. The chairman seemed reluctant but nodded his okay.

"So," she began, "I guess Miss Bivens is saying she's one of the few people willing to take in the strays, and do you know why? Because she isn't rescuing them. She's exploiting them. She's the one who should stop pretending. The only way to address this problem is to immediately stop her from taking advantage of people."

Still standing, Becky looked dejected. "I'm not exploiting. I'm offering a very shaky and tentative way for them to help themselves. And in response I've heard things like, 'those women should put their children up for adoption.'" She heard the townspeople shift in their seats. "And for boys? They're just told to just join the military."

A man in the middle of the audience snorted. "I don't disagree with any of that. I joined the U.S. Army. That's the American way!"

She squinted at the audience. "And that too, conveniently, supports the status quo. Addressing the problems I've highlighted seems less important that forcing people to conform to the current social order, whether it's filling army boots or filling church pews."

"You're out of line!" A man in the front row shouted. Others loudly voiced their agreement. "She's totally out of line, and obviously a communist!"

The chairman tried to intervene but the sound of his gavel was barely noticed.

"The point I'm trying to make," Becky raised her voice for a second time, "is that both sides, socialists and conservatives, are convinced their approach is the only way. Two philosophies with a huge gulf in between. Neither can keep people from falling into that void."

She gave the room an angry look. "So where does that leave us? Why don't you help?"

Becky's lip quivered again, but her message remained on-point. "That's all I can say. I'm trying to run my own business. And if I can give others a space to find their way, I will do that."

There were new murmurs of disapproval, but also a few cheers of support.

The gavel banged. There were shouts for order and the meeting continued. Other speakers were called. Other questions were asked. Becky was prodded to provide answers. But she always returned to her main message. "These people need to live somewhere."

As the crowd filed out, Mary Jane slipped forward and leaned over Becky's chair.

"But not here," she whispered. "They are never going to live here."

Chapter 48

Fractured

Honesty should be used more often as a negotiation tool. Honesty surprises people. It's a refreshing virtue that eliminates ulterior motives and superficial actions. Honesty can promote integrity and eliminate the need for manipulation. But it's a rare thing to find.

The Art of Truth and Politics, Shoreline Books, 1955

Yarrow sat through a morning police briefing. Then he headed out to his patrol car to start the day. But the chief called him aside.

"You're going to have a rider with you today."

"Really? Who?"

"The mayor asked if he could ride along with an officer today. He wants to see what we do on patrol and how we interact with citizens. That sort of thing."

Yarrow let out a long exhale. "And you chose me?"

"Actually, the mayor chose you. When he made the request, he mentioned your name."

Yarrow walked on, then turned back. "Come on, Chief. You know what's going on here."

The chief held up his hand. "All I know is the city is working on next year's budget right now and the department needs more of just about everything. If the mayor wants to see what we're doing, I welcome that. And, if you can work it into the conversation, tell him we need two new cars, one additional officer, and another mechanic out back. You are dismissed."

Fifteen minutes later he pulled up to the town hall and the mayor climbed in.

"Well, Officer Yarrow. How are you?"

"Okay, I guess."

"Good … good."

They rode in silence for a minute. Yarrow could see the mayor was hesitant to get the real conversation started. So, he broke the ice.

"So, here we are Mayor. Riding along. Maybe you can tell me what's up."

"All right, I will. Interesting town meeting last evening, don't you think?"

"I thought it was very interesting. A lot of good points were made. Maybe on both sides. What did you think?"

Mayor Driscoll ran his finger along the chrome edge of the car's oversized radio speaker. "Well, you know."

"That doesn't tell me much."

The mayor hesitated, then spoke openly. "I think we have a problem to deal with, Sargent Yarrow. I don't think any solution will be a perfect one. So, I think we just need to work toward the best outcome."

"And that is?"

"The one that will cause the least chaos for Riverbend."

"Ahh. Again, what do you think that is?"

The mayor brushed lint from his pants. "You may not want to hear this, Jim. Everyone knows you and Becky have some sort of personal relationship. But you understand the pressure we're under here, and you know there are plenty of reasons to shut down that farm. Hopefully none of this will reflect badly on you."

Yarrow said nothing. He just cranked the big steering wheel and drove onto the next street. He wasn't shocked, but hearing the message coming from the town's top elected official carried more weight than the complaints of the improvement society.

Nearly a minute passed without comment. Then the mayor spoke again—softly at first. "I'm not blaming you. There's plenty of blame to go around. I figure your friend Rocco probably told you I own a couple of those honey futures."

"Yup."

"Probably a big mistake."

"Depends, Mayor. What did you do with them?"

He shrugged.

"You know why I'm asking. I mean, did you … you know …?"

"I'm not saying anything."

Yarrow rounded another corner and pulled into a parking space. "Mayor, look, I'm not going to judge. You're young. You don't have a girlfriend. What the hell, what you do on your own time is your—"

"Damn it, I did *not* say I did anything."

"Yeah, well. All right."

More silence.

"Look, Mayor, you're the one who mentioned it. So, I guess one thing that might come up is whether you cashed in any of your futures. Did you?"

"I did. Partially."

"Do you want to tell me how you spent it?"

"I repeat, I'm not going to say."

Yarrow took a long breath. "Okay, so I'm guessing if this comes up, either soon or during your reelection, some shit could hit the fan for you. So, whatever you decide your story is, make sure to get it straight. The sooner the better."

The mayor seemed lost in thought. Then he raised his eyebrows. "Yeah, I understand maybe this whole thing doesn't portray me in the best light."

Just then the radio squawked.

"You there, Jim?"

He picked up the mic. "Affirmative Tina. And, just so you know, the mayor is here with me at the moment."

"Oh. Okay. Well, you're scheduled to be on patrol out by the Merrimack later today, so I'm passing along a request from the

Haverhill Police Department. They asked us to keep an eye out. There might be a body in the river."

"Ten-four. Any details?"

"Caucasian male. Age thirty-one. They think he jumped from their easternmost bridge last night."

Yarrow let a tone of skepticism seep into his voice. "Why are we looking for a body? That bridge is barely high enough to give you a sore belly if you land wrong."

He could hear Tina sigh. "I don't know, but some people are desperate. You know?"

He nodded. "Ten-four again. Let me know if you get any more details."

After Jim returned the mic to its holder, Mayor Driscoll asked, "Do you think a body would float all the way to Riverbend?"

Yarrow tried to picture the river. "Probably not. Some bodies have drifted for miles, but they're more likely to snag on something in the shallows. You never know though. I'll keep an eye out."

"I guess that's part of being a river town. You have to deal with whatever floats downstream."

"Well put, Mayor. But getting back to what we talked about, did you at least have a good time at the farm?"

"I had a very good time. I even made a new friend." He ran his fingers through his hair. "Shit, Jim. I can't believe I got fooled into this."

Yarrow bit his lip for a moment. "You weren't fooled, Mayor. Just like I wasn't fooled when I reestablished ties with Becky. No one who spends time at that farm can claim innocence. They just don't expect consequences."

In his peripheral vision, he saw the mayor rub the bridge of his nose. "I just never expected to see the town so divided. Remember when the farm first opened? Just one little table. I thought it was great. I wish I'd known she'd be such a catalyst."

Mayor Driscoll looked up at the trees. "And now it's going to be tough for the town to survive the trash Becky brought to our borders."

Yarrow felt a slow burn bubble up from under his collar. "Is that what you think? First, this town, like most, has survived both good and bad things for hundreds of years. It will continue to survive. Second, you're saying Becky brought trash here? What are you, quoting directly from Mary Jane's script?"

"I didn't mean it like that."

"Yeah, well, I hope you understand Mary Jane and her crew only want success for certain people, and those are the people who look and act exactly like them."

The mayor tried to answer, but Yarrow wasn't finished. "So, you've made your choice? You're joining the people who—" He struggled to find the right metaphor. "Who treat Riverbend like their own personal painting? You know what I mean. They paint it exactly the way they want, and no one else can touch the brush."

They talked more, but it was a stalemate. Yarrow would not pressure Becky on the mayor's behalf. But he did agree to stay mum on his indiscretions. "I can't erase the record though. I don't have access to Becky's ledger, Mayor."

"Can you confiscate—"

"No! Not without a court order. And you'd need to say why."

He pulled back onto the road and they rolled back into downtown.

"I guess you can drop me at the town hall."

"Sounds fine." Yarrow signaled and pulled over. "Here you go."

As the mayor walked away, Jim Yarrow realized his fingers ached. He'd been clutching the wheel far too tightly.

Chapter 49

Liquid Assets

If one looks at asset protection from a natural perspective, like we do for animals, we realize nature protects, not through fences or walls, but through their own internal and external immunities. The resilience of animals evolved over time. Walls are not a substitute for that.

Models for Asset Protection, The New England Business Library, 1957

A man in a dark suit parked on the road and walked into Becky's farm. Accompanied by an Essex County sheriff's officer, he carried a single white envelope.

"Miss Bivens?" he asked.

"Yes."

He handed her the letter and spoke. "We need to close your operations. This is an injunction. Details are inside."

She was aware efforts were underway to charge her with a crime, but it was not until she read the letter that she learned they planned to seize all her assets. The document listed several people as plaintiffs, including Mary Jane and the town itself.

As the sheriff placed a chain across the driveway, the man in the suit said she could appeal the order. A lock was snapped into place beneath a sign that read *Closed by Court Order*.

When they were gone, Becky jumped in her truck, drove around the chain, and rushed toward town. She went directly to her bank to see if she could protect her money by withdrawing it.

"I'm sorry, Miss Bivens," the teller informed her. "Your account has been frozen by the court."

Becky leaned against the counter. She stifled the urge to scream. Instead, she took a moment to collect her thoughts. "I'd like to speak to bank President Ted Markley please."

The teller walked to his office. Through the glass wall, Becky saw him shake his head. When the young woman returned, she avoided eye contact. "I'm sorry, ma'am. Mr. Markley won't be able to see you today."

Becky grabbed a deposit slip and wrote a hasty note. Folding it, she handed it to the teller. "Please give him this."

"I don't think I should—"

"Just do it. He'll want to read it."

Reluctantly the teller walked back into the office. The gray-haired man unfolded the note, read it, and looked troubled. He whispered something. The woman raised an eyebrow and emerged from the office. She motioned for Becky to step inside.

"You're quite persistent," Markley said when they were alone. Becky slid into one of the brown leather chairs facing his desk.

"I'm sorry. But sometimes I must be." She leaned in. "You have been supportive of the farm since you gave me our first loan. So, please tell me. What are your thoughts on this?"

He crumpled her note and threw it in his trash. "I think this is going to be a problem. For you, and yes, for me."

"So, Ted, is there anything you can do about it?"

He stood up and walked toward his bookcase. On those shelves, mostly for show, sat bound volumes containing the bank's earliest hand-written transactions. Some of the ledgers dated to before the country was founded.

"I don't know what to think, Becky. I'm not a fan of losing money, even if it's just a few thousand dollars."

Becky sighed. "Is that your main concern?"

"That and … everything that may come out."

"Well, let's talk about that. You hold the mortgage for the farm. I appreciate that you gave me that without a male cosigner. You are a visitor to our place too." She smiled demurely. "You even hold a couple of the futures contracts. By the way, two of your vice presidents are in my ledger too."

"Jesus, really? That I didn't know."

Becky gripped the arms of her chair. "And I assume the investment growth you all enjoyed was mentioned in the last quarterly report to your shareholders? Or perhaps it wasn't?"

"Okay. So—" he nervously ran his finger along the old registers.

"So, as of right now you have over thirty-two thousand dollars tied up in my farm. That's between your original mortgage and the growth of the futures you purchased with the bank's money. I won't talk about what a big loss that could be if everything is seized. I'll just ask how that it might affect your bank's integrity."

"Jesus, what do you want Becky?" He sat back down and tossed his glasses on his green desk blotter.

She smiled at him. "You'll help stop this?"

"I haven't decided yet. This is embarrassing, but it won't kill us to just take the loss."

"I know you face some difficult choices, Ted. I do hope you make up your mind soon." She stood and smoothed her skirt. "I just don't want to see any of my clients—excuse me, *investors*—end up on the front page of the papers."

For the rest of the morning, Becky stopped into other places and had similar conversations with her other investors. Most agreed having the farm audited would produce embarrassment and repercussions. But getting anyone to agree on a solution proved challenging.

At one point, a local businessman followed her out of his shop and walked with her along the sidewalk. They walked without speaking for several yards.

"I think you need a different tactic," he finally whispered. "At least for now."

"I'm listening."

"Appeal to the court and say they don't have the right to shut you off from all your assets. You should be able to keep some as living expenses. Also, was the letter addressed to you or to the Bivens Farm as a business?"

"To the farm."

"Some of the assets probably are under your own name, right?"

"Some are, yes."

"Then point that out. If the court order was not specific on exactly what they are authorized to seize, including a dollar amount, then point that out too. Ask for clarification. Ask for a stay until that clarification is made. Demand that they be much more specific. Ask if you can continue business until that happens. Force the proof back on them if you can."

"Do you think that will work?"

"I think it may buy you some time while you come up with a better strategy."

She thanked him, but he had already stepped away, hurrying back toward his shop.

Becky considered his words and wondered if she might indeed be able to force a delay. But she would need a little guidance.

She turned around and walked toward Rocco's Grill.

Chapter 50

Thousand Yard Stare

Medical personnel should not use the term "shell shock" in reports or conversations. Do not permit nurses or hospital corpsmen to use it. It's not a medical term. It's a piece of disrespectful military slang used to describe a group of conditions. "Shell shock" will not be accepted as a diagnosis of disability.

The Journal of Military Medicine, 1918

That evening, Rocco didn't do much talking as he and Yarrow sat at the bar. He spent long moments staring out the windows, wiping the counter, and cleaning glasses.

One of their old classmates, Lefty Hogan, was with them. A semi-regular, Lefty was the sort of guy who didn't belong to any one place or group of friends. He just appeared, hung around for a while, and disappeared again. People liked him well enough but, as Leon once said, Lefty chose to remain unknowable.

"I do so love this beer," Lefty said as he lifted a bottle of Frank Jones Portsmouth Ale. "You said this is the last of it? That's too bad."

"Huh?" Rocco seemed to come out of a daze. "Oh. Yeah. I have maybe three bottles left. The brewery closed last year."

Lefty shook his head. "That's a real shame. Old brands … a lot of them are fading away."

Yarrow agreed. "That's one of the beers my father used to buy. Hell, a lot of his old beers are gone now, especially the dark brews."

"Leaving us with what?" Lefty lifted his glass up to the light. Amber ale and bubbles. "Do I have to just drink Schlitz now? Or Budweiser? In Europe, we all got to taste some mighty fine beers. Then we come home, and the damn yellow lagers have taken over America. That's all I can find in the stores." He shook his head and emptied his bottle.

"That's just business Lefty. They're meeting demand."

"Yeah, maybe. Anyway, it's time for me to head home." He stood and grabbed his coat.

"Hang on." Rocco scrounged through his cooler and handed him the last three bottles of the Portsmouth Ale. "On the house, Lefty. Maybe they'll be collectors' items."

"Wow. Thanks Rocco! You sure?"

"All yours my friend."

They watched him leave, then Yarrow asked, "What's with that? The bar side of your business barely turns a profit and you're giving inventory away?"

"Eh, nobody orders those anymore. That's probably why they went out of business."

Yarrow started to ask another question, but realized Rocco was barely paying attention. He sat back and watched.

Rocco puttered around the back bar area. But he seemed aimless. When he wiped the same spot for the third time, Yarrow spoke up.

"What's going on Rocco?"

"Huh?"

"Something's going on with you. Your mind is in space."

Rocco tossed his rag on the bar. "I don't know. I may feel a little lost. Just for the moment."

"Like, how lost?"

Rocco shrugged. "I don't have an answer."

"Does this have anything to do with Becky stopping in here to talk to you today?"

"Oh. She told you she was here?"

"Word gets around."

Rocco leaned hard against the back counter. Bottles rattled. "Might have something to do with her visit. I think I was able to help her somewhat, but I also gave her hell for what she's put you through. Frankly, the whole situation with her, you, and the town has me feeling disconnected."

Yarrow pointed to a bottle on the back bar. "Why don't you pour us a couple of Old Granddads? Then we'll decide."

Rocco locked his front door, flipped over the closed sign, and came back to fill the glasses. Jigger and a half in each. Neat.

"Not much to add, Jim. Got the blues, you know? We all get that way."

Yarrow sipped then said, "Why don't you start with what you and Becky talked about? You said you were able to help her?"

"Maybe a little. Did that change anything? Maybe not." He saw Yarrow was waiting for details, so he took his own long sip. "Okay. Here's what we talked about. You know how downtown workers come here for lunch? Bankers, lawyers, and businessmen. So, at Becky's request, I talked to a few of them. In confidence, mind you. Maybe I'll hint that I think Mary Jane's vendetta against the Bivens Farm is creating more problems than it solves. So, after talking to several people, I realized I was hearing similar stories. If they had gotten involved with the farm, most were sorry they did. Most would like to see her gone, or at least they want her to change her business practices."

"I guess that last part is encouraging."

"Yup. No one was seeking an immediate showdown. And if they have money invested with her, they don't want to lose it."

"Understandable."

"Becky came to talk with me about the court order that froze her assets. She said she won't be able to repay her loans. Her records will be subpoenaed. Witness statements will be taken. No one is going to be happy, Jim."

"Interesting."

"So, yeah, I tried to slip those points into my conversations with others."

Yarrow rubbed his thumb over his scar. "Thanks for helping her, Rocco. I know you and Becky don't see eye to eye."

"True. But I don't want to see her crash and burn, Jim. She's a friend of yours."

Yarrow took another long sip of bourbon. "So, if people would rather avoid a big investigation, that's a good thing for Becky, right?"

Rocco was hesitant to answer. "It could buy her some time." He stared out the window again. "Remember back in the war? We watched huge groups of people trying to push each other around. I don't know about you but I hoped to leave all that behind when I came home. Yet the crap that's happening to Becky just reminds me it's always with us. Watching one group of people go all-in on destroying another? I guess that's brought up a lot of mixed feelings for me."

"You mean feelings like you had in Japan?"

Rocco looked toward the far wall and beyond. "Yeah. Exactly. That's basically what war is, right? One group violently wiping out another. And if you survive, you're scarred for life."

He walked to his cash register and started counting the evening's take. It was meager. "Like I've told you before, Jim, I didn't know what I wanted after seeing that. I bought the grill as my escape. I guess it sort of worked."

"It definitely worked. You've seemed happy here over the past few years. Just as happy as you were in high school, maybe."

"Yeah. You're right. But, when I first came home, God … I carried a lot of images in my head. Lord, the shit we all saw."

"Yup."

Rocco looked toward the floor. "I've never told this to anyone, but do you know what prompted me to buy this place? One day I was shaving and I looked in the mirror and saw no emotion in my own eyes. They were just dead. Right then I realized I had been avoiding eye contact with myself. Maybe for weeks. I didn't want to deal with that guy I saw. So that day, I forced myself to look into my own eyes for a moment. And you know what? I couldn't hold my own gaze. I kept looking away. Just think about that." Rocco blinked several times.

Yarrow drank his bourbon.

"But that moment also brought a realization. I still knew that guy in the mirror, and I knew he didn't deserve to be ignored or hated. So I forced myself to look again. That's when I knew it wasn't myself that I hated. It was the world."

"The world?"

"I mean the way the world works. It's brutal, tribal, and competitive to the point of ruin. Tribalism is what makes people feel completely justified when destroying others. You know, 'us versus them' and anyone different is a threat. Folks like us just get sucked into it. And then what? On a small scale, we see people like Becky getting pushed aside. On a larger scale, it's cities in ruins."

"But you're still here Rocco, and you found your place. This place. And mentally, you made it back. I did too, with help from my wife." He paused there, thinking of Linda, and what she once meant to him. He missed that. He missed her. He felt confusion setting in and hoped the bourbon would mute the feeling.

"I know, but I guess watching groups squaring off here brought back all the bad feelings. The us-versus-them shit. So, yes, I found solace here in this building. Now I fear I've grown complacent." Then he seemed to dismiss his own words with a wave of his hand.

"I don't think you've grown complacent about anything. But you do look unsettled. So, maybe you can finish that thought?"

"Okay. Here's the challenge: If I don't want to be complacent, what's the next step? Do we have to fight again? Or maybe stand in between as a peacemaker? I don't have an answer." He shook his head and slammed down the rest of his drink.

Yarrow did the same. The bottle was still on the bar, so he refilled both glasses. "Listen," he said in a low voice, "I've never talked much about this, but the first friend I made in the army was during boot camp. His name was Ronnie. Good guy. We ended up deploying together. In our very first battle, I saw him take three rounds in the chest from a big German GG-42. I was furious and I killed the Kraut who pulled the trigger. I even shot him once more when I knew he was dead. I kept his beast of a machine gun as a prize. But two days later I threw it in a deep creek. It turned out to be a terrible souvenir because every time I looked at it, it just reminded of Ronnie's death."

Rocco gave his friend a pat on his shoulder.

"So, yeah. I became detached too. And I liked being detached. It muted all the feelings. From that point on it was just a long, sad, and violent journey, and I was just determined to make it to the end."

They were silent again, then tried to force some small talk. It was Rocco who brought the conversation back around.

"Okay, this is going to sound weird, but I realized I could find peace and meaning through really simple activities. Making coffee. Cutting potatoes. It started to dawn on me that having a meaningful life has nothing to do with plugging myself into one tribe or one path. It was meaningful just to interact with the world in a small way. I watched other vets trying to move toward a higher-paying job or a bigger house. None of them seemed happy. By letting my ambition and anger go, I found each moment along the way could be as intriguing as the next, and as meaningful as I wanted to make it."

"Nice thought. Is that really practical?"

"I live a practical life, don't I? I think that when people strive for success, their lives become increasingly driven by a need to interact with material things. I don't mean cutting potatoes. I mean they try to acquire things. They like to display their success to others, because they think it says something about their own worth."

"Hasn't it been that way for ages?"

"Of course. Winners built castles. Rich men have their fine clothes and wine. But we end up letting our possessions speak for the way we value ourselves."

Yarrow shrugged and rolled a swizzle stick between his fingers.

Rocco shook his head. "Anyway, that's my crossroads right now. I'm far from a rich man. However, I am as guilty as the next veteran of coming home and immediately chasing the American dream. I bought this building and started my business. But now I feel stuck. I'm just here—with my stuff."

"Jesus. You're fine, Rocco. Get rid of any stuff you don't want."

Rocco gave Yarrow a look that told him he was missing the point. "You know what I read recently? Rudolf Peierls, a key physicist from the Manhattan Project, started rejecting the idea of materialism right after the war. He said the human urge to constantly acquire things in a world where resources are finite was a main cause of human conflict. Acquiring things creates haves and have-nots, in turn that stokes feelings of unfairness, which creates more clashes."

"Yeah? So, what's the alternative? Communism?"

"No, no. As far as I can see, communism is also focused on materialism. It's just that the property and production is communally owned. It still urges people to produce and achieve. That's drilled into them with posters and slogans. If they're lucky, their collective will become wealthy. Then other tribes grow jealous. And just like that, we're back to using war and destruction to take stuff from others."

Yarrow raised his eyebrows. "Hey, this bourbon tastes good, doesn't it?"

"Sorry, Jim. I know. I'm prattling on."

"No." He shook his head. "You're asking decent questions. So okay, maybe you're not falling under the realm of the socialists. But you're kind of leaning that way. Maybe we can call you an anti-materialist? Or just a non-conformist?"

"Huh. Maybe." Rocco looked around. "I suppose I have to be a bit of a non-conformist to end up in a place like this."

Chapter 51

The Dust

Historically, tensions between construction workers rose from a number of factors, including tension between labor groups, personality conflicts, racial discrimination, and organizational disputes. Construction jobs attracted tough men, and those men did not always get along.

Building Pains, Bartho Industries, 1972

Yarrow pushed the cruiser's accelerator to the floor. With siren and lights engaged, he headed toward a section of the new highway that was still under construction—just a ribbon of dirt that sliced through a long field.

When he arrived at the scene, he was waved around a pair of sawhorses. He raced up the makeshift road until he saw two men rolling on the ground, punching each other. A crowd was gathered nearby.

"What is this?" he shouted as he climbed out of the car. "You're all just watching? No one's tried to separate them?"

Someone at the back of the crowd called out, "We have some bets going."

Yarrow grabbed one of the fighters by the back of his shirt and pulled him up and away.

"Can someone drag the other one back? Come on!"

A few workers helped while the others just laughed. Once the fighters were separated, a string of cuss words spilled from both.

"That's enough. Want to tell me what's going on?"

The fighter with a cut lip shouted his response. "This son-of-a-bitch has been trying to get in good with my girl. He knew full well I was with her too."

"Yeah, says you," the other guy replied. "She ain't got no reserved sign on her. She's out of your league anyway."

They tried to reengage, but Yarrow tightened his grip and kept them apart. "Knock it off now, or I'm taking you in."

More words were exchanged. Yarrow asked if anyone wanted to file charges. Since neither spoke up, he sent them in different directions and told them to cool down.

"Now, where is the foreman?"

Turned out he was standing just a few yards away.

"What's your name?" he asked.

"Bernie," said the foreman.

"Come on, Bernie. We can't have this sort of thing going on out here. But you're just standing and watching with the others?"

Bernie gave a sheepish grin. "Yeah. I should have stopped 'em. But it's been a hot and dusty week, and we ran into delays. These two have been at each other and they just needed to blow off some steam."

Yarrow took a moment to look at the road itself. The cleared area was wider than he expected. He could see twenty bulldozers, graders, and other heavy equipment.

"Look, this place is getting busy and the impact you're having on the town is overwhelming. And when your guys get paid they flood into downtown. They hit the bars and cause all sorts of problems."

"I know. But it's a big state project and we need lots of workers."

"Just reel them in. Okay? And I don't want to see any more fights."

The foreman gave a mock salute and said he'd do what he could.

"Thanks, Bernie. And just so you know, I plan to contact the owner of your company. I'll remind him the town expects you to have better control of your guys."

As he drove away, he checked in with Tina and updated her on the fight.

"Always a lot of fun with these sorts of state projects, eh?"

"Yeah," Yarrow said. "Lucky us."

Chapter 52

The Plan

Organized crime has long been fueled by factors such as criminal markets, public demand, tolerance for illegal activities, corruption, and the need for local protection and resources. Organized crime is often able to flourish when there are weak or corrupt law enforcement environments and where social and economic factors create vulnerabilities.

Key Players in Urban Environments, Luka Urban Studies, 1961

Mary Jane Danforth first met Jake Harrison in nineteen forty-six. He was one of the sketchiest people she knew.

She maintained their relationship because Harrison had connections to all sorts of people who could do all sorts of things—legal or not. They first connected when she purchased a vacant lot in a nearby town. Cash, thanks to one of her divorce settlements. She wanted to build two houses there, but discovered the ground might be too wet to pass the town's required perc test.

"Don't sweat it," someone suggested. "Just talk to Jake."

She did so. Jake said he'd be happy to dig the hole in a special way. It would pass, he promised. When the town inspector came, he poured two buckets of water into the four-foot-deep hole. They watched the water quickly disappear. That meant it was percolating deeper into the ground, which in turn meant the lot was deemed dry enough to build on.

"This place is almost a swamp," Mary Jane said as the inspector drove away. "How did you manage that?"

"Quite simple," Jake replied. "I dug the hole about twenty inches deeper than what they required. Right before the inspector came, I tossed a dozen big sponges into the bottom and covered them with a little dirt. It was the hidden sponges that absorbed the water."

She was impressed by his creative solution and kept Jake's number handy. She ended up consulting with him several times over the years.

But Mary Jane didn't like to be seen with Jake. If they had to talk in person, they met in a different town, in a local park. That's where Mary Jane first asked Jake for ideas on how to force Becky Bivens to leave Riverbend.

"Now," Jake said as he rubbed his mustache. "When you say encourage; how much encouragement are we talking? A nudge? Or outright force?"

"I guess we could start with a nudge then work towards other methods if needed."

He admitted he knew someone who could help. But Mary Jane wasn't happy with his suggestion. At first, she outright rejected it.

"No Jake, there is no way I'm driving with you to visit the clubhouse of some biker gang. I can't believe you'd even suggest that." She looked at him with disdain. "Especially not when their club is in those god-awful swamps near Revere."

Jake Harrison took a long drag on his cigarette. "I understand. But, you have a job and you need it done. Correct?"

She looked away. "You know I do. That's why I'm here."

"Well, Gunner and his boys can help and probably at an affordable price. But the Swamp Riders don't come to you. You need to talk to Gunner in person."

She stewed on his words. "What if I go there and I'm never seen again? People dump bodies in those swamps, Jake. You know that's true."

He laughed. "Oh, I've read the news stories. But he won't just kill someone who doesn't need killing. There's no money in that."

She paced a bit. "How about if we do this? Let's say I pay you to meet with him and if you like his plan, we can hire him."

Jake Harrison snorted. "That's not going to work. He wants to meet whoever he's working for. Let's not piss off the bikers. These guys are all veterans and we won the war because of bad asses like them."

Mary Jane nodded then placed a brown envelope on the bench between them.

"What's this?"

"Open it."

He did and saw four crisp one-hundred-dollar bills. "Jesus, you really do want this to happen."

"And that's just for you. It's yours if you can get Gunner on board."

"Okay, you have my attention. Let me think for a minute." He leaned back, hands behind his head, and worked out a plan. "Maybe I can go see him. We'll have a beer. I'll describe what we need and then I'll just tell him how nervous you are about going into his club. I'll give him a couple of other C-notes, which you will also give me. That will show good faith. He may want to meet, so I'll ask him to join me at a bar that sits behind the amusement park near Revere Beach. You'll be there, waiting."

He looked her in the eyes. "Best I can do Mary Jane."

"Okay," she replied. "I guess that's reasonable."

It took a few days for Jake to make the connections, but they ended up gathering at the Oceanview Ballroom in Revere. Gunner came dressed in jeans and an army jacket with its sleeves cut off. Mary Jane explained what she wanted. He asked several questions and eventually took the money. He told her what they would do, then they parted ways.

"I think that went well," Jake said when they were outside. "Better than I expected actually."

"Agreed," said Mary Jane with a satisfied tone. "Even with tough guys, money talks. People listen."

Chapter 53

Shhh ...

Life is all about limitations, but you must know which limits to accept and which to overcome. If something bothers you, is it worth your energy to confront it? During the war, I learned that. You can't engage with every enemy you see. Focus your efforts on the most important battles.

Leon Davis, 1952

"Wow Leon, you're doing great! Look at how many books you've shelved. I think you're our hardest working volunteer."

The compliment came from Dorothy Belanger, director of the Riverbend Memorial Library. She saw Leon standing in section 810—American Literature—so she stopped to thank him.

Leon beamed. "I'm not always a volunteer. You do pay me for a few things around here, like moving tables and cleaning the windows. So, I figure I can put away a few books for free."

She watched him lift the last few books from a box then dragged it out of his way. "I also see you scanning books while you work. Looks like you're reading more all the time."

"I'm trying!" Leon dragged another box of books into the stacks. "I first came here to meet with your reading tutor. We practice every Saturday morning in your small conference room. She showed me some tricks for figuring things out whenever I can't tell the difference between some kinds of letters. I started with your early reading books. That's all I could understand at first, but I've made fast progress. I try to read everything now, from cereal boxes to signs."

Dorothy smiled. "I remember. I helped you track down some of the *Dick and Jane* books.

"Yup. Wow, those were boring. But they did help me."

"Now you're reading newspapers too."

"I'm trying. You know, I never even knew what dyslexia was. But understanding the challenge helps me learn the workarounds. Now I try to look at *The Boston Record*. *The Boston Globe* too. I got started by reading the comic pages. Now I look at the front pages too. Then sports."

"You've worked hard."

He beamed. "Thank you. It was my friend Jim who lit the fire under me. He said a man deserves to be able to read. I think I agree."

She helped him shelve a few books, then said, "Hang on. I want to look for something."

A few minutes later she returned with a dusty volume. The cover had faded gold lettering on green fabric.

"I think you might find this interesting." She handed him the thin book. Leon studied it, then read the title aloud. "*Learning to Read and Write*, by Frederick Douglass."

"Yes," Dorothy said. "It's an essay he wrote. It was originally part of a longer book he wrote about his life and times. But he also published this one separately because it became so popular." She opened the book to its first page. "He recounts how he learned to read at age twelve and how that allowed him to read newspapers. That was his gateway to educating himself. He was a slave and his owner supported his reading at first. But he eventually grew concerned about the books Frederick chose and tried to limit them. Frederick Douglas escaped slavery at age twenty and wrote his first book a few years later. So, learning to read completely changed his life."

Leon flipped through a few pages. "Why thank you. But I don't think I'm ready to tackle this."

"Well, maybe just try. You can renew the loan as many times as you need."

Then Dorothy thought for a moment. "I'm also going to see if I can order some things from the Orton Society. They have a teaching method that includes sound recordings and booklets."

"Oh, you don't need to go to that trouble."

"Nonsense, Leon," she said. "That's what libraries are for."

Leon worked for another hour, checked out his book at the main desk, and walked toward home. On his way, he saw a familiar face coming toward him on Main Street.

"Hello Becky. Haven't seen you in a while. What brings you downtown?"

"Leon!" She gave him a quick hug. They laughed as they recalled their boat theft and all the risks they took.

"I don't know if anyone told you, Leon, but now we have ten women living inside the hull. And they have a little wood stove in there."

Leon looked happy. "I can't believe we got away with it. And I can't believe people can live there. That's fantastic."

They made some more small talk, then Leon's voice took on a more serious tone. "So how are you doing now Becky? I've heard about the damage. And the threats people have made. I'm sorry you lost some of your bees."

"Well, you know how it is. Some people don't like what we do."

"Well, if they don't like it, they can just step in to help all the people you help."

She patted him on the back. "Thank you for saying that, Leon. But what I want is for people at my farm to be able to help themselves. I just help them get started, with the freedom to do what they want."

Behind Becky, Leon saw the large homes that lined the shady side of Main Street. "Not everyone wants that though, do they Becky? I may not read well, but I sure can read that writing on the wall."

She thanked him and they continued on their paths.

Chapter 54

Deterrence

Outlaw motorcycle gangs first emerged in America in the late 1940s. Within a few years clubs and their associated chapters appeared in many major cities, especially along the coasts. The clubs often were formed by veterans seeking to reestablish their sense of military brotherhood. Leathers, patches, and tattoos took the place of uniforms, chevrons, and medals.

Iron Brotherhoods, Paint Bucket Press, 1969

Becky managed to file the right paperwork with the court and she was permitted to temporarily reopen her business.

Two days later, as the traffic waned and the sun slipped low in the sky, she started her usual close-out of the day's business. She boxed up the honey and locked it in a shed for the night. Chairs and umbrellas were folded and placed beneath tables.

But on that fateful Thursday evening, things were different. She heard a deep rumble in the distance, which drew closer.

A minute later five motorcycles—two Harleys, two Indians, and a Triumph—rumbled into her lot. Gravel crunched. Men sat astride the loud machines and stared at her. Two of them wore goggles and leather vests. The others wore denim and sunglasses. As they stared menacingly in her direction, a biker on a grey panhead pulled a pint bottle from his pocket. He drained the last of its contents and shattered the bottle on the ground.

A woman who was driving past the farm saw him break the bottle. She slowed for a moment, then accelerated, disappearing around a bend.

Back in the parking area, under the gaze of the bikers, Becky stood tall and held their gaze. Some of the women who lived in the tents heard the roar and came up the hill to investigate.

The bottle-thrower climbed off his bike and walked toward Becky. He tightened the straps on his gloves.

"Sorry." Becky said as he approached. "We're closed."

"Are you Rebecca Bivens?"

"I said we're closed."

"I don't fucking care about that. I asked your name."

Becky stood silently as the camp women moved behind her.

"No matter," he sneered. "I can tell it's you."

As they stood facing each other, the other riders dismounted their bikes and walked behind him.

A thousand feet away, the woman who drove past stopped at the Blanchard General Store. She knew a police car often sat there in the late afternoon, watching for speeders. Sure enough, the patrol car was still there.

She rolled down her window. In the police car, Seargent Jim Yarrow did the same.

"Hello, officer. I don't want to be worry-wort. But when I drove by that honey farm, I saw something that bothered me. "

Yarrow closed his eyes and waited for a complaint. Since he started sitting near the store he'd been approached three times with questions about why the police weren't challenging Becky.

But his eyes popped back open when he learned this woman wasn't there to lodge a complaint.

"Wait," he held up a finger. "Say that again?"

"I saw a bunch of motorcycle riders at the farm. They looked kind of rough. Maybe angry too. And that lady who owns the place, you know, that one who always dresses so nicely? She looked worried and flustered."

Yarrow asked more questions and grew more concerned with each answer.

"Anyway," she continued, "I'm probably being silly. But some of those men had patches on their vests and one of them threw a bottle. So I wanted to look for you to let you know."

"You did the right thing. Thank you, Miss …?"

"Oh, just call me Helen."

In mere seconds he was accelerating up the road. He wasn't sure if it was a siren-worthy call, so he kept the trip quiet. But he did check in with Tina to say where he was heading. "Just looking into some suspicious activity," he said.

As he reached the farm, he saw a big biker standing in front of Becky, yelling and tapping his finger on her chest. Yarrow called for backup then climbed out, nightstick in hand.

"You! Let's back away. Then we'll talk about what's going on."

The biker held up his hand, palm facing Yarrow. "No concern of yours. We're talking business."

"Jim?" Becky called out, "I don't know these men. They're scaring me."

"Okay, I'm telling you again buddy, step back. Right now."

The man backed up just one step. Then he turned and sneered at Yarrow. "Yeah? Or what? Are you going to wave your little stick? Threaten to shoot us?" He looked at Yarrow like he was surveying a pile of dirt. "Like I said, we have business here. You don't need to be involved."

Becky walked over to Yarrow and stood beside him. "I don't know what to do, Jim."

"Have you asked them to leave?"

"Yes. Before you got here."

"Maybe you should say it again."

She took a long breath, then said it loudly. "Please leave, all of you. We're closed."

"All right then gentleman," Jim said. "This is her place, and you heard her. On your way."

He heard two sirens in the distance. Good. He hoped that would prompt them to back down. But the leader had other ideas.

"Jesus, you small town dicks are a pain in the ass. You show up and interrupt someone's private conversation? Nothing else to do?"

He started to turn away, but only enough to hide his hand as it curled into a fist. Then he spun quickly, shifting his weight and throwing a roundhouse punch.

But Yarrow noticed the suspicious change in his stance and was prepared. He raised his nightstick to block the blow and moved forward enough to nudge the big biker off balance. Then he used a move he hadn't used since he fought on the front lines. He swung a mighty punch of his own, but his curved upward, connecting directly under the biker's ribcage.

When he was in boot camp, there was a drill sergeant who told the recruits they should always visualize their first punch before it was thrown. He said to picture it as full power and on a path of maximum damage.

"Think of it like this," the sergeant said as he paced in front of them. "When you punch an enemy in the gut, it's not just about where it lands, it's mostly about where it goes after you make contact. If you want to knock that bastard down, you have to punch deep."

He ordered one of the recruits to stand in front of the others. Then the sergeant demonstrated in slow motion. "I'm telling you to think of your punch like a massive missile that moves so hard, so fast, and with so much of your weight behind it, that you can picture yourself punching all the way through him." He held his fist against the young soldier's shirt. "Picture it going right on through the spine too. Picture yourself hitting so hard that you even break the wall behind him. Deliver it that kind of energy."

Then the sergeant laughed like a man who had done a lot of fighting. "Now, you know no one can deliver that kind of impact. But if you're in hand-to-hand combat with no weapon besides your fist, that's what it will take to knock your enemy down. And they're not getting back up."

So Yarrow made that kind of swing and connected with the biker. The impact compressed the man's midsection and lifted both the stomach and the diaphragm up toward his lungs. The blow knocked the wind out of him, and he collapsed in a heap, face crunching against the gravel. He gurgled, as if trying to decide whether to vomit or pass out.

"Jim!" Becky shouted in a panic.

"It's okay. Fight's already over."

The other bikers moved forward, but two other police cars arrived and accelerated to get in front of them. Jim knew both of the arriving officers—Tony Clark and John Griffin. Good men. Both had been on the force for three years.

The officers jumped out with their hands resting on their guns. Yarrow held up his own hands, to calm the situation. "That's it. Okay? We can be done right now." As the fallen biker continued to gasp, Yarrow pulled the man's wallet from his pocket. He read the name, then tossed the billfold on the biker's back.

"If we decide to charge you, I know who you are and where to find you." Then he turned to the other bikers, "Get this bastard up, let him puke if he needs to, and get him back on his bike."

He pointed with his billy club. "I may still file charges against all of you. But for now, just get out of here. And if you cause more problems, we're going to make it open season on your club."

The bikers grumbled and eyed the police pistols. It took a couple of minutes to get their leader back on his feet. Someone kick-started his bike for him and he let it idle until his breathing settled. When they finally rode away he flipped his middle finger over his shoulder.

"Think you'll charge him later?" Clark asked.

"Maybe. I just wanted to get them out of here for now."

Becky saw Yarrow rubbing his knuckles, so she took his hand in hers. She rubbed them and massaged his wrist. "Are you okay? Is your hand okay?"

"Ehh, the soreness just confirms I delivered a good solid punch."

The other cops looked at each other. "I wouldn't have let them ride away," said Griffin. "You know he's just pissed off now."

"Then let him carry that message back to the rest of his club."

Yarrow motioned for Becky to step away with him. He spoke in a hushed tone. "This is getting worse here. You keep making enemies. We'll try to protect you, Becky. But, my God, we can't always be here! You're in danger and something's got to change."

"I know."

"So, you'll start reining things in?" He leaned close, whispering even lower. "Start moving this place toward legitimacy?"

"At some point, yes."

"What? When?"

"I don't know."

"You don't know? How can you not know what you should do when that just happened?"

Becky whispered as they kept their backs to the others.

"I'm not going to give up what we're building here, Jim. Not if it means abandoning these people. And the timing is wrong. The road construction is right on our doorstep. The workers' payday is just two days away. Some of my girls will make enough to—"

"Jesus, enough to what?"

"Enough to get out, Jim. To move on. That's what most are trying to do! They're trying to make enough money to move toward a different life. Maybe a better place to live. Maybe a job at a supermarket or something. I refuse to push any of them out before they can fly on their own!"

Jim looked lost. He gripped the brim of his hat and took a deep breath. "Look, Becky, those guys came here to intimidate you. When we stood up to them, it just made them mad. You know they planned to slap you around a bit, right? Maybe pretty hard, with black eyes and bruised ribs. You can't expect long-term police protection if you're out here running your own racket."

She nodded.

"So, yeah, Becky. Start shutting this down."

She raised her voice to a level that surprised him. "We're growing, Jim. We're not stopping. Not yet." Her tone was almost a hiss. "There's more money to be made, and I'm not walking away from that."

She picked up her cash box. "But thank you for helping me. That was very brave of you." She walked toward her truck.

He shook his head as he watched her walk away.

Officer Clark joined him. "So, Yarrow, exactly what is it with you and her?"

"Nothing."

"Bullshit."

"We knew each other back in high school, that's all."

"People are talking, Jim. Everyone knows Linda has moved out. So, are you Becky together? Or what?"

He remained silent, because he didn't know how to answer. He saw two distinct sides to Becky. One side was loving. Nurturing. Like a mother hen watching over her chicks. But her other side was ambitious, sometimes amoral, and with a hint of ruthlessness.

Becky had his respect. Maybe even his love. But that love came with a troubling dose of doubt and worry.

Chapter 55

Honesty

New Englanders are said to be standoffish when they meet new people. But that's really more of a myth. A better word is genuine. When you first meet a New Englander, they may be polite, but they won't pretend they like you until they think they know the real you. They're genuine, and they want to make sure you're genuine too.

Backrooms of New England, Red Wagon Book Binders, 1961

"I think I'm in trouble, Rocco."

"Yeah? Why? For flattening that biker? Wish I'd seen that."

Yarrow shrugged, "Starting with that. Yeah."

"If it happened like you said, you should be fine. He swung first, right? You protected yourself, and Becky too. You even have witnesses. If anything, you should get an accommodation."

"But I may be in trouble for letting the guy walk. The chief has already asked why, and he wants to see me tomorrow."

"Don't lose sleep. You're good at talking your way out of things."

"Thanks. I think. But this seems different."

He felt the need to get away from the bar. He picked up his bottle and walked to the window. Red neon splashed over wet pavement. Main Street always seemed bigger when it rained. More sprawling and abstract. It reminded him that a bigger Riverbend was what some people seemed to want.

"Look," Yarrow said. "I knew if I arrested the guy, it would bring scrutiny. Others would ask why he came there in the first place and why he threatened Becky."

"Is that bad? Let everyone find out. It's obvious Mary Jane or some rich benefactors were the driving force behind the bikers' visit."

"Of course. But that's tough to prove unless the bikers rat them out. Cooperating with police is not their strong point."

"Still, dots can be connected."

"Yeah. In many ways."

Rocco stretched. It had been a long day. "Okay, tell me what you're worried about."

Yarrow walked back, sat down, and propped his elbows on the bar. "I'm worried about the questions that will be asked. Asked of me. Asked of Becky. Others too. I see extra scrutiny coming down, and I'm worried. That's all. The chief will ask why I made the decision to knock the guy down if all I was going to do was send him off with a warning."

"Is that really your main real worry?"

Yarrow waited before answering. "I also worry that what I did was too obvious. Maybe it looks like I'm willing to break the rules to protect Becky."

"But you are, Jim. That's become obvious to everyone. Though maybe not to you."

Before he asked for another, Yarrow drained the rest of his beer. "Okay, I bent some rules. And here's why. I like that Becky not only helps people, but she also serves as a necessary thorn in the side of local authorities. She pushes them to get involved and won't let them turn away. She may skirt the laws, but she solves problems others won't even tackle."

"She skirts the laws? Or outright ignores them?"

Yarrow gave his friend a censorious look. "Damn it, she's doing what she has to do, Rocco. I thought you believed that too."

Rocco looked troubled as he placed a new beer on the bar. "Okay, Jim. Since you're being insistent, and a little contentious, I'll weigh in too. But it may not be what you think."

"Go on."

"To be honest, I still don't know what to think of Becky. And I've tried. She seems likable enough. I knew her a little in high school. Certainly not like you did. And in 1941 I understood why she and her mom ran."

He looked up at the ceiling, searching for his next words. "This summer she's back and I've watched this whole fiasco unfold. I've listened to both sides prattle on about how wonderful or terrible she is. But through it all, I've heard nothing that makes me want to choose a side."

Rocco lifted some glasses into the sink. "I mean, at her core, is she a good person? Is she bad? Does she help people?"

"Yes."

"Okay, so let's explore that. Does she help out of pure altruism? Or is it to also help herself?"

"Jesus, I don't know Rocco. Why can't it be both?"

"Fine. For now, let's say it can. But, like I said, I don't feel I know the real Becky. I don't feel like she lets people get to know her."

"Well, damn it, I know her. I mean …" His voice trailed off. "I think I do."

Rocco rubbed his eyes. "So, I'll admit I think of Becky as someone who is at least trying to do the right thing. But her approach is convoluted. So let's call her misguided."

"Okay. But only for the sake of this argument."

"The trouble is, Jim, we both know she's too smart to be misguided. She knows exactly what she's doing and that's why I have such an amoral position toward her. I do know she is trying to do good things in an impossible circumstance. So, for that, she has my respect. But I don't respect her willingness to unleash a flood of other problems to accomplish that."

Yarrow scraped at the label on his beer.

"I know you don't see her in that light, Jim. You mostly see the good."

"I do. But maybe I see more than you think."

Rocco stared at him. "If that's true, how much are you willing to ignore?"

Yarrow remained silent. The label was wet and it kept peeling off quite nicely.

Rocco lost his patience. "I understand why you don't want to answer. But I'm genuinely curious. The Jim I know is a decorated vet and a law-abiding citizen. So, I'm just going to say it. You can't support the law while also supporting what Becky's doing."

Yarrow lowered his beer with a thud, then looked Rocco in the eyes.

"Like fuck I can't."

"Then that's the impasse, right there."

Jim crumpled up the peeled label and threw it toward the trash. "You know, we've talked about coming back here as changed men." He felt his voice growing louder, so he stopped and patted the counter a few times. "Let me tell you about one thing that changed me, and I mean before I even got back to town."

Rocco walked around the bar and sat on one of the stools.

"It was forty-five. The war was wrapping up. I was an MP at that point and my job was to make sure the Yanks and Limeys didn't get too rowdy before we all packed up and headed home. But while we celebrated, I also saw the German people. Their leaders had started a war that they lost. They weren't going home like us. For a lot of them, their homes were obliterated. I saw the shock in their eyes. Their old lives were gone and a new struggle was beginning. Trying to survive. Trying to rebuild from nothing."

He knew Rocco was listening. Yarrow clenched his fists and pulled out his old memories like moldy strings of taffy.

"So many people, Rocco. So many homeless, destitute, and confused people. I saw them in Italy. I saw them in Germany. They needed food. Jobs. Hell, just having a bicycle was like a pot of gold. Almost every day, women approached me and my buddies, trying to sell their bodies just to feed their children.

Husbands? Lovers? They were dead. Food stations were set up by the Allies, but the lines were long and they ran out. So, what does it take to survive? We both saw it up close." He took a long swig from his bottle, then added, "And that, my friend, is like a sledgehammer to the heart."

Then he sat back and spoke in a calmer tone. "So, yeah. What I learned was to sometimes turn a blind eye to what people do just to live."

Rocco closed his eyes. "Okay, Jim. You've made it clear. You think prostitution might sometimes be acceptable."

"No! That's not what I mean. I mean … shit. Maybe sometimes? Depending on the circumstance. And only that."

"Did you feel that way before Becky started her farm? Or is this a recent development?"

Yarrow didn't answer.

"Okay, I have sympathy for everything you said, Jim. But over on the other side of the world I saw something different. Before the war, and during, Japan allowed the enslavement of women to provide companionship for their men in uniform. Look it up sometime. They called them Comfort Women. When U.S. occupation forces finally moved in, they expressed outrage at what they saw, yet they allowed some Comfort Women locations to continue. They tried to justify it. Some of the women had nowhere else to go, so they stayed right there, doing what they were doing. And you know what? Those women ended up 'comforting' American GIs too, at the end."

"I didn't know that."

"I only know it because I saw it with my own eyes. The Allies figured leaving it in place solved two problems: it gave those women a means of income, and it gave their own men in uniform an outlet. There was even some government funding during the transition. The Japanese transitional government that we set up called it the Recreation and Amusement Association. You can look that up too."

"Dang."

"Well, it got shut down in 1946 because it quickly became an embarrassment."

"Doesn't change my mind though. What I've recently come to believe is that the choice should be up to the women themselves. And only them."

Rocco looked exasperated. "Come on, Jim! It was just wrong! It was the wrong for the Japanese to do it and it was wrong for the Americans to let it continue. And it's wrong out at Becky's farm." Rocco felt the volume of his voice increasing. "No one wants to fuck for money. It's gross. It's demeaning. And if that's the only choice they have for survival, then something is way off track in a society."

Yarrow nodded slowly. "Well, on that much, we can agree my friend."

Rocco cleaned up. Returnable bottles clanked in their cases. Rags were dragged over the counter. After a while, he spoke again.

"I know Becky's survival was a challenge when she was growing up. So she, of all people, should understand why that's wrong. But I think that survival instinct is so deeply ingrained in her family that she knows no other way. So yes, she probably is a good person, but with a street urchin's instinct for staying alive."

Yarrow contemplated the words. "I guess it helped her endure."

"The problem is, she's smart. She's figured out how to ramp things up. She helps more people, but at a larger scale, shit falls apart and she gets noticed. Scrutiny brings trouble."

"Yeah. And here we are."

"So, how much is enough for her? Will she continue to grow? Where is she going to be next month? Next year? Or five years? And where will you be?"

Yarrow shrugged.

"Becky's not going to change. So, I'm asking. Can you change your ways to accommodate hers? Will you slip deeper ever into the legal gray area? Avoiding that day of reckoning?"

"No, Rocco. I mean, come on, I'm not going to become a criminal."

"Good. Because that's where you're heading my friend."

It was nearly midnight when Yarrow returned home. He walked to the end of his driveway, looked up at the stars, and opened his mailbox. Inside the house, he sorted through the stack of bills and advertisements. On the bottom of the pile, he found a handwritten envelope with a Maine return address.

He took a deep breath and tore it open—having no idea what Linda might want to say to him in a letter. *Why would she write rather than pick up the phone?*

He pulled out two white pages. Before scanning them, he decided to grab a drink. Then he slid into his easy chair and started to read.

Chapter 56

Handwritten

American society long prioritized family and marriage, but by the late 1940s, women leaving wartime jobs often felt frustrated at the pressure to return to a homemaking role. Many men again became sole providers for their families. Women again were expected to maintain the household and raise the children. But cracks soon appeared in the family facade.

Myth of the Nuclear Family, Condit University Imprints, 1970

Before he read the first word, Yarrow noticed something strange about the letter. The text seemed neat and the language was formal on the first page. But by the bottom of page two the words were shaky and emotional.

So, was this it? The end of his marriage? He took a deep sip and a deep breath. Then dug in.

Dear Jim,

It seems so strange to start a letter with those words. We've never addressed each other so formally. And, I'm just now realizing, you and I have exchanged very few letters. We didn't need to. We've been apart very little since that wonderful summer when we met.

The words "wonderful summer" caused him to pause. What was she saying?

"When we weren't together, we mostly talked by phone. Do you remember? Early on, we just enjoyed listening to the sound of each other's voices. We always had a lot to talk about, didn't we? And sometimes we didn't need to talk at all. We'd run out of words, and there was something comforting in just listening to each other breathe.

As I write this, Jim, I've been here in Maine for over three months. I don't know how this has gone on for so long. When I left with the kids

I thought we would reconnect in a matter of days. It was always my intention that we would resolve things between us.

"Yeah, Linda. Me too," he said aloud.

I was waiting for you to reach out to me. I realize now that was a stupid little power-play. It was a selfish way to behave since I was the one who left with no warning. I came to realize I was the one who should reach out. I think your last visit triggered my change of heart. I don't know why I yelled at you for taking the kids to see some stupid televisions. You were a good dad and that was a wonderful trip for them, and they still talk about it. They've been asking when we can get one.

I regret that your visit devolved into a fight. I think my real anger was that I felt so far away from you.

I also realize that I really want to hear your voice again, without it being part of an argument. I guess that's my blunt confession.

I miss you, Jim. More than I ever thought possible. And our kids miss you. They ask about you constantly. I read them every letter and postcard you send. They always ask when you're coming home.

Actually, let me correct that. They don't ask when you are coming here. They ask when they can go home. To them, home is still our house in Riverbend. To them, home is the place where all of us live together. I can't keep that place from them anymore. I hope you still feel that way too.

He stopped reading and stared into space. He did feel that way when Linda first left. But did he still feel it? He was so angry with her. But he also still felt love. It was a much different love than what he felt for Becky, and was more stable, grounded, and honest. And only Linda could unlock a sense of calm inside of him. After all, she was the one who pulled him back to life.

And he missed his kids most of all. He steeled himself and looked down at the letter. He was determined to finish it.

It breaks my heart to see our kids in limbo. And I know deep inside that our family does belong together. That means you and I, in my mind, should be together.

This separation was my messy and foolish gambit. I fully admit my fault, but it happened out of desperation. It was never supposed to be a breakup. I just wanted you to come to Maine with me. I still want that, but I won't let it tear our family apart. And I do admit I still have a great fondness for that charming little town on the river where you grew up.

Yarrow found himself nodding.

So, that's all I wanted to tell you, Jim. I have loved you since we first met on that beach almost seven years ago. My love has not diminished. It never will. I hope you still love me and that we can talk about that.

I understand our relationship is wounded but hope I haven't damaged the love.

Please don't answer this letter immediately. Give it a day or two to sink in. Give thought to what you want to do. Then please write to me or call me. Or just show up at my door. I will welcome you, even if my mother won't.

Home is wherever we can be together. All of us.

Love,

Linda

He sat for a long time. At some point he wiped away a tear, but only once. The moon drifted lower in the sky and he sat in total darkness.

When he and Linda first met, he was just one of many returning GIs. Proud and strong. But she saw behind his façade. The world had gone insane, and she saw the choices he had to make, both at war and at peace. She saw all the scars.

Back then, Linda didn't run away. She helped him.

He closed his eyes as a new realization set in. Linda was facing her own crisis right now. The collapse of her own confidence triggered her retreat to Maine. She too needed to heal, and he missed it.

At one time, having a family was what he wanted. Then it became a reality. He knew it was something he had to keep.

Chapter 57

The Call of the Road

By the middle of the twentieth century, many traditional New England mills were closing. Aging machines. Aging buildings. Competition from other places. Workers sought better opportunities. In the first half of the nineteen fifties, hundreds of thousands of people left New England for America's southern and western states. California saw greater growth than any other state. Its population grew by over four hundred thousand every year during the 1950s.

Why Americans Move, Pragmatic Press, 1961

"I'm sorry. Say that again?" Yarrow knew his voice sounded indignant. But he wanted it to.

"What do you mean you might close?"

Rocco's Grill had become a major part of his life. It never entered his mind that his friend might shut the doors.

"I haven't decided yet, Jim. But the idea shouldn't be a total surprise. I've mentioned it before."

"But I always thought you were kidding. Just like when I talk about moving to Hawaii. We know that's not going to happen."

For better or worse, it had become Rocco and Yarrow's custom to start drinking in the early evening. Most nights there were others at the bar, but the crowd always thinned out by ten.

That evening it was just Yarrow, Rocco, and a young couple sitting toward the back.

"I need change because I'm in a rut. Hell, you are too, Jim. Look around. Same barstools. Same drinks. This has become our life. The only variable is whether Leon or Lefty are here too."

Yarrow couldn't disagree.

"I could just close for a while. Maybe I'll travel and get rid of the restlessness."

Yarrow expressed his disappointment. "Just the idea of Rocco's Grill closing leaves me feeling lost. I've been a customer since you opened. This place became even more important to me when Linda and I split."

"Oh, so that's the reason you've been dropping in more often? You had nothing better to do?"

"Well, that and your wise counsel, you fucking psychology major."

"Philosophy."

"Whatever."

He stuck a paper-covered straw in Yarrow's beer and watched the glass fizz up and over.

Yarrow slid back. "Damn it!"

Rocco threw a towel on the puddle.

"Anyway, what did a philosophy degree get me? This? I'm on my feet all day, slinging hash, and washing dishes."

"Come on. You're a small business owner. That used to give you great pride."

Rocco watched as the couple in the back prepared to leave.

"I just feel like we're entering a different time. And not just us. The whole country. When the war ended, we had the GI bill. We built homes and families. But everything else seemed to stand still. We've been stuck in time for six years now. Doing our jobs and waiting for the other shoe to drop."

"Hell," Yarrow replied, "this town has been stuck in time for a hundred years."

"Exactly. In nineteen forty-five all we wanted was to return to our normal lives. And since then, we're scared to stray from 'normal.' I include myself in that club. I know what my whole day will be like before it begins. I see the same faces. People order the same breakfasts." He held up his bottle. "When evening comes I sit with the same friends and drink the same beer. To mix things up, we go to the VFW and hear the same war stories."

"Yeah."

"Turn on the radio and I hear the same damn music. Doris Day. The Andrews Sisters. Sinatra." Rocco sighed.

"What do you want though? This is small-town America. This is what you get."

Rocco looked toward the front door. "That's my point. Look at us. We're not even thirty years old yet. I'll bet most people would peg us as well over forty."

"Gee. Thanks a lot."

"What I mean is, it's 1951. We're barely into this decade. But I can see it's a different animal. Cars look different. Music is different. Faster roads are unspooling like ribbons. Supposedly we're going to start flying in jets in the next year or two. Yesterday I read about something called a microwave oven. It cooks things in a minute or two. I bet we'll have them in our homes someday. New things are happening everywhere, but what am I doing? I'm just sitting here watching the world go by."

The couple from the back table left four dollars and ninety cents on the counter and waved as they exited. As Rocco deposited the money in his cash register, Yarrow could almost hear the gears turning in his head.

"Okay," Rocco said. "Here's what I mean. We came back home with conformity drilled into us. I understand why. We were at war and we all had to work as one. But is everyone supposed to remain regimented forever? Jesus, look at this town. Everyone has a certain look. Every guy wears the same fedora, just in different shades of gray or brown. But is that what we want? Hey, do you fit in? Great! Welcome to the mainstream!!"

"You make it sound terrible, but I find it comfortable."

"Because you've always fit in quite nicely, Jim. I envy you for that. You're the breadwinner. Until you and Linda separated you were a perfect couple. Your wife stayed home. Raised kids. Always cooking, cleaning, and keeping the house perfect. But she was losing it. She had, what, three kids in just over five years? That's exhausting. She was collapsing inside and none of us noticed until she ran."

Yarrow looked hurt. "I knew. But I always thought—"

"You thought what you and Linda had was the American standard. Right? That's how life worked and we all just had to adjust." Rocco turned off the outside lights. "But things are changing. And like most change, it's welcomed by some people and hated by others."

Yarrow's slow agreement was almost imperceptible.

"Here's what I'm starting to realize, Jim. Over time, we all gather wounds and scars. They come from everything. Our ancestry. Our day-to-day lives. The dreams we can't achieve. We keep them hidden and they slowly turn our minds into haunted houses. You and I were lucky. We've set the damaged parts of our houses back in order. But not everyone can do that."

He looked directly at Yarrow. "Maybe that's what Linda's been trying to do, you know? To set her mind right. Maybe to set things back in order with you too."

"Yeah."

"And as for me, you know why I always have music playing here? Because I need to play it. Day and night. Here and at home. Music drowns out the other thoughts. The screams. The walking wounded. Music takes me away." Rocco walked to his radio, flicked it on, and tuned into a bebop jazz station from Boston. It was the type of music he'd never play if the place was full.

Yarrow said, "I understand Rocco. And I don't disagree with you about Linda."

"You probably thought the pressure Linda was feeling would be overcome by the pressure of our Yankee tradition.

Maybe you thought she'd fall in line, just like we fell into line in boot camp."

"That's not fair."

"I'm not blaming you. Tradition expects you to conform, both men and women. Cooking. Cleaning. Kids. Did you even think she might want something else? Most men don't."

"I thought that's the way life is."

"Exactly. And that's what I meant about sliding back into the things that have suited humans for generations. But now we have faster cars. Bigger roads, TVs, and a whole new world banging on our doors. Yet, here we sit. Another Massachusetts boy, Henry David Thoreau, said it best. 'The mass of men lead lives of quiet desperation'."

Yarrow looked Rocco in the eye. "Damn it, I like my life. And I like this town. I have everything I need here. And it's just a short drive to the coast. Or to the mountains, or to Boston. There's not much that I'd call bad here. Hell, there hasn't been enough crime to even arrest anyone in two weeks."

"I'm not saying Riverbend isn't nice. It's just … you know what? Maybe I have a way to explain it. Let's go back to music. You know how I like to listen to rhythm and blues sometimes?"

"Yeah."

Rocco adjusted the radio dial again.

"In the navy I mostly listened to big band music. But when I got back to the repair base in San Diego, I met some guys who always tuned in to musicians like T-Bone Walker out of LA. I heard other bands playing along Central Avenue there and I realized I really like rhythm and blues.

"Now, hear what's playing? That's Louis Jordan."

"Yeah, I'm listening."

"So, do you like this kind of music?"

"I never saw the appeal of R&B. I mean, I guess I do like the drums."

"All right. So now," Rocco gestured with his hands like he was trying to explain some new concept, "there's a brand-new type of music I've been hearing. My cousin Todd in Cleveland works for a music store. Sometimes he sends me new records. Last week he sent something that was really different."

"More R&B?"

"Not exactly. Todd listens to some disc jockey in Cleveland. His name's Alan Freed and he plays all sorts of new music, particularly some stuff he calls rock and roll."

Yarrow frowned. "What the hell does that mean?"

"I don't know. Maybe it's the way people dance when they listen to it? Or sex? Doesn't matter. It's a faster and more intense version of R&B, but it has other stuff mixed in too. Boogie-woogie. Jazz. A hint of country. Rock and roll is almost always played by smaller bands. Just a few guys with electric guitars and drums. Sometimes a piano. I have to tell you, Jim, I really like the stuff."

"So what does this have to do with you feeling restless and wanting to travel?"

"Maybe a little. It might make more sense if you hear it."

"Bring it on."

Rocco went to the kitchen and returned with the smallest portable record player Yarrow had ever seen. *RCA Victor* was printed on the front. The record Rocco pulled from a paper sleeve was also smaller than other records. It was maybe seven inches in diameter, with a big inch-and-a-half hole in the center.

"What the hell?"

"They call these forty fives—named after the number of rotations per minute."

"Is that why you had to buy a new record player?"

"Yeah," Rocco placed the disk on the turntable. "I got this one at Montgomery Ward. Not very expensive and it can play multiple speeds."

When the music started, Yarrow was confused at first. Then he smiled. "It's definitely … um, different." But even in his skepticism, he found himself tapping his foot. "What's this song called?"

"*Rocket 88*. Guitarist is a guy named Ike Turner."

"That's some intense piano too."

They listened to the whole song. Then Rocco played two others.

"Okay, I'll admit I like it. Couldn't take too much of it though. I still like my big bands."

"I know. But like I said, everything is changing. The era we all grew up in? It's over, Jim. We're not going back. We can't."

"Maybe you can't. But to me, things don't seem all that different."

"Come on, have you seen the display windows over at Frank's Furniture? Those tables and chairs are from Denmark. They're strange and modern. Sloping legs. Hanging canvas seats. Some are just wire frames."

"I've seen them."

"Did you like it?"

"Maybe. Wouldn't look right in my house though."

"And how about those new houses popping up over by the shore? Flat roofs and long narrow windows. We're right smack in the middle of the century and architecture is making a big shift too. Everything is going modern. Bolder colors and angles. Magazines and films too. I am stunned by all that's happening, and I think I want to be part of it. But instead, I'm stuck in here looking out. I'm just watching the world roll by through greasy windows."

Yarrow realized Rocco wasn't really looking at the windows. He was focused on something far beyond that.

They sat quietly, until Yarrow spoke. "If you leave, where will you go?"

"I don't know. Maybe New York. Maybe California."

Yarrow tapped his fingers on the counter. "You know what I think? I think you're going off to find Meadow, aren't you? I think you want to find that Navy nurse you were sweet on a when you were in San Diego.

"I've thought of it."

"That's where she is, right? California?"

"Yeah, but she left San Diego, and we lost contact."

"And you're thinking about giving up everything just to go look? California is one hell of a big state my friend."

"It's not definite. I'm weighing my options. Isn't that what everyone is doing? Seeking something?"

"Maybe not everyone. But you are."

"Hell, Jim, even your wife has been looking at her options. You have been too."

Jim paused before he admitted, "I have."

Then he felt his lip quiver, and his grip on his glass tightened.

Rocco began locking up for the night. "You know, people see you as a guy who followed the right path. High school football star. War hero. Family man. Police officer. That's a good mold for this town. It helps you fit right in."

Yarrow rolled his eyes. But he let Rocco talk.

"What you find here are unwritten rules. Join the common religion. Pledge to the same flag. Drink the same beer and fight the common enemy."

"What are you hinting at? That it all comes with a cost?"

"Damn right. What did our conformance get us, Jim? My mental baggage. Your hand. Cracks in your marriage. Like I said, we're all just haunted houses. Stoic and still standing."

Yarrow looked at his beer.

"This bar and grill really helped me heal my head. I feel that's nearly complete. Now I need to decide how to finish the job."

Rocco reached under the counter and pulled out a book.

"Anyway, besides the new music, I've been reading some stuff by this guy lately—Aldous Huxley." He plopped it on the counter. "I started with *Brave New World* and now I'm reading this one, *Ends and Means.* Fantastic musings on the nature of war, inequality, religion, and modern life. We like to say the ends justify the means. But is that always the case?"

Yarrow picked it up and looked at the simple yellow cover with a block of text. He wasn't sure what to make of it.

"So, that's all I can say. There are ways to leave the violent and uncertain times behind us. But we don't do it. There's a huge leap in human consciousness out there just waiting to happen. I don't want to miss it, Jim. I want to be part of it."

He flipped off the lights.

"You can keep the book."

Chapter 58

Olive Drab

The heyday of the American hobo came during the country's Great Depression. But smaller hobo subcultures remained into the 1950s. Homeless men, many of them veterans, moved from place to place as they took labor jobs. Some found it difficult to "settle down" as society expected. The transition from a respected man in uniform to an unwelcome vagrant could happen all too easily, and it could be emotionally taxing to a man who once saw himself as part of a powerful force.

When They All Came Home, Perspective Lens Journal, 1975

It had become rare for Becky to drive her old truck into town. She had enemies now. Being physically close to people she didn't know made her nervous. But sometimes she had to come in, and this was one of those times. The next shift for the police force was starting soon, so she parked across the street from the station.

She needed to talk to Jim. She saw something earlier in the day and she hoped he would know what to do.

In a few minutes, three police cars exited the station. The third one was driven by Yarrow. He spotted Becky and immediately slowed. She looked at him and pointed. Up the street, he pulled into an empty space. She climbed from her truck and walked to his window.

"Surprised to see you here in the morning," he said. "Is everything okay?"

She looked up and down the street, then shook her head. "No."

"Do you want to tell me what's up?"

"Yeah. I found something. Or someone. Do you remember a while ago, when you told me a man may have committed suicide by jumping from a bridge upriver?"

Yarrow leaned back and closed his eyes. "Wow. Don't tell me."

"Yup. I think I found the body. It's at the base of my hill, tangled in some weeds by the riverbank. I don't know how long it's been there. I smelled something when I was by the water, so I walked over to look."

"Jesus." He took a breath. "Okay, let's go look. I'll file a report and we'll get the poor guy out of there."

Becky reacted quickly. "No. We can't do that, Jim."

"What?"

"I know it needs to be reported. But the body can't be found on my property."

"Don't worry about that. It's not like it's your fault."

He saw her hands ball up into nervous fists. "Think for a minute! Remember the ship's hull on my property? It was stolen. The body is right near there. If people come for the body, they'll find the hull too."

Yarrow stared into space for a moment. The only response he could muster was, "Huh." He had become vaguely aware of Leon's wild ride when he delivered the ship. But he never wanted to ask many questions. Now he had to face the reality of Becky and Leon's theft.

"What else don't I know Becky?"

"Nothing. I figured Leon told you where we put the ship. Besides, it's not that big a deal. But the body certainly is, so, what can we do?"

"What can we do? We're not supposed to do anything. There needs to be an investigation. That's just the routine."

"Can you be the one who does it?"

"Yeah, but others will need to visit. The coroner, plus the guys who will haul the body out."

Becky looked upset.

"Okay. Look, why don't you take me there so I can see what's up?"

She agreed and he followed her back to the farm. Together they walked down the hill.

"When did you first see the body?"

"Around six thirty this morning."

"What kind of shape is it in?"

"I don't know, Jim. But not good, I didn't want to look too closely."

"Understandable."

As they came out onto the sand, Becky pointed. "Over there."

"Stay back if you want." He went to look, then walked back.

"Yup, that's a body all right. And it's probably the guy. Just go back up the hill. If anyone comes, walk back down here, singing loudly or something. That should give me some warning."

She agreed and climbed up the path.

The body was face down and partially submerged. He assumed the man was a veteran, since he wore an old army jacket. There were corporal stripes on the arm and a big red one on the shoulder. There wasn't a speck of grey in his hair.

Too young to end up like this, Yarrow thought to himself.

He found a long stick and used it to push the body away from the bank. If he could move it into deeper water, it might drift downstream. But he didn't want it to flow all the way to the Atlantic. The man was a vet and Yarrow would not let him end up completely lost.

He pushed sideways. But as he did so, the body started to sink.

No. No. Come on!

He waited to see if it would bob back up. But it kept sinking and it started to slide toward deeper water.

Shit.

Yarrow waded in, getting his shoes and pantlegs wet. He grabbed a handful of wet jacket and pulled the body back to shore. As he did so, it rolled over.

He looked down and stared into the face of a man who had been in the water for too long. Pale skin, turned green from algae. Empty eye sockets picked clean by crabs. Flesh was gone and bone was showing on the forehead and cheeks. Yarrow felt a terrible sensation wash over him. A pressure started to build deep inside. He tried to shake the feeling and he kept pulling on the coat because he wanted this guy back on the bank.

He looked at him again and stopped to catch his breath. He also tried to slow his heart, but it kept racing. His mind sputtered and he felt like he was falling.

His reaction surprised him. He'd seen many dead bodies in his life and most were far worse than this one. *What the hell is happening?*

He turned away, hands on his head.

He knew he wasn't just reacting to the condition of the body. Something much deeper had hit him. It was the entirety of what he saw. The face, the army jacket. The hopelessness of a strong man who couldn't function when he came home.

His old memories flashed forward. The close-in battles. Wounded soldiers. The dead floating at the bottom of wet trenches looking up but seeing nothing, just like this guy.

Yarrow felt something groan in his mind. He was not prepared for the shifting weight of it. Rocco was right. He was more of a haunted house than he wanted to admit. With more scars. Memories walled off, and for the first time, he was afraid the wall might not hold.

He left the body on the sand and paced, trying to will his mind back from the breaking point. He rubbed the back of his neck and he pictured his wife. He pictured their first summer. She was the first one he ever told about these feelings.

Linda. He thought. *Jesus, I think I need to talk with Linda.*

Slowly the panic passed. He stopped pacing and finished his work. In the end, he simply tied a rope to the man's feet and dragged the body through the shallows. He moved it two hundred yards past Becky's property. Then he pulled the body up and between a pair of rocks. He untied the rope and left the veteran there.

"I'm sorry corporal. But don't worry. We'll get you home. You can count on that."

Then Jim Yarrow strengthened his will, wiped all emotion from his face, and started his climb up the hill.

Chapter 59

Family

Pyrrhus of Epirus won a great triumph against the Romans in 227. But the victory came at an immense cost in terms of men and money. That effectively ended his campaign. "Pyrrhic Victory" became a term for winning a battle at too high of a cost.

The Road to Evacuation Day, New England Revolutionary Journal, 1948

The next morning, Yarrow plucked nickels and dimes from his coin bin. He tucked them deep in his pocket before heading out on patrol. As lunchtime approached, he parked at a gas station and walked to a phone booth. This would be his first conversation with Linda since he read her letter.

He wanted to use a phone booth because he wasn't ready to hear her voice inside the house. From the pay phone he still could keep her slightly at bay. It made him feel like he was in control of whether she would be allowed back into his life.

He also wanted to keep Linda at arm's length until he saw Becky again. Maybe to say goodbye? He didn't know yet. There was always an enigmatic uncertainty with Becky that turned everything into a wild card.

He dropped his coins in the slot and closed his eyes. The phone rang four times, then the voice of Linda's mother came on the line.

"Hello?"

"Hello, Barb. It's Jim."

"Oh," was all she said. Disappointment compressed into a single word.

He heard footsteps as she went to find Linda. In time, it was Linda's voice that he heard.

"Hello?"

"Hi, Linda."

There was a long pause.

"Jim. Hi, it's … it's good to hear your voice."

"Yeah. Yours too." He worried that his voice would break, but it held.

She was silent again. He could tell she was searching for her words. Eventually, she just said, "I guess you got the letter."

"Yes. A couple of days ago. I had to think about it for a bit."

"I understand. That's good."

It was his turn to be silent.

"So, what did you think?" she blurted out. "I mean, was that silly? Am I foolish, am I—"

"Linda. Stop! It's fine. I'm glad you wrote. It surprised me, but yes, I was glad." He closed his eyes and leaned his forehead on the metal doorframe. "I really was."

"Good, good. And, so?" He heard her hair brush against the phone's mouthpiece. He pictured her head drooping, surrendering to the gravity of the situation. "I'm sorry, Jim. I shouldn't rush into this part of the talk. Let's start with something easy. Curtis had a great day at school. He got an A on one of his assignments. And Bonnie has been blurting out full sentences. She always makes me laugh."

They exchanged small talk for a few minutes and then Yarrow said what was on his mind.

"Look, Linda, I called because I've been thinking about what you wrote. We've been apart and I think both of us maybe started to move on. But as that happened, maybe neither of us wanted to take that final step. Does that make sense?"

"It does, Jim." Her voice cracked a little. "And I agree." And then she called him Sweety.

They both used to call each other Sweetie, though he always thought it was corny. But now he realized how much he missed the word and what it meant. He tapped his fingers on the top of the black phone and reminded himself to go slowly.

"Look, I have to tell you, things are a little strange right now—at work and in my personal life too. I don't know Linda. Everything is all screwed up."

"I've heard."

"You have? I mean, heard wha—"

She interrupted him. "We have mutual friends, Jim. So I know. I don't want to know the details. We've been apart and we were both confused, angry, and lonely. But at some point, I'm going to want to know more."

"That's fair. But, before we go any further, I want to ask you something. Do you remember when we first started dating?"

"Of course. I remember it fondly. Even with love."

"Me too. We came to know each other well that summer." He laughed. "And you somehow discovered all those thoughts I was hiding."

Linda laughed too. "Don't be hard on yourself. You were always strong, including mentally."

He leaned against the booth's glass door. "Thank you for not running away the first time I woke up from a nightmare."

He could hear her breathing for a moment.

"I knew you came home with a lot of things that needed to be sorted out." Her voice dropped to a whisper. "I saw it happen to my brothers and cousins too. I wasn't scared of it."

The phone dinged. Yarrow dropped in another nickel and wiped his eyes.

"I know you weren't. Thank you for that."

"The first time I talked to you Jim, it was just because you seemed nice. You were interesting enough that I looked for ways for our paths to cross again. Then, I kept talking to you because I could tell you needed to talk, and I wanted you to."

Yarrow closed his eyes.

When they reopened he noticed his breath had fogged the glass. He dragged a finger through the condensation.

"I did need that." He tried to stop his voice from shaking. "You know what? At a time when nothing else mattered, you started to matter to me, Linda. That made you unforgettable."

He heard her voice crack. "So where does that leave us, Jim? You? Me? The children?"

Yarrow knew this question was coming. He had given it considerable thought before the call. Now it was time to answer.

"I'd like to do something with you before we get back together. I hope you'll indulge me."

She laughed. "What?"

"I want you to meet me at our neutral territory."

"Um ..."

"You know what I'm talking about. Let's meet for a weekend at Hampton Beach. Remember? It's not Maine. It's not Massachusetts. Just us, meeting in between. Maybe your mom can watch the kids."

"Yeah, Hampton Beach. Neutral territory."

"Whatever we had Linda, I need to know if we can still find that. Can you find it in me? Can I find it in you?"

"I think so. Don't you?"

"I do, Linda. But you—"

"What?" she interrupted. "I left? And you know the reason why I left. You know exactly why. And—" Suddenly she stopped herself. "I'm ... I'm so sorry, I don't want talk like that—"

"It's all right. We have a lot to work out."

"Yeah."

"And I have my own issues. We're never going to agree on everything, Linda. I don't think either of us should expect everything to be forgotten."

"Probably not."

"But haven't we always said our relationship should be bigger than any argument?"

She laughed. "Yeah, we do say that."

"So, we meet in New Hampshire then? Maybe in a week or so?"

"I think so. I'll have to make plans with my mom. But, yeah, that would be nice."

"Neutral territory!"

"Indeed," Linda said. "Neutral territory."

Chapter 60

Main Street

"It'll all go back to normal if we put our nation first. But the trouble with normal is it always gets worse."

The Trouble with Normal, Bruce Cockburn, *1983*

When Yarrow started his shift, he found an envelope on his desk. Plain white paper with his name typed on the front. No return address. No other markings.

He scanned the faces of his colleagues. "Did anyone see who dropped this off?"

"It was there when we all came in."

He tore it open. After reading the note, he headed toward the town hall. The day was bright but chilly, so he walked on the sunny side of the street and pictured the text in his head. It was just two lines.

We should talk. We both need a favor right now.

- AD

He knew AD stood for Arnie Driscoll, but he wasn't sure why the mayor was keeping his message so low-key. He walked to the town hall, and as he jogged up the steps, Yarrow had no idea that Becky Bivens was heading toward the other end of Main Street.

She quickened her pace and crossed over the street, gliding past faded yellow lines and patched potholes. Her path took her straight through the door of Rocco's Grill.

Rocco caught her eye as she entered, so he was forced to nod hello. But he made no effort to greet her. Becky sat at the counter and waited. She didn't pick up a menu. She just stared calmly in his direction.

Eventually, he gave in and approached her.

"Hello Becky." He pulled out his order pad. "What will you have?"

"I'm looking for Jim. I called his house this morning. I'm wondering if you've seen him."

Rocco slid his pencil back behind his ear. "I saw him earlier today."

"Well, that's good to know. I've been waiting for him to drive past the farm like he usually does. I worry about him. I know he's made some enemies recently."

"He has. But maybe you're also worried he's avoiding you?"

She closed her eyes. "Gee, thanks Rocco. But I don't think he would do that."

He started to attend to his other customers, but suddenly he turned back.

"You know, Becky, I'm not sure if Jim would want me to tell you this. But consequences be damned." He dropped his voice to a whisper. "I know the big favor he did for you out there. I know he moved that body."

She looked him in the eyes, unflinching.

"And?" he asked.

Becky looked confused. "And … what?"

"Jim is torn about that. He knows he crossed a line. I think you know it too."

At that point she finally picked up a menu. "I'm not sure what you mean."

Rocco leaned in. "I think, you do. A cop should never move a body before a death is investigated. It's tampering and you know it. Even though that guy drifted there totally by accident, and even though the police investigation will be minimal, you can't go erasing what little evidence there might be at the scene."

Becky slowly nodded. "I do understand that, Rocco. But still, I'm glad to have it off my property. That's all I can say."

He raised his eyebrows. "And you haven't seen Jim since?"

She shook her head.

"Any idea why?"

"I don't know. That's why I came here. And you're right, maybe I am worried he's avoiding me."

Rocco looked toward the bus station down the street.

"He's probably not mad or anything. My guess is he's torn about what to do. He needs to think things through."

"Does he think he was wrong to help me?"

"Maybe. But it may be deeper than that." He felt awkward delivering one more bit of news. "You should also know that Jim got a letter from his wife. He told me this morning."

He waited for the news to sink in. But Becky stared straight ahead.

"Linda wants him back, Becky. And she said she will come back here. They can live as a family in Riverbend."

Becky bit her lip and her eyes grew wide.

"I just thought you should know."

He could see the news seeping in. He watched her feelings of doubt, hurt, and loss burrow.

"I, I don't. I mean, what did he …" Her words wouldn't coalesce. Her feelings just gave way to other feelings mid-sentence. Finally, she sputtered, "What did he say? I mean, about all that?"

Rocco gave her a sympathetic smile. "Our conversation stopped there. So, I can't say for certain. But he's often said he misses his kids, and he seemed elated that he might be with them again."

"He did?" Her voice was soft and distant. Her mind didn't seem to be in the room anymore.

"I'm sorry Becky. I guess the rest is between you, Jim, and now Linda. For what it's worth, I do think he loves you. But he also understands life will never be normal when he's with you. Jim needs normal."

Becky looked away. When she turned back he saw defiance in her eyes, yet cracks were already forming. "But isn't that what we're all trying to do? Have a normal life? You with this restaurant? Me with my farm?"

Rocco shook his head. "The fact is, Becky, we don't all crave normal. I don't include Jim in that. The big galoot is a square peg that found a nice square hole. He is quite happy living here, being a cop and a family man. But others, like you and me, we don't fit so comfortably. Maybe that's because we notice things, and we see broader challenges to address. Hell, this whole town has had some sort of lingering collective trauma since the war ended. We just don't talk about it. And look at you. You more than anyone have tried to make changes to a place that fears the idea of change most of all.

Becky nodded.

"Jim also said something about visiting Hampton Beach with Linda. He felt that was important."

Those words made Becky rise quickly. She silently hurried to the exit, tears welling up in her eyes. She bit the knuckle of her index finger to stifle a cry that would otherwise pour out the door and follow her onto the street.

Chapter 61

Alternatives

A small New England town can seem different to different people. Simultaneously rich and poor. Threatening or welcoming. Familiar yet strange. Two people may visit the same place and come away with vastly different opinions on a New England town and its nature.

Main Streets and Common Destinies, James Cooter Publishing, 1963

The receptionist spoke first. "Good morning, Officer Yarrow. The mayor said to send you right in."

As he entered, Mayor Driscoll motioned for him to close the door. Yarrow plopped into a chair without being asked and gave the mayor an icy stare. "What's this all about?"

"I wanted to talk with you."

"Yeah? Here I am."

The office door opened again, and an older man calmly strolled in. Yarrow immediately recognized him. It was Driscoll's father.

The mayor smiled. "You and I both have serious problems right now, Jim."

Yarrow regarded him like a bothersome gnat. "I suppose that's true. Different problems for each of us, but probably the same root cause." Then he looked toward the father. "So, what's this? Teaming up with your dad? Looking for a fix?"

"In a way," the older man said.

"So," the mayor began, "I think you realize the Bivens Farm is on the verge of collapse. I don't know how soon. But we both know it's coming."

"What's your point, Mayor?"

He leaned forward. "My point is this. You are in this fiasco right up to your neck and your job is on the line."

"If you say so."

The father spoke up. "Jim, any legal threat to you is not coming from my son. In fact, we'd be quite happy to let you carry on with that Bivens woman in any way you want. But there are folks in this building, and within your police department, who see you as her chief enabler. That's the real issue. If we were to listen to them, you wouldn't just lose your job. You could be charged criminally."

"Yeah? I'd say that's a stretch." He looked around the big office. Leather desk pad. Fine cashmere coat on a brass hook. Out the window, he saw Arnie Driscoll's yellow Imperial parked in its reserved space. A big Coupe DeVille sat beside it. Yarrow assumed that belonged to the dad.

The elder Driscoll leaned back. "What if we offered you a way out?"

"How? Do you have a magic wand?"

"Actually, we might."

The mayor spoke next. "What if we were able to move you away from your current hotspot, Seargent Yarrow? That might be the bit of magic you need."

Yarrow frowned a bit. "I'm listening."

Driscoll placed his index fingers together. He rested them on the bridge of his nose.

"With all our rapid growth and new roads, the town applied for a state grant. Our goal is to establish a community development office that can handle planning for Riverbend's future expansion. The office will help balance the town's competing interests without blocking development."

"Okay. So?"

"So, big surprise, we actually received the grant. One stipulation is we're supposed to hire a commissioner to oversee the new office." He leaned forward. "I'm thinking maybe you might like that job. And it would come with a pay raise."

The mayor leaned back. "You can thank my father for the idea."

Yarrow looked stunned. "I … wow. I guess I'm flattered. But I don't think I'm qualified to do that."

"What do you think the qualifications are?" the dad asked.

"I have no idea."

"Nor does anyone else. That's the point."

Yarrow scratched his head.

"I can write the job description any way I want," said the mayor. So, I'll say we're looking for someone with deep roots in town. Maybe a guy who's lived locally for his whole life. But it should also be a guy who's smart enough to understand the benefit of growth, unlike some of these yokels. Also, maybe we want a guy who has been involved in some kind of community outreach before. You know, like in policing. I also want someone who people will respect. Like a war veteran. Shall I keep going?"

"I get the point."

"So, what do you think?"

Yarrow looked skeptical. "I don't think you're making this offer out of the goodness of your heart. I think you want something."

The mayor looked at his dad. He seemed reluctant to continue, but the father gave him a subtle nod. "Okay, as of now you, Becky, Rocco, and my dad are the only people who know about my visits to the farm. She cryptically wrote my name in her book. So that's good at least. Another plus: the woman I used to visit at the farm has moved on."

"Was she the one who always wore the low-cut—"

"Yes."

Yarrow raised his eyebrows. "Huh. Well, good for you." Then his voice took on a more somber tone. "But let's be clear. Are you asking me to lie?"

"No. I'm just asking you not to volunteer anything. I'll do the same for you, at least regarding your involvement with the farm."

"You have no idea what my involvement is."

"What we don't know, we'll find out," said the dad. "But only if we have to."

"I see. Old money, big resources, eh?"

"If you mean there's an advantage to having deep roots in a town, then yes."

Yarrow mulled the offer over. "Fuck. I don't know. It sounds like a possible escape plan, but maybe I should talk to a lawyer before I agree to any of this."

"Yes. Please do. I want you to do what's in your best interest. Of course, I'd appreciate it if you left the Driscoll family name out of those conversations. But please do ask your lawyer something. Ask him about the difference between withholding evidence if questions are asked, versus remaining mum and volunteering no details if no questions have been asked. The latter seems more defensible, for all of us."

Yarrow wasn't sure how to respond.

"So, tell me, Jim, how are your kids? I know you've been separated for a while."

"Kids are fine. I see them fairly often."

"Good. Good. I'm sure that's nice. I'm sure you'd like that to continue."

Yarrow shot him an angry look. "The conversation about my kids ends now. Understand Arnie?"

The mayor held up his hand. "Staying discreetly silent hasn't been your way of doing things, Jim. It hasn't been mine either. So please believe me when I say this: I fucked up. And so did you. But I feel we both got involved with this honey thing without realizing how slippery of a slope it would be."

A painting of Riverbend's first mayor hung on the far wall, and Yarrow focused his attention there. He wondered how much that first mayor knew about running a town when it was founded in sixteen sixty-six. Did he have experience? Or was he just winging it? But the community survived and thrived. Yarrow realized various mayors probably had been winging it ever since.

"A slippery slope," he repeated. "That much is certainly true."

"So, that is the offer. New job. You'll avoid the public embarrassment of being fired from the police. You simply transfer, keep a low profile, and ease into your new role. But there will be no more connection to the force or the conflicts that created. This is your way out."

Yarrow looked at the floor. "Maybe it's one way out." Then he looked back at the mayor. "But I need to know. What about Becky?"

"What about her?"

"Don't patronize me. I need to know she'll be okay. I need to know she's not going to be arrested and splashed across the news. And I need to know she won't lose her farm."

"We can't promise too much."

"Then tell me what you can promise."

The mayor looked at his dad. "Okay. I agree not to shut her down. Or have her arrested. Jesus, think of the investigation that would trigger for us too. I'll also promise to slow or redirect any attempt by town officials to pressure her. But, goddamn it Jim, we are going to have to push her toward legitimacy, and I mean immediately. Like with cattle prods and bulldozers."

Yarrow chuckled.

"Furthermore, I don't know what Essex County will try to do. Nor the state attorneys. Many things are outside our control, especially if people decide to file their own lawsuits."

"You think that will happen?"

"Let's just say there are wives and mothers who are upset with their men. But it's easier if they can blame someone else.

They want Becky's head on a platter. A few of them will figure out how to get that."

Yarrow sighed. The mayor sighed. The father shook his head.

"But anyway, I think you'd make an awesome commissioner."

"Whatever the hell that is."

"Exactly. Whatever. But I'm confident you'll figure that out and be good at it. Plus, you'll be out of uniform. Rumor is your wife would like to see that."

Yarrow made angry eye contact with the mayor. Then he rose and left the office. He didn't accept or reject the offer. But he knew it might be his only way out. Old money would triumph again. He suddenly realized why the young and inexperienced Arnie Driscoll was unopposed when he ran for mayor. No one wanted to go up against his family.

Old money. That's also what sent me off to war. He'd never had such a thought before, but the events of the summer were causing him to do some rethinking.

Chapter 62

Bee Free

Sometimes, the queen of a hive develops issues. If the worker bees sense that a new queen is needed, they may put the existing queen on the run. They may deprive her of sustenance. To encourage a split, they may allow a new queen to be raised. That queen will eventually rule the hive while the old queen, and those who remain loyal to her, will need to leave.

Becky's Guide to Raising Bees, Unpublished, 1951

The encampment at the Bivens Farm had grown so large that Becky no longer knew all the residents. They came and went. She welcomed newcomers when she could and always encouraged existing residents to make room.

She enjoyed taking evening walks around the grounds. She'd ask residents where they were from, how they ended up at the farm, and where they wanted to go next. She would always ask about their destinations because she wanted the residents to think of the farm as a waystation, not a permanent home.

During one of those walks, she met two women who came from Revere.

"Ah," Becky said, "We had some recent dealings with folks from there."

"I've heard," said the one with the light brown ponytail.

"You have?"

"Yes. I think you're talking about that Swamp Riders gang. My friend dates one of their members. Full patch guy. When I told her I was coming here, she told me about how they started a fight at the farm, then got chased off."

"Well, that did happen. Did she say anything else?"

"She said he doesn't like to talk much about the club. They can be all secretive-like. But I heard tell that some of them were plenty mad. They felt disrespected."

"And angry?"

"Well, yeah. Anger is just part of their nature. She said a couple of members talked about getting revenge. But the full club ain't on board. Apparently, the guy who got gut-punched by the cop has been an ongoing problem for the riders. He's always having run-ins with cops and other people. There's been talk of changing his standing and turning him out."

Becky asked more questions, but the woman had no other details.

Over the course of the evening, Becky found more newcomers to talk to. Only a few were from the North Shore and neither knew much about the Swamp Riders.

Then late in the evening, she met a second woman who had a passing acquaintance with the club. That's when Becky learned the Swamp Riders recently received an anonymous donation. It came with a request that they help with some issue.

"Do you know what the issue was?"

"No," the woman replied. "But whatever it is, I hear-tell there's some woman who now has a price on her head."

The next morning, Becky worked on her hives and kept a wary eye on the horizon. In the late morning, she saw Amy running toward her. As she tried to catch her breath, she haltingly whispered some words in Becky's ear.

Becky nodded. "How long?"

"Not even forty-eight hours. They're waiting for three guys who are coming out of town."

"I see."

That night, she walked through the camp and gave warnings. "Beware," she said, "and always be vigilant. Stay with a group and carry something you can use as a weapon."

"What should we do if trouble starts?"

"Be ready to run. Keep a bag packed. If you have to, just run into the woods. Hide there. Or follow the river. Do what you must."

Nearly half the residents packed up and left immediately Others moved to the riverbank. But some stayed and pledged their support.

"Please don't take that risk," Becky responded. "I'll never ask you to fight for me."

Becky barely slept that night. Before first light, she rose and slipped into her beekeeping outfit—full rig with boots, mask, and gloves. Smoker in hand, she walked into the field. No one was going to destroy her colonies.

It was a cool morning with medium fog. The sumacs and maples near the water had already turned red. Walking through the blurred landscape, she methodically moved from box to box, opening tops and pulling frames from their slots.

If she could quickly spot a queen, she'd pluck her from the group and then carry her, along with a handful of worker bees, to the edge of the meadow. If she could put the queen in a safe place, most of the colony would follow.

If the queen was not immediately visible, she would lay the frames on the open ground. The exposure to the air and the change of orientation would awaken the colony's defenses. That could be enough to make them swarm.

She also carried a spray bottle holding a mix of Citronella oil, garlic, and cinnamon. All three scents were offensive to bees. By mixing them, she hoped the liquid would trigger multiple alarm bells in their little bee minds.

The bees were slow and groggy in the morning chill. Some didn't want to move. But she was persistent. The buzzing grew loud, but her white suit gave her protection. When bees landed on her she gently shook them off.

For three hours she disassembled hives and when she was done the field had the look of a tornado zone. When she finished, she stood and looked at all the pieces. She had expected to cry, but the tears never came. For now, she was stoic and tenacious.

Becky watched individual colonies rise from the scattered frames. They buzzed in circles. Some gathered temporarily atop the places where they once lived.

She knew the process. Each group was trying to understand what happened. She watched one colony and then another make their decisions. Then each swarmed in their chosen direction, like static-filled clouds on a new mission.

Amy emerged from the woods and saw the damage. She ran to join Becky and was visibly upset as she watched the departing bees. "Where will they go?" she asked.

"I can't say for sure. Some may find their way to other farms. Maybe they'll be collected by another keeper. Some may travel deep into the forest and never live in a human-built hive again.

"They don't need us," Amy lamented. "You told me that once."

"No, they don't. But I do hope some may be gathered by other beekeepers. Good ones who can take better care of them than what I could provide."

Amy rested her head on Becky's shoulder and started to cry. Becky stroked her hair.

"Thanks for all you've done here, Amy. You still have your father's farm. You should go back there. I know you rented it to someone, so maybe tell the tenants you can't renew their lease when it's up. Just pitch your tent on the property until then. You're lucky enough to have more than most of these women.

She gave Amy a final hug, then sent her to gather her things.

Becky stood in her white beekeeper's outfit and took one last look. Then she turned and passed through the wreckage. Straggler bees buzzed around her. Some decided to follow. As she reached the field's far end, she resembled a staticky white ghost consumed by the anonymity of the mist.

Chapter 63

The Melting

For most of the nineteenth century, the waterways of New England were lined with textile, lumber, and grist mills. As water-powered machinery became a production powerhouse, young people often left their farms to work in the more lucrative factories. But after a couple of successful generations, international competition and plummeting textile prices forced outdated mills to close. With fewer places hiring, and no farms to return to, a mid-century working-class crisis began to emerge.

How the Rust Belt Was Lost, Wainright Journal, 1979

A stream of residents exited the farm all day. They carried bedrolls and backpacks. Some carried children.

Passing cars slowed, with drivers taking time to gawk. Occasionally a ride was offered, but only to those with children in tow.

As twilight came, the farm was nearly empty.

Around midnight a lone figure, small and dressed in black, stood on the other hill, across from the farm. Beside her was a truck, also black. The dark coverings allowed both to blend into the night. Shadows within other shadows.

Then came the roar, distant at first but with a familiar throaty bass. There were more motorcycles this time. Over a dozen. Bandanas concealed the riders' faces. There were no patches or other identifying marks on their clothing, but their noise and aggressive confidence gave them away.

Swamp Riders with incentive money in their pockets.

The dark figure watched from her hill as the bikers dismounted. Some unstrapped cylinders from their back saddles. They were Aeroil weed-burning torches—the kind sold at farm stores. Each was filled with kerosene.

The men used hand pumps to pressurize the tanks and lit small pilot flames on the tips of the three-foot wands. With a light squeeze of a trigger, those wands could squirt eighteen-inch jets of fire, like tiny flame throwers.

The bikers made their way toward various parts of the farm. Their actions were methodical as they moved like fireflies over the acreage.

They set fire to tarps, tables, and cloths. Those burned quickly and as tables collapsed, they, in turn, set fire to the boxes and equipment stored beneath.

Becky's produce stand burned first, followed by the camp area and the Quonset hut. The night grew brighter as the flames spread. The glowing dots made their way toward the fields and the hives.

The group's sheer cruelty was on display. They had no issue lighting fire to the remaining boxes and bees. Honey will burn if you get it hot enough.

It took the men less than fifteen minutes to set fire to every structure and hive on the land. They even made their way downhill to the old ship's hull, where they torched the interior. Flames stretched out from the portholes as they retreated.

The arsonists roared away as police lights appeared in the distance. Their bikes were pointed in a different, more northerly direction than before. A few minutes later fire trucks and police cars rolled in from the south. But there was nothing to be saved. Ashes and embers fluttered onto the gravel.

While firemen snuffed the remaining fires, the police spent over an hour searching for residents. Only two women were found. They were hiding in the woods and neither knew Becky's whereabouts.

At five in the morning the trucks departed and the farm was quiet. The woman in black still watched from the hill. When everything seemed clear she drove down the bumpy slope, out onto the road, then into the farm. She removed a box and two bags from the back of the truck and left them on the ground. She set a ledger on the top with bookmarks on several pages.

Then she drove away. Behind her, on the truck floor, lay the deed to the farm and some shoe boxes full of cash.

Chapter 64

Ripples

They swarmed around me like bees, but they were consumed as quickly as burning thorns.

Psalm 118:12

A ringing phone caused him to jolt awake. Rubbing the sleep from his eyes, Yarrow walked to the kitchen and grabbed the receiver on the seventh ring.

"Hello?"

"Jim?"

"Uh, yeah."

"It's Tina."

It took him a moment to realize he was talking with the police dispatcher.

"Oh. Hi Tina. Wow. Why are you calling me at home? And so late. Or early?"

"I had to let you know, you should go out to that farm. You know the one."

"What? Why?"

"Just go, Jim. Others are heading there, so you should be too. Get there first if you can." And with that, the line went dead.

He quickly donned his uniform and jumped in his car. Every time he reached a straight portion of the road his foot dropped hard on the accelerator.

At the farm he climbed from his car and was stunned by what he saw. Everything he remembered was now just black wreckage. The stand itself was a smoldering pile. In the field, scorches marked the earth where hives once stood. One remaining fireman stood watch by the hut—just a Jake on guard for sparks and flare-ups.

Yarrow nodded to him. Then, with a sense of trepidation, he jogged to where Becky's truck was always parked. He found the space empty. There was no evidence of a burned vehicle, but a scorched trashcan that held a dozen depleted cans of black spray paint.

He noticed the box and bags on the ground, and as he approached, he saw Becky's ledger sitting on top. He was confused. The ground beneath them was scorched, but none of the items appeared burned.

Those must have been placed there after the fire, he thought to himself.

He'd return to them. For now, he'd search for people.

He ran through the fields, then to where the tents once stood, then to the apiary. But everything looked different. Everything was gone. Burned or melted. Sticky honey oozed along the weeds. Some of the puddles still steamed.

His search became frantic, he found no evidence of Becky, or anyone else. Disheartened, he walked back to the boxes and ledger.

Just then, two other cars rolled in. One carried an officer from his department, the other was a county sheriff.

Damn!

He rushed toward the ledger. The other men were already out of their cars. They hurried toward him.

"Hold on Jim, we need to take that as evidence."

"That's exactly what I'm doing!"

"No, no. Leave it for us."

That's when Yarrow realized the Riverbend cop was one of the department's two detectives. That made him angry. Yarrow only knew him as Earl, and he knew he was a cousin of Mary Jane's. He'd only met him once because Earl seldom came into the station. The secretaries called him the ghost cop, but no one seemed willing to challenge his attendance record.

"No need to get involved, Earl. I'm already handling the investigation. You can stand down."

"What? Who assigned you?"

Yarrow raised his voice. "Who assigned you?"

Earl looked flustered, but only for a moment. "Look, Yarrow, I outrank you. I'm ordering you to drop that stuff."

"And I'm saying I was here first, and I'm aware that you have a conflict of interest in this case. So, unless you can tell me how you were assigned to this case, any claim you're in charge carries no weight." He looked Earl in the eyes. "In other words, back the fuck off."

Then he turned to the other officer.

"And I see we have a sheriff's deputy! Excellent. Since you're here too, I'm requesting that you be the one to take these items and log them into evidence. I'll trust you to make sure none of this disappears."

The sheriff stood stoically and switched his gaze back and forth between Yarrow and Detective Earl. Then he spoke. "Okay, officers, tell me what the hell's going on here."

Earl started to speak, but Yarrow talked louder and faster. "We need this ledger, and whatever is in those boxes, to be part of the record of what happened here. As you can see, everything else here burned. That tells me this stuff is supposed to be found. I suspect it will help us put some of this vandalism into context."

"Okay," the deputy responded. "And you don't want your detective to take it. Why?"

"Because Seargent Yarrow is a criminal." Earl shouted. The deputy held up a finger. "Stop. I'm asking him."

"Actually," Yarrow spoke softly, "it's because Earl here is a relative of the woman who may have played a part in this attack and all of this damage."

Earl looked angry. "That's a lie. He's the one that's in trouble."

The sheriff stared in bewilderment.

Detective Earl redirected his ire toward the sheriff. "Who called you here anyway? This isn't your jurisdiction. It's a local matter. And how did you even arrive here at the same time as me?"

"I think it was your town dispatcher. Tina. Now I understand what she meant about having a neutral third party."

Yarrow laughed. "Way to go, Tina."

Earl steamed.

The sheriff's deputy motioned toward the boxes. "Look, I don't know what's going on. But since you two can't agree, and since we don't need any accusations of evidence tampering, let's just open this stuff together. We're all lawmen. Let's write down the inventory and I'll take it back to the county evidence lock-up."

Earl started to protest but realized he was outvoted.

They opened the first box, and as if on cue each man's eyes widened. It was filled with neat bundles of U.S. bills; mostly fifties and hundreds. The other boxes held the same. A note on top read, "This is one-half of the total. I've left it here to settle accounts."

While Yarrow and Earl watched each other like hawks, the sheriff grabbed a camera from his car. When he returned, they spread the bundles on the ground. "This is bizarre," he said as he took photos. "What kind of criminal runs away, but leaves a note and half their stash?"

"You'd have to know Becky," Yarrow said. "It sort of runs in the family."

They counted the money together, with the total coming to twenty-eight thousand seven hundred dollars.

"All right," the sheriff said. "That's a nice amount of cash, and it's duly recorded. Now let's look at this book."

They flipped through the pages of the ledger and commented on specific names or deposits.

"Wow," the sheriff exclaimed as he photographed some pages. "Would it be fair to say this is going to cause some ripples in your town?"

"I think that is very much an understatement."

Earl walked toward his car. Yarrow knew there would be hell to pay in the morning. The chief and others would be furious at him for butting heads with a superior officer, and for involving the county sheriff's office. But he didn't care. He'd deal with the fallout.

By the time the sheriff left with the evidence, the sun was fully up. Gawkers drove by on the road. They slowed, then sped away when Yarrow glanced in their direction.

He took another walk through the farm, hoping to spot some remaining pieces of her life. But he found nothing. With hands thrust into his pockets he kept walking, through the sweet-smelling honey puddles and carcasses of bees. He passed the remains of cooking stoves and burned-out containers of white gas. He stopped and watched an old balled-up tarp roll like a tumbleweed toward the woods.

That's when he saw Amy Maye.

She emerged from the woods with tear streaks on her face and soot on her blouse. He ran to her and allowed her to collapse in his arms. She cried for only a minute, then wiped her face and tried to catch her breath.

"Were you hiding in there?"

"Yes," she said. "Most of the night. A few other women too."

"Is Becky—"

Amy closed her eyes. "She's gone. I mean, she's okay, but she wasn't here when they attacked. She left after she made sure we were safe. And she made me promise to tell you she was sorry."

Yarrow looked at her. "Sorry for what?"

"She said you would know. Maybe not today. But eventually. That's all. She said you would come to understand."

Not again, he thought.

He asked Amy to wait near his car. He wanted to do something before they left. He stepped over the old WPA sign, now lying scorched on the ground, and made his way down the path toward the river. The water was clear and the tide was low. A handful of minnows sensed his shadow and darted away.

That's when he saw the black words painted on the fallen tree that stretched over the water. That was where he and Becky had sat, sipping wine and getting reacquainted. He stepped into the water and waded toward the spot. The paint was still tacky and stuck to his skin as he ran his fingers over the letters.

HERE THERE WAS LOVE

That was all it said. But her message was clear. He had to turn away. He stared at the ground as he climbed the path.

Yarrow knew the painted words would cling to that tree for years, but he would never lay eyes on them again. He would never return to that stretch of sand.

Chapter 65

Temporary Nations

Once in place, the national highways provided some small-town people with a means to escape. A tank of gas could take you away from a declining neighborhood and toward a thriving one.

The Interstate Aftermath, Greendale University Press, 1981

By the time Rocco and Jim said goodbye, the big road was paved, marked, and opened to traffic. A SOLD sign sat in the window of the Grill, while Rocco stood with a gas station map unfolded on the hood of his pickup.

"What route are you taking?" Yarrow asked.

"Still trying to decide. I'll probably cut southeast toward Route 20. I'll take that west and stay well above New York City until I cross the Hudson. Maybe zig-zag south toward Virginia. Route 50 from there. Straight shot to the West Coast."

"You'll find places to stay. A lot of the tourist-cabin motels are still along the older routes and newer motels near the Interstate exits."

"I brought a tent too, just in case."

Rocco and Yarrow shook hands, then hugged, slapping each other's backs.

"Is your job working out for you?" Rocco asked.

"It is now. It took over a year for things to fall into place, but we found our niche. We've identified key development areas and I'm meeting with an investment group soon. Their specialty is building small plazas. And I've already given them Leon's name to help with any excavation."

Rocco gave an earnest smile. "That's good, I hope that all works out."

"Thanks. And I hope you find what you're looking for, my friend."

Rocco opened the truck door as Yarrow added, "Still don't know how you'll find your nurse friend Meadow."

Rocco slid behind the wheel and shut the door. "Yet, I think I will. I know the type of people she's drawn to. And the key is, I know she seeks communities where people live together and support each other. You know, utopian societies. Collective settlements. Communes. She's ever-hopeful like that. Even in California, that's a limited number of places."

"So, just a matter of putting on the mileage and asking around?"

"Yeah. Pretty much that."

Yarrow waited for a motorcycle to pass. "If you do find her, do you think she'll still be interested? And still be available?"

"A man can hope."

"And could you live the way she does?"

"I don't know the answers to any of those things, Jim. That's all part of the adventure. But I definitely see things differently now and am in even more agreement with the way she views the world." He thought for a moment. "You kept telling me I'm a socialist. But I disagree. I'm still a capitalist at heart, but more like Thomas Paine or Adam Smith. They believed in social safety nets. And that markets should be able to produce wealth without steep inequalities."

He wiped at a smudge on the windshield. "Anyway, I won't predict whether anything I do from here-on will be long-term. I've stopped expecting permanence."

Yarrow looked up Main Street, toward the place where the road disappeared. "You've talked a lot about that recently—how nothing is permanent. What was that expression you used last week? 'Temporary nations?'"

"Yup. That was something I thought about while looking at an old atlas. People. Towns. Countries. Every few decades, borders change. Names too. Battles occur. We barely remember most of them."

"Sadly, that's true."

"And it hit me that everything starts as temporary. People drift in and stake a claim. If a new empire takes root, maybe those people will thrive. If not, theirs is a nation that never becomes."

"And sometimes nations fight to survive. I guess that's what we went through."

Rocco grew pensive. "Funny thing though? When we were young, we were taught to hate the Germans and Japanese. But now I view them with pity. Or at least I pity the low-level soldiers. Even if they'd won instead of us, there would have been little reward for the average fighter. Wars are for the wealthy. The poor bear the wounds."

They watched a group of kids ride past on their bikes. Yarrow recognized one of them as the son of a classmate who was killed in France.

"Yeah," Yarrow agreed. "We won. That means everything should have been bright and good when we came back. Yet, it wasn't. Not for most."

Rocco sighed. "Let me just say, Jim, back when we had to pick a side, did we even think about the unfairness of who is called to serve? I certainly didn't. Sometimes it takes years to understand that."

"For some people, maybe. But I think we fought for the right reasons."

"I admire your confidence." He nodded toward Yarrow's hand. "I hope the scar you earned continues to give you that sense of pride."

Yarrow frowned. "And you? Any pride for your service?"

"Some. But cynicism too. And sometimes I wonder why it happened in our time. We would have been different people without it."

Yarrow stepped back as Rocco started the engine.

"You know Jim, I could never be as happy here as you. You always could fit right in. At least one of us adapted well."

"I just made my choice, I guess."

"And some of us realize we have to move on."

Something in Rocco's words made Yarrow think of Becky. He shook the feeling away. "You know what? Get out of here. Drive safely, you moron."

Before he pulled away, Rocco handed Yarrow a wrapped box. "Present for you."

Yarrow ripped it open and found himself holding the clanging bell that used to hang above the grill's front door.

"What? Really?"

"I thought you should have it."

"You know I'm going to throw this in the river, right?"

"Make sure someone gets a picture of that. And you know what? You never did order a slice of pecan pie!"

Yarrow watched the truck roll out of sight. Then he headed back to a home that was more than half paid for, where he knew he'd find a homecooked meal on the table and his kids watching their new television in the living room.

Chapter 66

June 18, 1967

These modern college kids? We don't really understand them. Very few join the ROTC. Instead, they focus on ideas like counterculture, ecology, and some kind of "higher consciousness" they can only find with psychedelics. What they call a radical new sensibility seems more like a threat to traditional values.

A letter from Boston, Author Unknown, 1967

Forest-green metal. Tan Landau roof.

Jim Yarrow was proud of his new car. It was a Thunderbird Special with three hundred and forty-five horses tucked beneath the hood. And it was the first car he owned with leather seats and air conditioning.

He paused for a moment to admire its sleek lines, then he climbed in and sped away from the Riverbend High School. Bonnie's graduation had been held outside. It was a sunny afternoon and everyone was sweating. But he didn't mind. It was amazing to see what a fine young woman she had become.

He watched Bonnie walk across the stage, head held high and tassel flowing. He was so proud of her. Proud of his boys too. Both were home from college and working their summer jobs.

The commencement speaker was a Congressional Medal of Honor recipient. With a VFW cap perched on his head and the blue ribbon and star hanging around his neck, he said something that still lingered in Yarrow's mind. The old soldier told the graduates to work diligently but be prepared for a life that might add up to little more than the sum of their griefs. He talked of lost friends and loved ones and world events they could not control. Sacrifice was a duty, he said, and one should feel like they can never do enough.

Jim Yarrow knew why the veteran felt that way. But he hoped his kids would live lives that were more than just accumulated sadness or remorse.

Linda planned a big post-graduation party for Bonnie, so he drove separately to the graduation. His wife had asked him to buy beer and soda on his way home and he also needed to get some fresh rolls and a platter of cold cuts.

The quest took him toward the Blanchard General Store, which also allowed him to feel the horsepower on his new ride. He accelerated into every straightaway and grinned at the T-Bird's kettle drum roar.

The state had widened the road twice in recent years and built a highway entrance ramp near the land once occupied by the Bivens Farm. The farmland itself had been vacant for some time.

As he roared past, something caught his eye. It was just a sign, painted white with two hand-lettered words.

Local Honey.

Yarrow frowned. Gravel crunched as he slowed and coasted onto the shoulder.

What the hell?

He looked in his mirror, then turned around.

As he entered the farm, he spied a young woman at a small table. She had straight hair and wore round sunglasses and a floppy hat. With cautious uncertainty, he killed the engine.

The woman waved.

He climbed out, noticing several jars of honey on the table.

"That looks like a fine crop," he said. "Are you the beekeeper?"

"Thank you. And yes, I am. These are all from my hives. I was lucky this year. Good healthy bees, with sweet clover and alfalfa nearby."

Yarrow estimated the girl to be about eighteen years old. She wore a bright paisley print dress and petite glass beads on a string around her neck. Love beads, the kids called them. He didn't recognize her as one of the local teens.

He picked up one of the jars. "Very nice. And, it says *B. Farms*." He tried to look her in the eyes but saw only his reflection in her wire-rimmed lenses. "Do you have any connection to the old Bivens Farm?"

"No. But I knew some of them. I admired them."

He placed the jar back on the table. "I see. So, does that mean you knew—"

"Becky? Of course."

He was silent for a moment, then asked, "So, tell me. How is she?"

The young woman smiled, but her face held a hint of sadness. "I lost touch with Becky a couple of years ago. She tended to move quite often."

"Yeah," he chuckled. "She certainly did."

She pulled down her sunglasses and gazed over the lenses. "Now, can I ask you a question?"

"I suppose so."

"How are you, Mr. Yarrow? Do you still wear your uniform?"

Her words took him by surprise. "I'm sorry. Do I know you?"

"No, no. We've never met. But Becky had many stories about her time in Riverbend. A lot of those stories included you. She showed me a photo of you once. She's the one who taught me all about raising bees. She was quite good at it."

"She genuinely was."

"I used to help her with her hives. Whenever we worked, she would tell me about all the places she lived over the years and how she tried to find perfect fields for her apiaries."

"Like this one?"

"Other places too. New Hampshire. Maine. But yes, Becky said her greatest memories were of this field and the people she knew when she was here."

Hearing Becky's name again after so long made him feel strange. When she disappeared, he always assumed he'd see her again. But that time never came. After a few years, he realized she'd managed to fade back into the landscape.

"Well," he said, "to answer your questions, I'm doing fine, thanks. And, no, I'm not a police officer anymore. That was a long time ago. I left the force right after Becky was run out of … I mean, when she left."

"It's okay, Mr. Yarrow. You don't need to sugarcoat things. I know the whole story."

"That, that's good to know." He took a deep breath. "So, when I left the police force, I had little choice. I was too involved with her, and it became apparent my time in uniform was done."

Something caught his eye just then. Clusters of yellowish-white flowers were growing in the spot where Becky had once parked her truck. He realized he was looking at wild Yarrow, just like his name. He wondered if someone had planted them there as a joke.

"Thanks for being honest," she replied. "I knew the basics of what happened. But I never knew the outcome for you." She studied his crisp suit, then his new car. "From the look of things, I'd say you did quite well."

"I guess I did," he said with a satisfied grin. "I certainly didn't feel lucky at the time, but things did work out in the long run."

"Why didn't you feel lucky at first?"

He began to feel more at ease and decided to provide some genuine answers. "Because at first, I was in trouble, mostly because I stood up for Becky. At that time, helping her meant I had to stand up to some powerful local people. That's when things started to go bad. Then Becky disappeared before I could even say goodbye. I was fortunate the town threw me a lifeline in the form of a job offer. I became the Riverbend Community Development Commissioner. That's been my job for nearly seventeen years.

She folded her sunglasses and placed them on the table. "What does that office do?"

"Mainly, we support economic growth. We try to expand local employment opportunities too. We try to stoke the town's development without letting it get out of control."

"That all sounds like very useful bullshit," she said.

Her comment caught him off guard. It was time for him to adjust his own glasses; prescription hornrims he had started wearing just a month before.

"Am I wrong?" she asked.

"Look," Yarrow replied, "we just met, but if you want honesty, yeah. It was a bullshit job for the first several weeks and it remained hit-or-miss for another year. But I found my stride, and the office has grown from just me to a staff of four. I think we've made a big difference. We recruit new businesses, give tax breaks, and prod the state for grant money. The town's old dirt roads are mostly paved now. We have two new economic development zones. Riverbend is a nice thriving community."

"I see. So, there's no riffraff slipping into town anymore?"

"No. Not at all—"

Yarrow stopped himself right there. He knew what she meant.

He changed the subject by picking up another jar. "This one looks nice. Collecting all that honey can be hard work."

"It is. But it's honest work. And I hope to keep it that way. I've heard the stories, Mr. Yarrow. I know what happened here. I know why things failed, both for Becky and Erin before her. That way of doing business seems broken. I won't follow it."

"I'd say that's a wise choice."

She rearranged the jars. As he watched her, Yarrow sensed there was something more she wanted to ask.

"You know," she finally spoke. "Becky told me how much you helped her back then. And how you came around and eventually supported the ideals she held. So tell me, do you still support them? Do you push back against power?"

"I like to think I do."

"So, when you plan your so-called economic development projects, do you try to include the types of people Becky was trying to help? Or are they left out of the equation?"

Yarrow looked away. He wanted to provide a positive answer but realized he couldn't. Instead, he asked, "You really don't know where Becky is now?"

"I really don't. I'm not sure anyone knows. She always lived on the edge. She'd raise bees and sell produce somewhere for a few years. But shantytowns always popped up around her, and the locals would grow angry. She could never break that pattern. Too ingrained, I guess."

"I'm sorry to hear that."

"I'm sure she'd appreciate your sympathy. But I know she's okay. She's a survivor."

He found himself looking toward the wildflowers. "Yes, she is. Impressively so."

Then he pointed to the jars. "So, the darker ones. How about if I take one of those?"

"Of course."

She took his money, placed the jar in a paper bag, and handed it to him.

Yarrow tucked it under his arm. His gaze lingered on the empty fields.

"I'm glad someone has reopened here. This farm always had the best honey and produce. Wonderful location too. If you can grow your business as fast as Becky, you should do quite well."

"Thank you. I'm confident I can, and I already have some help lined up."

"Oh?"

"Two friends are joining me next week. They're coming down from Portland."

"I hope it all works out."

"Thank you. And, if the word gets around, Mr. Jim Yarrow, I hope maybe my mother will hear about my efforts. Maybe she'll come back. Maybe she'll find me."

"Your mother ..."

"Yes. Becky."

Yarrow stood in stunned silence. It took him a moment to gather his wits. Then he spoke. "I'm sorry. Did you say Becky is your mother?"

"Yes. And it would be wonderful if I could see her again."

Yarrow was at a loss for words. As if in a daze, he turned without saying goodbye. He walked a few steps, then turned back. "If you don't mind me asking, how old are you?"

"I don't mind at all. I just turned sixteen. By the way, my name is Delta."

When the name and the number sunk in, he looked her in the eyes. That's when he saw it. She had a wink that looked just like her mother's.

Epilogue

The Centuries

Nothing is permanent in this wicked world – not even our troubles.
Charlie Chaplin in Monsieur Verdoux, *1947*

Other customers arrived. Delta had to cut the conversation short but asked if they could talk again. He promised to return.

"Before you go, Jim Yarrow, I must give you something. I've been carrying it for two years."

Delta rummaged through a worn suitcase and handed him an envelope.

"When my mother and I went our separate ways, she wrote this note. She knew I wanted to come here at some point, so she asked me to give this to you if we ever met. I've never opened it. She asked me not to."

He stared in bewilderment.

Ten minutes later, the Thunderbird purred, and he found himself driving in a different direction. Toward the low hills above the river. He needed a place to think.

He passed the big road, long since completed, with its asphalt, white lines, and cars passing through from other states.

He went by the remains of a grist mill, with its water wheel rusted in place for a century, then passed a historical marker describing how prehistoric stone tools were discovered nearby.

These scattered pieces of the past triggered a sudden clarity in his mind. People came and went. Societies too. Lingering remains of other life journeys, struggles, and tragedies.

Temporary nations.

On that sunny Sunday, everything around him seemed to merge into a fleeting moment, where he alone was granted clarity.

From the hilltop, he saw the river. And the ocean.

Looking behind him to the west he saw a vast land, once wild, now tamed, cleared, segmented, and settled. Endless stone walls. Picture-perfect villages. Old houses and new. Settled by the survivors. Populated by the lucky ones.

With a deep melancholy, he stared at the envelope, then tore it open.

April 18, 1965

Dear Jim,

It's nice to write your name. It's been such a long time since I've called you, Jim or set your name to paper.

I don't know if you'll ever read these words, and if you do, I don't know when that will be. But if this is in your hands, it means you've met our daughter, Delta.

She's a fine girl, Jim. Smart, capable, and hardworking. I guess she takes after her parents.

But, because of me, she's grown up as a vagabond. I was never able to give her the stability she deserved. Yet I've watched her endure, grow, and thrive. That says more about her strengths than mine.

And to ease your mind: No, Delta has not had to endure the same things I did as a teen. At least I was able to shield her from that.

As I write this, it's been many years since I fled Riverbend. I didn't realize I was pregnant when I left, but I found out within a few weeks. That changed everything.

You may be wondering why I never contacted you or told you about Delta. That's because I felt protective. Of you.

I knew your wife wanted to reconcile with you. I knew your kids missed their daddy. But most of all, I remembered how you said Linda was there for you when you so needed support and understanding. You told me about your wonderful summer at Hampton Beach. Your lip quivered, and your voice broke when you explained how she helped you to calm your mind and find your way back home.

At first, I felt angry and selfish, Jim. I loved that you and I were finely able to reconnect. I didn't want to lose you again. But I also knew if I tried to remain with you, I'd rob you of the one thing that brought peace and stability into your life.

I also knew stability was not something I could offer. My life has never been calm and steady. The most selfish thing of all would have been to draw you deeper into my chaos.

You needed to become a family again. There was no place in that family for me.

Did I make the right decision, Jim? God, I hope I did. I want to believe your marriage was restored, and your family endured. I hope they sustained you. I hope the years have been kind.

I'm writing this letter because Delta is fourteen now and she's been asking about Riverbend and my old farm. She's asked about you too – her father. I suspect she will want to visit the town within the next couple of years, so, I'm giving these words to her—to give to you.

As for me, I need to remain in hiding, for reasons I won't go into. So, even if this letter reaches you, please don't look for me. I am not, and never will be, an easy person to find.

On a different note, I have a friend who still reads the newspapers from Riverbend. She told me you now supervise long-term planning and development for the town. Congratulations.

Do you remember when we watched the new roads come through back in nineteen fifty-one? We stared in disbelief as the ground was scraped away and as we saw field after field cut up for development, like slices of pie.

Since planning is your job now, I'd like to ask you one thing, though I realize I will never hear your answer.

Does Riverbend still have a place for people like me? You know what I mean—for those who've been marginalized? You understand how important that was to me. I once saw that same concern growing in you.

So, Jim, in your role of deciding what Riverbend will become, have you been able to find a space for those who have no refuge? Or do your efforts focus on making Riverbend a polished jewel that includes some people, but not all?

No matter what the answer is, please don't think I'm judging you. I know you struggled to find a comfortable normalcy in your life. I believe you finally did. I hope you still help others find it too, especially the ones who were born to lives of very little comfort.

I remember something you told me about your time in the war. You said as battles unfolded, you sometimes watched in anger, wondering why the world had come to that. Why were men plodding through fields and openly killing each other? Why were ships covered in thick armor? I watched you try to explain that feeling. I knew you felt immensely proud of the battles you fought, yet there also was a side of you that hated the leaders who so determinedly sent young men to be killed or wounded.

But … I've said enough.

I still miss you, Jim. And I will always love you. The only thing I had to offer you was a bohemian existence. Your kids deserved more. Delta deserved more too.

Finally, I hope the demands of the town's ridged status quo didn't swallow you up again. I hope you still notice those who live their lives on the margins. I hope you still offer them a strong hand when you can.

Here, there was love,
Becky

Yarrow placed the letter on the seat beside him and stared out the window.

He thought of all of his painful losses. His father. The use of his hand. Ma Yarrow. His brother Will. He thought of the good things too. Home. Family. Success. For these, he felt grateful.

Would Becky be proud of him now? He didn't want to answer that. Instead he gripped the wheel and looked toward the river and the ocean, even though he knew they would give no answer.

Becky.

Through all the passing years he still thought of Becky.

Maybe Rocco, wherever he ended up, said it best. *We all become haunted houses.*

Riverbend remained a perfect little town where everyone felt pressure to live a perfect little life.

Losses? Wounds? Those must be painted over, like grey New England clapboards.

As he looked downriver, Yarrow didn't remember stretching out his hand. But there it was in front of him—holding one of his own deepest wounds, grasping for an understanding he couldn't quite reach.

How many of his children and generations beyond, he thought, *would ever know the crossroads their ancestors faced or the scars they carried from the choices they had to make?*

He found no answer in his thoughts, but he did know one thing: Like those offshore ships, close but ever elusive, his descendants would make their own journeys, bear their own scars, and endlessly move forward … toward a future that could take them anywhere, show them everything, but promise them nothing.

Did you enjoy this book? We always appreciate a review on your choice of book sites.

Also By Shawn P McCarthy

The Puzzle Box Chronicles Series

Wreck of the Gossamer - The Puzzle Box Chronicles: Book 1

The Lost, the Found and the Hidden - The Puzzle Box Chronicles: Book 2

Those Who Wander - The Puzzle Box Chronicles: Book 3

Wires and Wings - The Puzzle Box Chronicles: Book 4

North of Angel Falls - The Puzzle Box Chronicles: Book 5

The Beckoning Spark - The Puzzle Box Chronicles: Book 6

Short Stories

The Sea Glass Empire and Other Stories

www.ingramcontent.com/pod-product-compliance
Lightning Source LLC
LaVergne TN
LVHW020520100826
845148LV00010B/1298

* 9 7 9 8 9 8 5 6 8 8 2 3 8 *